SLEIGH RIDE WITH THE SINGLE DAD

BY
ALISON ROBERTS

A FIREFIGHTER IN HER STOCKING

BY
JANICE LYNN

MILLS
BOON

Christmas in Manhattan

All the drama of the ER,
all the magic of Christmas!

A festive welcome to Manhattan Mercy ER, a stone's throw
from Central Park in the heart of New York City.
Its reputation for top-notch healthcare is eclipsed only by
the reputation of the illustrious, wealthy Davenport family
and the other dedicated staff who work there!

With snow about to blanket New York over Christmas, ER
Chief Charles Davenport makes sure his team is ready for
the drama and the challenge…but when it comes to love,
a storm is brewing such as they've never seen before!

Available now:

Sleigh Ride with the Single Dad
by Alison Roberts

Dr Grace Forbes is reunited with old flame
Charles Davenport—but will the brooding father and
his adorable twins make her Christmas dreams come true?

A Firefighter in Her Stocking
by Janice Lynn

Dr Sarah Grayson can't resist a festive fling with
her playboy neighbour, hunky firefighter Jude Davenport,
even if she knows she's playing with fire…

And coming soon:

The Spanish Duke's Holiday Proposal
by Robin Gianna

The Rescue Doc's Christmas Miracle
by Amalie Berlin

Christmas with the Best Man
by Susan Carlisle

Navy Doc on Her Christmas List
by Amy Ruttan

SLEIGH RIDE WITH THE SINGLE DAD

BY
ALISON ROBERTS

Published in Great Britain 2017
By Mills & Boon, an imprint of HarperCollins*Publishers*
1 London Bridge Street, London, SE1 9GF

© 2017 Harlequin Books S.A.

Special thanks and acknowledgement are given to Alison Roberts for her contribution to the Christmas in Manhattan series.

ISBN: 978-0-263-92669-9

Printed and bound in Spain
by CPI, Barcelona

Alison Roberts is a New Zealander, currently lucky enough to be living in the south of France. She is also lucky enough to write for the Mills & Boon Medical Romance line. A primary school teacher in a former life, she is now a qualified paramedic. She loves to travel and dance, drink champagne, and spend time with her daughter and her friends.

Books by Alison Roberts

Mills & Boon Medical Romance

Paddington Children's Hospital

A Life-Saving Reunion

Christmas Eve Magic

Their First Family Christmas

Wildfire Island Docs

The Nurse Who Stole His Heart
The Fling That Changed Everything

Always the Midwife
Daredevil, Doctor...Husband?
The Surrogate's Unexpected Miracle

Mills & Boon Cherish

The Wedding Planner and the CEO
The Baby Who Saved Christmas
The Forbidden Prince

Visit the Author Profile page
at millsandboon.co.uk for more titles.

Praise for
Alison Roberts

'…the author gave me wonderful, enjoyable moments of conflict and truth-revealing moments of joy and sorrow… I highly recommend this book for all lovers of romance with medical drama as a backdrop and second-chance love.'

—*Contemporary Romance Reviews* on
NYC Angels: An Explosive Reunion

'This is a deeply emotional book, dealing with difficult life and death issues and situations in the medical community. But it is also a powerful story of love, forgiveness and learning to be intimate… There's a lot packed into this novella. I'm impressed.'

—*Goodreads* on
200 Harley Street: The Proud Italian

CHAPTER ONE

As AN OMEN, this wasn't good.

It could have been the opening scene to a horror movie, in fact.

Grace Forbes, in her crisp, clean set of scrubs— her stethoscope slung around her neck along with the lanyard holding her new Manhattan Mercy ID card— walking towards Charles Davenport who, as chief of Emergency Services, was about to give her an official welcome to her new job.

An enormous clap of thunder rolled overhead from a storm that had to be directly on top of central New York and big enough for the sound to carry into every corner of this huge building.

And then the lights went out.

Unexpectedly, the moment Grace had been bracing herself for became an anti-climax. It was no longer important that this was the first time in more than a decade that her path was about to cross with that of the man who'd rocked her world back in the days of Harvard Medical School. Taking control of a potential crisis in a crowded emergency room was the only thing that mattered.

In the brief, shocked silence that followed both the clap of thunder, a terrified scream from a child and the

startling contrast of a virtually windowless area bathed
in bright, neon lighting being transformed instantly into
the shadowed gloom of a deep cave, Charles Davenport
did exactly that.

'It's just a power outage, folks.' He raised his voice
but still sounded calm. 'Stay where you are. The emergency generators will kick in any minute.'

Torch apps on mobile phones flickered on like stars
appearing in a night sky and beams of light began to
sweep the area as people tried to see what was going on.
The noise level rose and rapidly got louder and louder.
Telephones were ringing against the backdrop of the
buzz of agitated conversations. Alarms sounded to warn
of the power disruption to medical equipment. Staff, including the administrative clerks from the waiting area,
triage nurses and technicians were moving towards the
central desk to await instructions and their movements
triggered shouts from people desperate for attention.

'Hey, come back…where are you going?'

'Help… I need *help*.'

'Nurse…over *here*…please?'

'I'm scared, Mommy… I want to go *home*…'

Grace stayed where she was, her gaze fixed on
Charles. The dramatic change in the lighting had soft-
ened the differences that time had inevitably produced
and, for a heartbeat, he looked exactly as he had that
night. Exactly like the haunting figure that had walked
through her mind and her heart so often when sleep had
opened portals to another time.

Tall and commanding. Caring enough to come after
her and find out what was wrong so he could do something about making it better…

Which was pretty much what he was doing right now.
She could see him assessing the situation and dealing

with the most urgent priorities, even as he took in information that was coming at him from numerous directions.

'Miranda—check any alarms coming from cardiac monitors.'

'Get ready to put us on bypass for incoming patients. If we don't get power back on fast, we'll have a problem.'

'Put the trauma team on standby. If this outage is widespread, we could be in for a spate of accidents.'

Sure enough, people manning the telephones and radio links with the ambulance service were already taking calls.

'Traffic lights out at an intersection on Riverside Drive. Multi-vehicle pile-up. Fire service called for trapped patients. Cyclist versus truck incoming, stat.'

'Fall down stairs only two blocks away. Possible spinal injury. ETA two minutes.'

'Estates need to talk to you, Dr Davenport. Apparently there's some issue with the generators and they're prioritising Theatres and ICU...'

Charles nodded tersely and began issuing orders rapidly. Staff dispersed swiftly to cover designated areas and calm patients. A technician was dispatched to find extra batteries that might be needed for backup for equipment like portable ultrasound and X-ray machines. Flashlights were found and given to orderlies, security personnel and even patients' relatives to hold. Finally, Charles had an instruction specifically directed to Grace.

'Come with me,' he said. 'I need someone to head the trauma team if I have to troubleshoot other stuff.' He noticed heads turning in his direction. 'This is Dr Grace Forbes,' he announced briskly. 'Old colleague of mine who's come from running her own emergency department in outback Australia. She probably feels right at home in primitive conditions like this.'

A smile or two flashed in Grace's direction as her new workmates rushed past to follow their own orders. The smile Charles gave her was distinctly wry. Because of the unusual situation she was being thrown into? Or was it because he knew that describing her as an old colleague was stretching the truth more than a little? It was true that she and Charles had worked in the same hospital more than once in that final year of medical school but their real relationship had been that of fierce but amicable rivals for the position of being the top student of their year. The fact that Charles knew where she'd been recently, when he hadn't been present for the interview she'd had for this job, was another indication that he was on top of his position of being head of this department. No wonder he'd won that final battle of the marks, even though it had only been by a small margin.

'Welcome to Manhattan Mercy, Grace… Trauma One is this way…'

It was hardly the best way to welcome a new member of staff but maybe it was better this way, with so many things to think about that Charles couldn't allow any flashes of memory to do more than float past the edges of his conscious mind.

He hadn't seen Grace since he'd noticed her in the audience when he'd walked onto the stage to accept the trophy for being the top student of their graduation party from medical school.

He hadn't spoken to her since…since *that* night…

'Warn people that waiting times are going to go through the roof for anything non-urgent,' he told the senior member of the administrative team as he passed her. 'But don't push them out the door. By the sound of this storm, it's not safe out there.'

A flicker in the ambient light filtering into the department suggested a flash of lightning outside and another roll of thunder could be heard only a second later so they were still right underneath it. Fingers crossed that the worst of the storm would cross the central city quickly but how long would it be before the power disruption was sorted? And how many problems would it cause?

The weather alone would give them a huge spike in traffic accidents. A sudden plunge into darkness could cause all sorts of trauma like that fall down stairs already on its way. And what about the people on home oxygen who could find themselves in severe respiratory distress with the power outage cutting off their support? They needed to be ready for anything in the ER and he needed to clear space for the potential battleground of dodging unexpected missiles of incoming cases and whatever ambush could be in store with equipment that might not be functioning until power came back on.

He hadn't faced a challenge like this for a long time but he had learned way back how to multi-task when the proverbial was hitting the fan and Charles knew he could function effectively on different levels at the same time.

Like knowing which patients could be sidelined for observation well away from centre-stage and directing staff members to transfer them as he passed their ed cubicles at the same time as fending off a request from a television crew who happened to be in the area and wanted to cover the fallout from what was apparently a record-breaking storm.

'Keep them out of here,' he growled. 'We're going to have more than enough to deal with.'

It never took long for the media to get their teeth into something, did it? Memories of how much damage had been done to his own family all those years ago had left Charles with a mistrust bordering on paranoia. It was a time of his life he had no desire to revisit so it was perhaps unfortunate that the arrival of Grace Forbes in his department had the ability to stir those memories.

And others...

A glance over his shoulder showed him that Grace was following his slightly circuitous route to Trauma One as he made sure he knew what was happening everywhere at the moment. The expression on her face was serious and the focus in those dark grey eyes reminded him of how capable he knew she was. And how intelligent. He'd had to fight hard back at medical school to keep his marks on the same level as Grace and, while they'd never moved in the same social circles, he'd had enormous respect for her. A respect that had tipped into something very different when he'd discovered that she had a vulnerable side, mind you, but he wasn't going to allow the memory of that night to surface.

No way. Even if this situation wasn't making it completely unacceptable to allow such a personal distraction, he wouldn't go there. It was in the same, forbidden territory that housed flirting and he had never been tempted to respond to opportunities that were only becoming more blatant as time crept on.

No. He couldn't go there. It would still feel like he was being unfaithful...

Nobody could ever accuse Charles Davenport of being less than totally loyal. To his family and to his work.

And that was exactly where his entire focus had to

be right now. It didn't matter a damn that this was a less than ideal welcome to a new staff member. Grace would have to jump into the deep end and do her bit to get Manhattan Mercy's ER through this unexpected crisis.

Just as he was doing.

Other staff members were already in the area assigned to deal with major trauma, preparing it for the accident victims they had been warned were on their way. A nurse handed Grace a gown to cover her scrubs and then a face mask that had the plastic eye shield attached.

'Gloves are on the wall there. Choose your size.'

Someone helpfully shone a torch beam over the bench at the side of the area so that Grace could see the 'M' for medium on the front of the box she needed. She also caught a glimpse of an airway cart ready for business, an IV cart, a cardiac monitor, ventilator and portable ultrasound machine.

Okay. She could work with this. Even in semi-darkness she had what she needed to assess an airway, breathing and circulation and to do her best to handle whatever emergencies needed to be treated to stabilise a critically injured patient. And she wasn't alone. As the shadowy figures of paramedics surrounding a gurney came rapidly towards them, Charles was already standing at the head of the bed, ready to take on the most important role of managing an airway.

'Male approximately forty years old,' one of the paramedics told them. He was wearing wet weather gear but his hair was soaked and he had to wipe away the water that was still trickling into his eyes. 'Hit by a truck and thrown about thirty feet to land on the hood of an approaching car. GCS of twelve, blood pressure ninety on palp, tachycardic at one-thirty. Major trauma to left arm and leg.'

The man was semi-conscious and clearly in pain. Despite wearing a neck collar and being strapped to a back board, he was trying to move and groaning loudly.

'On my count,' Charles directed. 'One, two...*three*...'

The patient was smoothly transferred to the bed.

'I need light here, please,' Charles said. He leaned close to their patient's head as someone shone a beam of light in his direction. 'Can you hear me?' He seemed to understand the muffled change to the groan coming from beneath an oxygen mask. 'You're in hospital, buddy. We're going to take care of you.'

A nurse was cutting away clothing. Another was wrapping a blood pressure cuff around an arm and a young, resident doctor was swapping the leads from an ambulance monitor to their own. Grace was watching, assessing the injuries that were becoming apparent. A mangled right arm and a huge wound on the left thigh where a snapped femur had probably gone through the skin and then been pulled back again. The heavy blood loss was an immediate priority. She grabbed a wad of dressing material and put it on the wound to apply direct pressure.

'We need to get back out there,' the lead paramedic told them. 'It's gone crazy. Raining cats and dogs and visibility is almost zero.'

'How widespread is the power cut?'

'At least sixteen blocks from what we've heard. Lightning strike on a power station, apparently. Nobody knows how long it's gonna be before it's back on.'

Charles nodded. 'Thanks, guys.' But his attention was on assessing his patient's breathing. He had crouched to put his line of sight just over head level and Grace knew he was watching the rise and fall of the man's chest to see whether it was symmetrical. If it wasn't, it could indicate a collapsed lung or another problem affecting his breathing.

She was also in a direct line for the steady glance and she saw the shift, when Charles was satisfied with chest movement and had taken on board what she was doing to control haemorrhage and his gaze flicked up to meet her own. For a split second, he held the eye contact and there was something in his gaze that made her feel…what? That he had confidence in her abilities? That she was already a part of the team?

That he was pleased to see her again?

Behind that emotional frisson, there was something else, too. An awareness of how different Charles looked. It shouldn't be a surprise. Thirteen years was a very long time and, even then, they had been young people who were products of their very different backgrounds. But everyone had known that Charles Davenport had the perfect life mapped out for him so why did Grace get the fleeting impression that he looked older than she would have expected? That he had lines in his face that suggested a profound weariness. Sadness, even…

'Blood pressure eighty on forty.' The resident looked up at the overhead monitor. 'And heart rate is one-thirty. Oxygen saturation ninety-four percent.'

'Is that bleeding under control, Grace?'

'Almost. I'd like to get a traction splint on asap for definitive control. It's a mid-shaft femoral fracture.'

Another nod from Charles. 'As soon as you've done that, we need a second line in and more fluids running. And I want an abdominal ultrasound as soon as I've intubated. Can someone ring through to Theatre and see what the situation is up there?'

The buzz of activity around the patient picked up pace and the noise level rose so much that Grace barely noticed the arrival of more paramedics and another patient being delivered to the adjoining trauma room, separated only by curtains. Working conditions were difficult, especially when some of the staff members were directed to the new arrival, but they were by no means impossible. Even with the murky half-light when a torch wasn't being directed at the arm she was working on, Grace managed to get a wide-bore IV line inserted and secured, attaching more fluids to try and stabilise this patient's blood pressure.

With the airway and breathing secured by intubation and ventilation, Charles was able to step back and oversee everything else being done here. He could also watch what was happening on the neighbouring bed, as the curtain had been pulled halfway open. As Grace picked up the ultrasound transducer and squeezed some jelly onto her patient's abdomen, she got a glimpse of what was happening next door.

Judging by the spinal board and the neck collar immobilising the Spanish-looking woman, this was the 'fall down stairs' patient they had been alerted to. What was more of a surprise was that Charles was already in position at the head of this new patient. And he looked... fresher, somehow. Younger...?

No... Grace blinked. It wasn't Charles.

And then she remembered. He'd had a twin brother who'd gone to a different medical school. Elijah? And hadn't their father been the chief of emergency services at a prestigious New York hospital?

This hospital. Of course it was.

Waiting for the image to become readable on her screen as she angled the transducer, Grace allowed herself a moment to think about that. The dynasty was clearly continuing with the Davenport family front and centre in Manhattan Mercy's ER. Hadn't there been a younger sister who was expected to go into medicine as well? It wouldn't surprise her if there was yet another Davenport on the staff here. That was how rich and powerful families worked, wasn't it—sticking together to become even more powerful?

A beat of something like resentment appeared. Or was it an old disappointment that she'd been so insignificant compared to the importance of family for Charles? That she'd become instantly invisible the moment that scandal had erupted?

Whatever. It was easy to push aside. Part of a past that had absolutely nothing to do with the present. Or the future.

'We've got free fluid in the abdomen and pelvis,' she announced. 'Looks like it's coming from the spleen.'

'Let's get him to Theatre,' Charles ordered. 'They've got power and they've been cleared to only take emergencies. He's stable enough for transfer but he needs a medical escort. Grace, can you go with him, please?'

The metallic sounds of brakes being released and sidebars being raised and locked were almost instant. Grace only had time to ensure that IV lines were safe from snagging before the bed began moving. This was an efficient team who were well used to working together and following the directions of their chief. Even in the thick of what had to be an unusually stressful shift for this department, Grace could feel the respect with which Charles was regarded.

Behind her, as she stayed close to the head of the bed to monitor her patient's airway and breathing en route to Theatre, Grace could hear Charles moving onto a new task without missing a beat.

'Any signs of spinal injury, Elijah? Want me to see if the CT lab is clear?'

And then she heard his voice change. 'Oh, my God... *Maria?*'

He must know this patient, she realised. And he was clearly horrified. She could still hear him even though she was some distance on the other side of the curtain now.

'What happened? Where are the boys?'

A break from the barely controlled chaos in a badly lit emergency department was exactly what Grace needed to catch her breath but it was a worry how crowded the corridors were. And a glimpse into the main waiting area as they rushed past on their way to the only elevators being run on a generator suggested that the workload wasn't going to diminish any time soon.

This was a different planet from the kind of environment Grace had been working in for the last few years and the overall impression was initially overwhelming. Why on earth had she thought she could thrive with a volume of work that was so fast-paced? In a totally new place and in a huge city that was at the opposite end of the spectrum from where she'd chosen to be for such a long time.

Because her friend Helena had convinced her that it was time to reconnect with the real world? Because she had become exhausted by relying solely on personal resources to fight every battle that presented itself? Because the isolation of the places she had chosen to practise medicine had finally tipped the balance from being a welcome escape to a bone-deep loneliness that couldn't be ignored for ever?

Like another omen, lights flickered overhead as neon strips came alive with a renewed supply of power. Everybody, including the porters and nurses guiding this bed towards Theatre, looked up and Grace could hear a collective sigh of relief. Normal life would be resumed as soon as the aftermath of this unexpected challenge was dealt with.

And she could cope, too. Possibly even thrive, which had been the plan when she'd signed the contract to begin work in Manhattan Mercy's ER. This was a new beginning and Grace knew better than most that to get the best out of new beginnings you had to draw a line under the past and move on. And yes…some things needed more time to heal but she had taken that time. A lot more time than she had anticipated needing, in fact.

She was ready.

Having stayed longer than the rest of the transfer team so that she could give the anaesthetist and surgeons a comprehensive handover, Grace found that she needed to find her own way back to the ER and it turned out to be a slightly more circuitous route than before. Instead of passing the main reception area, she went past an orthopaedic room where casts were being applied, what looked like a small operating theatre that was labelled for minor surgery and seemed to have someone having a major laceration stitched and then a couple of smaller rooms that looked as if they had been designed for privacy. Were these rooms used for family consultations, perhaps? Or a space where people could be with a loved one who was dying?

A nurse was peering out of one of the doors.

'Oh, thank goodness,' she said, when she saw Grace

approaching. 'I'm about to *burst*... Could you please, please stay with the boys in here for two minutes while I dash to the bathroom?'

The young nurse, whose name badge introduced her as 'Jackie', certainly looked desperate. Having had to grab a bathroom stop herself on her way back from Theatre, Grace could sympathise with the urgency. She was probably already later in her return to the ER than might have been expected so another minute or two wouldn't make any difference, would it?

'Sure,' she said. 'But be as quick as you can?'

Jackie sped off with a grateful smile and vigorous nod without giving Grace the chance to ask anything else—like why these 'boys' were in a side room and whether they needed any medical management.

She turned to go through the door and then froze.

Two small faces were filling the space. Identical faces.

These two children had to be the most adorable little boys she had ever seen. They were about three years old, with tousled mops of dark hair, huge curious eyes and small button noses.

There was something about twins...

For someone who'd had to let go of the dream of even having a single baby, the magic of twins could pack a punch that left a very physical ache somewhere deep inside Grace.

Maybe she wasn't as ready as she'd thought she was to step back into the real world and a new future...

CHAPTER TWO

'WHO ARE YOU?'

'I'm Grace. I'm one of the doctors here.'

It wasn't as hard as she'd expected to find a smile. Who wouldn't smile at this pair? 'Who are *you*?'

'I'm Cameron,' one of the boys told her. 'And he's Max.'

'Hello, Max,' Grace said. 'Hello, Cameron. Can I come into your room?'

'Why?' Cameron seemed to be the spokesman for the pair. 'Where's Jackie gone?'

'Just to the bathroom. She'll be back in a minute. She asked me to look after you.'

'Oh… 'Kay…'

Grace stepped into the room as the children turned. There was a couch and two armchairs in here, some magazines on a low table and a box of toys that had been emptied.

'Are you waiting for somebody?' Grace asked, perching on the arm of the couch.

'Yes. Daddy.' Cameron dropped to his knees and picked up a toy. His brother sat on the floor beside him. 'Here…you can have the fire truck, Max. I'm going to have the p'lice car, 'kay?'

Max nodded. But as he took hold of the plastic fire

truck that had been generously gifted with both hands, the back wheels came off.

'Oh…no…' Cameron sounded horrified. 'You *broke* it.'

Max's bottom lip quivered. Grace slid off the arm of the couch and crouched down beside him.

'Let me have a look. I don't think it's very broken. See…?' She clipped the axle of the wheels back into place. 'All fixed.'

She handed the truck back with a smile and, unexpectedly, received a smile back. A delicious curve of a wide little mouth that curled itself instantly right around her heart.

Wow…

'Fank you,' Max said gravely.

'You're so welcome.' Grace's response came out in no more than a whisper.

Love at first sight could catch you unawares in all sorts of different ways, couldn't it? It could be a potential partner for life, or a gorgeous place like a peaceful forest, or a special house or cute puppy. Or it could be a small boy with a heartbreaking smile.

Cameron was pushing his police car across the top of the coffee table and making muted siren noises but Max stayed where he was, with the mended fire truck in his arms. Or not quite where he was. He leaned, so that his head and shoulder were pressed against Grace's arm. It was impossible not to return this gesture of acceptance and it was purely instinctive to shift her arm so that it slid around the small body and let him snuggle more comfortably.

It would only be for a moment because Nurse Jackie would be back any second. Grace could hear people in the corridor outside. She could feel the draught of air as the door was pushed open behind her so she closed her eyes for a heartbeat to help her lock this exquisite fraction of time into her memory banks. This feeling of connection with a precious small person…

'Daddy…' Cameron's face split into a huge grin.

Max wriggled out from under Grace's arm, dropping the fire truck in his haste to get to his feet, but Grace was still sitting on the floor as she turned her head. And then astonishment stopped her moving at all.

'Charles?'

'Grace…' He sounded as surprised as she had. 'What on earth are you doing in here?'

She felt as guilty as a child caught with her hand in a forbidden cookie jar. 'It was only for a minute. To help out…'

'Jackie had to go to the bathroom.' Cameron had hold of one of his father's hands and he was bouncing up and down.

'She fixed the truck,' Max added, clearly impressed with the skills Grace had demonstrated. 'The wheels came off.'

'Oh…' Charles scooped Cameron up with one arm. Max was next and the ease with which two small boys were positioned on each hip with their arms wrapped around their father's neck suggested that this was a very well-practised manoeuvre. 'That's all right, then…'

Charles was smiling, first at one twin and then the other, and Grace felt her heart melt a little more.

She could feel the intense bond between this man and his children. The power of an infinite amount of love.

She'd been wrong about that moment of doubt earlier, hadn't she? Charles did have the perfect life.

'Can we go home now? Is Maria all better?'

Grace was on her feet now. She should excuse herself and get back to where she was supposed to be but something made her hesitate. To stand there and stare at Charles as she remembered hearing the concern in his voice when he'd recognised the new patient in ER.

He was shaking his head now. 'Maria's got a sore back after falling down the stairs. She's going to be fine but she needs to have a rest for a few days.'

He looked up, as if he could feel the questions buzzing in Grace's head.

'Maria is the boys' nanny,' he said. 'I'll be taking a few days' leave to look after them until she's back on her feet. Fortunately, it was only a sprain and not a fracture.'

That didn't stop the questions but Grace couldn't ask why the head of her new department would automatically take time away to care for his children. Where was their mother? Maybe she was another high-achieving medic who was away—presenting at some international conference or something?

Whatever. It was none of her business. And anyway, Jackie the nurse had come back and there was no reason for her to take any more time away from the job she was employed to be doing.

'I'd better get back,' she said. 'Do you still want me to cover Trauma One?'

'Thanks.' Charles nodded. 'I'll come with you. Jackie, I just came to give you some money. The cafeteria should be up and running again now and I thought you could take the boys up for some lunch.'

Planting a kiss on each small, dark head, he deposited the twins back on the floor.

'Be good,' he instructed. 'And if it's not still raining when we go home, we'll stop in the park for a swing.'

He led Grace back towards the main area of the ER.

'It's still crazy in here,' he said. 'But we've got extra

staff and it's under control now that we've got power back on.'

'I'm sorry I took so long. I probably shouldn't have stopped to help Jackie out.'

'It's not a problem.'

'They're gorgeous children,' Grace added. 'You're a very lucky man, Charles.'

The look he gave her was almost astonished. Then a wash of something poignant crossed his face and he smiled.

A slow kind of smile that took her back through time instantly. To when the brilliant young man who'd been like royalty in their year at med school had suddenly been interested in her as more than the only barrier he had to be a star academically and not just socially. He had cared about what she had to say. About who she was…

'Yes,' he said slowly. 'I am.'

He held open one of the double doors in front of them. 'How 'bout you, Grace? You got kids?'

She shook her head.

'Too busy with that exciting career I was reading about in your CV? Working with the flying doctors in the remotest parts of the outback?'

Her throat felt tight. 'Something like that.'

She could feel his gaze on her back. A beat of silence—curiosity, even, as if he knew there was a lot being left unspoken.

And then he caught up with her in a single, long stride. Turned his head and, yes…she could see the flicker of curiosity.

'It's been a long time, Grace.'

'It has.'

'Be nice to catch up sometime…'

People were coming towards them. There were obviously matters that required the attention of the chief and Grace had her own work to do. She could see paramedics and junior staff clustered around a new gurney in Trauma One but she took a moment before she broke that eye contact.

A moment when she remembered that smile from a few moments ago. And so much more, from a very long time ago.

'Yes,' she said quietly. 'It would…'

The rest of that first shift in Manhattan Mercy's emergency department passed in something of a blur for Grace. Trauma related to the storm and power outage continued to roll in. A kitchen worker had been badly burned when a huge pot of soup had been tipped over in the confusion of a crowded restaurant kitchen plunged into darkness. A man had suffered a heart attack while trapped in an elevator and had been close to the end of the time window for curtailing the damage to his cardiac muscle by the time he'd been rescued. A pedestrian had been badly injured when they'd made a dash to get across a busy road in the pouring rain and a woman who relied on her home oxygen supply had been brought to the ER in severe respiratory distress after it had been cut off.

Grace was completely focused on each patient that spent time in Trauma One but Charles seemed to be everywhere, suddenly appearing where and when he was most needed. How did he do that?

Sometimes it had to be obvious, of course. Like when the young kitchen worker arrived and his screams from the pain of his severe burns would have been heard all over the department and the general level of tension rocketed skywards. He was so distressed he was in danger of injuring himself further by fighting off staff as they attempted to restrain him enough to gain IV access and administer adequate pain relief and Grace was almost knocked off her feet by a flying fist that caught her hip.

It was Charles who was suddenly there to steady her before she fell. Charles who positioned security personnel to restrain their patient safely. And it was Charles who spoke calmly enough to capture a terrified youth's attention and stop the agonised cries for long enough for him to hear what was being said.

'We're going to help you,' he said. 'Try and hold still for just a minute. It will stop hurting very soon...'

He stayed where he was and took over the task of sedating and intubating the young man. Like everyone else in the department, Grace breathed a sigh of relief as the terrible sounds of agony were silenced. She could assess this patient properly now, start dressing the burns that covered the lower half of his body and arrange his transfer to the specialist unit that could take over his care.

She heard Charles on the phone as she passed the unit desk later, clearly making arrangements for a patient who'd been under someone else's initial care.

'It's a full thickness inferior infarct. He's been trapped in an elevator for at least four hours. I'm sending him up to the catheter laboratory, stat.'

The hours passed swiftly and it was Charles who reminded Grace that it was time she went home.

'We're under control and the new shift is taking over. Go home and have a well-deserved rest, Grace. And thanks,' he added, as he turned away. 'I knew you would be an asset to this department.'

The smile was a reward for an extraordinarily testing first day and the words of praise stayed with Grace as she made her way to the locker room to find her coat to throw on over her scrubs.

There were new arrivals in the space, locking away their personal belongings before they started their shift. And one of them was a familiar face.

Helena Tate was scraping auburn curls back from her face to restrain with a scrunchie but she abandoned the task as she caught sight of Grace.

'I hear you've had quite a day.'

Grace simply nodded.

'Do you hate me—for persuading you to come back?'

She shook her head now. 'It's been full on,' she said, 'but you know what?'

'What?'

Grace felt her mouth curving into a grin. 'I loved it.'

It was true, she realised. The pace of the work had left no time for first day nerves. She had done her job well enough to earn praise from the chief and, best of all, the moment she'd been dreading—seeing Charles again—had somehow morphed into something that had nothing to do with heartbreak or embarrassment or even resentment. It almost felt like a reconnection with an old friend. With a part of her life that had been so full of promise because she'd had no idea of just how tough life could become.

'Really?' Helena let out a huff of relief. 'Oh, I'm so happy to hear that.' She was smiling now. 'So it wasn't weird, finding that someone you went to med school with is your boss now?'

Grace had never confessed the real reason it was going to be awkward seeing Charles Davenport again. She had never told anybody about that night, not even her best friend. And certainly not the man she had married. It had been a secret—a shameful one when it had become apparent that Charles had no desire to remember it.

But today it seemed that she had finally been able to move past something that had been a mere blip of time in a now distant past life.

'Not really,' she told Helena. 'Not that we had time to chat. I did meet his little boys, though.'

'The twins? Aren't they cute? Such a tragic story.' Helena lowered her voice. 'Nina was the absolute love of Charles's life and she died minutes after they were born. Amniotic embolism. He'll never get over it…'

Shock made Grace speechless but Helena didn't seem to notice. The hum of voices around them was increasing as more people came in and out of the locker room. Helena glanced up, clearly refocusing on what was around her. She pulled her hair back again and wound the elastic band around her short ponytail. 'I'd better get in there. You can tell me all about it in the morning.'

The door of her locker shut with a metallic clang to reveal the figure arriving beside her to open another locker. Charles Davenport glanced sideways as Helena kept talking.

'Have my bed tonight,' she told Grace. 'I'll be home so late, a couple of hours on that awful couch won't make any difference.'

And then she was gone. Grace immediately turned to look for her own locker because she didn't want to catch Charles's gaze and possibly reveal that she had just learned something very personal about his life. She turned back just as swiftly, however, as she heard him speak.

'You're sleeping on a couch?'

'Only until I find my own place.' Grace could see those new lines on his face in a different light now and it made something tighten in her chest. He'd suffered, hadn't he?

She knew what that was like…

'It's a bit of a squash,' she added hurriedly. 'But Helena's an old friend. Do you remember her from Harvard?'

Charles shook his head and Grace nodded a beat later. Why would he remember someone who was not only several years younger but, like her, had not been anywhere near the kind of elite social circles the Davenports belonged to? Her own close friendship with Helena had only come about because they'd lived in the same student accommodation block.

'She was a few years behind us. We've kept in touch, though. It was Helena who persuaded me to apply for the job here.'

Charles took a warm coat from its hanger and draped it over his arm. 'I'll have to remember to thank her for that.' He pulled a worn-looking leather satchel from his locker before pushing the door shut. He looked like a man in a hurry. 'I'd better go and rescue my boys. Good luck with the apartment hunting.'

'Thanks. I might need it. From what I've heard, it's a bit of a mission to find something affordable within easy commuting of Central Manhattan.'

'Hmm.' Charles turned away, the sound no more than a sympathetic grunt. But then his head turned swiftly, his eyes narrowed, as if he'd just thought of something important. 'Do you like dogs?'

The random question took Grace by surprise. She blinked at Charles.

'Sorry?'

He shook his head. 'It's just a thought. Might come to nothing but...' He was pulling a mobile phone from the pocket of his scrubs and then tapping on the screen. 'Give me your phone number,' he said. 'Just in case...'

What had he been thinking?

Was he really intending to follow through with that crazy idea that had occurred to him when he'd heard that the newest member of his department was camping in another colleague's apartment and sleeping on an apparently uncomfortable couch?

Why would he do that when his life had suddenly become even more complicated than it already was?

'It's not raining, Daddy.' Zipped up inside his bright red puffer jacket, with a matching woolly hat covering his curls, Cameron tugged on his father's hand. 'Swing?'

Max's tired little face lit up at the reminder and he nodded with enthusiasm. 'I want a swing, too.'

'But it's pouring, guys.' Charles had to smile down at his sons. 'See? You're just dry because you're under my umbrella.'

A huge, black umbrella. Big enough for all of them to be sheltered as they walked beneath dripping branches of the massive trees lining this edge of Central Park, the pavement plastered with the evidence of the autumnal leaf fall. Past one of the more than twenty playgrounds for children that this amazing space boasted, currently empty of any nannies or parents trying to entertain their young people.

'Aww...'

The weight of two tired small boys suddenly increased as their steps dragged.

'And it's too dark now, anyway,' Charles pointed out. 'We'll go tomorrow. In the daytime. We can do that because it's Sunday and there's no nursery school. And I'm going to be at home to look after you.'

'Why?'

'Because Maria's got a sore back.'

'Because she fell down the stairs?'

'That's right, buddy.'

'It went dark,' Cameron said.

'I was scared,' Max added. 'Maria was *crying...*'

'Horse was barking and barking.'

'Was he?'

'I told Max to sit on the stair,' Cameron said proudly. 'And Mr Jack came to help.'

Jack was the elderly concierge for their apartment block and he'd been there for many years before Charles had bought the penthouse floor. He was almost part of the family now.

And probably more willing to help than his real family would be if he told them about the latest complication in his home life.

No, that wasn't fair. His siblings would do whatever they could but they were all so busy with their own lives and careers. Elijah would have to step up to take his place as Chief of Emergency in the next few days. His sister Penelope was on a much-needed break, although she was probably on some adrenaline-filled adventure that involved climbing a mountain or extreme skiing. The youngest Davenport, Zachary, was back from his latest tour of duty and working at the Navy Academy in Annapolis and his half-sister, Miranda, would try *too* hard, even if it was too much. Protecting his siblings had become second nature to Charles ever since the Davenports' sheltered world had imploded all those years ago.

And his parents? Hugo Davenport had retired as Chief of Emergency to allow Charles to take the position but he'd barely had time for his own children as they were growing up and he would be at a complete loss if he was left with the sole responsibility of boisterous twin almost three-year-olds. It would be sole responsibility, too, because Vanessa had led an almost completely separate life ever since the scandal, and playing happy grandparents together would never be added to her agenda.

His mother would rush to help, of course, and put out the word that she urgently needed the services of the best nanny available in New York but Charles didn't want that. He didn't want a stranger suddenly appearing in his home. His boys had to feel loved and totally secure at all times. He'd promised them that much when they were only an hour old—in those terrible first minutes after their mother's death.

His grip tightened on the hand of each twin.

'You were both very brave in the dark,' he told them. 'And you've both been a big help by being so good when you had to stay at Daddy's work all day. I'm very, very proud of you both.'

'So we can go to the park?'

'Tomorrow,' he promised. 'We'll go to the park even if it's still raining. You can put your rubber boots on and jump in all the puddles.'

They could take some time out and make the outside world unimportant for an hour or two. Maybe he would be able to put aside the guilt that he was taking emergency leave from his work and stop fretting that he was creating extra pressure for Elijah or that his other siblings would worry about him when they heard that he was struggling as a single parent—yet again. Maybe he could even forget about the background tension of being part of a family that was a far cry from the united presence they could still display for the sake of a gala fundraising event or any other glittering, high-society occasion. A family whose motto of 'What happens in the family stays in the family' had been sorely tested but had, in recent years, regained its former strength.

A yellow taxi swooped into the kerb, sending a spray of water onto the pavement. Charles hurried the twins past a taco restaurant, souvenir shop, a hot dog stand and the twenty-four-seven deli to turn into the tree-lined avenue that was the prestigious address for the brownstone apartment block they called home.

And it was then that Charles recognised why he'd felt the urge to reach out and try to help Grace Forbes.

Like taking the boys to the park, it felt like he had the opportunity to shut the rest of the world out to some extent.

Grace was part of a world that had ceased to exist when the trauma of the family trouble had threatened everything the Davenport family held dear. It had been the happiest time of Charles's life. He had been achieving his dream of following in his father's footsteps and becoming a doctor who could one day be in charge of the most challenging and exciting place he had ever known—Manhattan Mercy's ER. The biggest problem he'd had was how to balance a demanding social life with the drive to achieve the honour of topping his class, and the only real barrier to that position had been Grace.

He'd managed to succeed, despite the appalling pressure that had exploded around him in the run-up to final exams, by focusing only on the things that mattered the most—supporting his mother and protecting his siblings from the fallout of scandal and passing those exams with the best possible results. He had been forced to dismiss Grace, along with every other social aspect of his life. And he'd learned to dismiss any emotion that could threaten his goals.

But he had never forgotten how simple and happy his life at medical school had been up until that point.

And, if he was honest, he'd never forgotten that night with Grace...

He could never go back, of course, but the pull of even connecting with it from a distance was surprisingly compelling. And what harm could it do? His life wasn't about to change. He had his boys and he had his job and that was all he needed. All he could ever hope for.

But Grace had been special. And there was something about her that made him think that, perhaps— like him—life hadn't quite turned out the way she'd planned. Or deserved?

'Shall we stop and say hello to Horse before we go upstairs?'

'*Yes...*' The tug on his hands was in a forward direction now, instead of a reluctant weight he was encouraging to follow him. 'Let's *go*, Daddy...'

CHAPTER THREE

'So here's the thing…'

'Mmm?' Grace was still trying to get her head around hearing Charles Davenport's voice on a phone for the first time ever.

The twang of a New York accent had probably been mellowed by so many years at exclusive, private schools but his enunciation was crisp. Decisive, even. It made her think of someone in a suit. Presenting a killer summary in a courtroom, perhaps. Or detailing a take-over bid in the boardroom of a global company.

She was sitting cross-legged on the couch in Helena's apartment, a take-out container of pad Thai on her lap and a pair of chopsticks now idle in her hands. She was in her pyjamas already, thanks to getting soaked in the tail end of the storm during her long walk home from the nearest subway station.

Was her attire partly responsible for hearing that slightly gravelly edge to Charles's voice that made her think that he would sound just like that if his head was on a pillow, very close to her own?

'Sorry…did you say your neighbour's name was *Houston*? As in "Houston, we have a problem"?'

The chuckle of laughter came out of the phone and went straight for somewhere deep in Grace's chest. Or maybe her belly. It created a warmth that brought a smile to her face.

'Exactly. It's their dog that's called Houston and they chose the name on the first day they brought him home as a puppy when they found what he'd left in the middle of their white carpet.'

The bubble of her own laughter took Grace by surprise. Because it felt like the kind of easy laughter that she hadn't experienced in such a long time? The kind that made her think of a first date? Or worse, made her remember *that* night. When Charles had found her, so stressed before the start of their final exams that she was in pieces and he'd tried to reassure her. To distract her, by talking to her rather like this. By making her laugh through her tears and then…

And then there'd been that astonishing moment when they couldn't break the eye contact between them and the kiss that had started everything had been as inevitable as the sun rising the next morning.

It was an effort to force herself to focus on what Charles was actually saying as he kept talking.

'The boys call him Horse, because they weren't even two when he arrived and they couldn't pronounce Houston but he's quite big so that seemed to work, too.'

Grace cleared her throat, hoping her voice would come out sounding normal. How embarrassing would it be if it was kind of husky and betrayed those memories that refused to stay where they should be. Buried.

'What sort of dog is he?'

'A retro doodle. Half poodle, half golden retriever. One of those designer, hypo-allergenic kind of dogs, you know? But he's lovely. Very well behaved and gentle.'

Grace closed her eyes for a moment. This was *so* weird. She hadn't seen Charles Davenport in more than a decade but here they were chatting about something completely random as if they were friends who caught up every other week. And they'd never been *friends*, exactly. Friend*ly*, certainly—with a lot of respect for each other's abilities. And they'd been passionate—so briefly it had always seemed like nothing more than a fantasy that had unexpectedly achieved reality. But this?

Thanks to the memories it was stirring up, this was doing Grace's head in.

On top of that, her noodles were getting cold and probably wouldn't appreciate another spin in the microwave.

The beat of an awkward silence made her wonder if this apparently easy chatting was actually just as weird for Charles.

'Anyway… I'm sorry to disturb your evening but it occurred to me that it could be a win-win situation.'

'Oh?'

'Houston's parents are my neighbours on the ground floor of this block—which, I should mention, is about two minutes' walk to Central Park and ten at the most to Manhattan Mercy.'

'Oh…' How good would that be, not to have to battle crowds in the subway and a long walk at the end of the commute?

'Stefan's an interior designer and his husband, Jerome, is an artist. They're heading off tomorrow for a belated honeymoon in Europe and they'll be gone for about six weeks. They're both fretting about Houston having to go into kennels. I suggested they get a dog-sitter to live in but…' Charles cleared his throat as if he was slightly embarrassed. 'Apparently Houston is their fur child and they couldn't find someone trustworthy enough. When I got home this evening, I told them about you and they seem to be very impressed with the recommendation I gave them.'

'Oh…?' Good grief, she was beginning to sound like a broken record. 'But… I work long hours. I couldn't look after a dog…'

'Houston has a puppy walker that he loves who would come twice a day on the days that you're working. That's another part of his routine that Stefan and Jerome are worried about disrupting because he gets to play with his dog friends who get taken out at the same time. Even more importantly, if he was still in his own home, he wouldn't miss his dads so much. And I thought that it could give you a bit of breathing space, you know? To find your feet in a new city and where you want to be.'

Not just breathing space. Living space. Sharing a tiny apartment, even with a good friend, was a shock to the system for someone who had guarded their privacy so well for so long.

'I know it's all very last minute with them being due to drop Houston at the kennels in the morning but they're home this evening and they'd love to meet you and have a chat about it. Stefan said he'd be delighted to cover your taxi fares if you were at all interested.' Charles paused and Grace could hear something that sounded like a weary sigh. 'Anyway… I've only just got the boys to bed and I need to have a hunt in the fridge and see if I can find something to eat that isn't the boys' favourite packet mac and cheese.'

Again, Grace was aware of that tightness in her chest. Empathy? Charles might have the blessing of having two gorgeous children but he had lost something huge as well. Something that had changed his future for ever—the loss of a complete family.

They had a lot more than he realised in common.

Her new boss had also had a very difficult day, coping with a crisis in his department and the added blow of having to deal with a personal crisis with his nanny being put out of action. And yet he'd found the time to think about her and a way to possibly help her adjust to a dauntingly huge change in her life?

How astonishing was that?

'Thank you so much, Charles.' Grace dropped the chopsticks into the plastic bowl and put it onto the coffee table as she unfurled her legs. It didn't matter that she would have to get dressed again and then head out into this huge city that never slept. Despite so much going on in his own life, Charles had made a very thoughtful effort on her behalf and she knew exactly how she needed to show her appreciation.

There was something else prompting her, too. A niggle that was purely instinctive that was telling her not to miss this unexpected opportunity. That it might, somehow, be a signpost to the new path in life that she was seeking. The kind of niggle that had persuaded her, in the end, to come to New York in the first place.

'Let me grab a pen. Give me the address and I'll get there as soon as I can.'

'Morning, Doc.'

'Morning, Jack. How's the weather looking out there?' Not that Charles needed to ask. The view from his penthouse apartment over Central Park and the Manhattan skyline had shown him that any residual cloudiness from the storm of a few days ago had been blown well clear of the city. It was a perfect October day. But discussing the weather was a ritual. And it gave him the chance to make sure that the twins were well protected from the chill, with their jackets fastened, ears covered by their hats and twenty little fingers encased in warm mittens.

'It's a day for the park, that's fo' sure.' Jack had a passion for following meteorology and spent any free time on door duty surfing weather channels. 'High of sixteen degrees, thirty-two percent clear skies and twenty-one percent chance of light rain but that won't happen until after two p.m.'

'Perfect. Nice change, isn't it?' As usual, Cameron's mittens were hanging by the strings that attached them to his jacket sleeves. Charles pulled them over the small hands. 'That was some storm we had the other day.'

'Sure was. Won't forget that in a hurry. Not with poor Maria crashing down the stairs like that.' Jack shook his head. 'How's she doin'?'

'Good, but I don't want her coming back to work too soon. She won't be up to lifting small boys out of trouble for a while.' Charles tugged Max's hat down over his ears. 'You guys ready?'

'Can we say "hi" to Horse?'

Charles glanced behind the boys, to the door that led to one of the two ground-floor apartments. He'd been tempted to knock on that door more than once in the last few days—ever since he'd heard the news that Grace had taken on the dog-sitting gig—but something had held him back.

Something odd that felt almost like shyness, which was ridiculous because hanging back had never been an attribute that anyone would associate with the Davenport family.

Maybe he was just waiting for it to happen naturally so that it didn't seem like he was being pushy? He was her boss, after all. Or he would be, as soon as he got back to work properly. There were boundaries here and maybe Grace didn't want to cross them, either. That might explain why she hadn't knocked on *his* door.

He turned, holding out his hands. 'Let's go. Or you'll be wanting a hotdog before we even get to the playground.'

Jack was holding open the front door, letting sunlight stream in to brighten the mosaic tiles of the entrance foyer, but the boys weren't moving to take their father's hands. They were going in the opposite direction, as the door behind Charles swung open.

'Horse...'

The big woolly dog looked as pleased to see the twins as they were to see him. He stood there with what looked like a grin on his face, the long plume of his tail waving, as Cameron and Max wrapped their arms around his neck and buried their faces in his curls.

Grace was grinning as well, as she looked down at the reunion.

'Oh, yeah...cuddles are the best way to start the day, aren't they, Houston?'

She was still smiling as she looked up. The black woollen hat she was wearing made a frame that seemed to accentuate the brightness of that smile. A smile that went all the way to her eyes and made them sparkle.

'We're off to the park,' she said. 'It's my first day off so I'm on dog-walking duty today.'

'We're going to the park, too,' Cameron shouted. 'You can come with us.'

'I want to throw the ball for Horse.' Max nodded.

'I think he has to stay on his lead,' Grace said. 'I've been reading the rules this morning.'

Charles nodded. 'And he's not allowed in the playgrounds. But we can walk with him for a while.'

Grace's smile seemed to wobble, as if a shadow was crossing her face, and Charles had the impression that this was a bigger deal than he would have expected.

'If Grace doesn't mind the extra company, that is,' he added.

'I'd love it,' Grace said firmly. She was clipping the dog's lead onto his harness so Charles couldn't see if she really meant that but then she straightened and caught his gaze.

'You can show me the best places to walk. I don't know anything about Central Park.'

Her smile was strong again and he could see a gleam in her eyes that he remembered very well. He'd seen it often enough in the past, usually when they were both heading in to the same examination.

Determination, that was what it was.

But why did she need to tap into that kind of reserve for something that should be no problem? A pleasure, even...

It was puzzling.

'Have you never been to New York before?' Juggling two small children and a dog on the busy pavement meant that Charles had to wait until they were almost at the gates of the park to say anything more to Grace.

'Never. I was born in Australia and then my family moved to Florida when my dad got a job with NASA.' She was smiling again. 'He thinks it's hilarious that I've got a job looking after a dog called Houston. Anyway... coming here was always a plan once I got to medical school in Boston but there never seemed to be enough time. I was too busy studying...' The glance Charles received was mischievous. 'Trying to keep up with you.'

'I think it was the other way round.' Charles kept a firm grip on small mittened hands, as he paused to wait until a horse-drawn carriage rolled past, carrying tourists on a relaxed tour of the park, but he was holding Grace's gaze as well. They would have to part company very soon and it felt…disappointing?

'Okay…we have two favourite playgrounds close to here but…'

'But dogs aren't allowed, I know. When I looked on the map, there was a track called the Bridle Path? That sounds like a nice place to walk.'

'It is. Come with us as far as the playground and I'll show you which direction to take to find it. Next time, I'll bring the boys' bikes and we can all go on the Bridle Path.'

The way Grace's eyes widened revealed her surprise, which was quite understandable because Charles was a little surprised himself that the suggestion had emerged so casually. As if this was already a thing—this walking in the park together like a…like a *family*? A whole family, with two parents and even a dog.

And her surprise quickly morphed into something else. Something softer that hadn't been fuelled by determination. Pleasure, even? Was she enjoying their company as much as he was enjoying hers?

Charles was silent the rest of the way to the playground. Not that anybody seemed to notice because Cameron and Max were making sure that Grace didn't miss any of the important attractions.

'Look, Gace…it's a *sk-wirrel*…'

'Oh, yes… I *love* squirrels.'

'Look at all the leafs. Why are they all on the ground?'

'Because it's autumn. The trees get undressed for winter. Like you do when you're getting ready for bed. Aren't they pretty?'

Why had it felt so natural up until now, Charles wondered, to add feminine and canine company to his little troupe when it could be seen as potentially disturbing? He and his boys didn't need extra people in their lives. Against quite a few odds, he had managed perfectly well up until now and his children were happy and healthy and safe…

At least things would go back to normal any second now. Grace would continue her dog walk and he'd stand around with the other parents, watching the children run and climb and shout, until he was summoned to push the swings.

But when they got to the wrought-iron fence surrounding the playground, it seemed that his boys wanted a larger audience for their exploits.

'I want Horse to watch me on the slide,' Cameron said.

'And Gace,' Max added. His face was serious enough to let them know that this was important. 'Gace can push me on the swing.'

'Um…' Grace hadn't missed the slightly awkward edge to the atmosphere in the last minute or two because it had left her feeling just a bit confused.

She'd been happy to have company on her first walk to Central Park because it was always so much easier to go somewhere new with somebody who knew the way. And because it had been so good to see the twins again. Especially Max. Cameron's smile was identical, of course, but there was something a little more serious about Max that pulled her heartstrings so hard it was too close to pain to be comfortable. That was why, for a heartbeat back at the apartment block, she had wondered if it wasn't a good idea to share even a part of this walk. But she'd pushed aside any deeply personal misgivings. Maybe it did still hurt that she would never be part of her own family group like this, but surely she could embrace this moment for what it was? Being included, instead of watching from a distance?

Having Houston walking by her side helped a lot. In fact, the last few days had been a revelation. Due to her work hours and never settling in one place for very long, Grace had never considered adopting a dog and getting to know Houston had been a joy. She wished she'd learned years ago that a companion like this could make you feel so much less alone in the world.

Charles's company was surprisingly good, too. When she'd told him of her father's amusement about the dog's name, the appreciative glint in his eyes made her remember how easy that telephone conversation the other night had been. How close to the surface laughter had felt. He'd caught her memory of how focused life had been back in medical school, too, but twisted it slightly, to make it sound as if he'd been a lot more aware of her than she had realised.

And then he'd made that comment about them all coming to the park again together, as if this was the start of something that he'd expected to happen all along? That was when the awkwardness had sprouted.

Had he somehow heard the alarm bells sounding in her own head or did he have a warning system of his own?

Maybe she should just say goodbye and head off with Houston to explore the park and leave Charles to have time with his boys.

Except…it felt like it would suddenly be less interesting. A bit lonely, even?

And the way Max was looking up at her, with those

big, blue eyes, as if her being here was the most important thing in the world to him. He had eyes just like his father, she realised. That amazingly bright blue, made even more striking by the darker rim around the irises.

'I have to stay here, on this side of the fence. To look after Horse.' She smiled at Max. 'But I could watch Daddy push you?'

Houston seemed perfectly happy to sit by her side and Grace was grateful for the dog's warmth as he leaned against her leg. She watched Charles lift the little boys into the bucket seats of the swings, side by side, and then position himself between them so that he could push a swing with each hand. She could see the huge grins on the children's faces and hear the peals of their laughter as the arc of movement got steadily higher. And Charles finally looked exactly as she'd remembered him. Happy. Carefree. Enjoying all the best things in life that automatically came his way because he was one of life's golden people that always had the best available.

Except she knew better now. Charles might have had a very different upbringing from her solid, middle-class existence, but he hadn't been protected from the hard things in life any more than she had. His world had been shattered, maybe as much as hers had been, but he was making the best of it and clearly fatherhood was just as important to him as his work. More important, perhaps. He hadn't hesitated in taking time off when his children needed him.

That said a lot about who he was, didn't it? About his ability to cherish the things that were most important in life?

A beat of something very poignant washed through

Grace as she remembered those whispered words in the locker room.

'Nina was the absolute love of his life...he'll never get over it...'

The death of his wife was utterly tragic but how lucky had they both been to find a love like that? She certainly hadn't been lucky enough to find it in her marriage and she wasn't about to stumble across it any time soon.

Grace closed her eyes for a heartbeat as she let her breath escape in a sigh. How good was this kind of weather, when she could snuggle beneath layers of warm clothes and a lovely, puffy jacket? Nobody would ever guess what she was hiding.

Charles was smiling again as he came back towards her. He hadn't bothered with a hat or gloves and he was rubbing his hands together against the chill of the late autumn air. The breeze was ruffling his hair, which looked longer and more tousled than Grace remembered. Maybe he didn't get much time for haircuts these days. Or maybe how he looked wasn't a priority. It would be ironic if that was the reason, because the tousled look, along with that designer stubble, actually made him look way more attractive.

'That's my duty done. Now I get to watch them run around and climb things until they either get hungry or need to go to the toilet. Probably both at the same time.'

'I should get going. Horse isn't getting the exercise I promised him.'

'Wait a bit? The boys won't forgive me if you disappear before they've had a chance to show off a bit.'

'Sure.'

With the bars of the fence between them and Charles's attention back on his children, it felt curiously safe to be standing this close to him. It was safe anyway, Grace reminded herself. The last thing Charles Davenport would want would be another complication in his life and nobody could take the place of the twins' mother, anyway. With another wash of that empathy, the words came out before Grace thought to filter them.

'You must miss their mom so much…'

The beat of silence between them was surprisingly loud against the backdrop of happy shrieks and laughter from the small crowd of children swarming over the playground attractions. She couldn't miss the way Charles swallowed so carefully.

'So much,' he agreed. 'I can only be thankful that the boys will never feel that loss.'

Grace was silent but she could feel her brow furrowing as Charles slid a brief glance back in her direction.

'Oh, they'll know that something's missing from their life as they get older and notice that all the other kids have moms but they never knew Nina. She didn't even get to hold them.'

'I'm so sorry, Charles,' Grace said quietly. 'I had no idea until Helena mentioned it the other day. I can't even imagine how awful that must have been.'

'We had no warning.' His voice sounded raw. 'The pregnancy had gone so well and we were both so excited about welcoming the twins. Twins run in the family, you know. My brother Elijah is my twin. And we knew they were boys.'

Grace was listening but didn't say anything. She couldn't say anything because her treacherous mind was racing down its own, private track. Picking the scab off an old, emotional wound. Imagining what it would be like to have an enormous belly sheltering not one but *two* babies. She could actually feel a wash of that excitement of waiting for the birth.

'The birth was textbook perfect, too. Cameron arrived and then five minutes later Max did. They were a few weeks early but healthy enough not to need any intervention. I had just cut Max's umbilical cord and was lifting him up to put him in Nina's arms when it happened. She suddenly started gasping for breath and her blood pressure crashed. She was unconscious even before the massive haemorrhage started.'

'Oh… *God*…' Grace wasn't distracted by any personal baggage now. She was in that room with Charles and his two newborn sons. Watching his wife die right in front of his eyes. Her own eyes filled with tears.

'Sorry…' Charles sucked in a deep breath. 'It's not something I ever talk about. I feel…guilty, you know?'

'What? How could you possibly feel *guilty*? There was nothing you could have done.'

'There *should* have been.' There was an intensity to his voice that made the weight of the burden Charles carried very clear. 'It was my job to protect her. I was a doctor, for God's sake. I should have seen something. Some warning. She could have had a medically controlled birth. A Caesarean.'

'It could still have happened.' Grace could hear an odd intensity in her own voice now. Why did it seem so important to try and convince Charles that he had nothing to feel guilty about? 'A C-section might not have made any difference. These things are rare but they happen—with no warning. Sometimes, you lose the babies as well.' She glanced away from Charles, her gaze drawn to the two happy, healthy little boys running around in the playground. 'Look at them,' she said softly. 'Feel blessed…not guilty…'

Charles nodded. 'I do. Those boys are the most important thing in my life. They *are* my life. It's just that it gets harder at this time of year. It sucks that the anniversary of losing Nina is also the twins' birthday. They're old enough to know about birthdays now and that they're supposed to be happy. And it's Halloween, for heaven's sake. Every kid in the country is getting dressed up and having fun.'

'That's next week.'

'Yeah.' Charles pushed his fingers through his hair as he watched Max follow Cameron through a tunnel at the base of the wooden fort. 'And, thanks to their little friends at nursery school, they're determined to go trick or treating for the first time. And they all wear their costumes to school that day.'

Clearly, it was the last thing Charles wanted to think about. The urge to offer help of some kind was powerful but that might not be something Charles wanted, either. But, he'd opened up to her about the tragedy, hadn't he? And he'd said that he never talked about it but he'd told her. Oddly, that felt remarkably special.

Grace bit her lip, absently scratching Houston's ear as he leaned his head against her leg.

'I wonder if they do Halloween costumes for dogs,' she murmured.

Clearly, Charles picked up on this subtle offer to help make this time of year more fun. More of a celebration than a source of painful memories. His startled glance reminded her of the one she'd received the other day when she'd told him what a lucky man he was to have such gorgeous children. As if he was unexpectedly looking at something from a very different perspective.

If so, he obviously needed time to think about it and that was fine by Grace. Maybe she did, too. Offering to

help—to become more involved in this little family—
might very well be a mistake. So why did it feel so much
like the right thing to do?

Charles was watching the boys again as they emerged
from the other end of the tunnel and immediately ran
back to do it all over again.

'Enough about me,' he said. 'I was trying to remember the last time I heard about you and it was at a conference about ten years ago. I'm sure someone told me
that you'd got married.'

'Mmm.'

Charles was leaning against the wrought-iron rails
between them, so that when he turned his head, he
seemed very close. 'But you're not married now?'

'No.'

He held her gaze. He'd just told her about the huge
thing that had changed his life for ever. He wasn't going
to ask any more questions but he wanted to know her
story, didn't he?

He'd just told her about his personal catastrophe that
he never normally told anyone. She *wanted* to tell him
about hers. To tell him everything. To reveal that they
had a connection in grief that others could never understand completely.

But it was the recognition of that connection that
prevented her saying anything. Because it was a time
warp. She was suddenly back in that blip of time that
had connected them that first time. Outside, on a night
that had been almost cold enough to freeze her tears.

She could hear his voice.

'Grace? Oh, my God...are you crying? What's wrong?'

He hadn't asked any more questions then, either.
He'd known that it didn't actually matter what had gone
wrong, it was comfort that she'd needed. Reassurance.

'Come with me. It's far too cold to be out here...'

He could see that there was something huge that had gone wrong now, too. And maybe she wouldn't need to say anything. If that rail wasn't between them, maybe Charles would take her in his arms again.

The way he had that night, before he'd led her away to a warm place.

His room.

His bed.

It was a very good thing that that strong rail was there. That Charles couldn't come through the gate when he had to be in that playground to supervise his children.

Even though she knew it couldn't happen, Grace still pulled her layers of protective clothing a little more tightly around her body. She still found herself stepping back from the fence.

'I really should go,' she said. 'It's not fair to make Houston wait any longer for his walk.'

Charles nodded slowly. His smile said it was fine.

But his eyes told her that he knew she was running away. That he could see a lot more than she wanted him to.

He couldn't see the physical scars, of course. Nobody got to see those.

Grace had been confident that nobody could see the emotional scars, either.

Until now...

CHAPTER FOUR

IT MIGHT WELL have been the two cops standing outside a curtained cubicle that attracted his attention as he walked past.

If he'd had any inclination to analyse it, though, Charles would probably have realised that it was the voice on the other side of the curtain that made him slow down.

Grace's voice.

'Looks like we've got an entrance wound here. And…an exit wound here. But it's possible that they're two entrance wounds. We need an X-ray.'

One of the cops caught his gaze and responded to the raised eyebrow.

'Drive-by shooting,' he said. 'He's lucky. It was his arm and not his head.'

With a nod, Charles moved on. Grace clearly had things under control. She always did, whenever he noticed her in the department and that was almost every day now that he had adjusted his hours to fit around nursery school for the twins. More than once a day, too. Not that he went out of his way to make their paths cross or anything. It just seemed to happen.

Okay, maybe he was choosing to do some necessary paperwork at one side of the unit desk instead of tucked away in his office but that was because he liked to keep half an eye on how the whole department was functioning. He could see the steady movement of people and equipment and hear phone calls being made and the radio link to the ambulance service. If anybody needed urgent assistance, he could be on his feet and moving in an instant.

It had nothing to do with the fact that Grace would be in this area before too long, checking the X-rays that would arrive digitally on one of the bank of departmental computer screens beside him.

He had a sheaf of statistics that he needed to review, like the numbers and types of patients that were coming through his department and it was important to see how they stacked up and whether trends were changing. Level one patients were the critical cases that took the most in the way of personnel and resources, but too many level four or five patients could create barriers to meeting target times for treatment and patient flow.

Grace Forbes certainly wasn't wasting time with her patients. It was only minutes later that she was logging in to a computer nearby, flanked by two medical students and a junior doctor. As they waited to upload files, she glanced sideways and acknowledged Charles with a smile but then she peered intently at the screen. Her colleagues leaned in as she used the cursor to highlight what she was looking at.

'There… Can you see that?'

'Is it a bone fragment?'

'No. Look how smooth the edges of the humerus are. And this is well away from it.'

'So it's a bullet fragment?'

'Yes. A very small one.'

'Do we need to get it out?'

'No. It's not clinically significant. And we were right that it's only one entrance and an exit wound but it was also right to check.'

'Want me to clean and dress it, then?' The junior doctor was keen to take over the case. 'Let the cops take him in to talk to him?'

'Yes. We'll put him on a broad-spectrum antibiotic as well. And make sure he gets a tetanus shot. Thanks, Danny. You're in charge now.' Grace's attention was swiftly diverted as she saw an incoming stretcher and she straightened and moved smoothly towards the new arrival as if she'd been ready and waiting all along.

'Hi, honey.' The girl on the stretcher looked very young, very pale and very frightened. 'My name's Grace and I'm going to be looking after you.'

Charles could hear one of the paramedics talking to Grace as they moved past to a vacant cubicle.

'Looks like gastro. Fever of thirty-nine point five and history of vomiting and diarrhoea. Mom called us when she fainted.'

'BP?'

'Eighty systolic. Couldn't get a diastolic.'

'I'm not surprised she fainted, then…'

The voices faded but Charles found himself still watching, even after the curtain had twitched into place to protect the new patient's privacy.

His attention was well and truly caught this time.

Because he was puzzled.

At moments like this, Grace was exactly the person he would have predicted that she would become. Totally on top of her work. Clever, competent and confident. She got along well with all her colleagues, too. Charles had heard more than one report of how great she was to work with and how generous she was with her time for staff members who were here to learn.

Thanks to the challenge that had been thrown at her within the first minutes of her coming to work here, Charles already knew how good Grace was at her job and how well she coped with difficult circumstances. That ability to think on her feet and adapt was a huge advantage for someone who worked in Emergency and she demonstrated the same kind of attitude in her private life, too, didn't she—in the way she had jumped on board, under pressure, to take on the dog-sitting offer.

But…and this was what was puzzling Charles so much…there was something very different about her personality away from work.

Something that felt off-key.

A timidity, almost. Lack of confidence, anyway.

Vulnerability? The way she'd shrunk away from him at the park yesterday. When he'd ventured onto personal ground by asking her about her marriage. He'd been puzzled then and he hadn't been able to shake it off.

He didn't want to shake it off, in fact. It was quite nice having this distraction because it meant he could ignore the background tension he always had at this time of year when he was walking an emotional tightrope between celebrating the joy of the twins' birth and being swamped by the grief of losing Nina, which was a can of mental worms that included so many other things he felt he should have done better—like protecting his family during the time of that scandal.

A nurse appeared from behind the curtain, with a handful of glass tubes full of blood that were clearly being rushed off for testing. He caught a glimpse of Grace bent over her patient, with her stethoscope in her ears and a frown of concentration on her face.

Grace had understood that grief so easily. He could still see those tears shimmering in her eyes when she'd been listening to him. Perhaps he'd known that she would understand on a different level from anybody else and that was why he had chosen to say more to her than he would have even to members of his own family.

But how had he known that?

And why was it that she did understand so clearly?

Who had she lost? Her husband, obviously, but the tone of her limited response to his queries had made him think that it was a marriage that simply hadn't worked out, not one that had been blown apart by tragedy, as his had been.

He wanted to know, dammit.

More than that, and he knew that it was ridiculous, but he was a bit hurt by being shut out.

Why?

Because—once upon a time—she had fallen into his arms and told him everything she was so worried about? That the pressure of those final exams was doing her head in? That it was times like this that she felt so lonely because it made her miss the mother she'd lost more than ever?

He'd had no intention of revisiting the memories of that night but they were creeping back now. The events that threatened to derail his life that had crashed around him so soon after that night had made it inevitable that it had to be dismissed but there was one aspect he'd never completely buried.

That sense of connection with another person.

He'd never felt it before that night.

He'd been lucky enough to find it again—with Nina—but he'd known that any chance of a third strike was out of the question. He wasn't looking because he didn't want to find it.

But it was already there with Grace, wasn't it? It had been, from the moment he'd taken her into his arms that night to comfort her.

And he'd felt it again at the park, when he'd seen her crying for his loss.

She'd been crying that night, too…

'You okay?'

'Huh?' Charles blinked as he heard the voice beside him. 'I'm fine, thanks, Miranda.'

'Okay…' But his half-sister was frowning at him. 'It's not like you to be sitting staring into space.'

Her frown advertised concern. A closeness that gave Charles a beat of something warm. Something good. Because it had been hard won? Miranda had come into their family as a penniless, lonely and frightened sixteen-year-old who was desperately missing her mother who had just died. It had been Charles who'd taken on the responsibility of trying to make her feel wanted. A little less lonely. Trying to persuade her that the scandal hadn't been *her* fault.

'I was just thinking.' About Grace. And he needed to stop because he was still aware of that warmth of something that felt good but now it was coming from remembering something Grace had said. The way she had tried to convince him that he had no valid reason to feel guilty over Nina's death—as if she really cared about how he felt.

Charles tapped the pile of papers in front of him. 'I'm up to my eyeballs in statistics. What are you up to?'

'I need a portable ultrasound to check a stab wound for underlying damage. It looks superficial but I want to make absolutely sure.' Miranda looked around. 'They seem to have gone walkabout.'

Charles glanced towards the glass board where patient details were constantly updated to keep track of where people were and what was going on. Who could be currently using ultrasound to help a diagnosis?

'It could be in with the abdo pain in Curtain Two.'

'Thanks. I'll check.' Miranda turned her head as she moved away. 'How are the party plans going? Do we get an invitation this year?'

Charles shook his head but offered an apologetic smile. 'I'm keeping it low-key. I'm taking them to visit the grandparents the next day for afternoon tea and I'm sure you'll be invited as well, but my neighbours have said they'd be delighted to have an in-house trick or treat happen on the actual birthday and that's probably as much excitement as two three-year-olds can handle.'

Miranda's nod conveyed understanding of the need to keep the celebration private. She'd seen photographs of the Davenport extravaganzas of years past, before she'd become a part of the family—when there had been bouncy castles, magicians and even ponies or small zoos involved.

Buying into Halloween was a big step forward this year but there was going to be a nursery school parade so the costumes were essential. Charles found himself staring again at the curtain that Grace was behind. Hadn't she said something about finding a costume for Houston? Maybe she'd found a good costume shop.

And maybe Houston could join in the fun? The boys loved that dog and he could be an addition to the private party that would delight them rather than overwhelm them, like a full-on Davenport gathering had the potential to do.

Grace would have to be invited, too, of course, but that wasn't a big deal. Somehow, the intrigue about what had happened to change her had overridden any internal warning about spending time with her. He wanted an answer to the puzzle and getting a little closer was the only way he was going to solve the mystery. Close enough to be friends—like he and Miranda had become all those years ago—but nothing more. And that wouldn't be a problem. The barrier to anything more was so solid he wouldn't have the first idea how to get past it.

And he didn't want to. Even the reminder that that barrier was there was enough to send him back to safe territory and Charles spent the next fifteen minutes focused on the graphs he needed to analyse.

But then Grace appeared from the cubicle and headed straight to the computer closest to where he was sitting. It was tempting to say something totally inappropriate, like asking her whether she might be available for a while in two days' time, to go trick or treating but this wasn't the time or place. It was a bit of a shock, in fact, that the urge was even there. So out of character that it wasn't at all difficult to squash.

'Looking for results?'

'Yep. White blood count and creatinine should be available by now. I've got cultures, throat swabs and urine pending.'

'More than a viral illness, then?'

Grace didn't seem surprised that he was aware of which patient she was dealing with.

'I think she's got staphylococcal toxic shock syndrome. Sixteen years old.'

Charles blinked. It was a rare thing to see these days,

which meant that it could be missed until it was late enough for the condition to be extremely serious.

'Signs and symptoms?'

'High fever, vomiting and diarrhoea, muscle aches, a widespread rash that looks like sunburn. She's also hypotensive. Seventy-five over thirty and she's onto her second litre of fluid resus.' Grace flicked him a glance. 'She also finished her period two days ago and likes to leave her tampons in overnight.'

Charles could feel his mouth twisting into a lopsided smile. An impressed one. That was the key question that needed to be asked and could be missed. But not by Grace Forbes, apparently.

'Any foreign material left? Had she forgotten to take a tampon out?'

'No, but I still think I'm right.' Grace clicked a key. 'Yes… Her white count's sky high. So's her creatinine, which means she's got renal involvement. Could be septic shock from another cause but that won't change the initial management.'

'Plan?'

'More fluids, vasopressor support to try and get her BP up. And antibiotics, of course.'

'Flucloxacillin?'

'Yes. And I'll add in clindamycin. There's good evidence that it's effective in decreasing toxin production.' Grace looked past Charles to catch the attention of one of the nursing staff. 'Amy, could you see if there's a bed available in ICU, please? I've got a patient that's going to need intensive monitoring for a while.'

'On it, Dr Forbes.' The nurse reached for the phone.

Grace was gone, too, back to her patient. Charles gave up on the statistics. He would take them home and do his work later tonight, in those quiet hours after the boys were asleep. He was due to go and collect them soon, anyway.

Maybe he should give up on the idea of inviting Grace and Houston to join their party, too. He could give his boys everything they needed. He could take them out later today and let them choose the costumes they wanted themselves.

A sideways glance showed that Amy had finished her urgent arrangements for Grace's patient. She noticed his glance.

'Anything you need, Dr Davenport?'

He smiled at her. 'Not unless you happen to know of a good costume shop in this part of town?'

It seemed like every shop between Manhattan Mercy and home had decorated their windows for Halloween and it made Grace smile, despite her weariness after a couple of such busy days at work, to see the jack-o'-lanterns and ghosts and plastic spiders hanging on fluffy webs.

She'd missed this celebration in Australia.

As she turned towards the more residential area, there were groups of children already out, too, off to do their trick or treating in the late afternoon. So many excited little faces peeping out from beneath witches' hats or lions' ears, dancing along in pretty dresses with fairy wings on their backs or proudly being miniature superheroes.

What a shame that Charles hadn't taken her up on her subtle offer to share Halloween with him and his boys. She'd been thinking about him all day, and wondering just how difficult it had been for him when he had to be reliving every moment of this day three years ago when the twins had been born and he'd lost the love of his life.

Her heart was aching for Charles all over again, as she let herself into the apartment building, so it came as a surprise to hear a peal of laughter echoing down the tiled stairway with its wrought-iron bannisters.

The laughter of small people. And a deeper rumble of an adult male.

Grace paused in the foyer, looking upwards, and was rewarded by a small face she recognised instantly, peering down through the rails. His head was covered by a brown hood that had small round ears.

'Gace... Look at us...'

'I can't see you properly, Max.'

The face disappeared but she could still hear him.

'Daddy... Daddy...we have to visit Gace now...'

And there they were, coming down the stairs. Charles had hold of each twin's hand to keep them steady. In their other hands, the boys clutched a small, orange, plastic bucket shaped like a pumpkin. She could see plenty of candy in each bucket.

The brown hoods were part of a costume that covered them from head to toe.

'You're monkeys.' Grace grinned. 'But...where are your tails?'

The twins gave her a very patient look.

Charles gave her a shadow of a wink. 'Curious George doesn't have a tail,' he explained.

'Oh...'

'Trick or treat!' Cameron shouted. He bounced up and down on small padded feet. 'We want *candy...*'

'Please,' Charles admonished. 'Where are your manners, buddy?'

'*Please!*' It was Max who was first to comply.

'Grace might not have any candy. Maybe we could just say "hi" to Horse?'

'Actually, I *do* have some candy.' Grace smiled at Charles. 'I have a personal weakness for M&M'S. Would they be suitable?'

'A very small packet?' Charles was smiling back at her but looking slightly haunted. 'We already have enough candy to last till Christmas.'

'They're tiny boxes.' Grace pulled her keys from her bag. 'Come on in. Horse will be so happy to see you.'

Charles had probably been in this apartment before, visiting Stefan and Jerome, but he hadn't come in since Grace had taken over and it felt like a huge step forward somehow. The huge, modern spaces had felt rather empty and totally not her style, although she was slowly getting used to them. With two small boys rolling around on the floor with Houston and Charles following her into the kitchen, it suddenly felt far more like a home.

'Let me open the French doors so that Houston can get out into the garden. It's been an hour or two since Kylie took him out for his last walk.' Grace headed for the pantry next, where she knew the big bag still had plenty of the small boxes of candy-covered chocolate she kept for an after-dinner treat.

She had a bottle of wine in the fridge, too. Would it be a step too far to offer one to Charles? She wanted to ask how the day had gone because she knew that she would be able to see past any cheerful accounts and know how hard it had really been. But she could see that anyway. Charles was looking tired and his smile didn't reach his eyes.

And she wasn't about to get the chance to say anything, because his phone was ringing. He took the call, keeping an eye on the children, who were now racing around the garden with the dog, as he listened and then started firing questions.

'Who's there? How long ago did you activate Code Red?'

Grace caught her breath. 'Code Red' was a term used in Manhattan Mercy's ER to indicate that the level of patient numbers was exceeding the resources the department had to deal with them. Like a traffic light that was not functioning correctly, a traffic jam could ensue and, with patients, it meant that urgent treatment could be delayed and fatalities could result.

He listened a moment longer. 'I'll be there as soon as I can.'

'I can go back,' Grace offered as he ended the call. She could get there in less than ten minutes and she was still in her scrubs—she wouldn't even need to get changed.

But Charles shook his head. 'It's the administrative side that needs management. I'll have to go in.' He looked out at the garden. 'I can take the boys.'

This time, it was Grace who shook her head. 'Don't be daft. I'll look after them.'

Charles looked stunned by the offer. 'But…'

'But, nothing. I'll take them back up to your apartment. That way I can feed them. Or get them to bed if you end up being late. Is it okay if I take Houston up, too?'

'Of course…but…are you sure, Grace? They're going to get tired and cranky after the day they've had.'

Grace held his gaze. 'Go,' she said quietly. 'And don't worry about them. They'll be safe.'

For a heartbeat, she saw the shadows on his face lift as his smile very definitely reached his eyes.

'Thank you,' was all Charles said but it felt like she was the one who was being given something very special.

Trust?

CHAPTER FIVE

IF IT HADN'T been for her small entourage of two little boys and one large, fluffy dog, Grace might have felt like she was doing something wrong, stepping into Charles Davenport's private life like this.

How weird was it that just a few hours of one's lifetime, over a decade ago, could have had such an impact that it could make her feel like…like some kind of *stalker*?

It was her own fault. She had allowed herself to remember those hours. Enshrine them, almost, so that they had become a comfort zone that she had relied on, especially in the early days of coming to terms with what had felt like a broken and very lonely life. In those sleepless hours when things always seemed so much worse, she had imagined herself back in Charles's arms. Being held as though she was something precious.

Being made love to, as if she was the only woman in the world that Charles had wanted to be with.

She could have had a faceless fantasy to tap into but it had seemed perfectly safe to use Charles because she had never expected to see him again. And it had made it all seem so much more believable, because it *had* happened.

Once…

And, somewhere along the way, she had allowed herself to wonder about all the things she didn't know about him. What kind of house he lived in, for example. What his favourite food was. Whether he was married now and had a bunch of gorgeous kids.

She probably could have found out with a quick internet search but she never allowed those secret thoughts any head space in daylight hours. And, as soon as she'd started considering working at Manhattan Mercy, she had shut down even the familiar fantasy. It was no more than a very personal secret—a rather embarrassing one now.

But…entering his private domain like this was…

Satisfying?

Exciting?

Astonishing, certainly.

For some reason, she had expected it to be like the apartment she was living in on the ground floor of this wonderful, old building with its high ceilings and period features like original fireplaces and polished wooden floors. She had also expected the slightly overwhelming aura of wealth and style that Stefan and Jerome had created with their bespoke furniture and expertly displayed artworks.

The framework of the apartment with the floors and ceilings was no surprise but Grace's breath was taken away the moment she stepped through the door to face floor-to-ceiling windows that opened onto a terrace looking directly over Central Park. The polished floors didn't have huge Persian rugs like hers and the furniture looked like it had once been in a house out in the country somewhere. A big, old rambling farmhouse, maybe.

The couch was enormous and so well used that the leather looked crinkled and soft. There were picture books scattered over the rustic coffee table, along with crayons and paper and even the curling crust of an abandoned sandwich. There were toys all over the place, too—building bricks and brightly coloured cars, soft toy animals and half-done jigsaw puzzles.

It looked like…*home*…

The kind of home that was as much of a fantasy for Grace as being held—and loved—by someone totally genuine.

She had to swallow a huge lump in her throat.

And then she had to laugh, because Houston made a beeline for the coffee table and scoffed the old sandwich crust.

'I'm hungry,' Cameron announced, as he spotted the dog licking its lips.

'Me, too.' Max nodded.

Cameron upended his pumpkin bucket of candy onto the coffee table. Grace gave Houston a stern look that warned him to keep his nose out. Then she extracted the handfuls of candy from Cameron's fists.

'You can choose *one* thing,' she told him. 'But you can't eat it until after your dinner, okay?'

Cameron scowled at her. 'But I'm *hungry.*'

'I know.' Grace was putting the candy back into the bucket. 'Show me where the kitchen is and I'll make you some dinner. You'd better show me where the bathroom is, too.'

The twins led her into a spacious kitchen with a walk-in pantry.

'I'll show you,' Max offered.

He climbed onto a small step and wobbled precariously as he reached for something on a shelf. Grace caught him as he, and the packet he had triumphantly caught the edge of, fell off the step. For a moment, she stood there with the small, warm body in its fluffy monkey suit in her arms. She could smell the soft scent of something that was distinctly child-like. Baby shampoo, maybe?

Max giggled at the pleasure of being caught and, without thinking, Grace planted a kiss on his forehead.

'Down you go,' she said. 'And keep those monkey paws on the floor, where they're safe.'

She stooped to pick up the packet as she set him down.

'Mac and cheese? Is that what you guys want to eat?'

'Yes...*yes*...mac and cheese. For Horse, too...'

Houston waved his plume of a tail, clearly in agreement with the plan, but Grace was more dubious. She eyed the fruit bowl on the table in the kitchen and then the big fridge freezer. Could she tempt them to something healthier first—like an apple or a carrot? Were there some vegetables they might like in the freezer to go with the cheese and pasta? And packet pasta? *Really?* If she could find the ingredients, it wouldn't be hard to throw a fresh version in the oven. Cooking—and baking—were splinter skills she had enjoyed honing over the years.

The twins—and Horse—crowded around as she checked out what she might have to work with. There wasn't much in the way of fresh vegetables but the freezer looked well stocked.

'What's this?' The long cylindrical object was unfamiliar.

'Cookie dough,' Cameron told her. 'Maria makes us cookies.'

'Can you make cookies, Gace?' Max leaned forward so that he could turn his head to look up at her as she crouched. 'I *like* cookies.' Again, she had to catch him before he lost his balance and toppled into the freezer drawer.

'I don't see why not,' she decided. 'You can help. But only if you both eat an apple while I'm getting things ready. And we won't use the frozen sort. If there's some flour in the pantry and butter in the fridge, we'll make our own. From scratch.'

Over an hour later, Grace realised that the grand plan might have been ill-advised. This huge kitchen with its granite and stainless-steel work surfaces looked like a food bomb had been detonated and the sink was stacked with dirty pots and bowls. A fine snowstorm of flour had settled everywhere along with shreds of grated cheese and dribbles of chocolate icing. Houston had done his best to help and there wasn't a single crumb to be found on the floor, but he wasn't so keen on raw flour.

Whose idea had it been to make Halloween spider cookies?

The boys were sitting on the bench right now, on either side of the tray of cookies that had come out of the oven a short time ago. They had to be so tired by now, but they both had their hands clasped firmly in front of them, their eyes huge with excitement as they waited patiently for Grace to tell them it was safe to touch the hot cookies. It was so cute, she had to get her phone out and take a photo. Then she took a close-up of the cookies. The pale dough had made a perfect canvas for the iced chocolate spiders that had M&M eyes. She'd used a plastic bag to make a piping tool and had done her best to guide three-year-old hands to position spider legs but the results were haphazard. One spider appeared to be holding its eyes on the ends of a very fat leg.

Should she send one of the photos to Charles?

A closer glance at the image of his sons made her decide not to. Still in their monkey suits, the boys now had chocolate smears on their faces and the curls of Max's hair that had escaped his hood had something that looked like cheese sauce in it. Her own hair had somehow escaped its fastenings recently and she was fairly sure that she would find a surprise or two when she tried to brush it later.

Hopefully, she would have time to clean up before their father got home but the children and the kitchen would have to take priority. Not wanting to look a wreck in front of Charles was no excuse to worry about her own appearance. She was still in her work scrubs, for heaven's sake—what did it matter?

She prodded one of the cookies.

'Still too hot, guys,' she said. 'But our mac and cheese has cooled down. You can have some of that and then the cookies will be ready for dessert.'

She lifted one twin and then the other off the bench. 'Do you want to take your monkey suits off now?'

'No. We want to be George.'

'And *watch* George,' Max added, nodding his agreement.

'Okay. Do you eat your dinner at the table?'

'Our table,' Cameron told her. 'With TV.'

'Hmm. Let's wash those monkey paws.'

Grace wasn't sure that eating in front of the television was really the norm but, hey…they were all tired now and it was a birthday, after all. She served bowls of the homemade pasta bake on the top of a small, bright yellow table that Cameron and Max dragged to be right in front of the widescreen television. The chairs were different primary shades and had the boys' names painted on the back. Fortunately, it was easy to see how to use the DVD player and an episode of *Curious George* was already loaded.

The smell of the mac and cheese made Grace realise how hungry she was herself. She knew she should tackle the mess in the kitchen but it wouldn't hurt to curl up on the couch with a bowl of food for a few minutes, would it?

The yellow table, and the bowls, were suspiciously clean when Grace came in later with the platter of cookies and Houston had an innocent air that looked well practised. She had to press her lips together not to laugh out loud. She needed some practice of her own, perhaps, in good parenting?

The thought caught her unawares. She'd been enjoying this time so much it hadn't occurred to her to realise that she was living a fantasy. But that was good, wasn't it? That day at the park, she had wanted to able to embrace a special moment for what it was and not ruin it by remembering old pain. She had done that with bells on with this unexpected babysitting job.

The laughter had evaporated, though. And her smile felt distinctly wobbly. It was just as well that Cameron turned his head to notice what she was carrying.

'*Cookies...*'

Max's chair fell over backwards in his haste to get up and Houston barked his approval of the new game as they all rushed at Grace. She sat on the couch with a bump and held the platter too high to be reached by all those small fingers.

'One each,' she commanded. 'And none for Horse, okay?'

They ended up having two each but they weren't overly big cookies. And the crumbs didn't really matter because a leather couch would be easy enough to clean. Not that Grace wanted to move just yet. She had two small boys nestled on either side of her and they were all mesmerised by what Curious George was up to on the screen.

'He's a very naughty monkey, isn't he? Look at all that paint he's spilling everywhere!'

The boys thought it was hilarious but she could feel their warm bodies getting heavier and heavier against her own. Houston was sound asleep with his head pillowed on her feet and Grace could feel her own eyes drooping. Full of comfort food and suddenly exhausted by throwing herself so enthusiastically into what would undoubtedly become an emotionally charged memory, it was impossible not to let herself slip into a moment of putting off the inevitable return to reality.

She wouldn't let herself fall asleep, of course. She would just close her eyes and sink into this group cuddle for a minute or two longer...

It was the last thing Charles had expected to see when he let himself quietly into his apartment late that evening.

He knew his boys would have crashed hours ago and he had assumed they would be tucked up in their shared bedroom, in the racing car beds that had been last year's extravagant gift from their grandparents.

They were, indeed, fast asleep when he arrived home after his hectic troubleshooting in a stretched emergency department, but they weren't in their own beds. Or even in their pyjamas. Still encased in their little monkey suits, Cameron and Max were curled up like puppies on either side of Grace, who was also apparently sound asleep on the couch. Houston had woken at the scratch of the key in the lock, of course, but he wasn't about to abandon the humans he was protecting. He didn't budge from where he was lying across Grace's feet but he seemed to be smiling up at Charles and his tail was twitching in a muted wag.

It might have been a totally unexpected sight, but it was also the cutest thing Charles had ever seen. He gazed at the angelic, sleeping faces of his sons and could feel his heart expanding with love so much it felt like it was in danger of bursting. They were both tucked under a protective arm. Grace had managed to stay sitting upright in her sleep but her head was tilted to one side. He had never seen her face in slumber and she looked far younger than the thirty-six years he knew she shared with him. Far more vulnerable than she ever looked when she was awake.

Maybe it was because she was a single unit with his boys at the moment that she was automatically included in this soft wash of feeling so protective.

So...blessed?

But then Charles stepped closer. What was that in Grace's hair? And smeared on her cheek?

Chocolate?

A closer glance at the twins revealed unexplained substances in odd places as well. Charles could feel his face crease into a deep frown. What on earth had been going on here? Walking quietly, he went through the sitting room towards the kitchen and it wasn't long before he stopped in his tracks, utterly stunned.

He'd never seen a mess like this.

Ever...

His feet were leaving prints in the layer of flour on the floor. The sink was overflowing with dirty dishes. There was a deep dish half-full of what looked like mac and cheese and a wire rack that was covered with cook-

ies. Cookies that were decorated with…good grief…
what were those strange blobs and squiggles with chocolate candies poked amongst them?

Ah…there was one with a recognisable shape.

A spider…

And then it hit Charles. Grace had been making Halloween cookies with the boys and clearly she had let
them do most of the decorating themselves.

Suddenly, the appalling mess in the kitchen ceased
to matter because Charles had glimpsed a much bigger
picture. One that caught his heart in a very different
way to seeing his boys sleeping so contentedly.

This was a kind of scene that he had never envisaged
in the lives of his precious little family. Because it was a
dimension that only a woman would think of including?

A *mother*?

Somehow, it wrapped itself into the whole idea of a
home. Of a kitchen being the heart of the house. Of putting up with unnecessary mess because that was how
children learned important things. Not just about how
to make cookies but about…about *home*.

About being safe. And loved.

For a moment, the feeling was overwhelming enough
to bring a lump to his throat and a prickle to the back
of his eyes that brought all sorts of other sensations in
their wake.

Feelings of loss.

And longing…

He had to cradle his forehead between his thumb
and finger and rub hard at his temples to stop himself
falling into a complete wreck.

It was too much. On top of such an emotionally
charged day riding that roller-coaster between remembered grief and the very real celebration of his boys'

lives, topped off with an exhausting few hours of high-powered management of a potentially dangerous situation, it was no wonder this was overwhelming.

It was too much.

But it was also kind of perfect.

It was the gentle extraction of a small body from beneath her arm that woke Grace.

For a moment, she blinked sleepily up at Charles, thinking that she was dreaming.

That *smile*...

She had never seen anything quite so tender.

He was smiling at her as if he loved her as much as she knew he loved his children.

Yep. Definitely a dream.

But then Max gave a tiny whimper in his sleep as he was lifted. And the warm weight on her feet shifted as Houston got up and then it all came rushing back to Grace.

'Oh, my God...' she whispered. 'I fell asleep. Oh, Charles, I'm *so* sorry...'

'Don't be.'

'But the *mess*. I was going to clean it all up before you got home.'

'Shh...' Charles was turning away, a still sleeping Max cradled in his arms. 'I'll put Max down and then come back for Cameron. Don't move, or you might wake him up.'

That gave Grace all the time she needed to remember exactly what state she'd left this beautiful apartment in. It was bad enough in here, with the television still going, scattered toys and dinner dishes where they'd been left, but the kitchen...

Oh, help… She'd been given total responsibility and she had created a complete disaster.

But Charles didn't seem to mind. He lifted Cameron with a gentleness that took her breath away. Maybe because his hands brushed her own body as he slid them into place and she could feel just how much care he was taking not to wake his son. His gaze caught hers as she lifted her arm to make his task easier and, amazingly, he was still smiling.

As if he didn't actually care about the mess.

Grace cared. She got to her feet and any residual fuzziness from being woken from a deep sleep evaporated instantly as she went back to the kitchen.

It was even worse than she'd remembered.

Should she start with that pile of unwashed dishes or find a broom and start sweeping the floor?

Reaching out, she touched a puddle of chocolate icing on the granite surface of the work bench. It had hardened enough that it would need a lot more than a cloth to wipe it clean. Where were the cleaning supplies kept? Grace pushed her hair back from her face as she looked around and, to her horror, she found a hard lump that had glued a large clump of hair together. Hard enough to suggest it was more chocolate icing.

She was still standing there, mortified, when Charles came to find her.

For a long moment, she couldn't think of anything to say that could encompass how embarrassed she was. Finally, she had to risk making eye contact. He had to be furious, surely, even if he'd been doing a superb job of hiding it so far.

He caught her gaze and held it firmly. Grace couldn't look away.

Yes…there was something stern enough there to let

her know he knew exactly how major the clean-up job would be. That he knew how carried away she'd been in her attempt to keep the twins entertained. That she'd surprised him, to say the very least.

But there was something else there as well.

A…twinkle…

Of amusement, laced with something else.

Appreciation maybe.

No…it was deeper than that. Something she couldn't identify.

'What?' she heard herself whisper. 'What are you thinking? That you'll never leave me in charge of your kids again?'

One corner of his mouth lifted into a smile that could only be described as poignant.

'I'm thinking,' he said quietly. 'That I've spent the last three years trying to be both a father and a mother to my kids and keep their lives as predictable and safe as I can and then someone comes in and, in the space of a few hours, wrecks my house and shows me exactly what I didn't realise was missing.'

Grace's brain had fixed on the comment about wrecking his house.

'I'm sorry,' she murmured.

Charles's gaze shifted a fraction. Oh, help…was he staring at the lump of chocolate icing in her hair?

'I've never even thought of making cookies with the boys,' he said. 'I wouldn't know where to start. I know Maria makes them sometimes, but all that's involved there is slicing up a frozen roll and sticking them in the oven. I'm surprised you even found a bag of flour in the pantry. Not only that, you let them draw spiders on the top.'

'Oh…' Grace could feel her lips curve with pleasure. 'You could tell what they were, then?'

'Only after I spotted one that you probably did. Some of them seem to have eyes on their legs.'

'Helps to see round corners,' Grace suggested. Her smile widened.

Charles was smiling back at her and that twinkle in his eyes had changed into something else.

Something that was giving her a very distinctive shaft of sensation deep in her belly.

Attraction, that's what it was.

A very physical and very definite attraction.

Maybe Charles was feeling it, too. Maybe that was why he lifted his hand to touch her hair.

'Chocolate,' he told her.

'I know…' Grace made a face. 'You might find you need to wash the boys' hair in the morning as well.'

'It's not a problem.' Charles was touching her cheek now, his finger feather-light. 'You've got some here, too.'

Grace couldn't say anything. She was shocked by the touch and the electricity of the current it was producing that flashed through her body like a lightning bolt to join the pool of sensation lower down.

The smile on Charles's face was fading fast. For another one of those endless moments, they stared at each other again.

Fragments of unformed thoughts bombarded Grace. Memories of another time when they'd looked at each other just like this. Before Charles had kissed her for the very first time. Snatches of the conversation they'd just had. What had he meant when he'd said that she'd shown him what he hadn't realised was missing in his life?

Surely he didn't mean *her*?

Part of her really wanted that to have been the meaning.

The part that held his gaze, willing him to make the first move…

He was still touching her cheek but his finger moved past any smear of chocolate, tracing the edge of her nose and then out to the corner of her mouth and along her bottom lip.

And then he shut his eyes as he bent his head, taking his finger away just before his lips took its place.

Another shock wave of unbearably exquisite pleasure shot through Grace's body and she had to close her own eyes as she fell into it.

Dear Lord…she had relived a kiss from this man so many times in her imagination but somehow the reality had been muted over the years.

Nobody else had ever kissed her like this.

Ever…

It was impossible not to respond. To welcome the deepening of that kiss. To press herself closer to the remembered planes of that hard, lean body. It wasn't until his hand shifted from her back to slide under her ribs and up onto her breast that Grace was suddenly blindsided by reality.

By what Charles was about to touch.

She could feel the adrenaline flood her body now, her muscles tensing instantly in a classic fight-or-flight reflex, in the same moment that she jerked herself back.

Charles dropped his hand instantly. Stepped back from the kiss just as swiftly.

And this time there was a note of bewilderment in his eyes. Of horror, even…

They both looked away.

'Um…' Grace struggled to find her voice. And a reason to escape. 'I… I really need to take Houston downstairs. He must be a bit desperate to get out by now.'

'Of course.' Was it her imagination or did Charles seem grateful for an excuse to ignore what had just happened? 'He needs his garden.'

'I can't leave you with this mess, though.'

'My cleaner's due in the morning. It really isn't a problem.'

No. Grace swallowed hard. They had another problem now, though, didn't they?

But she could feel the distance between them accelerating. She wasn't the only one who needed to escape, was she?

They hadn't just crossed a barrier here. They had smashed through it with no consideration of any repercussions.

And maybe they were just as big for Charles as they were for herself.

But Grace couldn't afford to feel any empathy right now. The need to protect herself was too overwhelming.

With no more than a nod to acknowledge her being excused from cleaning up the mess she had created, Grace took her leave and fled downstairs with Houston.

She had no mental space to feel guilty about escaping.

Besides, Charles had created a bit of a mess himself, hadn't he? By kissing her like that.

That was more than enough to deal with for the moment.

CHAPTER SIX

'OH, MY…' VANESSA DAVENPORT looked slightly appalled as she peered more closely at what was being held up for her admiration. 'What *are* they?'

'Cookies, Grandma.' Cameron was using that patient tone that told adults they were being deliberately obtuse. 'We *made* them.'

'And Gace,' Max added.

'Gace?' Vanessa was looking bewildered now but Charles didn't offer an explanation.

He was kicking himself inwardly. He should have known exactly what his mother's reaction would be to the less than perfect cookies, but he couldn't forgive the slap to his boys' pride that had prompted them to insist on bringing their creations to the family afternoon tea.

It was the complete opposite end to the spectrum that Grace was also on. She'd been just as proud of the boys at the results of their efforts. This morning, she'd sent him the photo she'd taken of them sitting on the bench, their hands clasped and eyes shining with the tray of cookies between them. It even had Horse's nose photobombing the bottom of the image and Charles had been so taken with it, he'd thought of using it for his Christmas cards this year.

Maybe not, if his mother was going to look like this.

'Let's give them to Alice.' Vanessa was an expert in ignoring anything that she didn't approve of. 'She can put them in the kitchen.'

Alice was hovering in the background, ready to help with hanging coats up in the cloakroom, but she moved swiftly when there was another knock on the massive front door of the Davenport mansion. His father, Hugo, was coming into the foyer at the same time and the twins' faces brightened.

'Look, Grandpa...look what we made.'

'Wow...cookies...they look delicious.'

'Did I hear someone mention cookies?'

Charles turned towards the door. 'Miranda. Hey... I'm glad you could make it.'

His half-sister had two brightly wrapped parcels under her arm and the twins' eyes got very round.

'Presents, Daddy. For us?'

But Charles had been distracted by someone who had followed Miranda into the house. He hadn't seen his youngest brother, Zachary, for such a long time.

'*Zac*... What are you doing here?'

'I heard there was a birthday celebration happening.'

'But I thought you were in Annapolis.'

'I was. I am. I'm just in town for the day—you should know why...'

Charles had to shake his head but there was no time to ask. The shriek of excitement behind him had to mean that Miranda had handed over the parcels and, turning his head, he could see his mother already moving towards the main reception lounge.

'For goodness' sake,' she said. 'Let's go somewhere a little more civilised than the doorstep, shall we?'

Charles saw the glance that flashed between Zac and Miranda. Would there ever come a day when Vanessa actually welcomed Miranda into this house, instead of barely tolerating her?

His father was now holding the platter of cookies.

'Shall I take those to the kitchen, sir?' Alice asked.

'No…no…they have to go on the table with all the other treats.'

Charles felt a wash of relief. Families were always complicated and this one a lot more than most but there was still a thread of something good to be found. Something worth celebrating.

He scooped up Cameron, who was already ripping the paper off his gift. 'Hang on, buddy. Let's do that in the big room.'

Zac had parcels in his hands, too. And when the door swung open behind him to reveal Elijah with a single, impressively large box in his arms, Charles could only hope that this gathering wasn't going to be too overwhelming for small boys. He thought wistfully of the relatively calm oasis of their own apartment and, unbidden, an image of the ultimately peaceful scene he'd come home to last night filled his mind.

The one of Grace, asleep on the couch, cuddled up with the boys and with a dog asleep on her feet.

So peaceful. So…perfect…?

'I can't stay,' Elijah said, as they all started moving to the lounge. 'I got someone to cover me for an hour at work. I'll be getting a taxi back in half an hour.'

'Oh…' Miranda was beside him. 'Could I share? My shift starts at five but it takes so long on the Tube I'd have to leave about then, anyway.'

'Flying visit,' Zac murmured. 'It's always the way with us Davenports, isn't it? Do your duty but preferably with an excuse to escape before things get awkward?'

'Mmm.' The sound was noncommittal but Charles

put Cameron down with an inward sigh. This vast room, with a feature fireplace and enough seating for forty people, had obviously been professionally decorated. Huge, helium balloons were tethered everywhere and there were streamers looping between the chandeliers and a banner covering the wall behind the mahogany dining table that had been shifted in here from the adjoining dining room. A table that was laden with perfectly decorated cakes and cookies and any number of other delicious treats that had been provided by professional caterers.

Cameron, with his half-unwrapped parcel in his arms, ran towards the pile of other gifts near the table, Max hot on his heels. A maid he didn't recognise came towards the adults with a silver tray laden with flutes of champagne.

'Orange juice for me, thanks,' Elijah said. Miranda just shook her head politely and went after the twins to help them with the unwrapping.

'So what's with your flying visit?' he asked Zac. 'And why should I know about it?'

'Because I'm here for an interview. I've applied for a job at Manhattan Mercy that starts next month.'

'Really? Wow…' Charles took a sip of his champagne. 'That's great, man. And there I was thinking you were going to be a navy medic for the rest of your life.'

Zac shrugged. 'Maybe I'm thinking that life's short, you know? If I don't get around to building some bridges soon, it's never going to happen.'

Charles could only nod. He knew better than anyone how short life could be, didn't he? About the kind of jagged hole that could be left when someone you loved got ripped from it.

But that hole had been covered last night, hadn't it?

Just for a moment or two, he had stepped far enough away from it for it to have become invisible. And it had been that perfect family scene that had led him away. His two boys, under the sheltering arms of someone who had looked, for all the world, like their mother. With a loyal family pet at their feet, even.

But now Zac had shown him the signpost that led straight back to the gaping hole in his life.

And Elijah was shaking his head. 'I hope you're not harbouring any hope of this lot playing happy families any time soon.'

They all turned their gazes on their parents. Hugo and Miranda were both down on the floor with the twins. Miranda's gifts of a new toy car for Cameron and a tractor for Max had been opened and set aside and now the first of the many parcels from the grand-parents were being opened. It looked like it was a very large train set, judging by the lengths of wooden rails that were appearing. The level of excitement was in-creasing and Charles needed to go and share it. Maybe that way, the twins wouldn't notice the way their grand-mother was perched on a sofa at some distance, merely watching the spectacle.

'Anyone else coming?' Zac asked. 'Where's Penny?'

'Still on holiday. Skiing, I think. Or was it sky-diving?'

'Sounds like her. And Jude? I'd love to catch up with him.'

'Are you kidding?' Elijah's eyebrows rose. 'Being a cousin is a perfect "get out of jail" card for most of our family get-togethers.'

Charles moved away from his brothers. It was always like this. Yes, there were moments of joy to be found in his family but the undercurrents were strong enough to mean that there was always tension. And most of that tension came from Vanessa and Elijah.

You had to make allowances, of course. It was his mother who'd been hardest hit by the scandal of learning that her husband had been having an affair that had resulted in a child—Miranda. That knowledge would have been hard enough, but to find out because Miranda's mother had died and her father had insisted on acknowledging her and bringing her into the family home had been unbearable for Vanessa.

Unbearable for everyone. The difference in age between himself and his twin might have been insignificant but Charles had always known that he was the oldest child. The firstborn. And that came with a responsibility that he took very seriously. That turbulent period of the scandal had been his first real test and he'd done everything he could to comfort his siblings—especially Elijah, who'd been so angry and bitter. To protect the frightened teenager who had suddenly become one of their number as well. And to support his devastated mother, who was being forced to start an unexpected chapter in her life.

Like the authors of many of the gossip columns, he'd expected his mother would walk away from her marriage but Vanessa had chosen not to take that option. She'd claimed that she didn't want to bring more shame on the Davenport family but they all knew that what scared her more would have been walking away from her own exalted position in New York society and the fundraising efforts that had become her passion.

To outward appearances, the shocking changes had been tolerated with extraordinary grace. Behind closed doors, however, it had been a rather different story. There were no-go areas that Vanessa had constructed for her own protection and nobody, including her husband, would dream of intruding on them uninvited.

Charles had always wondered if he could have done more, especially for Elijah, who had ended up so bitter about marriage and what he sarcastically referred to as 'happy families'. If he could have done a better job as the firstborn, maybe he could have protected his family more successfully, perhaps by somehow diverting the destructive force of the scandal breaking. It hadn't been his fault, of course, any more than Nina's death had been. Why didn't that lessen the burden that a sense of responsibility created?

But surely enough time had passed to let them all move on?

Charles felt tired of it all suddenly. The effort it had taken to try and keep his shattered family together would have been all-consuming at any time. To have had it happen in the run-up to his final exams had been unbelievably difficult. Life-changing.

If it hadn't happened, right after that night he'd shared with Grace, how different might his life have been?

Would he have shut her out so completely? Pretended that night had never happened because that was a factor he had absolutely no head space to even consider?

To his shame, Charles had been so successful in shutting it out in that overwhelmingly stressful period, he had never thought of how it might have hurt Grace.

Was *that* why she'd pretty much flinched during that kiss last night? Why she'd practically run away from him as hard and fast as she could politely manage?

Receiving that photo this morning had felt kind of like Grace was sending an olive branch. An apology for running, perhaps. Or at least an indication that they could still be friends?

The effect was a swirl of confusion. He had glimpsed something huge that was missing from his life, along with the impression that Grace was possibly the only person who could fill that gap. The very edges of that notion should be stirring his usual reaction of disloyalty to Nina that thoughts of including any other woman in his life usually engendered.

But it wasn't happening…

Because there was a part of his brain that was standing back and providing a rather different perspective? Would Nina have wanted her babies to grow up without a mom?

Would *he* have wanted them to grow up without a dad, if he'd been the one to die too soon?

Of course not.

He had experienced the first real surge of physical desire in three long years, too. That should be sparking the guilt but it didn't seem to be. Not in the way he'd become so accustomed to, anyway.

He wouldn't have inflicted a life of celibacy on Nina, either.

Maybe the guilt was muted by something more than a different perspective. Because, after the way she had reacted last night, it seemed that going any further down that path was very unlikely?

The more he thought about it, the more his curiosity about Grace was intensifying.

She had felt the same level of need, he knew she had. She had responded to that kiss in a way that had inflamed that desire to a mind-blowing height.

And then she'd flinched as though he had caused her physical pain.

Why?

It wasn't really any of his business but curiosity was becoming a need to know.

Because, as unlikely as it was, could the small part he had played in Grace's life in the past somehow have contributed to whatever it was?

A ridiculous notion but, if nothing else, it seemed like a legitimate reason to try and find out the truth. Not that it was going to be easy, mind you. Some people were very good at building walls to keep their pain private. Like his mother. Thanks to that enormous effort he'd made to try and keep his family together during the worst time of that scandal breaking, however, he had learned more than anyone about exactly what was behind Vanessa Davenport's walls. Because he'd respected that pain and had had a base of complete trust to work from.

He could hardly expect Grace to trust him that much. Not when he looked back over the years and could see the way he'd treated her from her point of view.

But there was something there.

And, oddly, it did *feel* a bit like trust.

Stepping over train tracks that his father was slotting together, smiling at the delight on his sons' faces as they unwrapped a bright blue steam engine with a happy face on the front, Charles moved towards the couch and bent to kiss Vanessa's cheek.

'Awesome present, Mom,' he said with a smile. 'Clever of you to know how much the boys love Thomas the Tank Engine.'

That kiss had changed everything.

Only a few, short weeks ago Grace had been so nervous about meeting Charles Davenport again that she had almost decided against applying for the job at Manhattan Mercy.

What had she been so afraid of? That old feelings might resurface and she'd have to suffer the humiliation of being dismissed so completely again?

To find that the opposite had happened was even scarier. That old connection was still there and could clearly be tapped into but... Grace didn't want that.

Well...she *did*...but she wasn't ready.

She might never be ready.

Charles must think she was crazy. He must have sensed the connection at the same moment she had, when they'd shared their amusement about the spiders that had eyes on their legs, otherwise he wouldn't have touched her like that.

And he must have seen that fierce shaft of desire because she had felt it throughout her entire body so why wouldn't it have shown in her eyes?

Just for those few, deliciously long moments she had been unaware of anything but that desire when he'd kissed her. That spiralling need for more.

And then his hand had—almost—touched her breast and she'd reacted as if he'd pulled a knife on her or something.

It had been purely instinctive and Grace knew how over the top it must have seemed. She was embarrassed.

A bit ashamed of herself, to be honest, but there it was. A trigger that had been too deeply set to be disabled.

The net effect was to make her feel even more nervous about her next meeting with Charles than she had been about the first one and he hadn't been at work the next day so her anxiety kept growing.

She had sent out mixed messages and he had every

right to be annoyed with her. How awkward would it be to work together from now on? Did she really want to live with a resurrection of all the reasons why she'd taken herself off to work in the remotest places she could find?

No. What she wanted was to wind back the clock just a little. To the time before that kiss, when it had felt like an important friendship was being cemented. When she had discovered a totally unexpected dimension in her life by embracing a sense of family in her time with Charles and his sons and Houston.

So she had sent through that photo she had taken of Max and Cameron waiting for the cookies to cool. Along with another apology for the mess they had all created. Maybe she wanted to test the waters and see just how annoyed he might be.

He had texted back to thank her, and say that it was one of the best photos of the boys he'd ever seen. He also said that they were going to a family birthday celebration that afternoon and surprised her by saying he didn't think it would be nearly as much fun as baking Halloween cookies.

A friendly message—as if nothing had changed.

The relief was welcome.

But confusing.

Unless Charles was just as keen as she was to turn the clock back?

Of course he was, she decided by the end of that day, as she took Houston for a long, solitary walk in the park. He had as big a reason as she did not to want to get that close to someone. He had lost the absolute love of his life under horrifically traumatic circumstances. Part of him had to want to keep on living—as she did—and not to be deprived of the best things that life had to offer.

But maybe he wasn't ready yet, either.

Maybe he never would be.

And that was okay—because maybe they could still be friends and that was something that could be treasured.

Evidence that Charles wanted to push the 'reset' button on their friendship came at increasingly frequent intervals over the next week or two. Now that his nanny, Maria, had recovered from her back injury enough to work during week days, he was in the emergency room every day that Grace was working.

He gave her a printed copy of the photograph, during a quiet moment when they both happened to be near the unit desk on one occasion.

'Did you see that Horse photobombed it?'

Grace laughed. 'No... I thought I'd had my thumb on the lens or something. I was going to edit it out.'

She wouldn't now. She would tuck this small picture into her wallet and she knew that sometimes she would take it out and look at it. A part of her would melt with love every time. And part of her would splinter into little pieces and cry?

She avoided looking directly at Charles as she slipped the image carefully into her pocket.

'Did your cleaning lady resign the next day?'

'No. She wants the recipe for your homemade mac and cheese.'

It was unfortunate that Grace glanced at Charles as he stopped speaking to lick his lips. That punch of sensation in her belly was a warning that friendship with this man would never be simple. Or easy. That it could become even worse, in fact, because there might come a time when she was ready to take that enormous step into a new life only to find that Charles would never feel the same way.

'I'd like it, too.' He didn't seem to have noticed that she was edging away. 'I had some later that night and it was the most delicious thing ever. It had *bacon* in it.'

'Mmm… It's not hard.'

'Maybe you could show me. Sometime…'

The suggestion was casual but Grace had to push an image from her mind of standing beside Charles as she taught him how to make a cheese sauce. Of being close enough to touch him whilst wrapped in the warmth and smells of a kitchen—the heart of a home. She could even feel a beat of the fear that being so close would bring and she had to swallow hard.

'I'll write down how to do it for you.'

Charles smiled and nodded but seemed distracted now. He was staring at the patient details board. 'What's going on with that patient in Curtain Six? She's been here for a long time.'

'We're waiting for a paediatric psyche consult. This is her third admission in a week. Looks like a self-inflicted injury and I think there's something going on at home that she's trying to escape from.'

'Oh…' His breath was a sigh. 'Who brought her in?'

'Her stepfather. And he's very reluctant to leave her alone with staff.'

'Need any help?'

'I think we're getting there. I've told him that we need to run more tests. Might even have to keep her in overnight for observation. I know we've blocked up a bed for too long, but…'

'Don't worry about it.' The glance Grace received was direct. Warm. 'Do whatever you need to do. I trust you. Just let me know if you need backup.'

Feeling trusted was a powerful thing.

Knowing that you had the kind of backup that could also be trusted was even better and Grace was particularly grateful for that a couple of mornings later with the first case that arrived on her shift.

A thirteen-month-old boy, who had somehow managed to crawl out of the house at some point during the night and had been found, virtually frozen solid, in the back yard.

'VF arrest,' the paramedics had radioed in. 'CPR under way. We can't intubate—his mouth's frozen. We've just got an OPA in.'

Grace had the team ready in their resuscitation area.

'We need warmed blankets and heat packs. Warmed IV fluids. We'll be looking at thoracic lavage or even ECMO. Have we heard back from the cardiac surgical team yet?'

'Someone's on their way.'

'ECMO?' she heard a nurse whisper. 'What's that?'

'Extra corporeal membrane oxygenation,' she told them. 'It's a form of cardiopulmonary bypass and we can warm the blood at the same time. Because, like we've all been taught, you're not—'

'—dead until you're warm and dead.'

It was Charles who finished her sentence for her, as he appeared beside her, pushing his arms through the sleeves of a gown. He didn't smile at her, but there was a crinkle at the corners of his eyes that gave her a boost of confidence.

'Thought you might like a hand,' he murmured. 'We've done this before, remember?'

Grace tilted her head in a single nod of acknowledgement. She was focused on the gurney being wheeled rapidly towards them through the doors. Of course she remembered. It had been the only time she and Charles had worked so closely together during those long years of training. They had been left to deal with a case of severe hypothermia in an overstretched emergency department when they had been no more than senior medical students. Their patient had been an older homeless woman that nobody had seemed to want to bother with.

They had looked at each other and quietly chanted their new mantra in unison.

'You're not dead until you're warm and dead.'

And they'd stayed with her, taking turns to change heat packs and blankets while keeping up continuous CPR for more than ninety minutes. Until her body temperature was high enough for defibrillation to be an effective option.

Nobody ever forgot the first time they defibrillated somebody.

Especially when it was successful.

But this was very different. This wasn't an elderly woman who might not have even been missed if she had succumbed to her hypothermia. This was a precious child who had distraught members of his family watching their every move. A tiny body that looked, and felt, as if it was made of chilled wax as he was gently transferred to the heated mattress, where his soaked, frozen nappy was removed and heat packs were nestled under his arms and in his groin.

'Pupils?'

'Fixed and dilated.'

Grace caught Charles's gaze as she answered his query and it was no surprise that she couldn't see any hint of a suggestion that it might be too late to help this child. It was more an acknowledgement that the battle had just begun. That they'd done this before and they could do it again. And they might be surrounded by other staff members but it almost felt like it was just them again. A tight team, bonded by an enormous challenge and the determination to succeed.

Finding a vein to start infusing warmed IV fluids presented a challenge they didn't have time for so Grace used an intraosseous needle to place a catheter inside the tibia where the bone marrow provided a reliable connection to the central circulation. It was Charles who took over the chest compressions from the paramedics and initiated the start of warmed oxygen for ventilation and then it was Elijah who stepped in to continue while Charles and Grace worked together to intubate and hook the baby up to the ventilator.

The cardiac surgical team arrived soon after that, along with the equipment that could be used for more aggressive internal warming, by direct cannulation of major veins and arteries to both warm the blood and take over the work of the heart and lungs or the procedure of infusing the chest cavity with warmed fluids and then draining it off again. If ECMO or bypass was going to be used, the decision had to be made whether to do it here in the department or move their small patient to Theatre.

'How long has CPR been going?'

'Seventy-five minutes.'

'Body temperature?'

'Twenty-two degrees Celsius. Up from twenty-one on arrival. It was under twenty on scene.'

'Rhythm?'

'Still ventricular fibrillation.'

'Has he been shocked?'

'Once. On scene.' Again, it was Charles's gaze that

Grace sought. 'We were waiting to get his temperature up a bit more before we tried again but maybe...'

'It's worth a try,' one of the cardiac team said. 'Before we start cannulation.'

But it was the nod from Charles that Grace really wanted to see before she pushed the charge button on the defibrillator.

'Stand clear,' she warned as crescendo of sound switched to a loud beeping. 'Shocking now.'

It was very unlikely that one shock would convert the fatal rhythm into one that was capable of pumping blood but, to everyone's astonishment, that was exactly what it did. Charles had his fingers resting gently near a tiny elbow.

'I've got a pulse.'

'Might not last,' the surgeon warned. 'He's still cold enough for it to deteriorate back into VF at any time, especially if he's moved.'

Grace nodded. 'We won't move him. Let's keep on with what we're doing with active external rewarming and ventilation. We'll add in some inotropes as well.'

'It could take hours.' The surgeon looked at his watch. 'I can't stay, I'm afraid. I've got a theatre list I'm already late for but page me if you run into trouble.'

Charles nodded but the glance he gave Grace echoed what she was thinking herself. They had won the first round of this battle and, together, they would win the next.

There wasn't much that they could do, other than keep up an intensive monitoring that meant not stepping away from this bedside. Heat packs were refreshed and body temperature crept up, half a degree at a time. There were blood tests to run and drugs to be cautiously administered. They could let the parents come in for a short time to see what was happening and to reassure them that everything possible was being done but they couldn't be allowed to touch their son yet. The situation was still fragile and only time would give them the answers they all needed.

His name, they learned, was Toby.

It wasn't necessary to have two senior doctors present the whole time but neither Charles nor Grace gave any hint of wanting to be anywhere else and, fortunately, there were enough staff to cover everything else that was happening in the department.

More than once, they were the only people in the room with Toby. Their conversation was quiet and professional, focused solely on the challenge they were dealing with and, at first, any eye contact was that of colleagues. Encouraging. Appreciative. Hopeful...

It was an odd bubble to be in, at the centre of a busy department but isolated at the same time. And when it was just the two of them, when a nurse left to deliver blood samples or collect new heat packs, there was an atmosphere that Grace could only describe as...peaceful?

No. That wasn't the right word. It felt as though she was a piece of a puzzle that was complete enough to see what the whole picture was going to be. There were only a few pieces still to fit into the puzzle and they were lying close by, waiting to be picked up. It was a feeling of trust that went a step beyond hope. It was simply a matter of time.

So perhaps that was why those moments of eye contact changed as one hour morphed into the next. Why it was so hard to look away, because that was when she could feel it the most—that feeling that the puzzle was going to be completed and that it was a picture she had been waiting her whole life to see.

It felt like…happiness.

Nearly three hours later, Toby was declared stable enough to move to the paediatric intensive care unit. He was still unconscious but his heart and other organs were functioning normally again. Whether he had suffered any brain damage would not be able to be assessed until he woke up.

If he woke up?

Was that why Grace was left with the feeling that she hadn't quite been able to reach those last puzzle pieces? Why the picture she wanted to see so badly was still a little blurred?

No. The way Charles was looking at her as Toby's bed disappeared through the internal doors of the ER assured Grace that she had done the best job she could and, for now, the outcome was the best it could possibly be. That he was proud of her. Proud of his department.

And then he turned to start catching up with the multitude of tasks that had accumulated and needed his attention. Grace watched him walking away from her and that was when instinct kicked in.

That puzzle wasn't really about a patient at all, was it?

It was about herself.

And Charles.

CHAPTER SEVEN

'Bit cold for the park today, isn't it, Doc? They're sayin' it could snow.'

'I know, but the boys are desperate for a bike ride. We haven't been able to get outside to play for days.'

Jack brightened at the prospect of leaving the tiny space that was his office by the front door of this apartment block.

'Stay here. I'll fetch those bikes from the basement. Could do with checkin' that the rubbish has been collected.'

'Oh, thanks, Jack.' It was always a mission managing two small boys and their bikes in the elevator. This way, he could get their coats and helmets securely fastened without them trying to climb on board their beloved bikes.

As always, he cast more than one glance towards the door at the back of the foyer as he got ready to head outside. He remembered wanting to knock on it when Grace had first moved in and that he'd been held back by some nebulous idea of boundaries. He didn't have any problems with it now.

They'd come a long way since then. Too far, perhaps, but they'd obviously both decided to put that ill-advised kiss behind them and focus on a friendship that was growing steadily stronger.

And Charles had news that he really wanted to share.

So he knocked on Grace's door. He knew she had a day off today because he'd started taking more notice of her name on the weekly rosters.

'Charles… Hi…' Was it his imagination or was there a glow of real pleasure amidst the surprise of a morning caller?

He could certainly feel that glow but maybe it was coming from his own pleasure at seeing *her*. Especially away from work, when she wasn't wearing her scrubs, with her hair scraped back from her face in her usual ponytail. Today, she was in jeans tucked into sheepskin-lined boots and she had a bright red sweater and her hair was falling around her face in messy waves—a bit like it had been when he'd come home to find her sound asleep on his couch.

Horse sneaked past her legs and made a beeline for the boys, who shrieked with glee and fell on their furry friend for cuddles.

'I have something I have to tell you,' Charles said.

Her eyes widened. 'Oh, no…is it Miranda? Helena texted me to say she was involved in that subway tunnel collapse—that she'd been trapped under rubble or something.'

Charles shook his head. 'She's fine. She didn't even need to come into the ER. A paramedic took care of her, apparently. No, it's about Toby. I just had a call from PICU.'

He could hear the gasp as Grace sucked in her breath. 'Toby?'

'Yes. He woke up this morning.'

'Oh…it's been forty-eight hours. I was starting to think the worst… Is he…? Has he…?'

'As far as they can tell, he's neurologically intact. They're going to run more tests but he recognises his parents and he's said the few words he knows. And he's smiling…'

Grace was smiling, too. Beaming, in fact. And then she noticed Jack as the elevator doors opened and he stepped out with a small bike under each arm.

'Morning, Jack.'

'Morning, Miss Forbes.' His face broke into a wide grin. 'Yo' sure look happy today.'

'I am…' There was a sparkle in her eyes that looked like unshed tears as she met Charles's gaze again. 'So happy. Thanks so much for coming to tell me.'

'Can Horse come to the park?' Max was beside his father's legs. 'Can he watch us ride our bikes?'

The glance from Grace held a query now. Did Charles want their company?

He smiled. Of course he did.

'Wrap up warm,' Jack warned. 'It's only about five degrees out there. It might snow.'

'Really?' Grace sounded excited. 'I can't wait for it to snow. And I'm really, really hoping for a white Christmas this year.'

'Could happen.' Jack nodded. 'They're predicting some big storms for December and that's not far off. It'll be Christmas before we know it.'

Charles groaned. 'Let's get Thanksgiving out of the way before we start talking Christmas. We've only just finished Halloween!'

Except Halloween felt like a long way in the past now, didn't it? Long enough for this friendship to feel like it was becoming something much more solid.

Real.

'Give me two minutes,' Grace said. 'I need to find my hat and scarf. Horse? Come and get your harness on.'

The boys had trainer wheels on their small bikes and needed constant reminding not to get too far ahead of the adults. Pedestrians on the busy pavement had to jump out of the way as the boys powered towards the park but most of them smiled at the two identical little faces with their proud smiles. Charles kept a firm hand on each set of handlebars as they crossed the main road at the lights but once they were through the gates of Central Park, he let them go as fast as they wanted.

'Phew… I think we're safe now. I'm pretty sure the tourist carriages don't use this path.'

'Do they do sleigh rides here when it snows?'

'I don't know. I've seen carriages that look like sleighs but I think they have wheels rather than runners. Why?'

Grace's breath came out in a huff of white as she sighed. 'It's always been my dream for Christmas. A sleigh ride in a snowy park. At night, when there's sparkly lights everywhere and there are bells on the horses and you have to be all wrapped up in soft blankets.'

Charles smiled but he felt a squeeze of something poignant catch his heart. The picture she was painting was ultimately romantic but did she see herself alone in that sleigh?

He couldn't ask. They might have reached new ground with their friendship, especially after that oddly intimate case of working to save little Toby, but asking such a personal question seemed premature. Risky.

Besides, Grace was still talking.

'Christmas in Australia was so weird. Too hot to do

anything but head for the nearest beach or pool but lots of people still want to do the whole roast turkey thing. Or dress up in Santa suits.' She rubbed at her nose, which was already red from the cold. 'It feels much more like a proper Christmas when it snows.'

The boys were turning their bikes in a circle ahead of them, which seemed to be a complicated procedure. And then they were pedalling furiously back towards them.

'Look at us, Gace! Look how fast we can go.'

Grace leapt out of Cameron's way, pulling Houston to safety as Cameron tried, and failed, to slow down. The bike tilted sideways and then toppled.

'Whoops…' Charles scooped up his son. 'Okay, buddy?'

Cameron's face crumpled but then he sniffed hard and nodded.

'Is it time for a hotdog?'

'Soon.' He was climbing back onto his bike. 'I have to ride some more first.'

'He's determined,' Grace said, watching him pedal after his brother. 'Like his daddy.'

'Oh? You think I'm determined?'

'Absolutely. You don't give up easily, even if you have a challenge that would defeat a lot of people.'

'You mean Toby? You were just as determined as I was to save him.'

'Mmm. But I'd seen that look in your eyes before, remember? I'm not sure if I would have had the confidence to try that hard when I had absolutely no experience, like you did back when we were students.' She shook her head. 'I still don't have that much experience of arrest from hypothermia. That old woman that we worked on is the only other case I've ever had. Bit of a coincidence, isn't it?'

'Meant to be,' Charles suggested lightly. 'We're a good team.'

'It's easier to be determined when you're part of a team,' Grace said quietly. 'I think you've coped amazingly with challenges you've had to face alone. Your boys are a credit to you.'

He might not know her story yet but he knew that Grace had been through her own share of tough challenges.

He spoke quietly as well. 'I have a feeling you've done that, too.'

The glance they shared acknowledged the truth. And their connection. A mutual appreciation of another person's strength of character, perhaps?

And Charles was quite sure that Grace was almost ready to tell him what he wanted to know. That all it would take was the right question. But he had no idea what that question might be and this was hardly the best place to start a conversation that needed care. He could feel the cold seeping through his shoes and gloves and he would need to take the boys home soon.

'Come and visit later, if you're not busy,' he found himself suggesting. 'The boys got a train set from my parents for their birthday and they'd love to show it to you.'

The twins were on the return leg of one of the loops that took them away from their father and then back again.

'What do you think, Max?' he called out. 'Is it a good idea for Grace to come and see your new train?'

Later, Charles knew he would feel a little guilty about enlisting his sons' backup like this but right then, he just wanted to know that he was going to get to spend some more time with Grace.

Soon.

It seemed important.

'*Yes*,' Max shouted obligingly, his instant grin an irresistible invitation. 'And Horse.'

'And mac and cheese,' Cameron added.

But Max shook his head. 'Not Daddy's,' he said sadly. 'It comes in a box. I don't like it...'

Charles raised an eyebrow. 'This is your fault, Grace. I have at least half a dozen boxes of Easy Mac 'n' Cheese in my pantry—my go-to quick favourite dinner for the boys—and they're useless. Even when I try adding bacon.'

'Oh, dear...' Grace was smiling. 'Guess I'd better teach you how to make cheese sauce, then?'

His nod was solemn. 'I think so. You did promise.'

Her cheeks were already pink from the cold but Charles had the impression that the colour had deepened even more suddenly.

'I think I promised to write it down for you.'

'Ah...but I learn so much better by doing something. Do you remember that class we did on suturing once? When we had that pig skin to practise on?'

'Yes... It was fun.'

'Tricky, though. I'd stayed up the night before, reading all about exactly where to grasp a needle with the needle driver and wrapping the suture around it and then switching hand positions to make the knots. I even watched a whole bunch of videos.'

'Ha! I knew you always stayed up all night studying. It was why I had so much trouble keeping up with you.'

'My point is, actually doing it was a completely different story. I felt like I had two left hands. You were way better at it.'

'Not by the end of the class. You aced it.'

'Because I was doing it. Not reading about it, or watching it.'

Why was he working so hard to persuade her to do something that she might not be comfortable with? Because it felt important—just like the idea of spending more time with her?

There was something about the way her gaze slid away from his that made him want to touch her arm. To tell her that this was okay. That she could trust him.

But maybe he managed to communicate that, anyway, in the briefest glance she returned to, because her breath came out in a cloudy puff again—the way it had when she'd sighed after confessing her dream of having a Christmas sleigh ride in the snow. Her chin bobbed in a single nod.

'I'll pick up some ingredients on my way home.'

'We don't want to go home, Daddy,' Cameron said. 'We want to go to the playground.'

With their determined pedalling efforts, their feet probably weren't as cold as his, Charles decided. And with some running and climbing added in, they were going to be very tired by this evening. They'd probably fall asleep as soon as they'd had their dinner and…and that would be the perfect opportunity to talk to Grace, wouldn't it?

Really talk to Grace.

He smiled at his boys. 'Okay. Let's head for the playground.'

'And Gace,' Max added.

But she shook her head. 'I can't, sorry, sweetheart. I have to take Horse home now.'

'Why?'

'Because Stefan and Jerome are going to Skype us and talk to him, like they do every Sunday. And he needs his hair brushed first. Oh… I've just had an idea.' She held the dog's lead out to Charles. 'Can you stand with the boys? I'll take a photo I can send them, so they can see that he's been having fun in the park today.'

It took a moment or two to get two small boys, two bikes, a large fluffy dog and a tall man into a cohesive enough group to photograph. And then a passer-by stopped and insisted on taking the phone from Grace's hands.

'You need one of the whole family,' he said firmly.

Grace looked startled. And then embarrassed as she caught Charles's gaze.

It reminded him of Davenport family photos. Where everyone had to look as though they were a happy family and hide the undercurrents and secret emotions that were too private to share. The kind of image that would be taken very soon for their annual Thanksgiving gathering?

Charles was good at this. He'd been doing it for a very long time. And he knew it was far easier to just get it over with than try and explain why it wasn't a good idea.

So he smiled at Grace and pulled Houston a bit closer to make a space for her to stand beside him, behind the boys on their bikes.

'Come on,' he encouraged. 'Before we all freeze to death here.'

Strangely, when Grace was in place a moment later, with Charles's arm draped over her shoulders, it didn't feel at all like the uncomfortable publicity shots of the New York Davenports destined to appear in some glossy magazine.

It was, in fact, surprisingly easy to find the 'big smile' that the stranger requested.

It wasn't a case of her heart conflicting with her head, which would have been far simpler to deal with.

This was more like her heart arranging itself into two separate divisions on either side of what was more like a solid wall than a battle line.

There were moments when Grace could even believe there was a door hidden in that wall, somewhere, and time with Charles felt like she was moving along, tapping on that solid surface, waiting for the change in sound that would tell her she was close.

Moments like this, as she stood beside Charles in his kitchen, supervising his first attempt at making a cheese sauce.

'Add the milk gradually and just keep stirring.'

'It's all lumpy.'

'It'll be fine. Stir a bit faster. And have faith.'

'Hmm…okay…' Charles peered into the pot, frowning. 'How did your Skype session go?'

'Houston wasn't terribly co-operative. He didn't want to wake up. I showed them the photo from the park, though, and they said to say "hi" and wish you a happy Thanksgiving.'

'That's nice.' Charles added some more milk to his sauce. 'Where are they going to be celebrating? Still in Italy?'

'Yes. They're fallen head over heels in love with the Amalfi coast. They've bought a house there.'

'What? How's that going to work?'

'They've got this idea that they could spend six

months in Europe and six months here every year and never have winters.'

'But what about Houston?'

'I guess he'll have to get used to travelling.' Grace pointed at the pot. 'Keep stirring or lumps will sneak in. You can add the grated cheese now, too.'

Charles was shaking his head. 'I don't think Houston would like summers in Italy. It'd be too hot for a big, fluffy dog.'

'Mmm…' Grace looked over her shoulder. Not that she could see into the living area from here but she could imagine that Houston hadn't moved from where the boys had commanded him to stay—a canine mountain that they were constructing a new train line around. From the happy tooting noises she could hear, it seemed like the line was up and running now.

'I'd adopt him,' Charles said. 'Max and Cameron think he's another brother.'

'I would, too.' Grace smiled. 'I love that dog. I don't think you ever feel truly lonely when you're sharing your life with a dog.'

The glance from Charles was quick enough to be sharp. A flash of surprise followed by something very warm, like sympathy. Concern…

She was stepping onto dangerous territory here, inadvertently admitting that she was often lonely.

'Right…let's drain that pasta, mix in the bacon and you can pour the sauce over the top. All we need is the breadcrumbs on top with a bit more cheese and it can go in the oven for half an hour.'

The distraction seemed to have been successful and Grace relaxed again, helping herself to a glass of wine when Charles chased the boys into the bathroom to get clean. She had to abandon her drink before their dinner was ready to come out of the oven, though, in order to answer the summons to the bathroom where she found Charles kneeling beside a huge tub that contained two small boys, a flotilla of plastic toys and a ridiculous amount of bubbles.

'Look, Gace. A snowman!'

'Could be a snow woman,' Charles suggested. 'Or possibly a snow dog.'

He had taken off the ribbed, navy pullover he'd been wearing and his T-shirt had large, damp patches on the front. There were clumps of bubbles on his bare arms and another one on the top of his head and the grin on his face told her that, in this moment, Charles Davenport was possibly the happiest man on earth.

Tap, tap, tap...

Would she be brave enough to go through that door if she *did* find it?

What if she opened her heart to this little family and then found they didn't actually want her?

'Nobody's ever going to want you again... Not now...'

That ugly voice from the past should have lost its power long ago but there were still moments. Like this one, when she was smiling down at two, perfect, beautiful children and a man that she knew was even more gorgeous without those designer jeans and shirt.

Even as her smile began to wobble, though, she was saved by the bell of the oven timer.

'I'll take that out,' she excused herself. 'Dinner will be ready by the time you guys have got your jimjams on.'

The twins were just as cute in their pyjamas as they had been in their monkey suits for Halloween but another glass of wine had made it easier for Grace. The pleasant fuzziness reminded her that it was possible to embrace the moment and enjoy this for simply what it was—spending time with a friend and being included in his family.

Because they were real friends now, with a shared history of good times in the past and an understanding of how hard it could be to move on from tougher aspects in life. Maybe that kiss had let them both know that anything other than friendship would be a mistake. It was weeks ago and there had been no hint of anything more than a growing trust.

Look at them…having a relaxed dinner in front of a fire, with an episode of *Curious George* on the television and a contented dog stretched out on the mat, and the might-have-beens weren't trying to break her heart. Grace was loving every minute of it.

Okay, it was a bit harder when she got the sleepy cuddles and kisses from the boys before Charles carried them off to bed but even then she wasn't in any hurry to escape. This time, she wasn't going to go home until she had cleaned up the kitchen. She wasn't even going to get off this couch until she had finished this particularly delicious glass of wine.

And then Charles came back and sat on the couch beside her and everything suddenly seemed even more delicious.

Tap, tap, tap…

For a heartbeat, Grace could actually hear the sound. Because the expression on Charles's face made her wonder if he was tapping at a wall of his own?

Maybe it was her own heartbeat she could hear as it picked up its pace.

He hadn't forgotten that comment about being lonely at all, had he?

'Have you got any plans for Thanksgiving tomorrow,

Grace? You'd be welcome to join us, although a full-on Davenport occasion might be a bit...' He made a face that suggested he wasn't particularly looking forward to it himself. 'Sorry, I shouldn't make assumptions. You've probably got your own family to think about.'

Her own family. A separate family. That wall had just got a lot more solid.

Grace didn't protest when Charles refilled her glass.

'I had thought of going to visit my dad but I would have had to find someone to care for Houston and I didn't have enough of a gap in my roster. It's a long way to go just for a night or two. He might come to New York for Christmas, though.'

'And you lost your mum, didn't you? I remember you telling me how much you missed her.'

Good grief...he actually remembered what she'd said that night when she'd been crying on his shoulder as a result of her stress about her final exams?

'She died a couple of years before I went to med school. Ovarian cancer.'

'Oh...that must have been tough.'

'Yeah...it was. Dad's never got over it.' Grace fell silent. Had she just reminded Charles of his own loss. That he would never get over it?

The silence stretched long enough for Charles to finish his glass of wine and refill it.

'There's something else I should apologise for, too.'

'What?' Grace tried to lighten what felt like an oddly serious vibe. Was he going to apologise for that kiss? Explain why it had been such a mistake? 'You're going to send me into the kitchen to do the dishes?'

He wasn't smiling.

'I treated you badly,' he said quietly. 'Back in med school. After...that night...'

Oh, help… This was breaking the first rule in the new book. The one that made that night a taboo subject.

'I don't know how much you knew of what hit the fan the next day regarding the Davenport scandal…'

'Not much,' Grace confessed. 'I heard about it, of course, but I was a bit preoccupied. With, you know… finals coming up.'

And dealing with the rejection…

He nodded. 'The pressure was intense, wasn't it? And I was trying to stop my family completely disintegrating. The intrusion of the media was unbelievable. They ripped my father to shreds, which only made us all more aware of how damaged our own relationship with him was. It tarnished all the good memories we had as a family. It nearly destroyed us.

'We'd always been in the limelight as one of the most important families in New York,' he continued quietly. 'A perfect family. And then it turns out that my father had been living a lie. That he'd had an affair. That there was a half-sister none of us knew about.'

He cleared his throat. 'I was the oldest and it was down to me to handle the media and focus on what mattered and the only way I could do that was to ignore how *I* felt. My only job was to protect the people that mattered most to me and, at that time, it had to be my family. It hit my mother hardest, as you can probably imagine, but they went to town on Miranda's mother, too. Describing her as worthless was one of the kinder labels. I didn't know her and I probably wouldn't have wanted to but I did know that my new half-sister was just a scared kid who had nobody to protect her. She was as vulnerable as you could get…'

Grace bit her lip. Charles couldn't help himself, could he? He had to protect the vulnerable. It had been the reason why they'd been together that night—he'd felt the need to protect *her*. To comfort her. To make her feel strong enough to cope with the world.

That ability to care for others more than himself was a huge part of what made him such an amazing person.

And, yes…she could understand why his attention had been so convincingly distracted.

Could forgive it, even?

'By the time things settled down, you were gone.'

Grace shrugged. Of course she had gone. There had been nothing to stay for. Would it have changed things if she'd known how difficult life was for Charles at that time?

Maybe.

Or maybe not. It was more likely that she would have been made much more aware of how different his world was and how unlikely it would have been that she could have been a part of it.

'I can't imagine what it must have been like. Life can be difficult enough without having your privacy invaded like that. I couldn't think of anything worse…' Grace shook her head. 'I get that a one-night stand would have fallen off your radar. You don't need to apologise.'

But it was nice that he had.

'It was a lot more than a one-night stand, Grace.' The words were quiet. Convincing. 'You need to know that. And I asked about you, later—every time I came across someone from school at a conference or something. That was how I found out you'd got married.'

Grace was silent. He'd been asking about her? Looking for her, even? If she had known that, would she have taken her relationship with Mike as far as marrying him?

Possibly not. She had thought she'd found love but she'd always known the connection hadn't been as fierce as the one she'd found with Charles that night.

'It was just after that that I met Nina,' he continued. There was a hint of a smile tugging at his lips. 'Even then, I thought, well…if you could get married and live happily ever after, I'd better make sure I didn't get left behind.'

The silence was very poignant this time.

'I'm sorry,' Grace whispered. 'Everybody knows how much you loved her. I'm so sorry you didn't get your happily ever after.'

'I got some wonderful memories. And two amazing children. You reminded me just how lucky I am, on your first day at work.' Charles drew in a deep breath and let it out slowly. 'I hope you have things to feel lucky about, too.'

'Of course I do.'

'Like?'

Grace swallowed hard. She was leaning against that wall in her heart now, as if she needed support to stay upright.

But maybe she needed more than that. To hear someone agree that she was lucky?

'I'm alive,' she whispered.

She could feel his shock. Did he think she was making a reference to Nina? Grace closed her eyes. She hadn't intended saying more but she couldn't leave it like that.

'I found a lump in my breast,' she said slowly, into the silence. 'I'd been married for about a year by then and Mike was keen to start a family. The lump turned out to be only a cyst but, because of my mother, they ran a lot of tests and one of them was for the genetic markers that let you know how much risk you have of getting ovarian or breast cancer. Mine was as high as it gets. And some people think that pregnancy can make that worse.'

'So you decided not to have kids?'

Grace shook her head, glancing up. 'No. I decided I'd have them as quickly as possible and then have a hysterectomy and mastectomy. Only…it didn't work out that way because they found another lump and that one wasn't a cyst. So… I decided to get the surgery and give up any dreams of having kids.'

She had to close her eyes again. 'Mike couldn't handle that. And he couldn't handle the treatment—especially the chemo and living with someone who was sick all the time. And later, my scars were just a reminder of what I'd taken away from him. A mother for his children. A woman he could look at without being…' her next word came out like a tiny sob '…disgusted…'

Maybe she had known how Charles would react.

Maybe she had wanted, more than anything, to feel his arms around her, like this.

To hear his voice, soft against her ear.

'You're gorgeous, Grace. There are no scars that could ever take that away.'

She could hear the steady thump of his heart and feel the solid comfort of the band of his arms around her.

'You're strong, too. I fought external things and I'm not sure that I did such a great job but you…you fought a battle that you could never step away from, even for a moment. And you won.'

Grace's breath caught in a hitch. She *had* won. She would never forget any one of those steps towards hearing those magic words…

Cancer-free…

'Your courage blows me away,' Charles continued. 'You not only got through that battle with the kind of obstacles that your jerk of a husband added but you took yourself off to work in places that are as tough as they get. You didn't let it dent your sense of adventure or the amazing ability you have to care for others.' His arms tightened around her. 'You should be so proud of yourself. Don't ever let anything that he said or did take any of that away from you.'

Grace had to look up. To make sure that his eyes were telling her the same thing that his words were. To see if what she was feeling right now was something real. That she could be proud of everything she'd been through. That she could, finally, dismiss the legacy that Mike's rejection had engraved on her soul. That she was so much stronger now...

How amazing was this that Charles could make her feel as if she'd just taken the biggest step ever into a bright, new future?

That she'd found someone who made it possible to take the kind of risk that she'd never believed she would be strong enough to take again?

And maybe she had known what would happen when they fell into each other's eyes again like this.

As the distance between them slowly disappeared and their lips touched.

That door in the wall in her heart had been so well hidden she hadn't even realised she was leaning right against it until it fell open with their combined weight.

And the other side was a magic place where scars didn't matter.

Where they could be touched by someone else. Kissed, even, and it wasn't shameful. Or terrifying.

It was real. Raw. And heartbreakingly beautiful.

No. It wasn't 'someone else' who could have done this. It could only have been Charles.

CHAPTER EIGHT

THE SOFT TRILL advertising an incoming text message on his phone woke Charles.

It could have been from anyone. One of his siblings, perhaps. Or a message from work to warn him that there was a situation requiring his input.

But he knew it was from Grace.

He just *knew*…

And, in that moment of knowing, there was a profound pleasure. Excitement, even. An instant pull back into the astonishing connection they had rediscovered last night that was still hovering at the edges of his consciousness as he reached sleepily for the phone on his bedside table.

Okay, he'd broken rule number one, not only by allowing female companionship to progress to this level but by allowing it to happen under his own roof and not keeping it totally separate from his home life—and his children.

And he'd broken an even bigger, albeit undefined, rule, by doing it with someone that he had a potentially important emotional connection to.

Had he been blindsided, because that connection had already been there and only waiting to be uncovered and that meant he hadn't been able to make a conscious choice to back off before it was even a possibility?

Maybe his undoing had been the way her story had touched his heart. That someone as clever and warm and beautiful as Grace could have been made to believe that she didn't deserve to be loved.

Whatever had pushed him past his boundaries, it had felt inevitable by the time he'd led Grace to his bed. And everything that had happened after that was a blurred mix of sensation and emotion that was overwhelming, even now.

Physically, it had been as astonishing as that first time. Exquisite. But there had been more to it this time. So much more. The gift of trust that she'd given him. The feeling that the dark place in his soul had been flooded with a light he'd never expected to experience again after Nina had died. Had never wanted to experience again because he knew what it was like when it got turned off?

It was early, with only the faintest suggestion of the approaching day between the gap of curtains that had been hastily pulled. Grace would be at work already, though. Her early shift had been the reason she hadn't stayed all night and Charles hadn't tried to persuade her. The twins might be far too young to read anything into finding Grace and Horse in their apartment first thing in the morning but what if they dropped an innocent bombshell in front of their grandparents, for instance, during the family's Thanksgiving dinner tonight?

He wasn't ready to share any of this.

It was too new—this feeling of an intimate connection, when you could get a burst of pleasure from even the prospect of communication via text.

He wasn't exactly sure how he felt about it himself

yet, so he certainly didn't want the opinions of anyone else—like his parents or his siblings. This was very private.

There was only one other person on the planet who could share this.

Can't believe I left without doing the dishes again. I owe you one. xx

For a moment Charles let his head sink into his pillow again, a smile spreading over his face. He loved Grace's humour. And how powerful two little letters could be at the end of a message. Not one kiss, but two...

Powerful letters.

Even more powerful feelings.

They reminded him of the heady days of falling in love with Nina, when they couldn't bear to be apart. When they were the only two people in the world that mattered.

Was that what was happening here?

Was he falling in *love* with Grace?

His smile faded. The swirling potentially humorous responses to her text message vanished. He'd known that he would never fall in love again. He'd known that from the moment Nina's life had ebbed away that terrible day and he hadn't given it a second thought since. That part of his life had simply been dismissed as he'd coped with what had been important. His babies. And his work.

It had been a very long time before his body reminded him that there were other needs that could be deemed of importance. That was when rule number one had been considered and then put into place.

And he'd broken it.

Without giving any thought to any implications.

The jarring sound of his phone starting to ring cut through the heavy thoughts pressing down and suffocating the pleasure of any memories of last night. His heart skipped a beat with what felt like alarm as he glanced at the screen.

But it wasn't Grace calling. It was his mother.

At this time of the day?

'Mom...what's up? Is everything all right?'

'Maybe you can tell me, Charles. Who is she?'

'Sorry?'

'I'm reading the *New York Post*. Page six...'

Of course she was. Anyone who was anyone in New York turned to page six first, either to read about someone they knew or about themselves. It was a prime example of the gossip columns that Charles hated above everything else. The kind that had almost destroyed his family once as people fed on every juicy detail that the Davenport scandal had offered. The kind that had made getting through the tragedy of losing his wife just that much harder as the details of their fairy-tale romance and wedding were pored over again. The kind that had made him keep his own life as private as possible ever since in his determination to protect his sons.

'Why now?' Vanessa continued. 'Really, Charles. We could do without another airing of the family's dirty laundry. Especially today, with it being Thanksgiving.'

He was out of bed now, clad only in his pyjama pants as he headed into the living area. His laptop was on the dining table, already open. It took only a couple of clicks to find what his mother was referring to.

The photograph was a shock. How on earth had a

journalist got hold of it when it had been taken only yesterday—on Grace's phone?

But there it was. The boys on their bikes on either side of Houston. Himself with his arm slung over Grace's shoulders. And they were all grinning like the archetypal happy family.

His brain was working overtime. Had that friendly stranger actually been a journalist? Or had Grace shared the photograph on social media? No… But she had shared it with Stefan and Jerome and they had many friends who were the kind of celebrities that often graced page six. Easy pickings for anyone who contributed to this gossip column, thanks to a thoughtless moment on his behalf.

'She's a friend, Mom. Someone I went to med school with, who happens to be living downstairs at the moment. Dog-sitting.'

'That's not what's getting assumed.'

'Of course it isn't. Why do you even read this stuff?' He scanned the headline.

Who is the mystery woman in Charles Daven-port's life?

'And why are they raking over old news? It's too much. Really, Charles. Can't you be more careful?'

Speed-reading was a skill he had mastered a long time ago.

It's been a while since we caught up with the New York Davenports. Who could forget the scandal of the love child that almost blew this famous family apart? Where is she now, you might be asking? Where are any of them, in fact?

Moving on with their lives, apparently. Dr Charles Davenport is retired, with his notoriously private firstborn son taking over as chief of the ER at Manhattan Mercy in the manner of the best dynasties. He's become something of a recluse since the tragic death of his wife but it looks as though he's finally moving on. And isn't it a treat to get a peek at his adorable twin sons?

We see his own twin brother Elijah more than any of the family members, with his penchant for attending every important party, and with a different woman on his arm every time. Their sister Penelope is a celebrated daredevil and the youngest brother, Zachary, is reportedly returning to the family fold very soon, in more ways than one. He has resigned from the Navy and will be adding his medical skills to the Davenport team at Manhattan Mercy. Watch this space for more news later.

And the love child, Miranda? Well...she's so much a part of the family now she's also a doctor and it's no surprise that she's working in exactly the same place.

Are the New York Davenports an example of what doesn't kill you makes you stronger? Or is it just window dressing...?

Charles stopped reading as the article went on to focus on Vanessa Davenport's recent philanthropic endeavours. His mother was still talking—about a fundraising luncheon she was supposed to be attending in a matter of hours.

'How can I go? There'll be reporters everywhere and intrusive questions. But, if I don't go, it'll just fuel speculation. *Everybody* will be talking about it.'

'Just ignore it,' Charles advised. 'Keep your head high, smile and say "No comment". It'll die down. It always does.'

He could hear the weary sigh on the other end of the line.

'I'm so sick of it. We've all been through enough. Haven't we?'

'Mmm.' Charles rubbed his forehead with his fingers. 'I have to go, Mom. The boys are waking up and we need to get ready. It's the Macy's Thanksgiving parade today and we'll have to get there early to find a good place to watch. I'll see you tonight.'

It should have been such a happy day.

Some of Charles's earliest memories were of the sheer wonder of this famous parade. Of being in a privileged viewing position with his siblings, bundled up against the cold, jumping up and down with the amazement of every new sight and adding his own contribution to the cacophony of sound—the music and cheers and squeals of excitement—that built and built until the finale they were all waiting for when Santa Claus in his sleigh being pulled by reindeer with spectacular gilded antlers would let them know that the excitement wasn't over. Christmas was coming...

This was the first year that Cameron and Max were old enough to appreciate the spectacle and not be frightened by the crowds and noise. They were well bundled up in their coats and mittens and hats and their little faces were shining with excitement. They found a spot on Central Park West, not far from one of their favourite playgrounds, and Charles held a twin on each hip, giving them a clear view over the older children in front of them.

The towering balloons sailed past. Superman and Spiderman and Muppets and Disney characters. There was a brass band with its members dressed like tin soldiers and people on stilts that looked like enormous candy canes with their striped costumes and the handles on their tall hats. There were clowns and jugglers and dancers and they kept coming. Charles's arms began to ache with the weight of the twins and their joyous wriggling.

He wasn't going to put them down. This was his job. Supporting his boys. Protecting them. And he could cope. The three of them would always cope. The happiness that today should have provided was clouded for Charles, though. He could feel an echo that reminded him of his mother's heavy sigh earlier this morning.

That it was starting again. The media interest that could become like a searchlight, illuminating so many things that were best left in the shade now. Things that were nobody else's business. Putting them out there for others to speculate on only made things so much harder to deal with.

He could still feel the pain of photographs that had been put on public display in the aftermath of the family scandal breaking. Of the snippets of gossip, whether true or not, that had been raked over. The fresh wave of interest in the days after Nina's death had been even worse as he'd struggled to deal with his own grief. Seeing that photograph that had been taken at their engagement party, with Nina looking so stunning in her white designer gown, proudly showing off the famed Davenport, pink diamond ring, had been like a kick in the guts.

What if that photograph surfaced again now, with gossip mills cranking up at the notion that he'd found a new partner? Grace was nothing like Nina, who'd been part of the kind of society he'd grown up in. Nina had been well used to being in the public eye. Grace was someone who kept herself in the background, working as part of a team in her job where the centre stage was always taken by the person needing her help.

Or making two small boys happy by baking cookies and trashing his kitchen...

She would be appalled at any media interest. She'd as much as told him how she wouldn't be able to cope.

'I can't imagine what it must have been like. Life can be difficult enough without having your privacy invaded like that. I couldn't think of anything worse...'

The cloud settled even more heavily over Charles as the real implications hit him.

He knew her story now. That she had been broken by the reaction of the man who had been her husband to the battle she'd had to fight. That she'd actually hidden herself from the world to come to terms with being made to feel less than loveable. Ugly, even...

He hadn't even noticed her scars last night. Not as anything that detracted from her beauty, anyway. If anything, they added to it because they were a mark of her astonishing courage and strength.

But he knew exactly how vulnerable she could still be, despite that strength.

As vulnerable as his younger siblings had been when the 'love child' scandal had broken. He'd learned how to shut things down then, in order to protect them.

Maybe he needed to call on those skills again now.

To protect Grace. He could imagine the devastating effect if the spotlight was turned on her. If someone thought to find images of what mastectomy scars looked like, perhaps, and coupled it with headline bait like *Is this why her husband left her?*

He couldn't let that happen.

He *wouldn't* let that happen.

He had to protect his boys, too.

They weren't just old enough to appreciate this parade now. They knew—and loved—the new person who had come into their lives. Someone who was as happy as he was to stand in the cold and watch them run and climb in a playground. Who baked cookies with them and fell asleep on the couch with them cuddled beside her.

He wouldn't be the only one to be left with a dark place if she vanished from their lives.

What about that different perspective he'd found the day after the twins' birthday, when he'd known that he wouldn't want his boys growing up without a dad, if the tragedy had been reversed? That he wouldn't have wanted Nina to have a restricted, celibate life?

It was all spiralling out of control. His feelings for Grace. How close they had suddenly become. The threat of having his private life picked over by emotional vultures, thanks to media interest and having important things damaged beyond repair.

Yes. He needed to remember lessons learned. That control could be regained eventually if things could be ignored. He had done this before but this time he could do it better. He was responsible and he was old enough and wise enough this time around not to make the same mistakes.

He had to choose each step with great care. And the first step was to narrow his focus to what was most important.

And he was holding that in his arms.

'Show's almost over, guys. Want to go to the playground on the way home?'

* * *

'There's something different about you today.' Helena looked up as she finished scribbling a note in a patient file on the main desk in the ER. 'You look…happy.'

Grace's huff was indignant. 'Are you trying to tell me I usually look miserable?'

'No…' Helena was smiling but she still had a puzzled frown. 'You never look *miserable*. You just don't usually look… I don't know…*this* happy. Not at this time of the morning, anyway.'

Grace shrugged but found herself averting her gaze in case her friend might actually see more than she was ready to share.

She'd already seen too much.

This happiness was seeping out of every cell in her body and it was no surprise it was visible to someone who knew her well. It felt like she was glowing. As if she could still feel the touch of Charles's hands—and lips—on her body.

On more than her body, in fact. It felt like her soul was glowing this morning.

Reborn.

Oh, help… She wasn't going to be as focused on her work today as she needed to be if she let herself get pulled back into memories of last night. That was a pleasure that needed to wait until later. With a huge effort, Grace closed the mental door on that compelling space.

'I have a clown in Curtain Three,' she told Helena.

Helena shook her head with a grimace. 'We get a lot of clowns in here. They're usually drunk.'

'No…this is a real clown. He was trying to do a cartwheel and I've just finished relocating his shoulder that couldn't cope. I want to check his X-ray before I discharge him. He has a clown friend with him, too.

Didn't you see them come in? Spotty suits, squeaky horns, bright red wigs—the whole works.'

But Helena didn't seem to be listening. She was staring at an ambulance gurney that was being wheeled past the desk. The person lying on the gurney seemed to be a life-sized tin soldier.

'Oh...of course...' she sighed. 'It's the Macy's Thanksgiving parade today, isn't it?'

'Chest pain,' one of the paramedics announced. 'Query ST elevation in the inferior leads.'

'Straight into Resus, thanks.' Grace shared a glance with Helena. This tin soldier was probably having a heart attack. 'I can take this.'

Helena nodded. 'I'll follow up on your clown, if you like.' She glanced over her shoulder as if she was expecting more gurneys to be rolling up. 'We're in for a crazy day,' she murmured. 'It always is, with the parade.'

Crazy was probably good, Grace decided as she followed her tin soldier into Resus.

'Let's get him onto the bed. On my count. One, two...*three*.' She smiled at the middle-aged man. 'My name's Grace and I'm one of the doctors here at Manhattan Mercy. Don't worry, we're going to take good care of you. What's your name?'

'Tom.'

'How old are you, Tom?'

'Fifty-three.'

'Do you have any medical history of heart problems? Hypertension? Diabetes?'

Tom was shaking his head to every query.

'Have you ever had chest pain like this before?'

Another shake. 'I get a bit out of puff sometimes. But playing the trumpet is hard, you know?'

'And you got out of breath this morning?'

'Yeah. And then I felt sick and got real sweaty. And the pain…'

'He's had six milligrams of morphine.' A paramedic was busy helping the nursing staff to change the leads that clipped to the electrodes dotting Tom's chest so that he was attached to the hospital's monitor. His oxygen tubing came off the portable cylinder to be linked to the overhead supply and a different blood pressure cuff was being wrapped around his arm.

'How's the pain now, Tom?' Grace asked. 'On a scale of zero to ten, with ten being the worst?'

'About six, I guess.'

'It was ten when we got to him.'

'Let's give you a bit more pain relief, then,' Grace said. 'And I want some bloods off for cardiac enzymes, please. I want a twelve-lead ECG, stat. And can some-one call the cath lab and check availability?'

Yes. Crazy was definitely good. From the moment Tom had arrived in her care to nearly an hour later, when she accompanied him to the cardiac catheter lab-oratory so that he could receive angioplasty to open his blocked artery, she didn't have a spare second where her thoughts could travel to where they wanted to go so much.

Heading back to the ER was a different matter.

Her route that took her back to bypass the main wait-ing area was familiar now. The medical staff all used it because if you went through the waiting area at busy times, you ran the risk of being confronted by angry people who didn't like the fact that they had to wait while more urgent cases were prioritised. If Helena was right, this was going to be a very busy day. Which made sense, because they were the closest hospital to where the parade was happening and the participants and spectators would number in the tens of thousands.

Had Charles taken the boys to see the parade?

Was that why he hadn't had the time to answer her text message yet?

Grace's hand touched the phone that was clipped to the waistband of her scrub trousers but she resisted the urge to bring the screen to life and check that she hadn't missed a message.

She wasn't some love-crazed teenager who was holding her breath to hear from a boy.

She'd never been that girl. Had never dated a boy that had had that much of an impact on her. She'd been confident in her life choices and her focus on her study and the career she wanted more than anything.

But she'd turned into that girl, hadn't she? After that first night with Charles Davenport. The waiting for that message or call. The excitement that had morphed into anxiety and then crushing disappointment and heartbreak.

And humiliation…

Grace dropped her hand. They were a long way from being teenagers now. Charles was a busy man. Quite apart from his job, he was a hands-on father with two small boys. History was not about to repeat itself. Charles understood how badly he had treated her by ignoring her last time. He had apologised for it, even. There was no way he would do that again.

And she was stronger. He'd told her that. He'd made her believe it was true.

Walking past the cast room, Grace could see an elderly woman having a broken wrist plastered. There were people in the minor surgery area, too, with another elderly patient who looked like he was having a skin flap replaced. And then she was walking past the small rooms, their doors open and the interiors empty, but that couldn't stop a memory of the first time she had walked past one of them. When she'd seen those two small faces peering out and she had met Cameron and Max.

It couldn't stop the tight squeeze on her heart as she remembered falling in love with Max when he'd smiled at her and thanked her for fixing his truck and then cuddled up against her. He was more cuddly than his brother but she loved Cameron just as much now.

And their father?

Oh… Grace paused for a moment to grab a cup of water from the cooler before she pushed through the double doors into the coal face of the ER.

It hadn't been love at first sight with Charles.

But it had been love at first *night*.

That was why she'd been so nervous about working with him again. He'd surprised her by calling her that night about the dog-sitting possibility by revealing that he'd been thinking about her.

And he'd made her laugh. Made her drop her guard a little?

She'd realised soon after that that the connection was still there. The way he'd looked at her that day at the park—as if he really wanted to hear her story.

As if he really cared.

Oh, and that *kiss*. In that wreck of a kitchen still redolent with the smells of grilled cheese and freshly baked cookies. Even now, Grace could remember the fear that had stepped in when he'd been about to touch her breast. As though the lumpy scars beneath her clothing had suddenly been flashing like neon signs.

Crumpling the empty polystyrene cup, she dropped

it into the bin beside the cooler, catching her bottom lip between her teeth as if she wanted to hide a smile.

They hadn't mattered last night, those scars. She'd barely been aware of them herself...

She was back in the department now and she could see a new patient being wheeled into Resus.

So many patients came and went from that intensive diagnostic and treatment area but some were so much more memorable than others.

Like the first patient she had ever dealt with here. That badly injured cyclist who'd been a casualty of the power cut when the traffic lights had gone out. And the frozen baby that she and Charles had miraculously brought back to life. Yep... Grace would never forget that one.

That time with just the two of them when it had seemed as if time had been somehow rewound and that there was nothing standing between herself and Charles. No social differences that had put them on separate planets all those years ago. No past history of partners who had been loved and lost. No barriers apart from the defensive walls they had both constructed and maybe that had been the moment when Grace had believed there might be a way through those barriers.

She'd been right. And Helena had been right in noticing that there was something different about her today.

The only thing that could have made her even happier would be to feel the vibration against her waistband that would advertise an incoming text message.

But it didn't happen. Case after case took her attention during the next few hours. An asthmatic child who had forgotten his inhaler in the excitement of heading to watch the parade and suffered an attack that meant an urgent trip to the nearest ER. A man who'd had his foot stepped on by a horse. A woman who'd been caught up in the crowd when the first pains of her miscarriage had struck.

Case after case and the time flew by and Grace focused on each and every case as if it was the only thing that mattered. To stop herself checking her phone? It was well past lunchtime when she finally took a break in a deserted staffroom and sat down with a cup of coffee and could no longer ignore the weight and shape of her phone. No way to avoid glancing at it. At a blank screen that had no new messages or missed calls flagged.

Anxiety crept in as she stared at that blank screen. Was Charles sick or injured or had something happened to one of the twins? She could forgive this silence if that was the case but it would have to be something major like that because to treat her like this again when he knew how it would make her feel was…well, it was unforgiveable. All he'd had to do was send a simple message. A stupid smiley face would have been enough. Surely he would understand that every minute of continuing silence would feel like hours? That hours would actually start to feel like days?

But if something major like that had happened, she would have heard about it. Like she'd heard about Miranda being caught up in that tunnel collapse. A thread of anger took over from anxiety. How could she have allowed herself to get into a position where everything she had worked so hard for was under threat? She had come to New York to start a new life. To move on from so much loss. The loss of her marriage. The loss of the family she'd dreamed of having. The loss of feeling desirable, even.

Charles had given her a glimpse of a future that could have filled all those empty places in her soul.

This silence felt like a warning shot that it was no more than an illusion.

That the extraordinary happiness she had brought to work with her was no more than a puff of breath on an icy morning. The kind she had been making as she'd walked to Manhattan Mercy this morning in a haze of happiness after last night.

Last night?

It was beginning to feel like a lifetime ago. A lifetime in which this scenario had already played out to a miserable ending.

Anxiety and anger both gave way to doubt.

Had she really thought that history couldn't repeat itself? This was certainly beginning to feel like a re-run.

Maybe it had only been in her imagination that her scars didn't matter.

Maybe having a woman in his bed had opened old wounds for Charles and he was realising how much he missed Nina and that no one could ever take her place.

Maybe it had been too much, too soon and everything had been ruined.

For a moment, Grace considered sending another message. Just something casual, like asking whether they'd been to the parade this morning or saying that she hoped they were all having a good day.

But this new doubt was strong enough to make her hesitate and, in that moment of hesitation, she knew she couldn't do it.

Her confidence was starting to ebb away just as quickly as that happiness.

CHAPTER NINE

ANOTHER HOUR WENT past and then another…and still nothing.

Nothing…

No call. No text. No serendipitous meeting as their paths crossed in the ER, which was such a normal thing to happen that its absence was starting to feel deliberate.

Grace knew Charles had finally come to work this afternoon because the door to his office was open and she'd seen his leather laptop bag on his desk when she'd gone past a while back. She'd heard someone say he was in a meeting, which wasn't unusual for the chief of emergency services, but surely there weren't administrative issues that would take hours and hours to discuss? Maybe it hadn't actually been that long but it was certainly beginning to feel like it.

She thought she saw him heading for the unit desk when she slipped through a curtain, intending to chase up the first test results on one of her patients.

Her heart skipped a beat and started racing.

She'd know, wouldn't she? In that first instant of eye contact, she'd know exactly what was going on. She'd know whether it had been a huge mistake to get this close to Charles Davenport again. To be so completely in love and have so many shiny hopes for a new future that were floating around her like fragile, newly blown bubbles.

She'd know whether she was going to find herself right back at Square One in rebuilding her life.

Almost in the same instant, however, and even though she couldn't see his face properly, she knew it wasn't Charles, it was his twin, Elijah. And she knew this because the air she was sucking into her lungs felt completely normal. There was none of that indefinable extra energy that permeated the atmosphere when she was in the same space as Charles. The energy that made those bubbles shine with iridescent colours and change their shape as if they were dancing in response to the sizzle of hope.

'Dr Forbes?'

The tone in her migraine patient's voice made her swing back, letting the curtain fall into place behind her.

'I'm going to be sick…'

Grace grabbed a vomit container but she was too late. A nurse responded swiftly to her call for assistance and her gaze was sympathetic.

'I'll clean up in here,' she said. 'You'd better go and find some clean scrubs.' Pulling on gloves, she added a murmur that their patient couldn't overhear. 'It's been one of *those* days, hasn't it?'

Helena was in the linen supply room.

'Oh, no…' She wrinkled her nose. 'You poor thing…'

'Do we have any plastic bags in here? For super-soiled laundry?'

'Over there. Want me to guard the door for a minute so you can strip that lot off?'

'Please. I'm starting to feel a bit queasy myself.'

'Do you need a shower?'

'No. It's just on my scrubs.' Grace unhooked her stethoscope and then unclipped her phone and pager from her waistband. She put them onto a stainless-steel trolley and then peeled off her tunic. 'What are you doing in here, anyway?'

'We were low on blankets in the warmer and everyone was busy. I'm due for a break.' Helena was leaning against the closed door, blocking the small window. 'Past due to go home, in fact. We both are.' Her smile was rueful. 'How come we were among the ones to offer to stay on?'

'We were short-staffed and overloaded. It was lucky Sarah Grayson could stay on as well.'

'I know. Well, I've hardly seen you since this morning. You okay?' She wrinkled her nose. 'Sorry—silly question. Crazy day, huh?'

'Mmm.' Grace was folding the tunic carefully so she could put it into the bag without touching the worst stains. 'I certainly wouldn't want another one like this in a hurry.'

Not that staying on past her rostered hours had bothered her, mind you. Or the patient load. She loved a professional challenge. It was the personal challenge she was in the middle of that was a lot less welcome.

'What are you doing after work? There's a group going out for Thanksgiving dinner at a local restaurant that sounds like it might be fun. I know you'd be more than welcome.'

But, again, Grace shook her head. 'I can't abandon my dog after being at work so much longer than expected. And I need to Skype my dad. I haven't spoken to him for a while and it's Thanksgiving. Family time.'

'Ah…' Helena's gaze was mischievous. 'And there

was me thinking you might be going to some glitzy Davenport occasion.'

Pulling on her clean scrub trousers, Grace let the elastic waist band go with more force than necessary. 'What?'

'You and Charles…?' Helena was smiling now. 'Is *that* why you were looking so happy first thing this morning? Everybody's wondering…'

A heavy knot formed in Grace's gut. People were gossiping about her? And Charles? Had he said something to someone else when he hadn't bothered talking to her? Or had someone seen something or said something to remind Charles that he would never be able to replace his beloved wife? Maybe *that* was why he was ignoring her.

'I have no idea what you're talking about,' she said. 'We're just friends.'

'That's what he said, too.'

'What?' Grace fought the shock wave that made it difficult to move. *'When?'*

'There was someone here earlier this afternoon. A journalist pretending to be a patient and she was asking for you. You'd taken a patient off for an MRI, I think. Or maybe you were finally having a late lunch. Anyway… Charles told her she was wasting her time. That you were nothing more than a colleague and friend. And never would be.'

Was it simply the waft of soiled laundry that was making Grace feel a little faint? She secured the top of the plastic bag and shoved it into the contaminated linen sack.

So she didn't need to make eye contact with Charles to know that the truth was every bit as gut wrenching as she had suspected it would be.

'I don't understand,' she murmured. 'Why was he even saying anything?'

'It's because of the gossip column. That photo. Any Davenport news is going to be jumped on around here. They're like New York royalty.'

'What gossip column? What *photo*?'

'You don't know?' Helena's eyes widened. 'Look. I can show you on my phone. I have to admit, you do look like a really happy little family…'

Focus, Charles reminded himself. Shut out anything irrelevant that's only going to make everything worse.

He had responsibilities that took priority over any personal discomfort.

His boys came first. He'd been a little later for work this afternoon, after getting home from the parade, because he'd needed to brief Maria about the renewed media interest in his life and warn her not to say anything about his private life if she was approached by a journalist. He was going to keep the boys away from nursery school for a day or two, as well, for the same reason.

He'd assumed that he'd see Grace at work and be able to have a quiet word and warn her that she might be faced with some unwelcome attention but she hadn't been in the department when he'd arrived. Instead, he'd been confronted with the reality that interest in the Davenport family's private lives was never going to vanish. How had someone found out that Grace worked here? Had it helped to deal so brusquely with that journalist who had been masquerading as a patient or had he protested too much?

At least Grace hadn't been there to hear him dismissing her as someone who would never be anything more significant than a friend but the echo of his own words was haunting him now.

It wasn't true. He might have no idea how to handle these unexpected emotions that were undermining everything in his personal life that he'd believed would never change but the thing he could be certain of was that his own feelings were irrelevant right now.

He was in a meeting, for heaven's sake, where his push for additional resources in his department was dependent on being able to defend the statistics of patient outcomes and being able to explain anomalies in terms of scientific reasoning that was balanced by morality and the mission statements of Manhattan Mercy's emergency room.

He had to focus.

One meeting merged into the next until it was late in the day and he was still caught up in a boardroom. The detailed report of how his department and others had coped in the power cut last month was up for discussion with the purpose of making sure that they would be better prepared if it should ever happen again.

It was hard to focus in this meeting as well. The day of the power cut had been the day that Grace Forbes had walked back into his life in more than a professional sense. It seemed like fate had been determined to bring her close as quickly as possible. How else could he explain the series of events that had led her to meet his sons and remind him of how lucky he actually was? That had been when his barriers had been weakened, he realised. When that curiosity about Grace had put her into a different space than any other woman could have reached.

The kind of determination to focus that was needed here was reminiscent of one of the most difficult times of his life—when he'd had to try and pass his final exams in medicine while the fallout of the Davenport scandal had been exploding around him. How hard that had been had been eclipsed by the tragedy of Nina's death, of course, but he'd somehow coped then as well.

And he could cope now.

'We can't base future plans on the normal through-put of the department,' he reminded the people gathered in this boardroom. 'What we have to factor in is that this kind of widespread disruption causes a huge spike in admissions due to the accidents directly caused by it. Fortunately, it's a rare event so we can't resource the department to be ready at all times. What we can do is have a management plan in place that will put us in the best position to deal with whatever disaster we find on our doorstep. And haven't there been predictions already for severe snow storms in December? If it's correct, that could also impact our power supply and patient numbers.'

By the time his meeting finished, a new shift was staffing the department and Grace was nowhere to be seen.

He could knock on her door when he got home, Charles decided, but a glance at his watch told him that he'd have to be quick. He was due to take the boys to their grandparents' house for Thanksgiving dinner tonight and he was already running late.

Was she even at home? He'd heard about the staff dinner at a restaurant being planned and, when there was no response to his knock other than a warning bark from Houston, he hoped that was exactly where she was.

Out having fun.

More fun than he was likely to have tonight, with his mother still stressed about renewed media interest in the family and the necessity of trying to keep two three-year-old boys behaving themselves at a very formal dining table.

Maria had got the boys dressed and said she didn't mind waiting while he got changed himself. A quick shower was needed and then Charles found his dinner jacket and bow tie. The formality was a family tradition, like getting the annual Davenport photograph that would be made available to the media to remind them that this family was still together. Still strong enough to survive anything.

Charles rummaged in the top drawer of his dresser, to find the box that contained his silver cufflinks. He didn't know how many of the family members would be there tonight but hopefully the table would be full. Elijah would definitely be there. And Zac, who was about to start his new job at Manhattan Mercy.

His fingers closed around a velvet box and he opened it, only to have his breath catch in his throat.

This wasn't the box that contained his cufflinks. It was the box that contained the Davenport ring. The astonishing pink diamond that Nina had accepted when she had accepted his proposal of marriage. A symbol of the continuation of the Davenport name. A symbol of their position in New York society, even, given the value and rarity of this famous stone.

As the oldest son, it had been given to Charles for his wife-to-be and there was only one person in the world who could have worn it.

Nina.

Shadows of old grief enclosed Charles as he stared at the ring. He could never give it to anyone else.

It wouldn't even suit Grace…

Oh, help…where had *that* come from?

Memories of how he'd felt waking up this morning came back to him in a rush. That excitement. The pleasure.

The...longing...

And right now, those feelings were at war with remnants of grief. With the weight of all the responsibilities he had been trying so hard to focus on.

The battle was leaving him even more confused.

Drained, even.

He left the ring in its opened box on top of the dresser as he found and inserted his cufflinks and then slipped on his silk-lined jacket.

He closed the box on the ring then, and was about to put it back where he'd found it but his hand stopped in mid-air.

He had no right to keep this ring shut away in a drawer when he had no intention of ever using it again himself. It could be hidden for decades if he waited to hand it on to his firstborn, Cameron.

He should give it to the next Davenport in line. Elijah.

Charles let his breath out in a sigh. He knew perfectly well how his twin felt about marriage. With his bitterness about the marriage of their parents and scepticism about its value in general, he wouldn't want anything to do with the Davenport ring.

He couldn't give it to Penelope, because it was traditional for it to go to a son who would be carrying on the family name. Miranda was out of the question, even if she hadn't been another female, because of the distress that could cause to his mother, given her reluctance to absorb his half-sister into the family.

Zac. Was that his answer? The youngest Davenport male in his own generation. Okay, Zac had always had a tendency to rebel against Davenport traditions but he was making an effort now, wasn't he? Coming back into the fold. Trying to rebuild bridges? Was it possible that could even extend to taking an interest in Dr Ella Lockwood, the daughter of family friends and the woman who everyone had once expected Zac to marry? Though he'd noticed Ella hadn't seemed too pleased to learn that Zac was joining the team, so maybe not. But whatever happened, he hoped his youngest brother would find the happiness he deserved.

Yes. Charles slipped the ring box into his pocket. Even if Zac wasn't ready to accept it yet, he would know that it would be waiting for him.

He'd have a word with Elijah, first, of course. And then Zac. Maybe with his parents as well. If he could handle it all diplomatically, it could actually be a focus for this evening that would bring them all a little closer together and distract them from directing any attention on his own life. It would also be a symbol that he was moving on from his past, too. For himself as much as his family.

Yes. This felt like the next step in dealing with this unexpected intrusion into their lives. And maybe it would help settle the confusing boundaries between his responsibilities and his desires. Between the determination to protect everyone he had cared about in his life so far and the longing to just be somewhere alone with the new person in his life that he also wanted to protect?

Grace heard the knock on her door.

But what could she do? Her father had just answered her Skype call and he was so delighted to see her.

If there'd been a second knock, she might have excused herself for a moment but, after a single bark, Houston came and settled himself with his head on her feet. There was obviously no one on the other side of the door now. Maybe it had been someone else who lived in this apartment block. After all, Charles had had an entire day in which he could have called or texted her. Or he could have found her at work this afternoon because she'd certainly hung around long enough.

And he hadn't.

History was clearly repeating itself.

She had offered him everything she had to give and he had accepted it and then simply walked away without a backward glance.

'Sorry—what was that, Dad?'

'Just saying we hit the national high again today. Blue skies and sunshine here in Florida. How's it looking in the big smoke?'

'Grey. And freezing. They're predicting snow tomorrow. It could be heavy.'

Her father laughed. 'We have hospitals in this neck of the woods, you know. You don't have to suffer!'

'Maybe I'll see what's being advertised.'

The comment was light-hearted but, as they chatted about other things, the thought stayed in the back of her mind.

She could walk away from New York, couldn't she? She didn't *have* to stay here and feel…rejected…

Grace had to swallow a sudden lump in her throat. 'I feel a long way away at the moment. I miss you, Dad.'

'Miss you, too, honey.' Her father's smile wobbled a bit. 'So tell me, what are you doing for Thanksgiving dinner? Have you got yourself some turkey?'

'No. Work's been really busy and, anyway, it seemed a bit silly buying a turkey for one person.'

'I'll bet that dog you're living with could have helped you out there.'

Grace laughed but her brain was racing down another track. It couldn't have been Charles knocking at her door because wasn't he going to some big Davenport family dinner tonight? A dinner that he had suggested she could also go to but then he'd made a face as if the idea was distasteful.

Why? Did he not enjoy the family gathering himself or was it more the idea that she would hate it because she wouldn't fit in?

Of course she wouldn't. As Helena had reminded her so recently, the Davenports were New York royalty and she wasn't even American by birth. She was a foreigner. A divorced foreigner. A divorced foreigner with a scarred body who wasn't even capable of becoming a mother.

Oh, help… Going down this track any further when she had a night alone stretching out in front of her was a very bad idea.

'Have you got some wine to go with your turkey, Dad?'

'Of course. A very nice Australian chardonnay.'

'Well… I've got something in the fridge. Prosecco, I think. Why don't we both have a glass together and we can tap the screen and say cheers.' It was hard to summon up a cheerful smile but Grace gave it her best shot.

She could deal with this.

She had, in fact, just had a very good idea of exactly how she could deal with it. When she had finished this call with her dad, and had had a glass or two of wine, she was going to do something very proactive.

It was ironic that it had been Charles who'd pointed out how far she had come from being someone vulnerable enough to be easily crushed. How strong she was now.

Ironic because she was going to write her resignation letter from Manhattan Mercy. And, tomorrow, as soon as she started her shift, it would be Charles Davenport's desk that she would put that letter on.

CHAPTER TEN

'THANKS EVER SO much for coming home, Dr Davenport.'

'It's no problem, Maria. You need to get to this appointment for the final check on that back of yours. I hope you won't need the brace any more after this.'

'I shouldn't be more than a couple of hours. I'll text you if there's any hold-up.'

'Don't worry about it. I've got more than enough work that I can do from home.'

His nanny nodded, wrapping a thick scarf around her neck. 'The boys are happy. They're busy drawing pictures at the moment.'

A glance into the living area showed a coffee table covered with sheets of paper and scattered crayons. Two tousled heads were bent as the twins focused on their masterpieces. Charles stayed where he was for a moment, pulling his phone from his pocket and hitting a rapid-dial key.

'Emergency Room.'

Charles recognised the voice of one of the staff members who managed the phone system and incoming radio calls.

'Hi, Sharon. Charles Davenport here. I'm working from home for a few hours.'

'Yes, we're aware of that, Dr Davenport. Did you want to speak to the other Dr Davenport?'

'No. I actually wanted to speak to Dr Forbes. Is she available at the moment?'

'Hang on, I'll check.'

Charles could hear the busy sounds of the department through the line but it sounded a little calmer than it had been earlier today. When he'd gone to his office to collect his briefcase after the latest meeting, there'd been security personnel and police officers there but Elijah had assured him that everything was under control and he was free to take the time he needed away.

Right now, the voices close by were probably doctors checking lab results or X-rays on the computers. Would one of them be Grace, by any chance?

He hadn't seen her when he'd been in at work earlier and this was getting ridiculous. It was well into the second day after their night together and they hadn't even spoken. His intention to protect everyone he cared about by ignoring the potential for public scrutiny on his private life had been so strong, it was only now that it was beginning to feel like something was very wrong.

No. Make that more than 'feel'. He knew that he was in trouble.

He'd met the Australian dog walker, Kylie, in the foyer on his way in, minutes ago. The one that looked after Houston when Grace was at work.

She'd introduced herself. Because, she explained, she might be in residence for a while—if Grace left before Houston's owners were due to return.

But Stefan and Jerome had been planning to come back in less than a couple of weeks as far as Charles was aware.

Why would Grace be thinking of leaving before then?

It had only been just over a day since he'd seen her. How could something that huge have changed so much in such a short space of time?

He needed to speak to her. To apologise for not having spoken to her yesterday. At the very least, he had to arrange a time when they could talk. To find out what was going on.

To repair any damage he had the horrible feeling he might be responsible for? He'd tried so hard to do things perfectly this time—to think through each step logically so that he could avoid making a mistake.

But he'd missed something. Something that was seeming increasingly important.

Sharon was back on the line.

'Sorry, Dr Davenport. Dr Forbes is in CT at the moment. We had a head injury patient earlier who was extremely combative. We had to call Security in to help restrain him while he got sedated and intubated.'

'Yes, I saw them there when I was leaving.'

'He was Dr Forbes's patient. She's gone with him to CT and may have to stay with him if he needs to go to Theatre so I have no idea how long she'll be. Do you want me to page her to call you back when she can?'

'Daddy... *Daddy*...' Cameron was tugging on his arm, a sheet of paper in his other hand. 'Look at *this*.'

'No, thanks, Sharon. She's busy enough, by the sound of things. I'll catch up with her later.'

He ended the call. Was he kidding himself? He'd been trying to 'catch up' with her from the moment he'd arrived at work yesterday and it hadn't happened. And suddenly he felt like he was chasing something that was rapidly disappearing into the distance.

'Daddy? What's the matter?'

The concern in Max's voice snapped Charles back

to where he was. He crouched down as Max joined his brother.

'Nothing's the matter, buddy.'

'But you look sad.'

'No-o-o…' Charles ruffled the heads of both his boys. 'How could I be sad when I get to spend some extra time with you guys? Hey…did you really draw that picture all by yourself?' He reached out for the paper to admire the artwork more closely but, to his surprise, Max shook his head and stepped back.

'It's for Gace,' he said solemnly.

'So's mine,' Cameron said. 'But you can look.'

The colourful scribbles were getting more recognisable these days. A stick figure person with a huge, crooked smile. And another one with too many legs.

'It's Gace. And Horse.'

'Aww…she'll love them. You know what?'

'What?'

'I'll bet she puts them in a frame and puts them on her wall.'

The boys beamed at him but then Max's smile wobbled.

'And then she'll come back?'

Why hadn't it occurred to him how much the twins were already missing Grace? How much they loved her as well as Horse. He hadn't factored that in when he'd chosen to distance himself enough to keep his family temporarily out of the spotlight, had he? When he'd left her text unanswered and had told that journalist that they were nothing more than friends.

And never would be.

How many people had overheard that comment? Passed it on, even?

Could *that* have been enough to persuade Grace that she didn't want to be in New York any more?

The sinking sensation that had begun with that chance meeting with Kylie gained momentum and crashed into the pit of Charles's stomach but he smiled reassuringly and nodded.

It was tantamount to a promise, that smile and nod. A promise that Grace would be back. Now he just had to find a way to make sure he didn't let his boys down.

'You guys hungry? Want some cookies and milk? And *Curious George* on TV?'

'Yes!'

At least three-year-old boys were easily distracted. Or maybe not.

'*Spider* cookies,' Cameron shouted. 'They're the bestest.'

'I think we've run out of spider cookies,' he apologised.

'That's okay, Daddy.' Max patted his arm. 'I'll tell Gace and we'll help her make some more.'

He had to sit down with the boys and supervise the milk drinking but Charles wasn't taking any notice of the monkey's antics on the screen that were sending the twins into fits of giggles.

His mind was somewhere else entirely, carried away by the echo of his son's words. The tone of his voice.

That confidence that everything would be put to rights when he'd had the chance to explain what was wrong to Grace.

It hadn't even occurred to either of his boys to suggest that *he* make them some more homemade cookies. It might be only a superficial example but it symbolised all those things a mother could do that perhaps he couldn't even recognise as being missing from their lives.

And that longing in Max's voice.

And then she'll come back?

It touched something very deep inside Charles. Opened the door he'd shut in his head and heart that was a space that was filled with the same longing. Not just for a woman in his life or for sex. That need was there, of course, but this longing—it was for Grace.

He had to do a whole lot more than simply apologise for leaving her text unanswered when he spoke to her. He had to make her understand how important she'd become to his boys. How much they loved her.

And…and he had to tell her that he felt the same way.

That *he* loved her.

That the idea of life without her had become something unthinkable.

There was a painful lump in his throat that he tried to clear away but that only made Max look up at him with those big, blue eyes that could often see so much more than you'd expect a small boy to see.

'You happy, Daddy?'

'Sure am, buddy.' Man, it was hard work to sound as though he meant it. 'You finished with that milk?'

He took the empty cups back to the kitchen. He glanced at his phone lying on the table beside his laptop on his return.

Was it worth trying to find out if Grace was available?

There was a sense of urgency about this now. What if she really was planning to leave? What if she was actually planning to leave New York? Surely she wouldn't do that without telling him?

But why would she?

He hadn't spoken to her since they'd spent the night together. He hadn't even answered her text message.

Okay, stuff had happened and events had conspired to prevent him seeing her the way he'd assumed he'd be able to, but the truth was there was no excuse for what the combination of things had produced. Without any intention of doing so, he had allowed history to repeat itself. He'd made love to Grace and then seemingly ignored her. Pushed her out of his life because something else had seemed more important.

So why wouldn't she just walk away?

He'd thought he was protecting her by not giving any journalists a reason to pry into her life when there were things that he knew she would prefer to keep very private.

Those same things that had made her so vulnerable to allowing herself to get close to another man.

Why had he assumed that she needed his protection anyway? As he'd reminded her himself, she was a strong, courageous woman and she had dealt with far worse things in her life than the threat of having her privacy invaded.

She had been courageous enough to take the risk of letting *him* that close.

And somehow—albeit unintentionally—he'd repeated the same mistake he'd made the first time.

He'd made everything worse.

He hadn't even been protecting his boys in one sense, either. He'd created the risk of them losing someone they loved. Someone they needed in their lives.

Charles rubbed the back of his neck, lifting his gaze as he tried to fight his way through this mess in his head. The view from the massive windows caught his attention for a blessed moment of distraction. It was beginning to snow heavily. Huge, fat flakes were drifting down, misting the view of the Manhattan skyline and Central Park.

Charles loved snow. He'd never quite lost that childish excitement of seeing it fall or waking up to find his world transformed by the soft, white blanket of a thick covering. But there wasn't even a spark of that excitement right now. All he could feel was that lump-inducing longing. A bone-deep need to be close to Grace.

He'd never thought he'd ever feel like this again. He'd never wanted to after Nina had died because the grief had been crippling and he never wanted to face another loss like that. He didn't want his boys to have to face that kind of loss, either.

But it had happened. He had fallen in love. Maybe it had always been there, in an enforced hibernation after that first night they'd been together, thanks to the life events that had happened afterwards.

And here he was, possibly facing the loss of this love and, in a way, it would be worse than losing Nina because Grace would still be alive. If she wasn't actually planning on leaving Manhattan Mercy, and was only thinking of finding a new place to live, he'd see her at work and see that smile and hear her voice and know that being together could have been possible if he'd done things differently.

There had to be some way he could fix this.

If Grace had feelings for him that were anything like as powerful as the ones he had finally recognised, surely there was a way to put things right.

But how?

A phone call couldn't do it.

Even a conversation might not be enough.

Charles took a deep inward breath and then let it out very slowly as he watched the flakes continuing to fall. This was no passing shower. This snow would settle. Maybe not for long. It would probably be slush by the morning if the temperature lifted but for the next few hours at least it would look like a different world out there.

A world that Grace had been so eager to see.

An echo of her voice whispered in his mind.

'It's always been my dream for Christmas. A sleigh ride in a snowy park. At night, when there's sparkly lights everywhere and there are bells on the horses and you have to be all wrapped up in soft blankets.'

He could have given her that. But how likely was it to be possible now? Christmas was weeks away and maybe she wouldn't even be here.

He needed a small miracle.

And as he stood there, watching the snow fall, Charles became aware of the spark that had been missing. Excitement about the snow?

Maybe.

Or maybe it was just hope.

The letter was still in her pocket.

Grace could feel it crinkle as she sat down on the chair beside her elderly patient's bed.

She could have gone in and put it on Charles Davenport's desk first thing this morning but she hadn't.

Because he'd been in the office. Sitting at his desk, his head bent, clearly focused on the paperwork in front of him. And it had been just too hard to know what it would be like to meet his eyes. To explain what was in the sealed envelope in her hands. To have the conversation that might have suggested they were both adults and surely they could continue working together. To be friends, even?

Nope. She didn't think she could do that. Okay, maybe it was cowardly to leave a letter and run away. She was going to have to work out her notice and that meant that they would be working in the same space for the next couple of weeks but she would cope with that the same way she was going to cope today. By immersing herself in her work to the exclusion of absolutely everything else.

And fate seemed set to help her do exactly that, by providing an endless stream of patients that needed her complete focus.

Like the guy this morning. A victim of assault but it was highly likely he'd started the fight himself. The huge and very aggressive man had presented a danger to all staff involved with his care, despite the presence of the police escort who'd brought him in. Security had had to be called and it had been a real challenge to sedate this patient and get him on a ventilator. Due to his size, the drugs needed to keep him sedated were at a high level and Grace had needed to monitor their effects very closely. Knowing what could happen if his levels dropped meant that she'd had to stay with him while he went to CT and then to Theatre so the case had taken up a good part of her morning.

Charles was nowhere to be seen when she was back in the ER but, even if he had been there, she could have kept herself almost invisible behind the curtains of various cubicles or the resuscitation areas. Patient after patient came under her care. A man with a broken finger who'd needed a nerve block before it could be realigned and splinted. A stroke victim. Two heart attacks. A woman who'd slipped on the snow that was apparently starting to fall outside and had a compound tib and fib fracture and no circulation in her foot.

And now she was in a side room with a very elderly woman called Mary who had been brought in a couple of hours ago in severe respiratory distress from an advanced case of pneumonia. Mary was eighty-six years old and had adamantly refused to have any treatment other than something to make her more comfortable.

'It's my time,' she'd told Grace quietly. 'I don't want to fight any more.'

Grace had called up her patient's notes. Mary had had a double mastectomy for breast cancer more than thirty years ago and only a few weeks back she had been diagnosed with ovarian cancer. She had refused treatment then as well. While it was difficult, as a doctor, to stand by and not provide treatment that could help, like antibiotics, it was Mary's right to make this decision and her reasoning was understandable. Very much of sound mind, she had smiled very sweetly at Grace and squeezed her hand.

'You're a darling to be so concerned but please don't worry. I'm not afraid.'

'Do you have any family we can call? Or close friends?'

'There was only ever my Billy. And he's waiting for me. He's been waiting a long time now...'

Helena had been concerned that Grace was caring for this patient.

'I can take her,' she said. 'I know how hard this must be for you. Your mum died of ovarian cancer, didn't she?'

Grace nodded, swallowing past the constriction in her throat. 'I sat with her at the end, too. Right now it feels like it was yesterday.'

'Which is why you should step back, maybe. We'll make her as comfortable as possible in one of the private rooms out the back. It could take a while, you know. I'll find a nurse to sit with her so she won't be alone.'

'She knows me now. And I don't care how long it takes, as long as you can cope without me in here?'

'Of course. But—'

'It's because of my mum that I'm the right person to do this,' Grace said softly. 'Because of how real it feels for me. I want to do this for Mary. I want her to know that she's with someone who really cares.'

So, here they were. In one of the rooms she had noticed on her very first day here when she had wondered what they might be used for. It might even be the room next door to the one that she had stayed in with the twins and fixed Max's fire truck but this one had a bed with a comfortable air mattress. It was warm and softly lit. There was an oxygen port that was providing a little comfort to ease how difficult it was for Mary to breathe and there was a trolley that contained the drugs Grace might need to keep her from any undue distress. The morphine had taken away her pain and made her drowsy but they had talked off and on for the last hour and Grace knew that her husband Billy had died suddenly ten years ago.

'I'm so glad he didn't know about this new cancer,' Mary whispered. 'He would have been so upset. He was so good to me the first time...'

She knew that they had met seventy years ago at a summer event in Central Park.

'People say that there's no such thing as true love at first sight. But we knew different, Billy and me...'

She knew that they'd never had children.

'We never got blessed like that. It wasn't so hard... we had each other and that was enough...'

In the last half an hour Mary had stopped talking

and her breathing had become shallow and rapid. Grace knew that she was still aware of her surroundings, however, because every so often she would feel a gentle squeeze from the hand her own fingers were curled around.

And finally that laboured breathing hitched and then stopped and Mary slipped away so quietly and peacefully that Grace simply sat there, still holding her hand, for the longest time.

It didn't matter now that she had tears rolling down her cheeks. She wasn't sad, exactly. Mary had believed that she was about to be reunited with her love and she had welcomed the release from any more suffering. She hadn't died alone, either. She had been grateful for Grace's company. For a hand to hold.

And she'd been lucky, hadn't she?

She had known true love. Had loved and been loved in equal measure.

Or maybe she *was* sad.

Not for Mary, but for herself.

Grace had come so close to finding that sort of love for herself—or she'd thought she had. But now, it seemed as far away as ever. As if she was standing on the other side of a plate-glass window, looking in at a scene that she couldn't be a part of.

A perfect scene.

A Christmas one, perhaps. With pretty lights on a tree and parcels tied up with bows underneath. A fire in a grate beneath a mantelpiece that had colourful stockings hanging from it. There were people in that scene, too. A tall man with dark hair and piercing blue eyes. Two little mop-topped, happy boys. And a big, curly, adorable dog.

It took a while to get those overwhelming emotions

under control but the company of this brave old woman who had unexpectedly appeared in her life helped, so by the time Grace alerted others of Mary's death, nobody would have guessed how much it had affected her. They probably just thought she looked very tired and who wouldn't, after such a long day?

It took a while after that to do what was necessary after a death of a patient and it was past time for Grace's shift to finish by the time she bundled herself up in her warm coat and scarf and gloves, ready for her walk home.

She walked out of the ER via the ambulance bay and found that it had been snowing far more than she'd been told about. A soft blanket of whiteness had cloaked everything and the world had that muted sound that came with snow when even the traffic was almost silent. And it was cold. Despite her gloves, Grace could feel her fingers tingling so she shoved her hands in her pockets and that was when she felt the crinkle of that envelope again.

Thanks to her time with Mary, she had completely forgotten to put it on Charles's desk.

Perhaps that was a good thing?

Running away from something because it was difficult wasn't the kind of person she was now.

Charles had told her how courageous she was. He had made her believe it and that belief had been enough to push her into risking her heart again.

And that had to be a good thing, too.

Even if it didn't feel like it right now.

She had almost reached the street now where the lamps were casting a circle of light amidst a swirl of snowflakes but she turned back, hesitating.

She hadn't even looked in the direction of Charles's office when she'd left. Maybe he was still there?

Maybe the kind of person she was now would actually go back and talk about this. Take the risk of making herself even more vulnerable?

And that was when she heard it.

Someone calling her name.

No. It was a jingle of bells. She had just imagined hearing her name.

She turned back to the road and any need to make a decision on what direction she was about to take evaporated.

There was a sleigh just outside the ambulance entrance to Manhattan Mercy.

A bright red sleigh, with swirling gold patterns on its sides and a canopy that was rimmed with fairy lights. A single white horse was in front, its red harness covered with small bells and, on its head—instead of the usual feathery plume—it had a set of reindeer antlers.

A driver sat in the front, a dark shape in a heavy black coat and scarf and top hat. But, in the back, there was someone else.

Charles…

'Grace…?'

Her legs were taking her forward without any instruction from her brain.

She was too stunned to be thinking of anything, in fact. Other than that Charles was here.

In a *sleigh*?

Maybe she'd got that image behind the plate-glass window a little wrong earlier.

Maybe *this* was the magic place she hadn't been able to reach.

Just Charles. In a sleigh. In the snow.

And he was holding out his hand now, to invite her to join him under the canopy at the back. Waiting to help her reach that place.

Grace was still too stunned to be aware of any coherent thoughts but her body seemed to know what to do and she found herself reaching up to take that hand.

She had been on the point of summoning the courage to go and find Charles even if it meant stepping into the most vulnerable space she could imagine.

Here she was, literally stepping into that space.

And it hadn't taken as much courage as she'd expected.

Because it felt…right…

Because it was Charles who was reaching out to her and there was no way on earth she could have turned away.

CHAPTER ELEVEN

HEART-WRENCHING...

That look on Grace's face when she'd seen him waiting for her in the sleigh.

He'd expected her to be surprised, of course. The sleigh might not be genuine but the sides had been cleverly designed to cover most of the wheels so it not only looked the part but was a pretty unusual sight on a New York street. Along with the bells and fairy lights and the reindeer antlers on the horse, he had already been a target for every phone or camera that people had been able to produce.

For once, he didn't mind the attention. Bundled up in his thick coat and scarf, with a hat pulled well down over his head, Charles Davenport was unrecognisable but the worry about publicity was a million miles from his mind, anyway. The sight of this spectacle—that had taken him most of the day to organise—didn't just make people want to capture the image. It was delighting them, making them point and wave. To smile and laugh.

But Grace hadn't smiled when she saw him.

She'd looked shocked.

Scared, almost?

So, so vulnerable that Charles knew in that instant just how much damage his silence had caused.

And how vital it was to fix it.

The sheer relief when Grace had accepted his hand to climb up into the carriage had been so overwhelming that perhaps he couldn't blame the biting cold for making his eyes water. Or for making it too hard to say anything just yet. How much courage had it taken for her to accept his hand?

He loved her for that courage. And for everything else he knew to be true about her.

And nothing needed to be said just yet. For now, it was too important to make sure that Grace was going to be warm enough. To pull one faux fur blanket after another from the pile at his feet, to wrap them both in a soft cocoon. A single cocoon, so that as soon as he was satisfied there was no danger of hypothermia, he could wrap his arms around Grace beneath these blankets and simply hold her close.

Extra protection from the cold?

No. This was about protecting what he knew was the most important thing in his life at this moment. Grace. So important in his boys' lives as well. The only thing he wasn't sure of yet was how important it might be in her life.

The steady, rocking motion of the carriage was like a slow heartbeat that made him acutely aware of every curve in the body of the woman he was holding and, as the driver finished negotiating traffic and turned into the lamplit, almost deserted paths of Central Park, he could feel the tension in Grace's body begin to lessen. It was under the halo of one of those antique streetlamps that Grace finally raised her head to meet his gaze and he could see that the shock had worn off.

There was something else in her gaze now.

Hope?

That wouldn't be there, would it? Unless this was just as important to her as it was to him?

Again, the rush of emotion made it impossible to find any words.

Instead, Charles bent his head and touched Grace's lips gently with his own. Her lips parted beneath his and he felt the astonishing warmth of her mouth. Of her breath.

A breath of life...

Maybe he still didn't need to say anything yet. Or maybe he could say it another way...

For the longest time, Grace's brain had been stunned into immobility. She was aware of what was around her but couldn't begin to understand what any of it meant.

Her senses were oddly heightened. The softness of the furry blankets felt like she was being wrapped inside a cloud. The motion of the carriage was like being rocked in someone's arms. And then she *was* in someone's arms. Charles's. Grace didn't want to think about what this meant. She just wanted to feel it. This sense of being in the one place in the world she most wanted to be. This feeling of being protected.

Precious...

Finally, she had to raise her head. To check whether this was real. Had she slipped in the snow and knocked herself out cold, perhaps? Was this dream-come-to-life no more than an elaborate creation of her subconscious?

If it was, it couldn't have conjured up a more compelling expression in the eyes of the man she loved.

It was a gaze that told her she was the only thing in the world that mattered right now.

That she was loved...

And then his lips touched her own and Grace could

feel how cold they were, which only intensified the heat that was coming from inside his body. From his breath. From the touch of his tongue.

She wasn't unconscious.

Grace had never felt more alive in her life.

It was the longest, most tender kiss she had ever experienced. A whole conversation in itself.

An apology from Charles, definitely. A declaration of love, even.

And on her part? A statement that the agony of his silence and distance since they'd last been together didn't matter, perhaps. That she forgave him. That nothing mattered other than being together, like this.

They had to come up for air eventually, however, and the magic of the kiss retreated.

Actions might speak a whole lot louder than words, but words were important, too.

Charles was the first to use some.

'I'm so sorry,' he said. 'It's been crazy...but when Kylie told me this morning that you were thinking of leaving, I got enough of a shock to realise just how much I'd messed this up.'

'You didn't even answer my text message,' Grace whispered, her voice cracking. 'The morning after we'd...we'd...'

'I know. I'm sorry. I woke up that morning and realised how I felt about you and...and it was huge. My head was all over the place and then my mother rang. She'd seen something in the paper that suggested we were a couple. That photo of us all in the park.'

Grace nodded. 'Helena showed it to me. She said that there'd been a reporter in the department pretending to be a patient. That you'd told her we were just colleagues. Friends. That it would never be anything more than that.'

She looked away from Charles. A long, pristine stretch of the wide pathway lay ahead of them, the string of lamps shining to illuminate the bare, snow-laden branches of the huge, old trees guarding this passage. The snow was still falling but it was gentle now. Slow enough to be seen as separate stars beneath the glow of the lamps.

'I'd thought I would be able to find you as soon as I got to work. That I could warn you of the media interest. I thought…that I was protecting you from having your privacy invaded by putting them off the scent. And…and it didn't seem that long. It was only a day…'

Grace squeezed her eyes shut. 'It felt like a month…'

'I'm sorry…'

The silence continued on and then she heard Charles take a deep breath.

'I can't believe I made the same mistake. For the same reasons.'

'It's who you are, Charles.' Grace opened her eyes but she didn't turn to meet his gaze. 'You're always going to try and protect your family above everything else.'

She was looking at the fountain they were approaching. She'd seen it in the daytime—an angel with one hand held out over a pond. The angel looked weighed down now, her wings encrusted with a thick layer of snow.

Their carriage driver was doing a slow circuit around the fountain. Grace felt Charles shift slightly and looked up to see him staring at the angel.

'She's the Angel of the Waters, did you know that?'

'No.'

'The statue was commissioned to commemorate the first fresh water system for New York. It came after a cholera outbreak. She's blessing the water, to give it healing powers.'

He turned to meet her gaze directly and there was something very serious in his own. A plea, almost.

For healing?

'I do understand,' Grace said softly. 'And I don't blame you for ignoring me that first time. But it hurt, you know? I really didn't think you would do it again...'

'I didn't realise I was. I went into the pattern that I'd learned back then, to focus on protecting the people that mattered. My mother was upset. It was Thanksgiving and the family was gathering. The worst thing that could happen was to have everything out there and being raked up all over again.'

Grace was silent. Confused. He had gone to goodness only knew how much trouble to create this dream sleigh ride for her and he'd kissed her as if she was the only person who mattered. And yet he had made that same mistake. Maybe it hadn't seemed like very much time to him but it had felt like an eternity to her.

'What I said to that reporter was intended to protect you, Grace, as much as to try and keep the spotlight off my family. I had the feeling that you never talk about what you've been through. That maybe I was the only person who knew your story. I didn't want someone digging through your past and making something private public. You'd told me that that was the worst thing you could imagine happening. Especially something that was perhaps private between just *us*—that made it even more important to protect.'

He sighed as the carriage turned away from the fountain and continued its journey.

'I needed to talk to you somewhere private and it just wasn't happening. I couldn't get near you at work. There was the family Thanksgiving dinner and I was running late. I knocked on your door but you weren't home.'

'I was Skyping my dad. I couldn't answer the door.' And she could have made it easier for him, couldn't she? If she'd only had a little more confidence. She could have texted him again. Or made an effort to find him at work instead of waiting for him to come and find her.

He hadn't been put off by her scarred body. He'd been trying to protect her from others finding out about it. It made it a secret. One that didn't matter but was just between them. A private bond.

'I know that you don't actually need my protection,' Charles said slowly. 'That you're strong enough to survive anything on your own, but there's a part of me that would like you to need it, I guess. Because I want to be able to give it to you.'

They were passing the carousel now, the brightly coloured horses rising and falling under bright lights. There were children riding the horses and they could hear shrieks of glee.

'The boys are missing you,' Charles added quietly. 'They were drawing pictures for you this morning and I said that you'd love them and probably put them in a frame and Max said...he asked if you'd come back then.'

'Oh...' Grace had a huge lump in her throat.

'We need you, Grace. The boys need you. *I* need you.'

He took his hands from beneath the warmth of the blankets to cradle her face between them.

'I love you, Grace Forbes. I think I always have...

The lump was painful to swallow. It was too hard to find more than a single word.

'Same…'

'You were right in what you said—I will always protect my family above everything else. But you're part of my family now. The part we need the most.'

They didn't notice they had left the carousel behind them as they sank into another slow, heartbreakingly tender kiss.

When Grace opened her eyes again, she found they were going past the Wollman skating rink. Dozens of people were on the ice, with the lights of the Manhattan skyline a dramatic backdrop.

'I thought I had to ignore how I felt in order to protect the people around me,' Charles told her. 'But now I know how wrong I was.'

He kissed her again.

'I want everybody to know how much I love you. And I'm going to protect that love before everything else because that's what's going to keep us all safe. You. Me. The boys…' He caught Grace's hand in his own and brought it up to his lips. 'I can't go down on one knee, and I don't have a ring because I'd want you to choose what's perfect just for you, but…will you let me love you and protect you for the rest of our lives— even if you don't need it and even if I don't get it quite right sometimes? Will you…will you marry me, Grace?'

'Yes…' The word came out in no more than a whisper but it felt like the loudest thing Grace had ever said in her life.

This sleigh ride might have been a dream come true but it was nothing more than a stage set for her *real* dream. One that she'd thought she'd lost for ever. To love and be loved in equal measure.

To have her own family…

She had to blink back the sudden tears that filled her

eyes. Had to clear away the lump in her throat so that she could be sure that Charles could hear her.

'Yes,' she said firmly, a huge smile starting to spread over her face. 'Yes and yes and *yes*...'

EPILOGUE

IT WAS A twenty-minute walk from the apartment block to the Rockefeller Center but the two small boys weren't complaining about the distance. It was too exciting to be walking through the park in the dark of the evening and besides, if they weren't having a turn riding on Daddy's shoulders, they got to hold hands with Grace.

'Look, Daddy…look, Gace…' It was Max's turn to be carried high on his father's shoulders. 'What are they doing?'

'Ice skating,' Charles told him. 'Would you like to try it one day soon?'

'Is Gace coming, too?'

'Yes.' Grace grinned up at the little boy, her heart swelling with love. One day maybe he would call her 'Mummy' but it really didn't matter.

'Of course she is,' Charles said. 'Remember what we talked about? Grace and I are going to be married. Very soon. Before Christmas, even. We're a family now.'

'And Gace is going to be our *mummy*,' Cameron shouted.

Max bounced on Charles's shoulders as a signal to be put down. 'I want to hold my mummy's hand,' he said.

'She's *my* mummy, too.' Cameron glared at his brother.

'Hey… I've got two hands. One each.' Grace caught

Charles's gaze over the heads of the boys and the look in his eyes melted her heart.

Mummy.

It *did* matter.

Not the name. The feeling. Feeling like the bond between all of them was unbreakable.

Family.

A branch of the Davenport family of New York—something which she still hadn't got used to—but their own unique unit within that dynasty.

Charles had shown her the Davenport ring last week, after that magical sleigh ride in the park.

'I've told Zac it's waiting for him, if he ever gets round to needing it. It belongs to the past and, even before you agreed to marry me, I knew it wouldn't suit you.'

'Because it's so flashy?'

'Because it represents everything that is window dressing in life, not the really important stuff.'

'Like love?'

'Like love. Like what's beneath any kind of window dressing.'

He'd touched her body then. A gentle reminder that what her clothes covered was real. Not something to be ashamed of but a symbol of struggle and triumph. Something to be proud of.

So she had chosen a ring that could have also made its way through struggle and triumph already. An antique ring with a simple, small diamond.

'We're almost there, guys.' Charles was leading them through the increasingly dense crowds on the Manhattan streets. 'Let's find somewhere we'll be able to see.'

Grace could hear the music now. And smell hotdogs and popcorn from street stalls. People around them were

wearing Santa hats with flashing stars and reindeer antlers that made her remember the horse that had pulled
her sleigh so recently on the night that had changed
her life for ever.

They couldn't get very close to the Rockefeller Center in midtown Manhattan but it didn't matter because
the huge tree towered above the crowds and the live
music was loud enough to be heard for miles. Charles
lifted Cameron to his shoulders and Grace picked up
Max to rest him on her hip. He wrapped his arms around
her neck and planted a kiss on her cheek.

'I love you, Mummy.'

'I love you, too, Max,' she whispered back.

A new performance was starting. If it wasn't Mariah
Carey singing, it was someone who sounded exactly
like her. And it was *her* song: 'All I Want for Christmas Is You'.

Grace leaned back against the man standing pro-
tectively so close behind her. She turned her head and
smiled up at him.

'That's so true,' she told him. 'It's now officially my
favourite Christmas song, ever.'

'Mine, too.'

When the song finished, the countdown started and
when the countdown finished, the magnificent tree with
its gorgeous crystal star on the top blazed into life.

The Christmas season had officially begun.

And Grace had all she had ever wanted. All she
would ever want.

The tender kiss that Charles bent to place on her lips
right then made it clear that they both did.

* * * * *

A FIREFIGHTER
IN HER STOCKING

BY
JANICE LYNN

Published in Great Britain 2017
By Mills & Boon, an imprint of HarperCollins*Publishers*
1 London Bridge Street, London, SE1 9GF

© 2017 Harlequin Books S.A.

Special thanks and acknowledgement are given to Janice Lynn
for her contribution to the Christmas in Manhattan series.

ISBN: 978-0-263-92669-9

Printed and bound in Spain
by CPI, Barcelona

Dear Reader,

Firefighter heroes are new territory for me. But creating Jude was so much fun! I will be revisiting his heroic profession again in future stories.

Having grown up poor and, having been burned by love more than once, Dr Sarah Grayson is focused on her career and not much more. Especially not her gorgeous neighbour. That is until he comes rushing into the ER with a little girl he's saved from a fire and she realises there's more to him than a pretty face.

Having loved and lost, firefighter Jude Davenport takes risks with everything except his heart. How can he risk something he gave away long ago? But there's something about his Plain Jane neighbour he just can't resist, and maybe—just maybe—with her help he can finally let go of the past...

I'd love to hear your thoughts on Jude and Sarah. My email is Janice@janicelynn.net or you can message me on Facebook.

Happy reading!

Janice

To James Mills, FDNY EMS Battalion 8,
and to Andrew Floied, Manchester Fire Rescue.
Thank you for your invaluable insight
and for being real-life heroes!!

Any mistakes are my own.

Janice Lynn has a Masters in Nursing from
Vanderbilt University, and works as a nurse
practitioner in a family practice. She lives in the
southern United States with her husband, their four
children, their Jack Russell—appropriately named
Trouble—and a lot of unnamed dust bunnies that
have moved in since she started her writing career.
To find out more about Janice and her writing visit
janicelynn.com.

Books by Janice Lynn

Mills & Boon Medical Romance

Flirting with the Doc of Her Dreams
New York Doc to Blushing Bride
Winter Wedding in Vegas
Sizzling Nights with Dr Off-Limits
It Started at Christmas…
The Nurse's Baby Secret
The Doctor's Secret Son

Visit the Author Profile page
at millsandboon.co.uk for more titles.

**Janice won The National Readers' Choice Award
for her first book**
The Doctor's Pregnancy Bombshell

CHAPTER ONE

It wasn't every morning that Dr. Sarah Grayson stepped out of her apartment and saw a couple making out.

It had happened, though.

Same man, different woman.

Nausea churned in Sarah's belly. She ordered her eyes away, but since a nice, but somewhat bland apartment building corridor offered nothing to snag her attention, her gaze stayed put.

Making out in her hallway might be a bit of a stretch. Still, the couple stood in her rather hunky neighbor's apartment doorway, sharing a far from innocent kiss.

Even if the kiss had been a mere lip peck, her neighbor's lean hips wrapped in only a towel knocked innocent right out of the ball park. Home run.

Grand slam.

Sarah ran her gaze over his chiseled torso. He rated pin-up-worthy—centerfold, for sure. Part of her couldn't blame the busty brunette for clinging to his broad shoulders. Or for totally ignoring the fact Sarah had stepped into the hallway. Common decency said they should pull apart and look a little embarrassed, right?

When Sarah's gaze collided with piercing blue ones, her breath caught. No embarrassment in those magnificent eyes. Just pure unadulterated sexual temptation.

Good grief. He probably was a grand slam.

What eyes. A color so intense they pulled you in and made you feel as if you were drowning, made you want to drown in everything promised in the enticing blue depths.

Not Sarah, of course.

She was immune to playboys like this guy. She'd built up her defenses years ago while listening to her mother harp about the blight of good-looking, fast-talking men.

Adulthood had fortified her defenses.

Still, she wasn't blind. Her neighbor was hot. She knew it and so did he.

Even as his lips lingered on the brunette's, those eyes crinkled with bad-boy amusement. Probably laughing at the fact Sarah had taken up full-fledged voyeurism.

Gaze locked with hers, he pulled back from the kiss.

"Baby," the brunette protested, still not noticing Sarah as she tugged downward on her cocktail dress skirt.

Good, the skimpy material barely covered her perfectly shaped bottom. A sticking plaster would cover more than the clingy sparkling spandex. Then again, if Sarah had curves like the brunette maybe she'd wear shrink-wrapped clothes, too.

She doubted it, but who knew? Sarah dressed to avoid drawing attention so she could focus on more important things than meaningless ogling. Either way, she'd never know because her stick-straight slender body lacked the brunette's hourglass shape.

"Brandy, we have company," her neighbor said, much in the way a parent would to a petulant child.

The brunette turned, flashing big almond eyes, raked her gaze over Sarah's shapeless body beneath her heavy jacket, scarf, and hat. She dismissed Sarah's importance and quickly turned back to towel boy.

He was better to look at than a ready-to-face-the-chill-of-a-Manhattan-November-early-morning Sarah.

Or Sarah on any morning, really.

"Jude," the woman practically cooed.

So that was his name. Jude.

He'd tried talking to her a few times when they'd bumped into each other in the hallway, but she'd ignored him. What would be the point? She wasn't interested in going through his revolving front door and he didn't seem the type to want to just be friends with a woman. Plus, he made her feel uncomfortable. Not a creepy uncomfortable, just a very aware of how male he was uncomfortable.

Realizing she was standing in the apartment hallway, gawking still, Sarah turned from the couple, locked her deadbolt, and pretended she couldn't hear Brandy begging to do anything he'd like her to do. Had the woman no pride?

Go home, girl. He used you.

Too bad Brandy's mother hadn't warned about men like him as Sarah's mother had repeatedly done.

At the woman's next words, Sarah's cheeks caught fire. Nope, no pride whatsoever.

Sarah turned and her gaze collided with Jude's amazing blue one again. She'd swear those eyes could see straight into her very being, knew her thoughts. Maybe they even had some type of superpower because her stomach fluttered as if it had grown thousands of tiny wings.

Nausea, she told herself. Men like him made her sick. Out all hours of the night, never seeming to work, always with a different woman. Sick. Sick. Sick.

Maybe he was a gigolo or some kind of male escort.

Her nose curled in disgust to go along with her flaming cheeks.

"I think you've embarrassed my neighbor."

His voice was full of humor, which truly did embarrass Sarah. What was wrong with her? Standing in her hallway, as if frozen in place, ogling the man as if she'd never seen a bare chest.

She'd never seen one like his outside magazines and television, but that was beside the point.

She needed to get her voyeuristic self to work.

She couldn't make out most of what Brandy replied but caught the words "prude" and "dumpy". Ouch.

Refusing to look that way again, Sarah dropped her keys into the oversized bag she carried to work, and got out of Dodge before she had to listen to Jude's reply.

She hurried down the stairs, through the apartment complex foyer, and out onto the sidewalk to walk the few blocks to the hospital. The cold November wind bit at her face, but her jacket shielded her from the worst.

Too bad she'd not had a shield against what she'd just witnessed. That image was going to be hard to erase.

No doubt her neighbor had dismissed her as unimportant just as the brunette had. Sarah didn't care what he thought. Or what any man thought. She knew her strengths, her weaknesses. She preferred to be known for her brain and her heart rather than for outward appearances.

She was quite proud of who Sarah Grayson's brain and heart was. A dedicated emergency room doctor whom she believed made a difference in her patients' lives.

She wouldn't let her revolving bedroom door neighbor make her feel badly about herself. After all, what did he do?

He never seemed to do anything.

Except beautiful women.

On that, the man was an over-achiever.

A neighbor from the floor below said she thought he came from old money. Either Sarah was onto something with her paid male escort theory, or he was nothing more than a carefree, lecherous playboy using his family to fund his depraved lifestyle.

Maybe she would get lucky and he'd move.

Adrenaline drove firefighter Jude Davenport as he pushed his way through the flame-filled building. Or maybe it was the heat that kept him moving. Sweat dripped down the back of his neck and his ears burned beneath his Nomex hood.

First checking temperature with his thermal imaging camera, Jude opened a door and thick black smoke billowed out, banking low.

"Engine Seven to command. We are entering structure and making a left-hand search."

"Command copies Engine Seven is entering structure, making a left-hand search."

As lead man, Jude crawled to the left-hand wall and, staying in contact with him, his partner made his way around the room, using his axe to search. Visibility was next to nil thanks to the rolling black smoke.

They had to find her.

A four-year-old little girl was trapped in this hellish inferno.

Somewhere.

Along with more than a dozen tenants, they'd already rescued her mother and sister. Jude did not want to have to look that woman in the eyes and say he'd not been able to find her daughter.

He knew first-hand the pain of losing someone you loved and that drove him as he crawled toward a closed door he could barely make out.

A child was in there, was alive. Every instinct said she was.

He just had to get there, get to her, and pray that when he did find her, that she was still alive and he'd be able to get himself and her out of the fire.

Finally, he reached the door.

Then what he'd been dreading happened, what he'd known was coming because of how long they'd been searching in the burning building.

The air horn on the truck blew.

Once. Twice. Three long times.

"Command to all units. Evacuate the building. Repeat, evacuate the building."

He hadn't needed the sound of the horn or command coming over the radio speakers in his air pack to know things were bad and the building was lost.

Things were bad.

Somewhere in this hellhole was a terrified four-year-old.

"Command says part of the stairs has collapsed," his partner, Roger Woods, yelled. "We gotta go."

Jude had to check the room. They were too close to turn back without doing so.

"Seriously, Davenport," his partner called from behind Jude. "Don't make me drag your butt out."

"As if you could."

Roger was one of his best friends and Jude trusted the man implicitly. There was a reason Roger was his partner. Because they had similar life philosophies.

They valued others' lives much more than their own. Roger wouldn't turn back any more than Jude would. Not when they were so close to where the girl was supposed to be.

Finally Jude got to the door. Using the back of his wrist and his thermal imaging camera, he checked the door for heat.

Hot, but not unbearable.

He reached up, grabbed the handle with his gloved hand, and opened the door.

The room wasn't quite as smoke-filled as the one he was leaving, but visibility was still barely above zero.

Reaching again for the camera hooked to the strap of his breathing apparatus, Jude scanned the room. The left and right walls glowed white, indicating that there was fire on both sides of the room. Jude was pretty sure the wall not lighting up, the opposite wall from him, was an exterior wall, which was good, because he was also pretty sure they weren't going out the way they'd come in.

Then, with the aid of the TIC cutting through the smoke and steam, the image of a little body not moving made his heart pound.

"Davenport? Do you hear me? Get out now," Command screamed in his ear.

It wasn't the first time Command had screamed at him.

He prayed it wasn't the last.

He didn't answer his boss. What was the point? He wasn't going anywhere. Not without the girl. He wouldn't leave her. He couldn't walk out of a burning building when the child's thermal image was in his sight. Reality was that Command wouldn't want him to. None of their crew would exit when a fire victim was within sight.

"There she is."

"Thank God," Roger called from behind him.

"Engine Seven to Command—we need a ladder to fourth division A-side window for rescue." God, he hoped there was a window on the exterior wall because he couldn't see a thing. "We have one victim."

Command acknowledged, repeating the call.

"Keeley?" Jude yelled, hoping the girl could hear him above the fire's loud roar. Hoping that she'd answer, that she'd move.

She didn't.

Please, don't let us be too late.

He couldn't see her with his bare eyes, but used the camera to guide himself toward her. The room was a sweltering hot box.

Then the thermal image on his TIC moved and Jude wanted to cry out in relief. She was alive. Who knew how much smoke she'd inhaled, what kind of burns she might have endured, but she'd moved so there was hope.

"Keeley," he called again, crawling toward her. "We're here to get you out of this place."

He had no idea if she could hear him over the deafening sound of the fire destroying the building. If she could, he wanted her to know he was on his way.

Finally, he reached the far corner of the room where she was huddled beneath her mother's bed.

Coughing, the little girl stared at him with watery eyes, but didn't make any move toward him or respond to his motioning for her to come to him. Was she asphyxiated?

In his gear, he couldn't fit under the huge low-rise bed she was hidden beneath and wasn't quite sure how he'd move the massive bed with her beneath it without risking hurting her, but he had to get to her fast. They had to get out of the building pronto.

"Keeley, we have to go." He tried again, tugging on the corner post of the solid wood monstrosity without any success. Was the thing nailed down? "Come to me, honey. Let me carry you out of this place."

"Don't leave me."

He could barely make out her words. Maybe he even lip-read them more than heard them, but they rang loudly through his very soul.

As did the terror in her big puffy eyes as she coughed again.

"I won't leave you, Keeley. I promise. Crawl to me, Keeley." He purposely said her name over and over, hoping to get through to her, to let her know to come to him. He stretched his arms as far beneath the bed as he could. "Just move close enough that I can pull you to safety, Keeley, so we can get out of this building."

He heard a crash and knew another section of the structure had given way.

Any moment the building could come collapsing down.

They had to go now.

"Keeley, come to me," he pleaded, pushing against the bedpost again to see if it would move. Nope. The piece was solid, low to the floor, and heavy as hell.

He and Roger could stand, use their weight against the frame to see if they could shift it, and pray Keeley got out of the way if they did manage to move the massive piece of furniture.

She was crying, but she scooted forward a little, then back to where she'd been against the exterior wall.

Precious seconds were ticking by. Despite his protective gear, Jude could feel the worsening heat.

Instincts kicking in that said bad was about to get a whole lot worse if he didn't get her and get her now.

"I know it's scary, Keeley, but you're going to have to crawl to me so I can pull you to safety."

That was when she moved.

Finally.

"Just a little closer, Keeley." He reached as far as he could beneath the bed. "Just a little closer."

Then her hand touched his glove.

"That's it, Keeley. Just a little more."

His hand closed around her wrist and he pulled her to him.

"I've got her."

He wrapped his arms around her, just as a window burst out on the exterior wall.

Thank God. An exit.

No doubt the aerial truck platform was just outside the window and some of his guys were waiting to pull Roger, Keeley, and him through to safety.

Thank God.

"Don't leave me," the girl repeated, clinging tightly to him and then going limp in his arms.

"Never," he promised again, praying he'd not been too late.

Just as it had every day since the brown-out a couple of weeks before, the emergency room was hopping and had been all day. Sarah had run from one patient to the next with very little down time. Everything from having slipped due to ice to a gunshot wound had come through the doors.

Currently, she was examining a fifty-seven-year-old

white male with chest pain and a history of triple bypass three years previously. The man admitted to smoking a pack a day for the past thirty years, drinking a pint a day, wasn't bothering to take his prescribed blood pressure and cholesterol medications, and was a good hundred pounds overweight. He had been a heart attack waiting to happen.

"Has your chest pain eased up, Mr. Brown?" she asked the clammy-looking man as she scanned back over the notes the nurse had made upon his arrival. He should have come by ambulance, but he'd walked into the emergency room.

"It has some," he said, squinting at her as if the light bothered his eyes. "But it's been hurting off and on for two days. This evening it got a lot worse and I couldn't catch my breath. This may just be another off spell."

His cardiac enzymes were running stat in the lab and his telemetry was showing a slight T-wave abnormality. She'd started him on a nitroglycerin drip and had called to have the cardiac cath lab readied.

"Has the shortness of breath gotten better since you started on the IV meds and oxygen?"

Although he still looked sweaty and pale, he nodded. "I am breathing easier."

If that labored mess was easier, she'd been right to call Cardiology. If the guy wasn't having a myocardial infarction, he was on the verge of a major cardiac event. She was sure of it.

"Hey, Sarah, we have incoming. House fire. Multiple victims. Most minor. One serious."

She cut her gaze toward the nurse who'd leaned into the emergency room bay. "Thanks, Shelley."

Sarah fought wincing. Burns, smoke inhalation, and asphyxiation were all patients who gave Sarah nightmares. A few times during residency she'd gone home and wept at the absolute horribleness she'd witnessed. And she was seeing burn victims after the paramedics had done some clean-up.

She took a deep breath and turned back to her patient. "Mr. Brown, Dr. Andrews is on his way. He's going to take you to the cardiac lab to check your heart further by doing an arteriogram. I don't like how your EKG looks."

The man grimaced. "I had one of those a few years ago, after my bypass. They found some more blockages."

Not surprised, Sarah nodded, then turned as, on cue, Dr. Andrews stepped into the bay.

"Mr. Brown, this is Dr. Andrews." She heard a commotion outside the bay and knew the incoming fire victims had arrived. She nodded at the cardiologist, then at her patient. "I'm leaving you in capable hands."

With that she rushed to help, but came to an abrupt stop at what she saw when she stepped outside the bay.

The paramedics were rushing in a stretcher with an unconscious child wearing a facemask delivering oxygen. Keeping up with the stretcher, his dark brown hair matted to his head from sweat, dirt, and who knew what, was none other than her neighbor, talking to the little girl as if she were awake and hearing every word while he held onto her arm with his grimy hand.

He wore an NYFD uniform and looked like he'd just stepped out of a quick trip to hell.

CHAPTER TWO

SARAH'S CAREFREE, WOMANIZING, towel-wearing neighbor worked for the fire department?

So much for her male escort theory.

Mentally willing her paralysis away, she rushed to where the paramedics were rolling the unconscious girl and took a quick report.

"She was conscious when NYFD got to her, but went out just before they got her out of the building," the paramedic, Paul, informed while they rolled the girl into a bay. "She got a twenty-cc bolus of normal saline via her intraosseous line, and then at one hundred and fifty cc per hour."

He'd given the precise amount infused thus far, as knowing exact fluid replacement was crucial in a burn victim—especially a pediatric one.

"Also, morphine for pain at point four cc per kilogram." Paul grimaced. "Although lower than normal, her oxygen saturation has remained steady, going at one hundred percent, and there aren't any face burns, so maybe she won't need intubation, but we both know how quickly that can change."

Intubating a child if she didn't really need to was never something Sarah wanted to do. However, waiting until an urgent need arose wasn't either. Edema from the smoke and toxins inhaled could make getting the tube into the airway almost impossible. If the girl's lungs were swelling, the quicker she got intubated, the easier the feat would be accomplished.

Looking at the child, Sarah knew she'd be intubating.

"Gag reflex still present?"

"As of two minutes ago, yes," Paul answered.

"Get a warming blanket on her stat," Sarah told a nurse, disinfecting her hands and gloving up as she did so. "Were you able to get all her clothing removed?"

"Had to wet down the area on her right side, but otherwise her clothes came off fairly easily. Most of the burns are superficial, except that one and her hands."

Sarah nodded, and lifted the thin sheet to run her gaze over the girl's body. First- and second-degree burns on her arms and neck. A third-degree on her right torso and hands.

Sarah's heart squeezed.

Injured children were her least favorite aspect of her job. Every protective instinct inside her cried out at the injustice of a hurt child.

"Sorry, man, but you're going to have to step back," Paul told her neighbor as the paramedic bumped into him on the opposite side of the stretcher from Sarah.

Her neighbor didn't budge. "I told you, I promised Keeley I wouldn't leave her and I'm not going to."

His tone said they'd have to call Security to have him forcibly removed. He'd let go of the girl's arm when Sarah had inspected her burns, had been holding onto one of the few areas on the girl's arms that hadn't had burns, but he'd quickly taken hold again, as if he needed to be touching the child to let her know he was still there. Was the child someone he knew?

Sarah didn't want to deal with a commotion that

might slow down Keeley's care. Plus, the thought of her neighbor being dragged out of her emergency department didn't sit well.

"I may need to ask him something about her injuries." Doubtful, but it sounded better than admitting she didn't want him forced to leave. "Let him stay."

Which was when Jude turned that blue gaze to her, really noticing her for the first time since entering the emergency room. Recognition immediately shone in his red-rimmed eyes.

Sarah's heart slammed against her ribcage like a ball bouncing around in a pinball machine, lights and bells going off all through her insides.

The absolute difference in Jude's appearance from the carefree, towel-wrapped sex god standing in his apartment doorway early that morning to this concerned, dirty, smelly firefighter determined to stay by a child's side messed with her mind. Could she have been so wrong? Was it even possible there was more to her sexy neighbor than met the eye?

Had recognition not lit in those amazing blue eyes of his she'd have sworn he must be a twin.

Part of her felt she should say something, to acknowledge him in some way during that millisecond moment of recognition. Instead, she returned her attention to where it belonged, on the unconscious girl.

The weird flutter in her stomach was back and on high speed.

Indigestion, she told herself. *It's just indigestion*.

Although she'd lived next to his apartment for several months, Jude hadn't paid a lot of attention to his next-door neighbor.

She kept to herself and barely acknowledged him,

even when he'd tried talking to her a couple of times when she'd first moved in.

Honestly, until that morning, when he'd really looked at her for the first time, he'd have guessed her to be a lot older than the thirty or so she was.

She dressed much older, acted much older, and had never even glanced his way, much less made eye contact before today.

Not that she necessarily was dressed older now, more just dressed to hide whatever was beneath.

She wore hospital-issue scrubs in a faded gray color that hung on her body much as sackcloth would, leaving her shapeless, plain, and, at first look, a bit drab.

Interesting, because, as he'd noticed that morning, she had really great eyes behind those hideous monstrosities posing as glasses. She should seriously consider investing in contact lenses.

She had good skin and amazing cheekbones, too. He'd dated models who'd gone under the knife for cheekbones that weren't nearly as impressive.

Not that his neighbor did a thing to accent them. Mainly, it seemed her goal was to hide every God-given physical attribute she'd been blessed with. Why? Why would a young, healthy woman underplay herself?

Because she was a doctor and wanted to be taken seriously? Or had something happened in her past that had made her not want men to notice her physically?

Why did it even matter how she dressed and what had made her choose to do so?

All that flashed through his mind in the half-second his gaze connected with hers and recognition hit.

Some other emotion punched him in the gut, too, but he figured that was exhaustion, worry, and adrenaline battling around for dominance.

"Thank you," he told her for giving him the okay to stay, not that he'd been going to leave.

Short of interfering with Keeley's care, he'd have stuck by her side.

Just as he had after he'd made it out of the building and back to the ground, Jude had ignored the exhaustion in his own body, ignored his boss's insistence that he get himself checked out and tended to, and had stayed with the child.

Just as he'd stayed with her in the ambulance.

Had Paul not been the paramedic in charge that might not have flown, but fortunately his friend had been.

If only he could have found Keeley a few minutes quicker.

Thank God they'd gotten out when they had because his instincts hadn't been wrong.

Within seconds of their clearing the building, one of the outer walls and the remainder of the roof had caved in.

Had they not already been outside the inferno, they wouldn't ever have been.

A sobering thought.

"Jude, man, step back," Paul said, grabbing Jude's arm. "Let the doctor check her patient."

"Seriously, he can stay," his neighbor repeated, then began examining Keeley while the paramedic gave her further run-down on what had happened and the girl's objective findings and care while in the ambulance.

Without pausing in her examination, his neighbor gave the nurse more orders. Then, without turning to Jude, she asked him, "You are who saved her from a burning building?"

He tried not to let her incredulousness as she'd said

"you", as if she didn't believe him capable of anything of the sort, get to him.

Watching as she parted Keeley's eyelids and shone a light into her eyes, checking her pupil reflexes, he shrugged. "Just did my job."

Although not as well as he should have because he should have found her sooner. If he had, her little body might not be marred from burns from who knew what she'd done prior to hiding underneath her mother's bed. She wouldn't be unconscious, wouldn't have needed the trip to the emergency room by ambulance. If only they could have gotten her out when they'd gotten the other tenants of the building, when they'd gotten her mother and sister out.

"Ha, don't let him fool you." Paul spoke up, gesturing to Jude and not stopping, despite Jude's shake of his head in hopes of silencing his friend.

"He should have been wearing a cape today, because everyone had already been ordered out of the building. He just didn't listen. Never does." Paul shook his head. "First one in, last one out."

"An adrenaline junkie, eh?" his neighbor asked, still not looking his way. She checked Keeley's gag reflex and continued with her assessment.

The weight of his uniform suddenly pulled at his shoulders as he went to shrug again, making the movement require a lot more effort than it should have. He was tired. So tired.

"Or someone who couldn't live with himself if he left a kid in a burning building," he heard himself admit.

Besides, there was no one waiting on him to come home to prevent him from taking risks. He purposely kept his relationships simple. Had never been tempted to do otherwise.

Not since Nina.

His neighbor's gaze lifted to his and something shifted in her blue-green eyes, giving them the effect of shimmering sea water behind her glasses.

Oh, hell.

Maybe he'd inhaled too many fumes, too.

Or maybe it was because he'd just thought of Nina.

Whatever the cause, his head spun and he felt off kilter.

Way off kilter.

Like he might have to sit down.

He probably did need to rehydrate and replenish electrolytes. He'd sweated a bucket in that inferno and his uniform clung to him like a second skin, as did his sweat-smashed helmet hair.

That's why he felt dizzy.

Not because of whatever the odd emotion in—he glanced at her name badge—Dr. Sarah Grayson's eyes had been.

Rather than say anything further to him, she gave more orders to the nurse, ordering tests and treatments and things that were vaguely familiar but went far beyond Jude's basic first-aid skills.

"I need to intubate stat," she told the nurse. "She has internal swelling that's going to get worse. We need to act now before her airway becomes too swollen to get the tube down."

She said what size intubation tube she wanted and what anesthetic she'd like Keeley to be given to ease the discomfort of having the line introduced down her throat and into her lungs. If the girl regained consciousness, she wouldn't want it to be due to discomfort while being intubated.

As if she'd predicted what was about to happen,

Keeley's oxygen saturation dropped several points and the monitor alarm sounded.

Everyone hurried, setting up trays, responding to whatever Sarah told them to do. A nurse asked Jude to step back and he did so, knowing he was in the way while holding Keeley's arm.

Letting the girl's wrist go left him feeling bereft. As long as he'd been feeling the warmth of her skin, he could tell himself she was going to be okay, that he hadn't been too late.

Exhausted, but running on adrenaline, Sarah went to the private waiting area where she'd had a nurse bring Jude hours ago.

The emergency room had calmed down just enough for Sarah to take a much-needed break. She'd suspected her neighbor would still be in the small private lounge, waiting until he was allowed to see the girl in the pediatric intensive care unit where Sarah had transferred her to once she'd established an airway and stabilized the girl.

Thank God she'd gotten the line in on the first try. Keeley's lung tissue had already swollen and Sarah had felt the extra resistance.

She'd checked on the girl's mother and younger sister, who'd also been checked into the emergency department. Apparently, they'd gotten out of the fire much earlier than Keeley as their injuries had been minor and they'd arrived by private car.

The young mother had been allowed to see Keeley for a few minutes, then the worn-out woman and her toddler daughter had left the hospital with a friend as her businessman husband spent a lot of time working overseas.

Sarah couldn't imagine what the mother was going through, to have lost her home, her things, and to have almost lost one of her daughters.

The woman had just left and, although Keeley wasn't allowed visitors, Sarah planned to let Jude see the girl if he was still there.

A firefighter? Who would have believed the sexy man she lived next door to was an everyday hero who risked his life to save others?

Not her that morning, for sure.

Good grief, he could have been killed.

Paul, one of her favorite paramedics, had later brought in a pedestrian who'd been hit by a taxi. He'd gone on and on about his buddy Jude and what a real-life hero he was.

A real-life hero who was apparently as dog-tired as she was.

Stretched out in a chair, his eyes closed, Sarah took advantage of the opportunity to freely look at him.

As much as was possible for someone as unbelievably handsome as he was, he looked awful. His hair was matted to his head. He reeked of smoke and sweat and dirty man. His heavy overcoat was in the chair next to the one he slept in.

He needed a shower.

Which, of course, brought her brain back to that morning when he'd been squeaky clean and wrapped in a towel.

She closed her eyes.

No. No. No.

She did not want that image in her mind. Not now. Not when she looked at him and saw a man who'd risked his life to save a little girl.

Not when she saw someone who might have substance beneath those chiseled abs.

She didn't want to like him.

He was a playboy.

Then again, maybe he went through so many women because of not wanting to get into a serious relationship due to his high-risk job.

No, she corrected herself again. No. No. No. She was not going to make excuses for his womanizing ways.

Wasn't going to happen.

Only then he opened his eyes and caught her staring.

The intensity in his baby blues warned she might make lots of excuses for this man.

CHAPTER THREE

"KEELEY," JUDE SAID, fighting a yawn as he sat up in the waiting-room chair.

Even as hyped up as he'd been from the fire search and rescue, he couldn't believe he'd fallen asleep. Then again, searching a burning building drained a man from the anxiety, the adrenaline, the extreme heat, the sweat. Sometimes after a rescue he'd feel so tired he thought he might sleep a week.

"Is she still alive?" He prayed so. He'd gotten to her as quickly as he could. He knew that. But sometimes as quick as a person could just wasn't enough.

"Yes, she's stable," his neighbor told him from where she stood a few feet away. "It was touch and go for a short bit due to her pulmonary edema, but she responded to the medications and is holding her own."

He let out a sigh of relief. "Thank you."

Looking more than a little tired herself, Sarah sank into the chair opposite him and stared across the few feet separating them.

Which gave him the opportunity to study her face full on.

She really did have amazing eyes. And great cheekbones.

Her lips were full and perfectly bowed. Kissable.

Where had that thought come from?

"Actually, all the thanks go to you. I shudder to think what would have happened if you hadn't found her."

He knew what would have happened and that was why he did his job. He loved being a firefighter. Not that he could save every person, but he gave it his best. Always.

"Every firefighter's nightmare. Not finding someone," he admitted, raking his fingers through his matted hair. "The kind of stuff that messes with your head."

Maybe he should have gone home, showered, then come back. He supposed that would have been better than passing out in a private waiting area. Yet he'd not been able to leave. Not until he'd known Keeley was okay.

Sarah's plump lower lip disappeared between her teeth for a brief second, and then she asked, "Does it mess with your head, Jude?"

Her saying his name for the first time messed with his head.

Big time.

Which made no sense.

As hadn't the fact he found her lips kissable.

She wasn't the type of woman he messed around with. He preferred women who knew the score and were okay with that. Dr. Sarah Grayson didn't seem the one-night-stand kind.

Yet he'd be lying if he didn't admit there was something about her that appealed to him in a major way.

Must be the day he'd had and that despite the fact he'd chugged a couple of sports drinks, he still felt dry to the bone.

"Some days more than others," he answered.

Today, for instance, everything was getting to him.

The woman sitting across from him had intrigued him that morning.

She intrigued him now.

The in between had been a living hell and maybe she was an angel sent to redeem him.

Lord knew, he needed redeeming.

"Like today?" She read his mind.

He shrugged. "You trying to map out my psyche on the DSM-V, Doc?"

At his question, her brow arched. Then she offered up a small smile and it was as if the sun had come out on a cloudy day.

"I'm not that type of specialist," she pointed out, the light shining in her eyes saying he wasn't going to get a further answer to his question. "Do you want to see Keeley?"

"Can I?" He hadn't expected to get to see the child. Not tonight when she was still so critical. He'd stayed to find out how she was and had then dozed off in exhaustion.

Odd, at the moment he felt oddly refreshed. Which was absolutely crazy because he was starved, dehydrated, and grimy as hell. He probably smelled like he'd been there, too.

Most of the women he knew would have been pinching their noses and ordering him to shower. Then again, most of the women he knew liked the wealthy Davenport side of him more than the real him firefighter side.

His neighbor didn't currently look bothered by his physical state one way or the other. But that morning, when she'd raked those sea-green eyes over him, she'd been bothered. He'd seen it in the way she'd swallowed hard, in the way her pulse had throbbed at her throat just above her loose scarf, in the way she'd nervously wet her lips.

Sweet heavens, she'd just gulped and licked her lips again.

Which meant what exactly? He wasn't sure. That she found him physically distracting even when he was a mess?

Why did that possibility make him feel all he-man?

"Isn't seeing Keeley what you've waited for?" She answered his question with one of her own.

"Either that or I just needed a quick nap to regain my strength."

"Busy night ahead?" Her sarcasm couldn't have been more obvious if she'd taken out a billboard.

"Aren't they all?" he answered, gauging her response. That he'd confused her was apparent on her lovely face.

She watched him from narrowed eyes. "If I didn't already know the answer, I'd ask if you ever take anything seriously. Thanks to this evening, I know you do."

"I should set the record straight, then. I only joined the fire department to get women."

Her cheeks turned a bright pink, then she gave him a disgusted, *I knew it* look. "I figured as much."

Jude stifled a chuckle at her defensive arm-crossing and chin-lifting. "Are you saying you think I'm shallow, Sarah?"

Cheeks still glowing, she rolled her eyes. "You like to tease, don't you?"

Not since Nina.

The thought blindsided him and he almost grimaced, but kept from doing so at the last second. No way was he letting thoughts of Nina into his head again today. Not now. Not at the hospital.

Not when his doctor cousin, Charles, could be around.

So, instead of letting his mind go to the past, he focused on the woman sitting across from him, grateful for the fire in her eyes.

"I'd be lying if I didn't admit to liking how you respond." He did like her intelligence, her quick wit, that spark in her eyes. He was used to being physically attracted to women. Women were beautiful creatures. But with Sarah the attraction was something more than her gorgeous eyes and amazing cheekbones. The flash in those eyes was what drew him in, made him want to know more about the woman beneath the deceptive outer layer.

A want he hadn't felt since…nope, he wasn't going to think of her.

"Why?" Sarah asked, studying him as if he were some gross bug under a magnifying glass.

"Why not?"

"Because I'm not one of your women."

He wouldn't pretend he didn't know what she meant. Hadn't he just been thinking the same thing a few moments before?

His women lived in the moment, were experienced in the ways of the world, and were no more interested in anything beyond immediate pleasure than he was.

Unlike the scowling woman sitting across from him.

The scowling woman whose smile had lit up dark corners of his very being, an addictive feeling he'd like to sample again.

Although some dark corners might be best left in the shadows.

Unable to resist teasing her further, he waggled his brows. "Would you like to be?"

Her jaw dropped. "No!"

He gave a low laugh at her outrage. "That was quick. I think I'm offended. Is it my cologne?"

"Right." She glared. "Because you're so easily offended that a woman saying no just breaks your heart."

She might be saying no, but her eyes were singing an entirely different tune. They were shooting fire of feminine awareness. Interesting.

"Sure you don't want to think about it?" he teased, enjoying the blush in her cheeks.

"Positive. Some things a girl just knows."

"Yeah?" He arched his brow. "There's some things a woman just knows, too."

Her gaze searched his and her voice cracked a little when she asked, "Such as?"

"How she responds to a man." There were definitely sparks flying back and forth. He might have had a rough day but he wasn't hallucinating the energy between them.

Not that he understood the chemistry, but he'd have to be brain dead not to recognize the man-woman pull.

"Don't go confusing me with one of your bimbos," she warned, chin notching upward. "I'm not interested in a guy like you."

"A guy like me? Oh, yeah." He grinned, refusing to be insulted. "We established that I'm shallow."

Her gaze narrowed further, but the outraged look wasn't working. Not when her lips twitched.

"I didn't call you shallow," she pointed out.

"You didn't correct me."

"Because you weren't wrong," she countered.

He arched his brow.

Rather than answer, she jumped up from the chair and gave him an expectant look. "Do you or do you not want to see Keeley with me?"

Standing, he grinned. "I most definitely want to see Keeley with you, Doc."

Her hands went to her hips. "Don't call me that."

"Why not?" He kind of liked the nickname. It fit. Plus, she needed a nickname to lighten her up a bit. "It's as good a nickname as any."

"You don't need a nickname for me."

"Sure I do, so I can call it out when you're ninja-ing in and out of your apartment."

"Ninja-ing?"

"That thing you do where you come and go and hope no one sees."

"Whereas you hang around in the hallway long enough to make sure everyone sees you in your God-given glory?"

Lord, he loved her sharp wit, that whatever he threw out, she had a quick response. "Does that bother you?"

"Of course not. You can do whatever you want. In your apartment. With your bimbos."

"They aren't bimbos."

"They're not bright and upstanding citizens."

"For all you know about them, they could be."

"I know they spent the night with a man who used them so that checks bright right off their list of attributes."

"Sex for mutual pleasure isn't my using them any more than it is their using me."

"So it's a case of mutual using and that somehow makes it okay? Keep fooling yourself if you want, but there are some of us smart enough to know better."

He was standing so close to her now that he was looking straight down into her eyes, was tempted to remove her glasses so he could more fully see into their depths.

"I suppose a really pessimistic, prudish person might see mutual pleasure that way." He egged her on, liking the spark his words elicited.

"And who are you? Mr. Optimism? Going around spreading happiness and cheer?" she scoffed with an exaggerated eye roll. "More like spreading something else with how many different women I've seen come out of your apartment."

His lips twitched. "You keeping tabs?"

"Hardly, but I'm not blind."

Arguable with those ugly glasses she wore.

"For the record, I'm not spreading anything." He wanted the record straight. He wouldn't let himself delve into why it mattered, but he needed her to know the truth. "I'm a safety kind of guy. Always."

"Who runs into burning buildings when everyone else is running out? Yeah, try selling me another one."

"Someone has to do it."

Her chin tilted upward and her gaze didn't waver behind the thick glasses. "Good thing there's you."

"Yeah, good thing."

A bone-weary Sarah ninja-ed down the hallway and stealthily let herself into her apartment, pausing in her open doorway to glance at Jude's closed door.

So much had happened since that morning when he'd been standing in that doorway.

He'd been flirting with her at the hospital.

She should have checked him for hypoxemia-induced psychosis related to smoke inhalation.

Because no way was he in his right mind.

Or maybe it was her who wasn't in her right mind.

Maybe she'd accidentally inhaled some anesthesia

or hallucinogenic medication that was messing with her head.

Something was messing with her head.

More like someone.

Because Jude's teasing and hot looks refused to leave her mind even long after he'd left the hospital.

For the rest of her shift and an hour into the next when she'd stayed to help catch up the overload of patients, she'd battled with the facts that Jude was a womanizer, an incurable flirt, heroic when he'd rushed into a burning building to save Keeley, and sweet when he'd waited at the hospital.

Heroic. Sweet. Not adjectives she'd have ever thought she'd attach to the incorrigible towel-wearing man from that morning.

Unable to stop herself, she glanced toward his closed apartment door again. Was he home?

Should she check on him, make sure he was all right, that the smoke truly hadn't gotten to him, that he'd rehydrated well?

Then again, he might not be alone and the absolute last thing she wanted was to see Jude Davenport with another woman twice in the same day.

Especially after he'd so blatantly flirted with her.

Especially after, despite her best attempts not to, she'd so blatantly liked his flirting.

So, her neighbor had a few redeeming qualities.

That didn't mean they should become friends or have anything to do with one another.

They shouldn't.

Best thing she could do was forget today had even happened and stay far, far away from the man at all costs.

Determined that she was going to do exactly that, Sarah quietly closed her apartment door.

She was going to shower, eat whatever she could find and quickly prepare, sleep, and not think about her neighbor.

After he'd left the hospital, Jude had returned to the fire hall, showered, filled out appropriate paperwork, then come home to make himself something to eat.

He'd had plans with friends, but had opted to cancel, deciding he'd rather have a simple meal at home, a glass of wine, relax, and enjoy his apartment's amazing view of the city he loved so much.

Jude enjoyed cooking, enjoyed throwing ingredients together that pleased his senses and filled his stomach. He'd never been formally trained, but was pretty good. Even Nina had thought so.

Nina. She'd snuck into his thoughts too often today. Why?

Then again, thinking he could go to the hospital where Charles worked and not think of his cousin's late wife was foolish. After all, hadn't Jude introduced the woman he had been in love with to his cousin and she'd fallen head over heels for the emergency room doctor instead?

That Nina had fallen for Charles, rather than Jude, had never sat well, had ruined his friendship with Nina and left him on edge around his cousin. That feeling hadn't gone away after Nina and Charles had married. If anything, it had gotten worse.

Nina trying to repair the damage to their friendship hadn't helped. Feeling betrayed, angry, Jude had refused to have anything to do with her. They'd fought and never spoken again.

Nina's heartbreaking death due to complications from giving birth to twins had left an inconsolable hole in Jude's heart that bled anew every time he saw Charles so he avoided him. Grief, guilt, anger, so many emotions ran rampant when his past collided with the present. Thankfully, he'd not bumped into his cousin during the hours he'd been at the hospital waiting on news of Keeley.

Which brought his mind back to who he had bumped into at the hospital.

His uptight neighbor.

Confusing, plain Jane Sarah Grayson who wasn't really so plain beneath her attempts to appear to be.

An emergency room doctor.

Like Charles.

Pulling the baking dish out of his oven with a potholder, Jude lifted the lid and made a small slice into the chicken. Almost done. Another fifteen minutes or so and it would be perfect.

Restless from thoughts of Nina, of his intriguing neighbor, from life, Jude walked into his living room, meaning to stand at his floor-to-ceiling glass windows to stare out at the New York City skyline.

Instead, he frowned and strained to figure out what the noise was that he could barely make out.

Then it hit him.

A smoke alarm was going off in the unit next to his.

Sarah's apartment.

CHAPTER FOUR

How could an intelligent woman who could save lives not cook a simple piece of toast without burning it?

Okay, Sarah didn't usually burn her food, but this wasn't the first time. But she didn't recall ever doing so to the point that her alarm went crazy.

How did she get the thing to go off?

Pulling the plug on the toaster oven, she closed the door, rushed to where the alarm blared over the doorway. The baggy sleeve of her way oversized sweatshirt flopped as she fanned a dishtowel back and forth, hoping it would clear the smoke and shut the thing up.

"Stop that," she ordered the shrill bell, dancing around beneath it as she waved the towel with gusto and thought about how much she detested cooking. Almost as much as she detested this horrible alarm. "Stop. Stop. Stop."

Was she going to have to call Maintenance? Or maybe they just automatically showed up when one of the apartment's smoke alarms went off?

A loud knock pounded at her apartment door.

Well, that answered that. Maintenance had just shown up.

Which was a good thing since her fanning wasn't working.

Only when, flustered, she flung her front door open, Maintenance wasn't who stood there.

The man she'd been thinking about not thinking about stood there, wearing jeans, a plain white V-necked T-shirt, and nothing on his feet.

Good grief. He'd metamorphosed back into a sexy beast.

Not that he hadn't been sexy at the hospital.

Clearly, he had, because he'd twitterpated her to the point of burning her toast and filling her kitchen with smoke.

His blue gaze raked over her, obviously satisfying any doubts as to whether or not she was okay, and then he grinned. "Miss me?"

Pretending all was fine, that there wasn't a loud shrill screaming behind her, she wrinkled her nose at him, wishing she had on her glasses to shield herself from his probing gaze. "No."

Why on earth would he think she had? Before that morning, they'd never even made eye contact, much less spoken to each other.

His eyes danced with humor. "You sure about that?"

Wishing the stupid ear-piercing alarm would go silent so it would quit rattling her brain, she lifted her chin and stared straight into his eyes, thinking it very unfair that a man had his stunning eyes and long lashes. "Positive. Go away."

He laughed. "That's not the sound of your smoke alarm beckoning your friendly neighborhood firefighter your way?"

Oh. That's what he'd meant?

"No." If she looked sure enough, haughty enough, despite the obvious alarm blasting in the background, he'd take the hint and leave, right?

Nope.

Looking way too comfortable in his perfectly fitting jeans and just right chest-hugging T-shirt, he arched a thick masculine brow.

"Yes," she corrected, because, really, it wasn't as if he didn't recognize that annoying sound. Pretending otherwise just made her look foolish. "It is my smoke alarm, but it's not supposed to beckon you. Go home."

He shrugged as if it was no big deal, then asked, "You don't want me to turn off your alarm?"

"Could you, please?" she heard herself say, moving aside to let him into her apartment as if his words had been some secret magic phrase to grant entrance. "I can't get the thing to shut up."

His lips twitched. "If you ask nicely."

What? Her mouth fell open. Was he kidding her? But before she could come back with some retort, he came into her apartment and was following the smoke signals and noise to her kitchen.

When her gaze dropped to his jeans-clad butt that could sell millions of pairs of pants if someone would stick an ad up on a Times Square billboard, Sarah blamed the noise for interfering with her brain waves. No way would she have otherwise visually ogled the man's bottom, lit-up-billboard-worthy or not.

Within seconds, he'd pulled over a chair and climbed onto it. Looking like some sexy god up on his perch, he reset her smoke alarm.

Despite how much he annoyed her, the silence had her wanting to wrap her arms around him in gratitude.

"Bless you!" she praised. "That thing was driving me crazy."

Turning, he stepped down from the chair and carried it back to where he'd grabbed it from. "No problem."

"How did you know?"

Facing her, hands on his narrow hips, he grinned. "Told you. I succumbed to the sound of your mating call."

She shook her head. Maybe in denial of his claim. Maybe in denial of memories of those hips wrapped in a towel and nothing more. Maybe in denial of the fact that for the first time in her life she was an ogler. She didn't like it. Not one bit.

Mating call. As if.

"I didn't lure you here," she choked out of her dry mouth. Seriously, her vocal cords felt like they'd been put through a dehydration machine.

His amusement apparent, he cocked a brow. "Really? You expect me to believe your smoke alarm accidentally set itself off on the same day you learned I'm a firefighter?"

It did sound fairly incredible.

"Admit it," he continued, his eyes dancing with mischief. "You wanted to see me and issued an invitation you knew I wouldn't refuse."

"I…" She grimaced. He made a good point. One that made any argument she issued lack credibility, even though she hadn't intentionally set off her smoke alarm. Neither had she wanted to see him.

Quite the opposite.

She'd seen him too much that day already.

Seen and liked. Even the dirty, worn-out endearing hospital version. Unfortunately.

Wincing, he took in the smoke still escaping from her toaster oven. "You didn't have to really set fire to anything, Sarah. A simple knock on my door and a verbal invitation would have done." He shrugged. "Or, if you wanted something more dramatic, a match next to that sensitive baby there would have had it screaming for me."

"I didn't…" She paused, flustered by his teasing, by how her heart pounded that he was there, inside her apartment, talking directly to her, that he was using the teasing flirty tone as he had at the hospital.

"Need rescuing?" He finished her sentence for her. He walked over to the toaster oven, opened the door, grimaced at the burned mess inside. "Sure you did. In more ways than one. What was that?"

"Toast."

His eyes widened. "That was toast?"

At his question, something inside Sarah snapped.

"Yes, it was. Toast. Toast that was going to be my dinner, because I was hungry and tired and… Don't you judge me…you…you…" She searched for a derogatory name, sure there were thousands just on the tip of her tongue. Unfortunately, none sprang forth.

That's when the day's events took their toll and she did something totally out of character.

She watered up and fought tears.

Uh-uh. No way.

She was not going to cry in front of him.

Not now. Not ever.

She was not going to cry period.

She did not cry and most certainly if she ever did it wouldn't be over burnt toast.

"Sarah?" His tone was no longer teasing, but showed concern. "Are you okay?"

Embarrassed, exhausted, ready to call it a night, she took a deep breath. "I'm tired and hungry and my dinner is chunks of charcoal and you annoy me. No big deal."

He eyed her way too closely for comfort.

"You were really going to have toast for dinner?" he asked, ignoring the rest of her comment.

"I was going to spread hummus on it," she defended. She'd showered, thrown on the baggy sweats, and had planned to eat a quick bite and crash. She did the same thing quite frequently on the days she worked the emergency room and got held up beyond her normal twelve-hour shift.

His nose curled again. "Hummus and toast. No, thank you."

"For your information, I like hummus and toast."

He didn't look convinced. "Your hummus and toast must be better than any I've ever had."

"It's good. Stick around and you can taste for yourself." Sarah heard herself say the words, but had no clue where they came from. Not in a million years would she invite her neighbor who started his days with a different woman every day of the week to stay for dinner.

Good grief. What would he think?

He had come to turn off her alarm, so she couldn't really retract her invitation, could she? Not without seeming ungrateful and rude.

"Tempting," he ventured, not sounding anything of the sort. "But I have a better offer."

Of course he did. Women probably lined up to cook gourmet meals for him. And she'd heard first-hand that morning what else they offered.

"Why don't you come to my place and let me cook for you?"

Surprised, she opened her mouth to refuse, but he continued speaking before she could.

"Before you say no, the food is already in the oven, the wine is chilled, and I have a view that's even more amazing than yours."

He'd noticed her view? He had food in the oven? Why did he have wine chilling?

Then it hit her.

"I pulled you away from company, didn't I?"

He frowned. "No. Why would you think that?"

Because his apartment door was like a model runway exit, always with some beautiful woman walking through it.

But his look said he'd been alone.

"You're cooking for just yourself?"

"I like to eat."

Wondering at his apartment view, at what he'd cooked and how edible it was, she eyed him suspiciously. "What's the catch?"

"No catch. Just offering to share my dinner." He glanced toward the burned remains of her toast. "And looking out for my own interests of having an uninterrupted meal, of course. I don't want you attempting more toast and setting your alarm off again."

"Ha-ha. Real funny. The only reason my toast caught fire is because I was so tired." And had been distracted by thoughts of him, but she wasn't telling him that part.

"Fine. You can take a cat nap on my sofa while I finish up dinner."

As if.

"What are you serving?" she ventured out of curiosity, but with no intention of even entertaining the possibility of actually agreeing to have dinner with him. "I might prefer burnt toast."

He laughed and shook his head. "You won't. We're having Chicken Marsala served on a bed of angel-hair pasta, steamed asparagus with a light butter sauce, and a red wine because I prefer red to white."

Of course he did. Red stood for passion and white was just bland, right? Jude was a red kind of guy.

She blinked. "Are you for real?"

"You could pinch me and find out."

His eyes twinkled with that sparkle that had her heart doing funny floppy things in her chest.

"You wish."

Jude did wish.

As crazy as the thought was, he wanted Sarah to pinch him.

Not to see if he was real, but to wake him up because he was moving in some type of haze.

What was he thinking, inviting her to dinner? Not about how beautiful she was without her thick glasses blocking her face.

She was, but he was being a good neighbor.

That was it.

He wasn't inviting her to his place for anything more.

Even if she did have gorgeous eyes, amazing cheekbones, and full, pink, kissable lips.

"Is that how you lure women to your apartment? With promises of feeding them?"

"Something like that," he answered, wondering why she thought the worst of him when it came to women.

Maybe through her eyes, there were too many women, and maybe, if he was honest, he'd admit to it as well.

But he never deceived any of them or made promises he had no intention of keeping. They all knew the score. He was a one-night-stand kind of guy and the women he invited to his apartment came for one reason.

It wasn't so Jude could cook for them.

Sarah wasn't like the women he brought to his apartment for sex.

"I'm not interested in being lured to your apartment."

Suddenly feeling weary, restless, and as if maybe Sarah was right not to want to come to his apartment, he sighed. "I'm inviting you to my apartment to eat dinner." He put emphasis on the word. "You're tired. I'm tired. We've both had a long day. I want a good meal, to relax, and a good night's rest, Sarah. Nothing more. My invitation to feed you is with no strings attached and no hidden motives to trick you into my bed."

He'd never had any need to trick women into his bed. There was always one ready and willing to fill the empty spot in his life.

Tonight he'd just wanted to be alone.

Which didn't quite jibe with his burning desire for Sarah to say yes.

"Because I'm not your type?" she questioned, confirming his earlier thoughts.

"You're not my type." He meant to say more, to elaborate on the reasons why, to elaborate on the fact that she intrigued him and he'd like to let down her hair, see her smile, hear her laughter so he'd know what it sounded like, but her sigh of relief had him holding his tongue.

"Fine." She didn't sound or look happy about agreeing so the smile and laughter might not be forthcoming anytime soon. "In that case, I'll eat with you, but I'm eating, checking out this view you bragged about, and then I'm leaving, *capisce*?"

Sarah had bought her beloved apartment for three main reasons. Its walking distance proximity to Manhattan

Mercy, it fitting within her budget, barely, and the spectacular view.

Just like the man, Jude's view really did blow her away.

As did his apartment.

At some point, someone had taken two, maybe three, apartments and converted them into one luxurious one. His living room dwarfed hers, as did the floor-to-ceiling views of the twinkling New York City nightlife. Just *wow*.

Forget needing food. She'd just sit here, sip on the glass of wine he'd given her to keep her occupied while he finished up their meal, stare out at the skyline, and soak up the energy of the busy city she adored, to revive her exhausted soul.

Having grown up in Queens in various dumpy housing projects, when they'd had a home, Sarah had great appreciation for how far she'd come, for the luxuriousness of her small apartment, and especially for the grandeur of the apartment she was currently in.

Listening to the soothing surround-sound music he'd turned on with the click of a remote control and a voice command, Sarah scanned the room. Simple, but high-quality furniture. Artwork that was probably originals. The gigantic remote control that seemed to control everything in the apartment. Jude lived way beyond a firefighter's salary.

Which meant he either came from money or had another, more lucrative side job.

For a moment, she let her mind again toy with the idea of him being a hired escort. Ha, if so, maybe she should consider his services for her upcoming holiday events so she didn't have to go by herself.

Not that she minded being single. Just that at certain events being solo stood out like a sore thumb. Like at engagement parties and weddings and various get-togethers with her coworkers.

Coworkers, which included her boss. Charles Davenport. Davenport. Jude Davenport.

Duh. How could she have been so blind?

The last name. The eyes. She'd not put two and two together, but her conclusion made perfect sense.

Jude's eyes were the same blue as her boss's.

His last name was also the same.

That couldn't be a coincidence.

No way.

He was one of those Davenports.

"You ready to eat crow?"

Startled by his question, she jerked toward him, watching as he walked out of the kitchen, stepped up a step to where there was a table for four, and put down two plates.

Good grief, the man did things for a pair of jeans that ought to be declared illegal in every state but Alaska. Maybe there, it was cold enough to offset the burning heat that rose inside her every time she looked at him. *Wowzers.*

"Crow?" She arched a brow, grateful she'd forced her gaze up above his waistline as he turned toward her. "You told me you were serving chicken."

He grinned. "I meant the view. It's phenomenal, isn't it?"

Yeah, it was and she didn't just mean the New York City skyline. Seeing the eagerness with which he waited for her to respond, she marveled at the unexpected layer to him. He appreciated his view of the city that much?

That surprised her, made her have to admit there were more dimensions to Jude than she'd already realized.

She didn't need to discover any more positive dimensions. The fact he'd risked his life to save a young girl's already had her softening way too much.

That had to be why she was looking at him and feeling all warm and fuzzy on the inside.

Or maybe it was the wine.

She wasn't much of a drinker and she'd finished one glass and started another.

On an empty stomach.

Definitely that was it.

What had she been thinking?

No matter. Life was good.

"Haven't seen any crows, not even any pigeons this high up." She took another sip of the wine, despite just thinking that she should probably slow down or stop altogether. "But it's not bad."

He laughed. "You don't like admitting to being wrong, do you?"

She batted her lashes all innocent like. "What was I wrong about?"

"My view."

"I never said anything about your view," she reminded him, holding his gaze. "You were the one who said your view was better than mine. Not me."

"You're right," he conceded, then gestured to the view from where he stood on the raised platform dining area. The floor-to-ceiling windows behind him displayed a city that sparkled like diamonds under perfect lighting. "But, admit it, I'm also right."

She ran her gaze across the skyline, wondering if the city would ever fail to amaze. "You have an amazing view, Jude Davenport. Much better than mine, even. Happy?"

"Yes. Thank you. I am."

She tore her gaze away from the window and looked at him. With his easygoing smile, he actually did look happy. And relaxed. And way too handsome in his jeans, T-shirt, and bare feet.

The view she was looking at was better than any she'd seen in her apartment. A smiling gorgeous man gesturing to the Manhattan skyline. Yeah, that had never happened in her apartment.

For that matter, until tonight she'd never had a man in her apartment other than movers as she'd not wanted her few dates since moving in to taint her beloved home. She'd known with each one that things weren't going to work out. Maybe she was too picky, but better picky than ending up with some loser. Just ask her mother. Not that you had to ask. Sarah's mother vocalized the plague of society—men—to anyone and everyone who got within earshot.

That morning Jude had seemed to fit her mother's horror stories to a T. But firefighter Jude and this relaxed, easygoing, comfortable, bare-footed domesticated Jude refused to be shoved into that preconceived mold.

He wiggled his toes, as if knowing she was looking at them. Sarah wasn't a foot fetish kind of girl, or any kind of fetish girl, really, but there was something about this man's bare feet that she found appealing.

Maybe it wasn't the bare feet, but the entire package that was getting to her.

She gulped back a drink, then fought to keep from coughing as the sweet wine went down all wrong. That's all she needed, to aspirate, and choke in front of him. He'd think her a total klutz, having already set off her smoke detector.

Or that she'd purposely choked so he'd have to come to her rescue again.

When her gaze met his again, he was studying her as intently as she was him.

"I get the impression you really can see my view, Sarah."

Um, yeah, she could. His point was?

"Not once have I seen you squint," he continued. "Which makes me question those glasses you wear. It's going to be a tough sell to convince me you need them. Are they prescription?"

Busted.

"They serve their purpose."

His brow arched. "Which is?"

To put a barrier between her and anyone who tried to look too closely. As Jude was currently doing.

She should have grabbed them off her bathroom sink before heading to his place. She just hadn't been thinking clearly, and that had been way before she'd drunk any wine.

"Something smells wonderful. You sure I can't help?" she asked, needing to pull herself out of whatever trance he was putting her in.

"Positive." He came to stand by where she sat, held out his hand. "It's all done and on the table. Hungry?"

Being careful not to slosh her wine, she slipped her hand into his, not surprised one bit by the warmth, the tingles that zapped her at the skin-to-skin contact, the burning heat that settled deep in her belly.

It was only fitting that the man had the powers of

Zeus to shoot lightning bolts through unsuspecting women.

"Starved."

And not just for food.

Oops. There went the wine again.

CHAPTER FIVE

"You may have ruined me to hummus and toast forever."
Sarah patted her mouth with a napkin, then leaned back
in her chair and smiled. "Shame on you, spoiling my
rather dull palate."

Jude felt rather spoiled himself, having gotten to
watch Sarah eat. And loosen up. Now, that he'd enjoyed.

Because once she'd relaxed she'd opened up and
talked.

Sarah talking was a pleasure.

She fascinated him. From her political views to her
dreading the holidays as much as he was to her fear of
taking the tunnels out of the city to her absolute love
of New York and the diversity of people, customs, res-
taurants, and things to do.

He couldn't quite believe she'd lived in New York
her entire life and had never been to a Broadway show.
How did anyone manage that? Even prior to adulthood,
he'd repeatedly gone during prep school field day trips.

He leaned forward, pinning her with his gaze. "If you
could see any one Broadway show, which one would
it be?"

"Phantom of the Opera," she said without hesitation
and with a wistful look in her eyes that even her hideous glasses wouldn't have hidden.

"Obviously, you've given this some thought. Why haven't you gone?"

Glancing away from him to stare out the window at the skyline, she shrugged. "I made plans to go once. He failed to show and I've just never made plans to go again."

He?

"What?" He exaggerated the word, a bit stunned at her reason. "Are you kidding me? Some guy stood you up?"

Meeting his gaze for a brief moment, she shook her head, then stared down into her glass, twirling the small amount of sparkling wine remaining. "I... It's okay, really."

"You were all dressed up and waiting on the guy to take you on a date and he never showed?" Maybe his question had been crass, but the possibility that some clown had blown her off just seemed unfathomable. And made him angry for her. He should get the guy's address and give him a lesson on how to treat a lady. Because, despite Sarah's denial, her voice conveyed that she'd been hurt.

As did how her eyes were downcast and her face pale.

"You were, weren't you?"

"I was what?" Her gaze lifted to his.

The glistening in her eyes almost undid him. She was fighting tears. His insides clenched as did his fingers.

"Dressed up and waiting on a man who never showed and didn't bother to let you know he wasn't coming."

Her expression pinched and that was all the answer Jude needed. Yeah, he should really look up this tool and give him a piece of his mind.

"Was he straight?"

Sarah's face turned that rosy shade of red it seemed to often wear and she nodded. "Yes, he was straight. Like I said, he just forgot we'd made plans."

"How?" If he'd exaggerated the word earlier, this time was even more drawn out with total disbelief.

Looking embarrassed, Sarah shrugged. "You're making a big deal of it. It wasn't. He got busy and forgot about our date. It's fine. After that, we realized we weren't meant to date, but are still friends. End of story."

Only not really because the beautiful woman sitting across from him had taken a blow to her confidence that never should have happened. The thought of Sarah, all dressed up and waiting for her date, and the guy not bothering to show or call, had Jude livid.

He shook his head. "The guy stood you up and you're still friends with him? You should have kneed him where it hurt, not still be defending his bad-mannered behavior."

Eyes wide, she gave him a horrified look. "Why on earth would I do that? Because he and I didn't click romantically? That doesn't mean he's a bad person. He's not. He's a nice man."

Most of the women he knew would have neutered the guy, not defended him.

Wondering at why Sarah was, if she still had feelings for the idiot who'd stood her up, Jude shook his head. "Nice guys don't invite a woman to a show and forget."

"Could we please talk about something else? Besides, what do you know about being a nice guy, Jude Davenport?" she scoffed, leaning forward, too, and pinning him beneath her blue-green gaze.

Knowing she was one hundred percent focused on him threw Jude. Good grief, her attention was heady.

"More than the guys you hang out with, apparently."

He stared right back, liking everything about the way he felt staring into her eyes and that this time she held his gaze, not backing down or looking away even as electricity sparked between them.

Excitement licked his imagination and visions of kissing that full mouth of hers danced through his mind, of placing his palms against those cheeks of hers, staring into her eyes, and kissing her until her taste filled his senses.

Visions of his taking her on that date and giving her the night she should have had and making up for what the idiot had done to her.

"Think whatever you will, Sarah." He even liked saying her name, how it rolled off his tongue almost melodically. "But I can honestly say that if you'd been dressed up for a date with me, I wouldn't have forgotten you no matter what the hell came up."

"That's good to know." Eyes glinting, she pursed her lips.

At her comment, Jude raised his brow, to which her lips parted, tempting him further. His mouth craved hers with a dizzying intensity.

"That's not what I mean," she began, looking flustered. "I mean... Oh, you know what I meant and what I didn't mean."

"Do I?" His lips trembled from unfamiliar restraint at not taking what he wanted. She was so close, yet he knew he shouldn't kiss her, that he had no right to kiss Sarah.

"Oh, get real, Jude. I am not your type and you are certainly not mine. What your dating practices are really don't pertain to me." Even as she protested, he heard the question in her voice and understood why. Normally, he'd have already kissed those disapproving pink lips of hers.

He wanted to kiss them.

Wanted to kiss her.

All of her.

That he hadn't kissed her said something, but he wasn't sure he understood exactly what or why he was so hesitant to make a move.

"Certainly not your type?" he pushed, knowing he wasn't reading her wrong, that, despite whatever she thought of him, there was powerful chemistry burning between them.

"Certainly," she repeated with a slight slur, making him wonder how many glasses of wine she'd had while he'd been finishing their dinner.

"Why is it that I'm certainly not your type, Sarah?"

She blinked, then gave a haughty little tilt to her chin. "Because I'm not into men who sleep with so many different women."

Were they back to that?

"I think you overestimate my prowess."

She broke eye contact and laughed. "Nice try, Casanova."

He watched her toy with her wine. "What type of men are you into?"

Not answering for several moments, she seemed to search for the answer in her glass.

"Ones who aren't like you," she finally said.

Although her response didn't surprise him, he frowned. "That's not an answer."

"Sure it is."

"How so?"

"It means I'm into men who aren't adrenaline junkies, who have steady, stable jobs, who don't feel the need to have the most notches on their bedpost."

Her response gained passion with each word, making him wonder if she was trying to convince him or herself.

"You know, guys who aren't like you." She emphasized the last word.

Was that how she saw him? The same way the rest of the world did, no doubt. Still, her words stung in ways the words of a woman he'd technically only met that day shouldn't sting. They had no relationship, had just lived next to each other since she'd bought the apartment next to his. Thank goodness he'd not bought the place as he'd considered to expand his own again, mainly to widen his view of the city. He'd hate to have gone through life without the pleasure of having met his neighbor.

"None of those things disqualify me," he pointed out, taking in every nuance of her facial expression. "Because none of those things describe me."

She didn't look convinced at his denial. "You aren't an adrenaline junkie?"

"No."

"Right." She rolled her eyes. "A man who runs into a burning building?"

"I run into burning buildings because there are people inside who need help or when there's a chance of putting out the fire and saving the building from total destruction."

Emotion flickered in her gaze, like the shimmering of the sea. She didn't break eye contact, just narrowed her gaze, as if she fought letting herself believe him. "You don't get a rush out of fighting fires?"

"I didn't say that." He shrugged. "I get a rush when I save someone's life, but not from the actual going into the burning building or risking my own life."

Although doing so did make him feel more alive,

more like the man he'd been before Nina had fallen for Charles and then died.

Maybe every time he saved a life he somehow felt vindicated that he'd not been able to save the woman he'd loved, that he'd turned his back on her and their friendship when he couldn't have more. Not that he could have saved Nina. She'd chosen Charles, had died due to childbirth complications. There had been nothing anyone could have done. Had there been, Charles and Jude both would have given their lives for Nina's.

Except when he fought fires, Jude had felt half-dead since the moment he'd cut Nina completely out of his life, lost his best friend, and destroyed the closeness he'd once shared with his cousin.

He didn't feel half-dead now. Quite the opposite.

He didn't recall ever feeling as alive as he felt at this moment, staring into the eyes of a woman who didn't think much of him, but who was as intrigued by him as he was her, despite the fact that she didn't want to be.

Which meant what exactly? He didn't want a relationship, was no longer a relationship kind of guy. These days, he took women to his bed, not to his dining room to feed them a meal he'd cooked.

He sure didn't long to take women on dates where he showered them with romance and attention to make up for every wrong they'd ever endured.

Yet, looking into Sarah's eyes, that was exactly what he wanted. Hell.

"I think I'm more your type than you want to admit, Doc."

As Sarah helped Jude clear the table and load his dishwasher, his words kept running through her head.

Surprisingly, this was the first silence they'd had as

they'd chatted away during dinner. Jude was a great conversationalist. He made intelligent comments, listened with eager ears, and responded with insightful observations.

The few dates she'd ever gone on had left her feeling awkward and socially inept. Eventually, she'd almost quit dating, because why bother? She wasn't looking for a man in her life, knew what being involved with the wrong man could cost a woman, and didn't appreciate giving up a night of her life to feel inadequate at the end of the evening.

The few times she'd made exceptions had never ended well.

For instance, the night interesting Kenny Goodall had asked to take her to her first Broadway show. She'd lost the glasses, donned mascara and lipstick, put on a decently fitting dress, and anxiously awaited what had promised to be a wonderful evening.

She'd never felt so mortified, unattractive, and convinced her mother was right in all her life as when she'd discovered he'd forgotten their plans.

Never again would she allow herself to be so humiliated at the hands of a man.

Nothing about her dinner with Jude made her feel inadequate, though. Quite the opposite. She'd enjoyed sharing the meal with him more than she'd have dreamed possible. Maybe because she knew there could never be anything between them.

The fact he'd seemed perturbed she'd written him off as not her type and given him her reasons why surprised her, though. Why would he care?

Sure, she'd felt heat when looking at him and he'd made flirty comments at the hospital and tonight, but the reality was she wasn't Jude Davenport's type.

He hadn't bothered to deny that, had just questioned that he wasn't hers.

Before having seen that different side of him at the hospital and tonight, she'd have said it was because he was so arrogant he assumed he was every woman's type.

If gorgeous, intelligent, witty, and full of testosterone were the criteria, then he was.

Sarah glanced around the kitchen, surprised at how quickly they'd gotten everything cleared. Surprised at how amazingly stocked and spacious his kitchen was. She liked the granite countertops, the workstation island, and the stainless-steel appliances.

What she didn't like was that now there was nothing to occupy her hands, more awkwardness was setting in.

"You want another glass of wine?"

Looking at him in relief, she exclaimed, "Yes!"

He must think her a total slush and she rarely drank. She'd just been grateful for something to do with her hands to ward off her own mental demons. She should leave before the awkwardness and inadequacy set in, reminding that she had nothing in common with him.

He poured her another glass, then one for himself. "Let's sit on the sofa and look out at the city. It's my favorite way to end a stressful day."

So maybe they did have a few things in common. Besides chemistry.

Sarah sat, but couldn't relax to enjoy the view as she had earlier because Jude sat down beside her. His body wasn't touching hers, but he was closer than he should be since they were the only two people on his large sofa.

Why had he sat so close? If she took a deep breath, she'd probably brush up against his arm.

She finished off her glass of wine in record time, set

the glass on an end table coaster, and stood. Enough was enough. She'd had a mostly enjoyable night with him and wasn't going to ruin it by staying longer.

"Thank you for the delicious meal, for turning off my smoke detector, and for letting me enjoy your view."

First placing his glass next to hers on the table, he stood, stared down at her. "You are very welcome, Sarah, but I should be thanking you."

The intensity in his blue eyes about had her almost sitting back down because of wobbly legs. "For what?"

"Providing excellent dinner company and turning my night into something memorable."

She hadn't done that. Wasn't going to do that. Was that what he thought she was there to do?

"I'd best be going," she ventured, not breaking eye contact with him but taking a step back.

His eyes twinkled. "In a rush?"

"It's been a long day. I look forward to going to sleep." Yes, she had put emphasis on the word "sleep". "I'm sure you feel the same."

One side of his mouth crooked upward. "Then I guess I have no choice but to say good night."

Sarah barely held back her sigh of relief. Which was just as well, because Jude did the unthinkable.

He kissed her.

Just a short peck on her mouth with his warm lips, but one she felt ricochet all the way to her toes and bring every nerve cell to life along the way. The power of Zeus, she thought again, knowing she'd been struck by lightning.

"Goodnight, Sarah," he said, his lips still so close she could feel his warm breath caress her sensitized mouth. He looked straight into her eyes, his full of what she could only describe as desire.

Desire. For her.

No doubt hers shone the same way.

Because she felt desire. For him.

His lips touched hers again, this time slower, exploring her mouth with his soft, tender touch. He stared into her eyes, searching them as surely as his mouth explored her lips.

She shouldn't be kissing him. He was a scoundrel, a good-for-nothing womanizer who used women.

Only, deep down, he wasn't.

She shouldn't be kissing him. He wasn't her type.

Only, deep down, he was.

She shouldn't be kissing him. She wasn't his type.

Only he was looking at her, kissing her, as if she was.

His kiss was so sweet, so addictive, so electrifying, that she didn't want him to stop.

So she kissed him back.

Kissed him with the same exploration of his lips, his mouth, that he had kissed her with. At some point her hands found their way to his shoulders, to his neck, to his soft dark hair that she now threaded her fingers through, toying with the silky strands.

Never had she experienced a kiss like this.

Never had she felt a man's body like his.

Strong, hard, capable of amazing things, focused completely on her every movement, her every response, her every breath.

She didn't stop him when he cupped her face to kiss her more fully, when his hands worked their way down her shoulders, to her back to settle low and pull her against him.

Oh.

He was long and lean and hard. All man, the kind who rushed into burning buildings to save little girls.

The kind who could sweep a woman off her feet without having to catch his breath. The kind whose eyes seduced with just a glimpse.

The kind whose body made a woman want to explore every inch, feel every inch, claim every inch as her own.

That's how she kissed him, not bothering to hold anything back. What was the point? The moment was some anomaly in time that would never happen again. She'd worry about regrets and recriminations later. Much later.

Jude kissed with a passion she found addictive and she gave in to how she craved him.

His hands shifted to her shoulders, and to her surprise he pulled back, stared into her eyes with ones that appeared as dazed as she felt.

Which was saying a lot. Her legs had all the strength of melted butter. Which was a pretty accurate description of how the rest of her felt, too.

"That was some goodnight kiss, Doc."

She wasn't sure how to take his comment. Was he making fun of how she'd kissed him after claiming he wasn't her type?

"Um, y-yeah, it w-was," she stammered. "Nothing like any I've encountered, for sure."

"Really?"

He seemed intrigued by her comment and Sarah regretted her wine-induced confession. At least, she was blaming her blurting out that she'd never been kissed like that before on the wine.

Honestly, she could just as easily blame it on his kiss because the man's mouth had outright intoxicated her.

Squaring up her shoulders and trying to achieve a look of nonchalance, she nodded. "Don't act like it's a big deal because I'm sure you get that a lot."

"Get what a lot?"

Oh, the things she could respond with, but, even though she should be blaring a reminder over and over in her head, the last thing she wanted to do at the moment was think about him with other women.

"The reaction that you are a way above average kisser."

Looking more than a little pleased at her answer, he chuckled. "Way above average?"

His pleasure in her response, that he was looking at her with affection rather than mockery, freed Sarah of her embarrassment at her confession.

Or maybe it was the wine freeing her of her inhibitions. Yep, she was going to keep blaming the wine. Nasty inhibition-lowering stuff.

"Okay," she admitted with a little roll of her eyes and a smile of her own. "You're phenomenal and make my previous kissing experiences seem like they were conducted by preschoolers."

He stroked his thumb across her cheek. "Preschoolers?"

"They weren't," she assured him, thinking she should quit talking any moment now. "I have been kissed since preschool."

His thumb made a circular caress over her cheekbone and her brain went a little fuzzy for a moment. For a moment? Ha, her brain had been fuzzy all evening. Looking at him made her brain fuzzy. Kissing him had completely fuzzed her.

"I wasn't actually kissed in preschool," she clarified. "Not even once, although this little boy named Johnny chased me around saying he was going to kiss me when he caught me, but I never let him catch me." She should shut up, because why was she telling him about Johnny from preschool? "I have been kissed. By grown men. Good, decent men who were my type."

At least, she'd thought they were her type. Now she wasn't so sure.

"But they didn't kiss like you." Yeah, she really should quit talking.

The color of Jude's eyes deepened, darkening with an emotion Sarah couldn't label. Instinctively, she liked his warm expression, though. She liked it a lot.

"How did I kiss, Sarah?"

He cupped her face now, stared into her eyes, and his voice had a husky tone to it that made her want to listen to him say her name over and over.

All night long.

Wine, stop it.

"Like you could set my body on fire and make me happy to go up in flames."

Oops. That had slipped out. Maybe she needed to zip her lips.

Zip her lips?

She was reverting to preschool.

Or maybe the way Jude was looking at her, touching her, had her intelligence on hold.

He quirked a brow. "You know my job is to put out fires, right?"

"My guess is that you've started more than a few, too." She swallowed, half expecting him to sweep her off her feet and carry her to his bedroom all Rhett Butler style.

Would she stop him?

Or would she give in to the curiosity of how good Jude Davenport could make her feel? Because she knew being the focus of this man's attention in bed would be unlike anything she'd ever imagined possible.

Before that moment, that was, because right now her imagination was endless.

Jude stared into her eyes for long moments. "What are you doing tomorrow evening, Sarah Grayson?"

CHAPTER SIX

CONFUSED, SARAH BLINKED. Tomorrow evening? Shouldn't he be worried about what she was doing right then? At that moment? In the next fifteen minutes? No, Jude wouldn't be a fifteen-minute man. He'd be hours and hours.

There went her imagination again. Endless.

"Working," she answered, thinking he couldn't really have just asked if she was busy, because she didn't expect him to want more than just a rumble between his sheets.

Or was that his normal routine? Make the woman think he was interested in more than just one night before luring her into his bed?

Hadn't he already figured out that she needed no further luring? She was curious and purring for more.

"How about Friday evening?" he asked, his thumb sliding across her cheek. "Are you working then?"

Her forehead scrunched. "No, but—"

"Plans?"

"No, but—" She was going to tell him she didn't want idle promises of seeing him again. If she agreed. And she would. Why not let a man like Jude introduce her to what all the sex hype was about? *Sexual Orgasm for Beginners?*

Ha! She'd bet anything he'd move straight into an advanced course. Maybe *Advanced Multiple Wows*, or something along those lines.

"Would you give me the privilege of taking you to your first Broadway show on Friday evening?"

Their minds clearly on two different subjects, Sarah's head spun and she frowned at him in bewilderment. "Why would you want to do that?"

Why was he talking about Friday evening when they were in the here and now and his bedroom was only a few feet away?

"I'd like to take you to watch *Phantom of the Opera*."

"What? Why?"

"I'd like to fulfill that desire of yours."

Which was where her brain had been, not on watching a play. But he meant…he was saying…asking…

"As a…" she'd been going to say "friend", but, whatever they were, they weren't friends "…neighbor?"

He chuckled. "As someone who'd like to kiss you goodnight again. Soon."

"Oh." She bit her lower lip. Part of her wanted to throw caution to the wind and say yes, and to please just go ahead and kiss her again right now, like she'd thought he was going to do. Would that be soon enough? But she wasn't a throw-caution-to-the-wind kind of girl. She was a logical girl who avoided men like him because they used women. She knew he used women. She saw the parade of usees leaving his apartment the morning after.

She was not a usee. She'd been thinking about becoming one, had even been thinking of using him to give her the pleasure wielded at his fingertips, which would make her a user, too. What she hadn't been thinking of was going on a date with Jude Davenport.

That terrified her much more than the thought of having sex with him.

Sex was nothing to Jude. Maybe dates weren't either. But to her, at that moment, dragging him into his bedroom and stripping him naked felt safer than agreeing to a date.

No.

She would not set herself up for that particular disappointment again.

"I can tell you are way over-thinking this," he pointed out, lifting her chin to where she was looking into his eyes again. "It's just a date, Sarah."

Just a date. She hadn't misread what he'd been offering. Jude wanted to take her on a date. A real date.

"I'm not your type," she reminded him, positive that agreeing to go with him would be a bad idea, that to do so would be setting herself up for disappointment the way Kenny had never come close to.

What if she grew emotionally attached?

No, she knew better than to do that with a man like Jude. If they went out, it would be because he was tired tonight, but was interested in pursuing the sexual chemistry between them at a later time. On Friday night. Taking her to watch a Broadway show was no big deal to Jude, merely a form of foreplay.

She needed to be careful not to make his offer into more than what it was.

"And I'm not your type," he countered her response, his eyes full of delicious promise. "So how about you say you'll go to dinner and to see *Phantom of the Opera* with me? We will have a good time. I'll be on my best behavior and give you a night you'll never forget. I give my word."

The man could sell sand in the middle of the desert.

"And then what?" she ventured, trying to play out in

her mind what would happen after their "date". "You expect me to sleep with you and then me to sneak out of your apartment the next morning?"

His expression didn't waver. "I would never ask you to sneak out of my apartment, Sarah."

Right. He'd just kiss her goodbye, while standing in his doorway with only a towel covering his lean hips, while she craved more of whatever he'd done the night before.

If she wasn't careful, she'd be the one with no pride, offering to do whatever he wanted for just a little bit more of his delicious body.

She had to put a stop to this. Her sexual need had ebbed a little and she felt stronger, more able to walk away, and that's exactly what she was going to do.

She went to turn from him, but he stopped her.

"I like you, Sarah," he told her, his voice clear, sincere, imploring. "I've enjoyed tonight more than I've enjoyed talking with a woman in a long time. Stop judging me on what you think you know. Pretend you met me for the first time at the hospital today and listen to what your heart is saying right now."

If she'd met him at the hospital and not had preconceived ideas she might think he was wonderful and not at all like the men her mother had warned her about.

"My heart isn't saying anything right now." Okay, so it was beating fast, and a little erratically, but that wasn't speech.

He put his palm over her heart, as if interpreting an unspoken language.

Beating a *lot* erratically, she corrected, wondering why his hand on her chest made breathing so difficult.

"Maybe you just aren't listening closely enough, because I think it is."

"Don't use lines on me, Jude Davenport," she warned,

reminding herself not to get caught up in what he was saying. The man was a practiced womanizer. "I'm not one of your women."

Looking frustrated, he sighed. "How about we go to dinner and the show Friday evening and then just have some fun between now and Christmas? You get to decide how much, or how little, happens between us physically."

No doubt shock registered in her eyes because his question floored her. That a lot would happen between them physically wasn't in question. If she spent time with him, she would end up in his bed. She didn't fool herself otherwise. She didn't even deny to herself that a big part of her wanted to be in his bed, to know what it felt like to have him give her body pleasure.

"Christmas?" she finally croaked. "Christmas is weeks away. Wouldn't Thanksgiving make more sense?"

Which almost sounded as if she was considering his outrageous suggestion. She wasn't, was she?

He shrugged. "Why not Christmas? Thanksgiving is only a few weeks from now. We've already admitted that we're dreading the holidays. Why not spend them together so maybe they won't be so bad?"

Sarah mentally shook her head. Jude was asking her to date him through Christmas?

Had she passed out in her kitchen from smoke fumes and only dreamed he'd come to rescue her?

That made more sense.

Reality was that she was unconscious, suffering from smoke intoxication, and having one heck of a hallucination.

Either that, or Jude must have enjoyed their kiss.

She had enjoyed their kiss.

Had truly never been kissed that way, had never felt so much passion bubbling within her.

Yep, she must be hallucinating.

She bit the inside of her lip. Ouch. The pain was real. Which meant this was real. That Jude was searching her eyes, looking for an answer.

The truth was that she wanted to know him better, too.

If she said no, she'd only be denying herself. But there was that thing she didn't really want to think about. Before she could consider agreeing to any of this, she had to address it or else it would be a constant thorn.

"What about the other women?"

"What other women?" He glanced around his living room. "I only see you."

"You know what I mean."

"I'm not that shallow, Sarah."

When she didn't relent, he sighed. "You want me to sign my name in blood that I won't see other women?"

"You can do whatever you want. Whoever you want," she clarified. "Just not on my time. If I agree to this, then I don't want other women in your apartment."

Surprisingly, he didn't tell her she was crazy, that she had no right to make demands. Instead, he regarded her a moment, then asked, "You'll do the same?"

His question was laughable.

"I don't have men come and go out of my apartment."

"You go to their apartments?" he pushed.

"No."

His brow arched. "You do date?"

Not often. Dating wasn't high on her list of things to do. Never had been. She'd watched too many women squander their lives away chasing after that elusive "the one". Most of the time, she was smarter than that.

At the moment she didn't feel smart. She'd thought Jude wanted to take her to bed and instead he was trying to talk her into agreeing to spend the next several weeks dating him.

A smart woman would have already agreed.

Or was it that a smart woman would have already left his apartment? Or never been there to begin with?

"That guy, the one who stood you up, you have been on a date since that night?"

She winced at the reminder of just how miserable dating gone wrong could make her feel. Instead, she'd cling to how good his kiss had made her feel, to the knowledge that he wanted to kiss her again.

"Occasionally," she answered, trying to stay focused on their conversation rather than all the things running through her mind. "My priorities haven't been on how many notches I could put on my bedpost."

Although she'd been striking out, he didn't seem offended by her comment.

"What have your priorities been?"

"Not on getting laid."

"I think it's safe to say you've established that." His gaze narrowed. "You do think notches are my priority?"

They were talking in circles. She took another step back, determined she was going to make her way to her apartment.

"I don't know you well enough to know your priorities."

"Which I plan to remedy," he countered.

Flustered, she put her hands on her hips and glared. "You seriously want to take me to a Broadway show? To date me, just me, through Christmas?"

Eyes glimmering, he grinned. "Absolutely."

She had to say yes, didn't she? Only a fool would say

no to what he was offering. As long as she stayed focused on the facts, that they weren't in a real relationship but a temporary one, that she didn't want a real relationship any more than he did, everything would be fine.

She met his gaze and even before she said a single word, victory shone in his eyes.

"You know if you stand me up I'll put cockroaches under your apartment door," she warned.

Not looking worried, he grinned. "Cockroaches?"

"Or worse."

Rather than say something teasing back, he cupped her cheek. "I won't stand you up, Sarah. But I'm glad to hear that you refuse to let any man, myself included, treat you shabbily." His hold tightened ever so slightly. "Make sure you don't stand me up."

As if.

The emergency room had been busy. Busy enough that Sarah hadn't been able to dwell on her date with Jude the following night.

Not so busy that she hadn't paused outside her apartment to stare at his closed door that morning.

Not so busy that she hadn't answered his text messages saying good morning, then telling her to have a good afternoon, then messaging her that he'd been called in to the station that night but looked forward to seeing her the following evening.

He really planned to take her out.

If he stood her up, she'd be devastated. As much as she hated to admit that truth, she acknowledged it. Wasn't that why she'd never let a man pick her up at her new apartment? Because she didn't want her beloved home tainted by painful memories of being stood up?

Yet she'd agreed to go out with Jude.

Which meant she needed to figure out what she was going to wear.

Typically she dressed to avoid attracting any type of attention from the opposite sex. Doing so had just made life easier through med school and as an emergency room physician. Trying to appear attractive garnered attention she didn't want, hence the thick glasses sitting on her face that weren't prescription but that she wore any time she left her house.

Camouflage? Or self-defense?

While typing up the report on the last patient she'd seen, for a kidney stone, she mentally ran through the items in her closet.

Nothing there suitable for a dinner and show with Jude Davenport.

Unless she wanted to put on the dress she'd worn the night Kenny had been a no-show. Not going to happen.

She wasn't much of a shopper, but she supposed she could search tomorrow to find something. Not on Fifth Avenue, where most of Jude's dates probably shopped, but surely she could find something decent at an upscale department store or second-hand shop?

Maybe she'd even stop by the make-up counter and have her face done while there.

Or maybe she was being ridiculous in considering trying to spiff herself up to impress Jude. If she spiffed non-stop between now and tomorrow evening, she'd never rival the beauties she'd seen leaving his apartment.

Plus, the last time she'd spiffed up had gone horribly wrong and had ended with her looking like a raccoon from the tears she'd cried when she'd called Kenny and realized he'd forgotten he'd asked her out...and was out on a date with someone else. She'd not bothered to tell Jude that part. Why humiliate herself even further than she already had?

She finished up her notes on the patients she'd cared for during her shift, then logged off the computer system.

"You heading out?" her friend Shelley asked.

Sarah stood, stretching her spine. "Yes. Today wasn't as bad as yesterday, thank goodness, but it's definitely been another long one."

"Speaking of yesterday, how's the little girl? The one rescued by that hunky firefighter who saved her life and made me want to take him home to give him some tender loving care and a good scrub down."

Sarah's cheeks flamed at Shelley's mention of Jude. He'd been the one to give her the tender loving care, along with a delicious meal. No scrub down. They'd both already showered by the time she'd set off her alarm.

"Keeley's good," she said, thinking of the little girl she'd checked on several times throughout her shift. She'd even gotten permission from Keeley's mother to text Jude to let him know about the child. "She recovered consciousness this evening. Hopefully, she'll be weaned off the vent before the night is through."

Sarah spoke with her friend a few more minutes, considered mentioning that she had a date with the hunky firefighter, but decided not to. They hadn't actually gone on a date so she shouldn't jump the gun, just in case.

Not that she thought Jude would stand her up. With her history, she should be terrified he would change his mind, that he'd find some excuse to cancel their date. There was a tiny part of her that acknowledged the possibility, but her gut instinct was that he wouldn't do that. Something about him exuded honor and integrity.

Which was ridiculous when she knew he was a scoundrel when it came to women.

But if she didn't live next door to him, if she hadn't seen the plethora of women parading in and out of his apartment, if they really had met yesterday at the hospital, she'd have thought him a really great guy. A hero kind of guy.

Which might be testament to how foolish she was being over the man.

She was still thinking about Jude when she said hi to their apartment building doorman, while she rode the elevator up to their floor, when she stepped out of the elevator and made her way down the corridor. She'd not taken but a few steps when she noticed the large, brightly wrapped box with a huge gold bow propped against her apartment door.

A present?

She didn't have to wonder from who, because there could only be one person who'd do such a thing.

CHAPTER SEVEN

SARAH DIDN'T WANT to be excited, but was as she bent and pulled the card with her name on it off the box.

Heart pounding, goofy smile tugging at her mouth, reminding herself not to read too much into anything Jude did, she ripped into the envelope.

I planned to give you this in person, but got called to the fire hall. Can't wait to see you in this tomorrow night. Wear your hair up and forget your glasses so I can see your lovely face.

Her heart muscles squeezed a little too tight at his last line. Because of the past, she told herself.

Besides, if the man had bought her underwear she was going to place the order for cockroaches.

Not really. She'd put whatever skimpy piece of silk and lace the box held on and model for him. She'd probably be wearing a goofy smile to go with it, too.

But even if the size of the box hadn't already suggested otherwise, when she picked up the box, she knew whatever was inside was more than underwear.

Feeling like a kid in anticipation of Christmas morning and trying to remind herself there wasn't really a Santa Claus and she shouldn't be so keyed up, she unlocked her door, stepped inside, stripped off her winter layers, then carried the box to her coffee table.

Rather than open it, she sat on her sofa and stared at the package as if it might contain a rattlesnake.

Or the cure to cancer.

She was both eagerly excited to see what the box held but also afraid of what gift he might have given.

Or maybe it was a consolation prize because he planned to cancel after all?

No, he'd said he couldn't wait to see her in it and, truly, she couldn't see him doing that, not with how passionate he'd been about Kenny having done so.

Taking care, she pulled the ribbon off from around the box, then lifted the lid, and moved aside the tissue paper.

Oh, my.

Inside were a small gold-foil-covered box, a shoe-sized box, and the most beautiful dress she'd ever seen.

Had she gone shopping she never could have found anything so perfect in color and style.

Not that the items were likely to fit right. Not with her lack of curves, and how would Jude have known her size? But the sea-green dress was gorgeous, modestly cut, and very close to the color of her eyes.

She ran her finger over the silky material. Not too flashy, not too revealing, yet definitely something more figure-flattering than she'd ever worn. What size was it?

She moved the material aside to where she could see the label. Oh, wow. She dropped the material for fear she might damage the dress. She might be a fashion wreck, but even she recognized the designer and that the dress would have had a hefty price tag.

Christmas morning excitement or not, she couldn't wear the dress. She didn't want Jude spending money on her. That wasn't who she was. As a matter of fact, she'd planned to offer to pay for her show ticket and dinner.

Not that she'd thought he'd let her, but she would have been sincere in her offer to do so.

With shaky hands she picked up the shoe box, knowing what she'd find inside, and lifted the lid. Matching designer shoes in her exact size with medium-height heels. Smart man in choosing a pair that wouldn't make her feet hurt or make her walk like a shaky newborn fawn.

Again, the designer name on the shoe was one she recognized, but not one she'd ever splurged to purchase.

Unless he'd seen her size in the shoes she'd slipped off her feet while snuggled up on his sofa, drinking her wine, she had no clue how he'd known what size to buy. Good grief, the man paid attention to details.

A dress, shoes…she could only guess what was in the small box. The skimpy panties she'd imagined earlier?

She was wrong. Very wrong.

Inside was a velvet jewelry case.

If she'd thought her hands had been shaky before, now they shook with full-blown tremors. Earthquake-sized ones that probably had some Richter-scale-watching scientist freaking out as he tried to track down the source.

Holding her breath, she flipped open the box lid.

Inside was a stunning pair of dangling, sparkling earrings that surely to goodness weren't real diamonds, and a folded piece of paper with a handwritten message.

I won't forget.

Her eyes watered. He wouldn't. He'd be there. He'd bought her a dress, shoes, and earrings to wear. She'd never been given clothes or jewelry by a man. Not ever.

The only jewelry she owned was a gold chain with a quote pendant on it that her mother had given her at her high school graduation and that she rarely took off.

To thine own self be true

She pulled the chain from beneath the layers of her scrubs and long-sleeved undershirt and fingered the charm.

She wasn't quite sure how to take Jude's gifts.

Obviously, from his luxurious apartment, he didn't live on a firefighter's pay but on the deep Davenport dollars. He probably had trust funds. The gifts meant nothing to him, but were likely commonplace things he did for women.

If so, no wonder they came to him in droves.

What was she saying? If he gave them no gift except his time and body, women would come to Jude in droves.

She would come to him.

She didn't want gifts. She wanted…him.

She closed her watery eyes, took a deep breath, then pulled out her phone to text him a "thank you, but not necessary" note. She'd barely hit send when her phone rang with his number showing on the screen.

"Sorry I wasn't there to give them to you in person. I'd like to have watched you open them," he said by way of greeting. "Tell me you were smiling."

"I was smiling," she admitted. "They are lovely, Jude, but I have clothes and if I needed new ones I can afford to go shopping." Not on the scale of what he'd sent her, but she did make a decent living. "Like I said in my text, buying me gifts wasn't necessary."

Unless he had wanted her dressed a certain way, up

to a certain social standard in case they ran into friends?
She couldn't convince herself of that from a man who
hung out in a fire hall, who hadn't cared who'd seen
him dirty and smelly at the hospital. He didn't come
across as a social snob, but she supposed anything was
possible.

"I didn't think it necessary," he countered over the
phone. "I wanted to give them to you."

Sarah fought sucking in a deep breath.

"I want tomorrow night, my taking you to your first
Broadway show, to be everything you ever dreamed, to
make up for the last time you thought you were going."

She bit the inside of her lower lip and squeezed the
phone a little tighter in hope of steadying her hand.
"You don't need to make up for another man's wrongs,
Jude."

Which was the first time she'd ever admitted out loud
that Kenny had done something wrong. Even to him,
she'd accepted his explanation that he'd forgotten, made
other plans, but that she understood, right? Because he
and Sarah were just going as friends anyway, right?

"No," Jude agreed. "But I want to."

She closed her eyes, told her heartbeat to slow down
before it pounded out of her chest. "You always do what
you want?"

"Not always."

"Most of the time?"

"Yes."

Did that mean he hadn't wanted to have sex with her
the night before? She'd thought…no, she'd known that's
what he'd wanted. He'd just been tired. She'd been tired.
He'd promised he wouldn't trick her into his bed if she
came to dinner and he'd kept his promise.

Not that he would have had to trick her. All he'd

had to do was crook his finger and she'd have followed wherever he led.

Just like Brandy. Ugh.

"Should I remind you that I'm not like the women you usually date?" She definitely needed to remind herself of the women he usually dated.

"No reason to. I already know you're not like the women I usually date."

She'd swear she could hear amusement in his voice, but what he found funny, she wasn't sure. Regardless, his light-hearted tone eased some of her tension. Some, but not all.

"You giving expensive gifts makes me uncomfortable."

"You shouldn't be uncomfortable, Sarah," he assured her in a more serious voice. "I don't want you to think the gifts came with strings attached. They didn't. I gave them to you because I wanted you to have them, because giving them to you gave me pleasure, and my only regret is that I wasn't there to watch your face while you opened them."

She wasn't sure she believed him. She had no reason to. Then again, she had no reason not to other than her mother's voice blaring through her head.

"Okay," she ventured, leaning back on the sofa and staring at her presents. "Thank you. They are lovely."

"So are you. Did the dress fit?"

He thought she was lovely? Good grief, why was a man's compliments and excitement flabbergasting her so? She was logical, reasonable, too smart to be swayed by pretty words.

"I don't know," she admitted, swayed by his pretty words because she was smiling that goofy smile again and no matter how she tried to wipe it off her face, she couldn't. So much for logic and reason. "I haven't tried it on."

"What?" He sounded truly surprised. "I thought you would have done so first thing."

"I just walked in the door from work," she reminded him, pulling off her shoes and tucking her feet up under her on the sofa.

"Busy day?"

"I work in the emergency department at Manhattan Mercy. Every day is a busy day."

"Touché."

"Speaking of which, are you related to my boss?" She'd almost asked Charles today, but hadn't wanted to risk his asking why she wanted to know. She could have just said she lived next door to Jude, but she'd been afraid Charles might see things she didn't want seen.

There was a moment of silence, then Jude said, "He's my cousin."

Jude hadn't asked who she meant, which meant he'd already made the connection. Of course he had. He'd seen her at the hospital where his family was practically royalty.

"I thought you must be related. Your eye color is so similar to his. You should have told me. Might have helped your cause to mention your relationship to Charles. I'd be hard-pressed to name a man I admire more."

There was another brief silence, then, rather than take advantage of the opening she'd given him, he ignored her compliments about his cousin and said, "Try on your dress, Sarah."

She frowned at her phone.

"Why are you changing the subject? I adore Charles. If I had family of the caliber of Charles Davenport I'd make sure the whole world knew we were related."

"Yeah, well, when you're a Davenport the whole world tends to know a lot about you, whether you want them to or not." His voice had lost its happy edge and had taken on a dark one.

Apparently, Jude did not want to discuss his family with her. Fine. So they weren't that kind of dating. Not the kind that shared about their family and met each other's families and were invited to family functions.

Well, that was good to know. Helped her keep things in perspective.

Not that she wasn't planning to do that already.

She knew they were only temporary.

"I'm not going to try on my dress until after I've taken a shower." Maybe because she had hospital grime on her. Maybe because she was feeling contrary. "And then, I still might not tonight."

Her bets were leaning toward the latter.

"If you don't then I'll question if you're female."

The teasing tone she was used to was back and a tightness inside her unwound.

"I'm definitely female. Been that way my whole life," she assured him, glad that the dark edge had left his voice as quickly as it had appeared. "But whether the dress fits or not really isn't relevant, because even if it's a perfect fit, I'm not sure I'll wear it. It's not my usual style."

The dress was a perfect fit and Sarah was wearing it.

At the moment.

She'd contemplated changing a dozen times. Every time she'd walked to her closet and tried to come up with something else to wear to her Broadway show date, she'd not seen anything to tempt her to change.

Instead her gaze would fall on the black dress she'd

worn the last time she'd planned to go to see *Phantom of the Opera* and an uneasy feeling would twist her gut.

Maybe she should have spent the day shopping.

Instead, she'd done laundry, cleaned her apartment, bought groceries. All the things she typically did on her day off even when she didn't have a date with her hunky neighbor.

Her very handsome neighbor whom she'd not seen since he'd kissed her goodnight two nights ago.

What if he saw her and was disappointed?

What if she'd been wrong and he didn't show?

Her nervousness was just foolishness, wasn't it?

No, it wasn't. He wasn't going to stand her up. No matter how many ghosts from the past haunted her mind, she refused to let them take hold. Her nervousness stemmed from so much more than fear of rejection and humiliation.

Her fears came from what would happen after their date.

Jude might have said he didn't expect anything in return, but a man didn't bother sending a woman a dress, shoes, and jewelry unless he wanted something.

She knew what he wanted. It was what they both wanted. Her question was why? He didn't have to do gifts to get women into his bed, to get her into his bed. If anything, his gifts made her that much more skeptical. Was he toying with her? Seeing her as a challenge?

A make-over challenge?

Wouldn't he be in for a surprise? Although she had on the dress he'd sent, the shoes that were surprisingly comfortable or she'd not have kept them on fifteen seconds, and the sparkly earrings, she'd not done anything more than brush a little mascara across her lashes and gloss on some lip balm to prevent chapping.

She glanced down at her glasses sitting on the bathroom sink counter. She didn't need them to see, but she had a feeling she'd need them in other ways before the night ended. She slid them onto her face and instantly felt calmer.

She had this. She was in control. Not Jude. What happened tonight was up to her. Even he'd said so.

When she opened her apartment door and he stood there, in a tux, holding flowers, she wasn't so sure about that control.

He looked like the hero straight from a romantic movie. Only she was no fun, quirky heroine. She was... just her.

A just her that felt prickles in her eyes. Prickles she fought because she was not going to end up with raccoon eyes tonight.

"You are beautiful."

She went to deny his claim and chide him for his use of lines again, then realized he was sincere. He looked at her with true appreciation, with true admiration in his blue eyes. So she just stared at him in a bit of awe, blushed, and murmured thanks.

"I was wrong about wanting you to put up your hair. I like it better loose the way you have it. I'd never seen you with your hair down or I'd have suggested it to begin with. It's gorgeous."

Ha. She'd left it loose because she had felt contrary about being a yes girl who did everything he said and she hadn't wanted her neck exposed. At least, she'd thought she didn't want that. Maybe she did.

He didn't comment on her glasses, but she knew he'd noted that she'd put them on despite his knowing she didn't need them and that he'd asked her not to.

She wasn't sure why, but in her mind contrariness to

being a yes girl equaled control of what was happening between them. Or as close as she was going to manage.

"Do you have a coat?"

"I'm not going out there like this. I'd freeze," she countered, then realized how brusque and rude she sounded. She needed to just embrace the wonderfulness of what he was doing for her and forget contrariness. "Sorry. I'm a bit on edge."

"I'd never let you freeze." His eyes had that twinkle that told he'd come up with all sorts of interesting ways to keep her warm. "I don't want you tense, Sarah. This is supposed to be a fun night for you."

"It's impossible for me not to be on edge when I don't understand why you're doing this," she admitted, pushing her glasses up a little on the bridge of her nose.

He watched her movement, grinned. "Doing what?"

"Taking me on a date."

"You are a beautiful, intelligent woman who I had a great time with a couple of nights ago and who I want to get to know better." He leaned forward and dropped a kiss on her forehead. "Smile, Sarah. You have no reason to be nervous of me. My priority is for you to have the best night of your life."

Sarah sucked in a deep breath. She couldn't help it. She was positive that at no point in her life had anyone wanted to give her that. Not her mother. Not anyone.

"That's a good priority."

"Isn't it, though?" He brushed a long strand of hair away from her face, and smiled a smile that made her heart skip a beat. "Grab your coat and let's head out. The car is waiting."

Expecting to see a taxi, Sarah's feet froze in her new heels when she caught sight of the long black stretch limo pulled up to the curb in front of the building.

Taking in his proud smile, she choked, "What have you done?"

His pleasure at her reaction was as obvious as the huge smile on his face. "Arranged a ride to the theater."

"A taxi would have done just fine."

He squeezed her hand. "Tonight's not a taxi kind of night."

She cut her gaze to him. "Why not?"

He lifted her gloved hand to his lips and pressed a kiss there. "I promised the best night of your life, remember?"

"Mission accomplished."

His smile widened. "Good."

"I know I've said it before, but I'll say it again. All this isn't necessary."

"All this is very necessary," he assured. "Tonight is a night of firsts."

He had no idea.

Or maybe he did. Maybe that was why he was going to the extra trouble. Although if he was really the womanizer she'd initially labeled him as she supposed it didn't make sense that he'd go to so much trouble.

"Your first Broadway show," he clarified, grinning, and his eyes sparkling with mischief. "Our first date."

"Probably our last," she added, with an eye roll because she was scared if she kept looking at him he might see just how touched she was by how much effort he'd gone to.

"Such an optimist," he teased, and tucked her hand between his. "You agreed to through Christmas. I'm holding you to that. Don't you expect to enjoy yourself?"

She did expect to enjoy tonight. Very much. Like a fairy-tale princess on her way to the ball with the handsome prince. A heroic prince who fought fire-breathing dragons and carried her away in his chariot.

"Also my first limo ride," she said, offering him a small smile.

When her gaze connected with his, what she saw there stole her breath. So did his next words.

"Then I'm even happier I didn't go for a taxi."

The driver opened the passenger door and held out his hand to assist her. Sarah climbed into the car, slid across the seat to make room for Jude.

Make room for him? Half their apartment complex could fit inside the thing.

"The driver will take us to the Majestic and pick us up afterward. We have reservations for dinner at—" he named a French restaurant she'd heard of, but had never been to "—and then afterward I have a surprise I think you'll enjoy."

Sarah wasn't really a surprise kind of girl. There had been too many unknowns during her childhood for that. None of them ever good. She liked having a plan and knowing what to expect so she could prepare.

Besides, afterward? The show would last a few hours, then dinner. That would put them well past ten, probably close to eleven. Just what did he have planned? Maybe he really was some type of superman, but she needed sleep.

She wasn't scheduled in the emergency room the next day, but she did have things she planned to do.

She glanced around the inside of the limo, at the pure luxuriousness of the interior, then over at the man sitting beside her.

Looking like an eager kid to give her whatever his surprise was, he grinned and her heart jerked.

Careful, Sarah. Not only is Jude exactly what your

mother has warned you about your whole life, he's got more layers than you'd have ever given him credit for.

Because the man sitting beside her looked completely comfortable in his tuxedo. Completely and utterly breathtaking, too.

No more so than he'd been in his jeans and T-shirt the other night.

Or in his towel.

Or even in his dirty uniform.

She might even prefer the dirty uniform look because it had been one she could relate to, one that had cracked through the preconceived ideas she'd had about him.

A look that made him real, human, vulnerable.

Vulnerable?

Ha! The man sitting next to her looked about as vulnerable as a double zero agent from a British spy flick.

"This is the quietest you've been since we've met."

"That's not true. I didn't say a single word on the morning you were telling Brandy goodbye."

Why did the memory of him kissing the woman sting so deeply? Why did she always revert to throwing other women between them?

Because she needed something to keep her from forgetting none of this was real, that she didn't want it to be real.

CHAPTER EIGHT

"THAT MORNING DOESN'T COUNT."

At his comment, Sarah glanced toward Jude.

"You and I hadn't met," he clarified. "I didn't even know your name, despite the fact that I had said hi to you a couple of times."

He had. Sarah had ignored him, pretending not to hear, or had just mumbled a reply without looking his way.

Why was that? She wasn't a rude person, wasn't unfriendly. She'd made friends with other tenants in the building. But for some reason she'd felt the need to keep a safe distance from Jude.

Because he was a womanizing playboy.

Only she couldn't say he'd been anything other than a gentleman to her. At the hospital. When he'd rescued her from her screaming alarm. When he'd cooked dinner for her and shared his magnificent view of the city.

When he'd kissed her goodnight.

When he'd surprised her with presents, shown up at her door with flowers, arranged for a limousine for their date, and promised the best night of her life.

He'd been pretty close to perfect since they'd met, which made him about as unsafe as was possible.

Unable to stop herself, she faced him, stared at his

mouth. She didn't question whether or not he'd kiss her tonight. He would.

He wouldn't push or force himself upon her. He'd be just as he had been the other night. He'd give her control as to how far they went and seemed to have no issue with relinquishing that power to her.

She was in control of what happened between them. Her.

As long as she remembered that, held onto that control, she was fine.

"Can I?"

"Can you what?" she asked, wondering if she'd been so lost in her thoughts that she'd missed his having said something.

"Kiss you."

The man's powers of observation were quite terrifying.

"It wouldn't be a goodnight kiss."

His lips turned up a little at one corner. "I guess that depends on your definition of a good night."

Because he planned to give her a good night.

And not kiss her goodnight, but good morning, instead. She could see it in his eyes.

And feel it to her very core.

He was wining and dining her so she'd be agreeable. Which she already was.

So instead of answering his question, she turned to look out the window. "I love the city, you know. Not just the skyline, but the people, too. Where else in the world can you see so many people from different walks of life within just a few blocks?"

"Not many."

"There's nowhere else like Manhattan," she defended the city she adored.

"True. Have you visited many places, Sarah?"

Heat rushed into her face again. He must think her such an uncultured bumpkin compared to the social circles he traveled in as a Davenport.

"Not many," she admitted. She had barely left Manhattan. There was no need. She loved everything about where she lived.

"Your favorite place?" Apparently, realizing what she was about to say, he added, "Besides the obvious."

"London," she answered, although she'd never been. Had never even flown. It was just a place she'd thought she'd like to visit someday. A city whose heartbeat reminded her of her own beloved New York's. "Look." She gestured out the limo's window. "We're about to see Times Square."

His grin was infectious. "You're one of those who stand out there every New Year's Eve to watch the ball drop, aren't you?"

"Absolutely, and don't you dare laugh at me." It was something she'd done for as long as she could recall. She and her mother would stand in the crowded throng of happy partygoers and cheer in the New Year, thinking January was going to bring good things into their lives. Those hopeful moments were some of Sarah's best memories.

The one time her mother was optimistic rather than full of negativity.

"So no worries that you'll turn into a pumpkin at the midnight hour?"

Her lips twitched. "Not on New Year's Eve, at any rate."

The driver pulled the limo to the curb and came around to open their door.

Sarah's breath caught. She was at the Majestic. To

watch a real, live Broadway show. One she'd fantasized about for years.

Another throwback to her mother, no doubt, as she recalled them watching the film over and over while Sarah had been growing up.

Now she was going to watch the show live, had arrived in style with a gorgeous man.

Maybe she really had suffered smoke inhalation from her burnt toast and was still locked away in some fantasy world where men like Jude Davenport showered attention on women like her.

If so, she'd enjoy every moment of her delirium.

Excitement burned through her veins and, as she took Jude's outstretched hand and stepped out of the limo, she smiled. A real smile. One that filled all of her being and left no room for anything other than pure joy.

"Thank you."

"For?" Jude almost stumbled backward. Not because of the people moving around him but because of the woman radiating inner beauty toward him.

Sarah was breathtaking.

How he'd not noticed that months ago was mind-boggling, but now that he had, he wanted to soak in her exquisiteness.

Just as he wanted to see that smile over and over and was apparently willing to go to great lengths to do so.

Which made him question why he was going to such lengths with Sarah. Possibly the hurt he'd seen in her eyes over the idiot who'd stood her up and Jude wanting to erase that pain, to replace those memories with ones so magical she'd never doubt her value again. That she'd never let any man dump on her, because she'd not seen herself as worthy of better. He'd show her how she deserved to be treated so in the future she'd not settle for some man who didn't appreciate what a treasure she was.

Not that Jude liked to think of her with another man, but he wasn't a relationship kind of guy. He'd been a fool to think he had been with Nina. He'd learned better and that wasn't a lesson he'd forget.

Keeping Sarah's hand tucked in his, he guided them through the crowd and into the line to enter the theater.

"This. Thank you. Thank you. Thank you." She glanced around, taking in the ornate decorations visible through the open doors. "This is so beautiful."

Her excitement was contagious and Jude couldn't keep the smile off his face. Everything about Sarah was delightful. Any moment he expected her to spin around as if she were in a dream. Good. That's how he wanted her to feel.

"Just wait until you are inside the actual theater."

Excited blue-green eyes met his. "That good, huh?"

He hadn't necessarily thought about it being so on his previous visit, but he knew seeing the theater, the production, through Sarah's eyes was going to be an entirely different experience for him.

That everything, through Sarah's eyes, was new.

"That good," he agreed, pulling their tickets out of his jacket's inside pocket.

They made their way to their seats and he was glad they were as good as the sales agent had promised. He wanted tonight to be as amazing as Sarah had dreamed of. Better.

Her face shone with the excitement of someone who had looked forward to this moment for a long time and he was the lucky guy who got to share it with her.

Why hadn't she gone on her own when it was something she'd wanted to do for years? Why hadn't she gone with a friend? With a family member? By herself?

"Look. There's the chandelier!"

He chuckled. "Shh, you're supposed to be pretending that you don't see that yet."

She laughed and ran her gaze over the ornate ceiling. "I can't believe I'm here. I'm really here."

At one point in the show, she grabbed his hand and, not seeming to notice, held on.

Jude didn't mind. He enjoyed Sarah's warm, capable hand holding his.

A hand that could save a life.

A hand that could pull him closer or push him away.

No doubt before everything was said and done she'd do both.

A heaviness settled over his chest.

Sarah was different from any woman he'd known. He'd recognized that immediately, had been intrigued by her outside his apartment door, impressed by her at the hospital, fascinated by her at her apartment, protective of her at his, enthralled by her tonight.

There had been few times in his life when he'd made an effort to impress a woman.

Nina. He'd tried to impress her. And he had. As her friend. They'd been great friends, the best, had had lots in common, but Charles was who she'd given her heart to. Wonderful, perfect, brilliant Charles.

He wondered a moment if he was crazy when he began comparing the past with the present, when he wondered if there was something dark inside him that had caused Nina to fall for Charles instead. Jude had wanted to love her, to give her the world, and protect her. She'd loved his cousin and Jude hadn't been able to forgive her for that, not even when it had cost him her friendship and undermined his relationship with his family.

Since then, he'd not dated anyone, just had a flurry of one-night stands that had meant nothing more than physical satisfaction and reminders he didn't have to be alone but chose to be.

He glanced at Sarah, his mind racing in a thousand directions as he watched the play of expressions behind her ridiculous glasses.

Perhaps sensing he was looking at her, she squeezed his hand, her gaze glued to the lavishly dressed cast on the stage. "This is amazing," she whispered.

She was right. This was amazing, but he didn't mean the production.

He lifted her hand to his lips and pressed a kiss there, momentarily distracting her from the show.

She blinked at him. "What was that for?"

"For coming with me tonight."

"I should be the one kissing you for inviting me tonight."

Wanting his melancholy thoughts gone, he waggled his brows. "I'd be okay with that."

Smiling, she rolled her eyes. "I bet you would."

The stage caught her attention again and Jude forced his attention back there, too. Not that his focus lasted more than a few seconds. Because to his surprise Sarah leaned over and pressed a kiss to his cheek, then went back to watching the show as if nothing had happened.

Something had happened.

Something intense and deep and as swirling with rich emotion as the show.

Sarah had kissed him and he'd swear whatever that dark something inside him was, her sweet kiss had just cracked it wide open.

* * *

Sarah doubted Jude would accuse her of being quiet again that night. From the moment the show had ended and they'd gotten back into the limo, she'd been talking non-stop.

With an amused look on his face, he let her chat away, which was just as well because she didn't think she'd have been able to hold back her excitement if she'd had to.

"I thought my heart was going to stop when…" She elaborated on one of the scenes.

"I noticed tears rolling down your cheeks in that part," he pointed out, his smile indulgent.

"My glasses were supposed to keep you from noticing things like that."

His brow rose. "Is that what they were for?"

She knew what he meant and she wasn't going there. "That and the things glasses are usually for."

"Have you forgotten that I know you don't need those things to see?"

"I haven't forgotten."

"But felt the need to wear them tonight to shield yourself from whatever it is you don't want me to see?"

Something like that, she admitted to herself. They were part of the armor she'd been wearing for years.

"I think you see plenty despite the fact I have my glasses on," she accused.

"You hungry?" he asked, surprising her by his subject change.

"Starved," she confessed, telling the truth. "I didn't eat much earlier. I was nervous about tonight."

"Your nerves have settled now?"

"Now my nerves are so electrified from that amazing show that everything else pales in comparison," she gushed, not caring he probably thought she was silly for being so excited. "I have such a rush from the show I'm surprised I even notice I'm hungry."

He laughed and the sound reverberated through her chest and mind, setting off happy bells.

"Just you wait," he promised. "The best is yet to come."

"No food is going to compare to what we just witnessed."

"I take it back," Sarah recanted an hour later as her lips closed around her spoon. The most delightful sugary concoction melted in her mouth and sent pleasure through her from head to toe. "Pretty sure this stuff is straight from heaven."

"Like it?"

Rather than answer him, she took another bite and slowly withdrew her spoon from her mouth. "I'm positive it's illegal and some type of mind-altering goodness that makes the whole world seem absolutely euphoric."

He chuckled. "I assure you it's perfectly legal."

"I know," she admitted, meeting his gaze. "I didn't mean to imply you'd drug me. I don't think that at all."

"I never thought that's what you meant." His eyes twinkled. "Neither would I ever do that to you."

"You wouldn't have to.

Her admission had Jude swallowing hard and her mouth watering. Not because of the dessert.

He'd been the perfect date. Kind, thoughtful, generous, attentive, sweet.

"I've enjoyed myself tonight, Sarah."

"You make it sound as if you don't usually enjoy yourself and we both know better than that," she reminded him, as much for herself as him. She might not do this kind of thing often—ever—but Jude did.

"You're referring to sex. I'm not."

She didn't bother to hide her disbelief. "You're saying sex isn't enjoyable?"

"Sex is extremely enjoyable," he clarified. "That's why it's so popular. But I was referring to a different kind of enjoying myself."

Her heart pounded, the beat echoing through her head. "Does that mean we're friends?"

"No, Sarah, I don't think that's what that means."

"I'm confused." She took another pleasurable bite, trying not to let the fact that he'd stopped eating altogether and was just watching her do so bother her.

"No need for confusion. I meant I enjoyed your company in ways that have nothing to do with sex."

She wasn't sure whether to be insulted or complimented. What was she thinking? Wasn't she the girl who always claimed to want to be appreciated for her mind? For her personality? For what was inside rather than her physical appearance? For her brain rather than her body? Wasn't that why she downplayed her physical appearance to keep from attracting the wrong kind of attention?

The wrong kind? She hadn't attracted any attention in a long time. Not that she'd been trying. She hadn't. The opposite, actually, because she didn't want a relationship.

Her efforts had worked. No one had noticed her. Not her brain or her personality or anything about her.

Not until Jude.

He'd noticed her buried beneath her coat, scarf, and hat. The memory of how his eyes had glinted when he'd looked at hers that morning assured that.

He'd immediately recognized her at the hospital. *Sans* hat, coat, and scarf, even.

Sure, he had seen her in the apartment hallway a few times, but he'd never looked at her prior to that morning, and when he had looked, he'd noticed.

Despite all the reasons he shouldn't have—like that she'd been hidden beneath a dozen, figurative and literal, layers and that he'd been with another woman.

"You're a complicated man, Jude."

He laughed. "Me? Complicated? I'm the least complicated Davenport you'll ever meet."

She shook her head. "That's not true. You have so many aspects to how you really are you make my head spin."

That was why she felt a little dizzy when looking at him, thinking of him. There couldn't be any other reason.

"What you see is what you get," he pointed out, as if that somehow made his claim true.

She knew better.

"Every time I see you, I see something different."

That seemed to intrigue him. "In what way?"

"For instance, right now, you are the very opposite from the man who stayed at the hospital with Keeley."

With a look of disappointment, he shook his head in denial. "I'm exactly the same man who stayed with Keeley. What's 'very opposite' is what's on the outside."

"Explain," she said, hoping he would because she knew his doing so would give her insight he rarely revealed.

"What you see on the outside tonight is what you lump into being a Davenport. That's not who I am."

"You're not a Davenport?"

"By blood, yes, but I'm not like my family."

"In what ways?" Because she'd swear he was a lot like her boss. A good man, only Jude was a whole lot sexier than his handsome cousin could ever hope to be.

"I don't fit in with them, Sarah. Neither do I want to."

"More of a 'march to the beat of your own drum' kind of man?"

He shrugged. "I suppose. From an early age, I knew I wasn't going to grow up to make the family proud."

Which sounded odd to Sarah because he was a man who risked his life on a regular basis. Surely that he was so heroic made his family proud?

"Tell me about growing up as a Davenport," she said, because she wanted to know everything there was about him, to understand why he didn't think he belonged in his prestigious family.

He shrugged. "Not much to tell that you couldn't read in the papers or assume about the kid of a wealthy family. I went to all the right schools, did all the socially expected things of the wealthy, and was fairly miserable."

"A poor little rich kid kind of thing?"

He snorted. "I guess. But don't feel sorry for me. My parents loved me. Still do. They're just waiting on me to get my wild ways out of my system and take my right place within the family."

"Which is?"

"Not being a firefighter."

"Is that why you do it?"

He shook his head. "Not even on days when I'm most frustrated with my family."

"How did you end up running into buildings on fire? I doubt you just woke up one day and realized that's what you were meant to do in life."

"When I was fifteen I lived at the private school I was attending. One of the kids in my dormitory decided

to give smoking a try late one night and ended up setting the building on fire. The place was old, couldn't
have met fire codes, and went up in flames."

"Oh, no! Was anyone hurt?"

He shook his head. "Because of where the fire had
started, everyone on my floor was trapped. Even now I
remember the terror of my classmates, and how, when
the fire department rescued us, I was fascinated by
those who risked their lives to save others. From that
point on, much to my family's disappointment, fighting fires is the only profession I can imagine making
me happy."

She took his hand and squeezed it. "For whatever it's
worth, I'm very proud of you and what you do, Jude."

He didn't say anything, just stared at her in a way that
made her feel as if he were trying to see inside her head.

Trying not to be overly self-conscious at the intensity of his stare, she finished her dessert.

After he'd paid for their lavish meal and their coats
had been brought to them, Sarah was still fighting self-
consciousness.

"Don't do it," Jude said from beside her.

"What?" she asked, letting him help her into her coat.

"Whatever it is you're thinking."

She turned, met his gaze, and felt her tension ease
at the sincerity she saw there. Goodness, he was unlike
anyone she'd ever known. In a good way.

She arched her brow and gave him what she hoped
was a flirty look. "Fine. I won't, but it's your loss."

He gave a wry grin. "Because you were going to
throw yourself at me in the foyer of an exclusive French
restaurant?"

Pretending shock, she covered her mouth with her
fingertips. "How did you know?"

His eyes darkened and he took her hand into his. "You win," he conceded, pressing his lips to the top of her hand, as he continued in a tone that was only half teasing. "I take it back. Do it. Please, just do it."

The fact his words tempted her to do exactly that, that his lips were soft, warm, electrifying against her fingertips, should probably worry her. But at the moment she just felt glorious and as if she was the envy of every woman who'd seen them that night, as if she were floating through some amazing fantasy that was too good to be true.

"Too late," she teased. "The moment is lost forever." But as she stared into his sparkly blue eyes, she mentally corrected herself.

This moment was forever.

CHAPTER NINE

JUDE MIGHT BE in over his head.

Way over his head.

He'd never told anyone, not even Nina, about how he'd felt about his family, about why he'd become a fire-fighter. Why had he opened up to Sarah?

He'd not even thought about it, just answered when she'd asked, as if what he was saying was no big deal.

What was it about Sarah that made telling her things easy? As if spilling his guts to her was the most natural thing in the world?

That she hadn't judged him, hadn't found him lacking for not embracing what it meant to be a Davenport, surprised him. He was used to women who were with him as much due to the Davenport name as they were for him.

Not that there weren't advantages to being born wealthy and a part of the Davenport clan.

For instance, Sarah's surprise.

Penny, his daredevil cousin, had been over the moon at his request. Then again, she'd have likely agreed just to meet Sarah.

He'd made the mistake of mentioning a name, of mentioning how much Sarah loved the city, of how he wanted to show New York to her in a way she'd never seen it.

What better way than from Penny's helicopter?

Or so he'd thought until that moment.

Sarah's face had gone a ghastly pale shade at the sight of the helicopter.

"We're going somewhere in that?" she asked, her voice strained.

"You're not afraid of flying, are you?" He'd not considered that possibility, but knew there were lots of people who didn't fly.

"No." Her tone didn't sound confident. "At least, I don't think I am. I don't know." She gave him a trembling smile and shrugged. "I've never been in a helicopter."

Protectiveness swept over him. An odd protectiveness that felt different from any he'd ever experienced until she'd been telling him about her failed date. Just as then, he wanted to take on her fear, her doubt, and give her the world.

He gave her hand a reassuring squeeze.

"You'll like this," he assured her, hoping he was correct. "Penny is a great pilot. You'll like her."

Still eyeing the helicopter, she asked, "Penny?"

"My cousin Penny," he clarified. "She said she knew you. Among other things, she's a paramedic with Manhattan Mercy's air ambulance."

"Penny Davenport. Your cousin. Charles's younger sister. Of course." She glanced at him and a new uncertainty crept into her eyes. "You get along with her, then?"

He nodded. "She's crazy, like me."

"You don't care if she knows you're with me?"

Not what he'd been expecting Sarah to ask, neither did he understand why she had.

He frowned. "Why would I care if she knows?"

Insecurity shone behind her glasses. "I... I just wondered. I wasn't sure how much your family knew about your women."

Maybe because he was concerned he'd miscalculated on the helicopter trip or maybe in retaliation for the vulnerability he felt at the intense protectiveness she evoked in him, Sarah's comment made him angry. Enough was enough.

"You're not one of my women, Sarah."

She wasn't. She was...hurt by his outburst.

He could see it in how she averted her gaze, in how she looked even more tentatively at the helicopter, in how her grip on his hand loosened.

"That didn't come out right," he began, wanting to rake his fingers through his hair but knowing Penny was watching from where she now stood next to the helicopter. "Let's not talk about other women, Sarah. They don't matter." They never had, but especially they didn't at that moment, when he was looking into Sarah's eyes and wanting to recapture the magic that had sparkled there when they'd left the theater, when they'd been at the restaurant, before he'd spilt his guts to her. "Okay?"

"Fine by me." But there was no sparkle as she eyed the helicopter, just wariness.

"Sarah?" His pretty cousin with long, wavy chocolate-brown hair greeted them. Her eyes were the same blue as Jude's, that piercing Davenport blue that his family was famous for and that they couldn't escape.

"I know we've bumped into each other in the emergency department from time to time," Penny continued. "But we've never officially met. It's nice to meet you."

Sarah went to shake the woman's hand, but got pulled into a hug instead.

Seconds later, Penny had him in a death-grip hug, too. To be so tiny, his cousin packed a punch. He'd always connected to Penny on a level he hadn't with the rest of his family. Maybe because they were both risk-takers and didn't fall into line with family expectations.

"It's good to know my cousin's taste is improving," Penny teased, giving him a playful punch in the shoulder, much as one of his male friends might do.

Sarah's gaze cut to him, as if assessing how she was supposed to respond to Penny's comment since they'd just agreed not to discuss other women.

"As if yours is any better," he teased his cousin back, determined he was going to recapture the joy from earlier. "You ready for this?"

"Absolutely." Penny turned excited eyes toward Sarah. "I'd have sworn Jude didn't have a romantic bone in his body. I was so impressed by his call there was no way I could say no."

Sarah's feet shifted. Jude doubted it was because of her new shoes. "Romantic?"

"Quit giving away my surprise, cuz."

Smiling, Penny rushed them into the helicopter, gave them a quick safety rundown, headsets to put on, and then they were off.

Sarah's hand gripped his for dear life. He glanced at her and questioned himself again. Maybe he should have saved the helicopter for another night.

"Open your eyes, Sarah."

"No." She shook her head back and forth in tiny little movements. The rest of her body was stiff, as if she was afraid to move for fear she might trigger a tailspin that would send them crashing to the ground. "I can't."

Her hand had become clammy against his and Jude mentally swore.

"Have you ever flown in any type of aircraft, Sarah?"

She shook her head.

"Another first, eh?"

Which he probably should not have said as Penny's gaze briefly cut toward them.

"My stomach is still on the ground." Her face was pale, her hand clammy, her lower lip half-hidden between her teeth.

Then she trembled.

Aw, hell. Jude's stomach dropped to the ground, too, because there went that crazy, strange protectiveness again.

So he did what he had to do.

He pressed his lips to Sarah's.

Her eyes sprang open and her teeth freed her swollen lower lip.

Eyes locked with hers, he continued to kiss her, to taste her, to caress her mouth with his. Slowly, she relaxed, her grip on his hand taking on new purpose.

"Hi," he whispered against her lips when they finally separated a few millimeters.

Gaze locked with his, full of trust and so much more, she smiled the sweetest smile he'd ever seen. "Hi back."

His insides flooded with emotion, he searched her eyes. "You okay?"

"I am now."

"Good answer." He leaned his forehead against hers, the top of her glasses pressing against his face as he stared into her eyes. "I can have Penny take us back."

Sarah shook her head. "I think I'm okay now."

Brave girl.

"But you're missing your surprise."

To which she turned to look out the helicopter.
"Wow."

In a few seconds, she relaxed further, but still held onto his hand with a bit of death grip as she stared out at what he'd wanted her to see.

What he'd wanted to share with her.

The New York City skyline from the air.

Penny flew them over the bay, along acceptable flight routes, lingered at all the right places, as if she could somehow hear Sarah's breath catch over the loud buzz of the helicopter.

When they arrived back at the helicopter pad, Sarah gushed her thanks to Penny, who waved off the praise, hugged Sarah again, and gave Jude an approving thumbs-up that caused heat in his cheeks that some might have called a blush, but he knew better.

Within minutes, Jude and Sarah were back in the limo on their way home.

Home.

To his home.

Or her home.

Or to each their own?

As she leaned her head against his shoulder, squeezed his arm and thanked him for the most amazing night of her life, he knew the answer.

Sarah grew more and more antsy as the elevator made its way to their floor. Did she invite Jude into her apartment? Was that how this worked?

Or would he invite her into his?

Either way, she wanted what this night would bring. She couldn't imagine any better conclusion to their wonderful evening than to spend the night in bed with Jude.

That would be the grand finale.

The real surprise.

The first of all firsts.

What would make her stomach soar and drop in ways Penny's helicopter never could.

Feeling self-conscious, she reached out and took his hand, startling him in the process.

He'd been lost in thought for most of the limo ride home. Which had been okay by her, because she'd rested up against him and felt an inner peace at where they were.

Did she have any expectations of Jude beyond the night?

No. She knew better. She didn't even expect him to stay interested until Christmas. She was just another in a long line of women to enjoy the wonderful man he was.

Which didn't exactly thrill her, but he hadn't made any pretense of anything else. Other than that he'd said they'd enjoy each other through Christmas.

Which was so much more than she'd had to distract her from the holiday blah just a few days ago.

She walked beside him down the hallway, planning to take his lead on whether to invite him to her place or to eagerly follow him into his.

He stopped outside her apartment, so she dug into her coat pocket and pulled out her key.

Fumbling a little, she unlocked the door, but didn't turn the handle, just looked up at him. "Are you coming inside with me, Jude?"

He closed his eyes. "Do you want me to come inside with you, Sarah?"

"What do you think?"

"That I want you to come with me tomorrow evening to a party at my station."

Stunned, Sarah blinked. "A party at your fire station?"

He nodded. "The crew will be cleaned up and have their partners with them. It's an annual pre-Thanksgiving meal, of sorts. I'd like you to go with me."

"But...won't they wonder who I am?"

A V formed on his forehead. "Why would they? I'll introduce you. They're a rowdy bunch, but I wouldn't trade them for any other."

He was inviting her to go with him to a party at his fire hall. To introduce her to his coworkers. He was letting her know tonight wasn't a one-night stand, that there would be a tomorrow night.

Smiling, she nodded. "I'd love to go with you, Jude."

"Great." He let out a sigh of relief, then bent and kissed her with the quickest of pecks on her eagerly waiting lips. "I'll text you the exact details in the morning and pick you up about seven tomorrow evening. We'll take a taxi if that's okay with you?"

Did he think he'd set a precedent with the limo that he'd have to constantly repeat?

"I usually walk most places I go," she reminded him, not wanting him to confuse her with someone who expected grand gestures all the time. "We can do that, or take a taxi if walking to your station is too far."

"It's not that far, but we'll take a taxi." With that he took a step back from her and didn't quite meet her eyes as he said, "See you tomorrow, Doc."

With that he opened her apartment door, practically picked her up and set her inside, handed her keys to her, then pulled the door closed.

With him on the other side.

Jude leaned against Sarah's door and fought the urge to rip it off to get back to her.

What had he just done? Turned down an offer from a woman he wanted more than he'd ever wanted any other?

He'd lost his mind. Had to have.

But going into her apartment with her, knowing what would happen, wouldn't have been right.

Not with Sarah.

Not when spending the night with her would make her think she was no different from any other woman he'd ever known.

She was. So very different.

He wasn't playing for keeps so what she thought shouldn't matter so much, but it did.

She wasn't one of his women.

He wouldn't, couldn't, treat her as if she was.

CHAPTER TEN

ALTHOUGH SARAH HAD other plans, she spent the day at a mall instead. Not her favorite thing to do any time of year but as the holiday season was getting under way, the crowds made the whole outing that much more intimidating.

She was intimidated.

She bought clothes to hide her body, to blend in with her surroundings, to not be noticed, things she ordered online and didn't care if they hung on her body all wrong.

That wasn't going to work today.

She wanted to be noticed as a woman.

She didn't want to blend into the background and be a faceless, shapeless, asexual person.

She wanted Jude to notice her.

Correction, she wanted Jude to want her. To want her in every way a man could want a woman.

Which seemed a silly thought. He did want her.

She'd seen desire in his eyes repeatedly throughout the evening before. She wasn't blind. Desire had been there and real. What she didn't understand was why he'd shoved her inside her apartment and high-tailed it.

Her towel-wearing, bedroom revolving door wielding neighbor had not taken what she'd wanted to give him.

Had he thought she'd follow him out of her apartment, to perhaps beg for more, as Brandy had?

Wrong. She'd wanted to spend the night with him, but was not pathetic. She had her pride, her morals. She would not cling or beg. Ever.

She didn't want to have to beg.

Funny, she believed one hundred percent that had she been willing on the night he'd cooked her dinner he'd have taken her to his bed. Last night she had been, and he'd sent her to bed alone. What had changed?

The man really was complicated.

Had he not asked her to go with him tonight she might have questioned whether or not he'd been as attracted as she'd thought, if he'd really enjoyed himself. He'd seemed to, smiling, flirting, charming her hesitations away, but what did she know of such things?

Not much. Too little experience.

Now she wanted to seduce him, to be irresistible to him. Was that even possible?

Ugh. Her head hurt from just considering all the things that had happened between now and the morning when she'd stepped out of her apartment and found a towel-and-woman-wrapped Jude.

"Quit squinting your eyes," the sales clerk ordered, stepping back to survey her work. She turned Sarah first one way in the swivel chair and then the other. "That is so much better. Girl, I'd kill for those eyes. And those cheekbones. Are they implants?"

Sarah blinked at the woman whose name tag read "Cher". "What?"

"Your cheekbones." She studied Sarah's face. "Are they fake?"

Fake cheekbones?

"Um, no, they're all mine."

Had Sarah chosen implants, they sure wouldn't have been the cheekbones she had. She'd always thought them too prominent. Besides, if she ever got implants, she had other, mostly flat, areas that could use curves more than her face.

"Lucky you, girl."

"Thank you," Sarah answered automatically, reminding herself the woman complimented customers for a living.

"What color is your dress so I know how to do your eye make-up?"

"I don't know," Sarah admitted. "I ended up in the make-up department before I made it to dresses. I'm going there next to find something."

Cher's eyes widened. "No dress? Girl, we've got to get your dress before I do your eyes. What's your budget?"

Sarah told her what she planned to spend.

The clerk laughed. "You're funny. Leave this to me. My roommate is a personal shopper in Women's. I'll give her a call and she'll fix you right up."

Sarah started to protest then recalled how much she disliked fighting the crowds. "I guess that would work, but make sure she knows I…" She what? Wanted something that would blow Jude's mind, but that still left a lot to the imagination because Sarah wasn't used to skin showing and didn't want to feel self-conscious in front of Jude's coworkers? Did such a dress exist?

The dress Jude had given her for the evening before had been beautiful, had covered up her body, yet had gently hinted at what was beneath. She'd felt feminine without feeling like she was hanging everything out. He'd done a great job. Maybe she should have hired him to buy a dress for tonight.

Only she couldn't afford the name brands he'd sent.

"Something nice, but not too revealing," she told the clerk, who was patiently waiting for Sarah to finish the comment she'd started making. "It's for a date at a fire department party. I've never met any of them except my date and it's only our second date." Or was it third? Did the night she'd set off her smoke detector count? "I don't want to feel as if I'm pulling up my top and tugging down my skirt all night. I will feel out of place as it is, so anything I can do to raise my comfort level is a plus."

Cher smiled and waved away Sarah's concerns. "Like I said, leave this to me. You want sexy without looking as if you're trying. My friend can do subtly sexy. No problem. You'll be the belle of the fire ball and make your firefighter want to take you for a spin on his truck."

Taking out her cellphone and punching in a number, she walked away from a blushing Sarah and began talking. Sarah couldn't make out her exact words but imagined they consisted of things like plain Jane, boring, out of her league.

Not that the clerk knew Sarah was out of her league.

Not once had Sarah told anyone who she was going out with, or even that she was going out at all. Part of her still couldn't fathom why Jude had asked her out, much less asked her a second time to attend a party at his fire hall.

Maybe he wanted someone more normal to take to where he worked than someone a Davenport would typically date. Someone who'd fit in with ordinary people who didn't sing, act, model, or been born into wealth or prestige.

At least that theory made sense, because his wanting to date her for real seemed too far-fetched.

* * *

"Wow!" Jude gushed when Sarah opened her apartment door. "I should have sprung for the limo."

Lowering her lashes, layered with mascara, Sarah bit the inside of her painted bottom lip. "Is it too much? You didn't say what I should wear."

Eyeing her like she was the sweetest piece of candy, he shook his head. "It's perfect. You're perfect."

"You don't think I have on too much make-up?" she asked, still not feeling comfortable with the creams and powders Cher had brushed onto her face.

Subtly sexy, that's what Cher had said, promising she was going for a natural, but gorgeous look. Sarah had stared at the finished product in the mirror for a long time, wavering between surprised pleasure and uncertainty at what stared back.

"You are beautiful without the first speck of make-up," Jude assured her. "Tonight you are absolutely stunning."

With the way he was looking at her, she couldn't doubt him. He looked stunned in the best possible way.

Sarah smiled. "Thank you."

"Thank you." He took her hand, spun her around, and whistled. "I'll be the envy of every man there."

That he was verbalizing her thoughts from the night before made Sarah smile.

"Doubtful, but thank you."

They chatted during the short taxi ride over to the fire hall. He paid the driver, and they went into the fire hall. Small groups of friendly people of all sizes and shapes milled around.

"Hey, Davenport!" someone called when they stepped inside the large open area where normally their trucks would be parked, rather than just outside the building.

Jude greeted the man and his wife, then introduced Sarah. "This is my girlfriend, Sarah Grayson."

Sarah couldn't hide her surprise. His girlfriend? Was that what she was? Not just a date, but his girlfriend?

She owed Cher big time.

"Nice to meet you." The man grabbed her hand. "We always suspected this one was holding out on us."

"Oh?" Sarah asked, smiling at the man as she shook his hand, then his wife's. "Does Jude not usually bring someone to these things?"

Shaking his head, the man looked at his wife for confirmation and she said, "Never."

The woman's answer surprised Sarah and she glanced toward Jude, who looked as if he'd rather not be the topic of conversation.

"We were hoping the calendar would help him out. Guess it did."

Expression terse, Jude made a slashing motion, trying to silence the man.

Curiosity piqued, Sarah arched a brow. "The calendar?"

"You don't know?" The man slapped Jude on the back. "Hey, fellas, Davenport didn't tell his girl about his modeling debut."

Jude winced.

"What kind of modeling?" she asked the older man, who was all too eager to tell her.

"Here," another said, coming over to join them. "We'll show you."

"Let's not," Jude interjected, sounding flustered.

"Oh, let's," another added, laughing and joining in as the first flipped the pages of a calendar. "Check out Mr. December."

Jude did something Sarah had never seen him do.

He blushed.

Which made it difficult to look away from him to what the men were shoving in front of her. When she glanced down her eyes bulged at what she saw.

Jude Davenport in his fire uniform pants, boots, helmet, and suspenders, but no shirt.

She'd seen him shirtless.

That week.

She knew he boasted a major six pack.

But seeing the visual reminder in print stole her breath. There was nothing subtle about Jude. He was sexy. Seriously sexy.

Knowing his friends were waiting for a response from her, she glanced up and made a scolding noise with her tongue. "Now, honey, you know January is my favorite month, it being the beginning of a new year and all. December is so…commercialized."

Looking relieved at her teasing, Jude shrugged. "December was all they'd give me."

She flipped the calendar pages and let out a low wolf whistle when she got to January. "This guy from the Bronx fire department beat you out?" She gave a disappointed shake of her head, enjoying the men's good-hearted laughter around her. "Clearly, you are way hotter than him. He must have paid off someone."

"Clearly." He leaned forward and pressed a quick kiss to her lips.

"You must have this one hoodwinked, Davenport," the man who'd brought the calendar over accused with a big grin.

"Nah, she's a smart one. A doctor."

Sarah tried not to beam under Jude's praise, but she puffed out a little at the pride she heard in his voice.

"I think I feel sick," a male voice said from some-where in the crowd. "I need some mouth to mouth."

Wow. Sarah needed to go back to the mall and give Cher a bigger tip than the generous one she'd slipped into the girl's hand. Obviously, she'd performed mir-acles.

Subtly sexy.

Sarah would take it.

"Ha, ha." Jude greeted the man, grabbing hands and leaning in toward him in what Sarah called a "bro shake". "Sarah, I'd like you to meet my best friend. Roger, this is Sarah Grayson."

Sarah smiled at the handsome African American man standing next to Jude. "Nice to meet you."

Roger looked her over from top to bottom. Not in a sexual way, more a checking her out to see if she mea-sured up to what his best friend deserved. He must have approved, because his face split with a big smile and he pulled her to him for a hug. "The pleasure is all mine."

"Quit hitting on my girl," Jude warned in a stern voice.

"If you aren't man enough to keep your woman, then it's your own fault if I steal her. Always wanted to date a doctor."

They verbally sparred back and forth a little, all in fun, then Sarah was grabbed by a couple of wives and girlfriends who pulled her over to where several more were uncovering food.

"It's about time he found himself a nice girl to bring with him. And did I hear right? A doctor?"

Cheeks warm, Sarah nodded. "Is there anything I can do to help?" Obviously, the party was potluck. "I'm sorry I didn't know to bring something. Jude failed to mention that."

Then again, after her burnt toast it was possible he had purposely not mentioned the party was potluck for fear she'd burn down their apartment building.

The older woman waved her hand in a dismissive motion. "Jude does too much as it is. You just enjoy yourself and that sweet man tonight."

Jude did too much?

"Jude sent food?"

The woman nodded and motioned to where beverages were set up and the huge stack of canned and bottled drinks behind the drink table. "He has all that sent every year. And every year there's always enough to last everyone for their Christmas party and halfway into the new year."

Sarah wasn't crazy about sodas or sport drinks, but she supposed a bunch of people hanging out at a fire hall went through quite a few. Jude's generosity probably saved the crew a pretty penny.

"Plus, he springs for the turkey and ham, has it delivered," another added.

"And he always caters the fire hall Christmas party. He's a good man," one of the women praised.

"I think so," Sarah automatically replied, then realized what she'd said and that she'd meant her words.

Despite her thoughts to the contrary just a few days previously, she did think Jude was a good man.

She glanced toward him, realized he was looking at her, and just to throw him off kilter as much as he threw her off kilter, she winked.

His grin won out on the off-kilter causing, though, because her knees wobbled at how he was looking at her.

"You're a lucky woman."

Sarah turned to the young blonde woman who'd spoken from behind her.

"I'm Cassidy, Roger's on again, off again girlfriend." She smiled and held out her hand. "Currently on again."

Okay. She smiled at the woman. For the next thirty minutes, Sarah talked with the women while the guys did their thing across the room. Every time she glanced Jude's way, he was either looking at her or quickly did, as if he sensed her gaze. Or couldn't go long between looks.

They shared smiles and winks. Sarah was surprised at how comfortable she felt at the party with the group of women. Then again, they were a friendly bunch and all had wonderful things to say about Jude, praising him for his generosity, which apparently extended way beyond what he did at the holiday parties as one commented on how he'd saved him from losing his home when he'd fallen behind due to his wife's medical expenses. Another commented on how Jude had saved the day when he volunteered at every community outreach event. Another went on and on about he'd started a scholarship program for kids of the NYFD.

His crew and their significant others couldn't say enough good things about him. Sarah took their praise in, marveling at just how deep Jude ran.

When the chief called their attention to say grace, Jude made his way over to Sarah, took her hand into his as they bowed their heads.

For the rest of the night he was by her side. Not once did Sarah feel out of place or awkward.

She felt like she was right where she should be.

With Jude.

Her mother's voice rang in her head, warning she was being taken in, but Sarah ignored the warning. Her mother had never known a man of the caliber of Jude, not by far. As long as Sarah kept in mind that neither she nor Jude wanted a long-term commitment, everything would be fine.

For the second night in a row, Jude kissed her goodnight outside her apartment door, shoved her inside, and shut the door with him on the other side.

It took her all of thirty seconds to come to terms with the fact that he'd done nothing more than kiss her goodnight again. If that's what you could call it when she snapped out of her shock and flung her door open.

To do what she wasn't sure had he been out in the hallway still.

He wasn't.

He had gone inside his apartment.

For the briefest moment she considered beating on his door, demanding he let her in.

Didn't he know she was subtly sexy tonight for a reason? For him?

Instead, she stared at his closed door a moment, then went back into her apartment, confused that she was the only woman Jude didn't seem willing to sleep with despite her attempt at being irresistible. Go figure.

He hadn't bothered to make plans to see her again.

But she knew he would, that they would see each other again, because they weren't through with each other.

Far, far from it.

CHAPTER ELEVEN

WAS JUDE WORKING? Sarah wondered for the hundredth time that day. Or was he at home? Or doing whatever it was he did on his days off from the fire department? Probably do-gooder things like helping the needy and starting scholarship programs for public servants or—

"Dr. Grayson, the CT results are back on the abdominal pain in Trauma Six," Shelley said, pulling Sarah's thoughts back to the here and now.

"Thanks. I'll be right there." She finished charting despite her distraction, then clicked open the CT results.

Gallstones. Which was consistent with the man's right upper quadrant pain radiating to his shoulder blade, nausea, vomiting, and significantly elevated liver enzymes.

The rest of her shift passed in a busy blur. She didn't have time to pull out her phone to check her messages until right before leaving the hospital.

Excitement hit when she saw the message from Jude. Did she want to have dinner with him at his place?

Yes. Yes, she did.

At his place. Tonight must be the night.

Only it wasn't.

Oh, she had an amazing time with him. First, she'd shared the wonderful meal he'd prepared. Then, snuggled up next to him on his sofa looking out at the city they loved, she'd told him a little about her childhood, about her determination to excel, and the academic scholarships that had funded much of her education.

But when their sofa kisses had heated up to the point Sarah had wanted to rip off his shirt and get up close and personal with Mr. December, he'd pulled back. Quickly thereafter, he'd walked her to her apartment on the grounds they both had to work the following day.

As if that had ever slowed him down in the past.

The next night was similar, almost to the point Sarah found it humorous when she found herself yet again alone on the inside of her apartment door.

The next night Jude questioned his will power when Sarah decided to take matters into her own hands.

Literally.

They were kissing hot and heavy on his sofa and Sarah wanted more. Lots more.

"Sarah." He attempted to pull back when she fumbled with the snap of his jeans. "Do you like cheesecake?"

"What?" She blinked at him as if he'd lost his mind. He had.

"Do you like cheesecake?"

"Is that a trick question? Some secret code for an amazing sexual act you want to introduce me to?"

Jude fought groaning. He wanted to introduce Sarah to amazing sexual acts. Lots of them. Not doing so was getting more difficult, but the timing wasn't right.

He wasn't sure what exactly it was that wasn't right, but they should wait longer before having sex.

"I bought dessert but forgot until just now," he blurted out, sensing her frustration. She wasn't the only one frustrated. He was tired of cold showers, but would be taking a murderously long one again tonight. "I wasn't sure which topping you preferred so I got strawberry, blueberry, and cherry."

She frowned. "Are you for real?"

"Last time I checked. Why don't we try some of each topping and see which is best?"

When he started to stand, Sarah grabbed his arm. "Am I doing something wrong?"

She was doing everything right. Too right.

Rather than stand, he leaned back, swept his fingers through his hair, then shook his head. "You couldn't be further from the truth."

"I'm confused."

He felt confused, too, so it only made sense that she'd feel that way. She deserved an explanation. Maybe he could give one without muddling up things.

"I want to take things slow with you," he began.

Her brows formed the V of a deep frown. "Because I'm slow?"

He shook his head. "Because you're different."

She took a few moments before asking, "Is that a bad thing?"

He faced her, clasped her hand with his. "It feels as if it's a good thing, a very good thing that's worth taking our time and not rushing sex. Don't you agree?"

Gaze locked with his, she squeezed his hand. "You don't have to go slow with me, Jude."

"You're wrong. I need to take things slow."

He couldn't explain it to himself so he sure couldn't explain it to her, but he had to take things slow with Sarah. How much longer he'd have to wait, he wasn't sure, just that sex too soon would ruin things with her.

He'd ruined his relationship with Nina. The circumstances were different, but he wouldn't risk doing the same with Sarah. When this was all said and done, she'd look back on their relationship with a smile, would know she'd been special, would still be his friend.

Anything else was unthinkable.

The following week passed quickly. The emergency department had been crazily busy and Sarah doubted it would slow until after the holidays.

She never knew what would be in the next bay. She'd even taken care of a person who'd been trapped in a collapsed subway. She and Jude spent their evenings together, sometimes late into the night, but he always said goodnight at her door.

Her sexual frustration grew every time she saw him, kissed him, ran her fingers over his strong shoulders.

Sunbeams of happiness sprang to life inside Sarah that he wanted to take things slow with her, but that didn't mean she wasn't above trying to speed him up.

She worked a long shift on Thanksgiving, getting home much later than planned. Jude texted to come over to his place when she had showered after her shift.

She wasn't sure how he'd had time to prepare the scrumptious meal, but was appreciative of the traditional food he served. It had been years since she'd had turkey and dressing on the holidays. She'd gotten her non-existent cooking skills from her mother, unfortunately.

Her mother. She'd called her earlier that day, but had had to leave a message, which hadn't surprised Sarah. Her mother stayed busy with her women's home.

"You're quiet," Jude accused.

Not wanting to talk about her mother, she said the first thing that popped into her head.

"Everyone at the hospital was talking about the photo of Charles and Grace in the paper. Did you see it?"

Not meeting her gaze, Jude fiddled with his fork and didn't answer.

"Apparently they're an item," she continued. "Did you know?"

"No, neither do I care to talk about it."

Sara frowned. "Sorry, I didn't know discussion of family was off limits."

He sighed. "I'd rather hear about your day."

"I was telling you about my day, that everyone was talking about how happy Charles looked in that photo. I had to sneak a peek at break and I agree. I've never seen him so happy."

Why did Sarah want to talk about Charles so much? Not that she knew the reasons why Jude didn't want to think of his cousin, but she seemed to bring him up way too often.

"That's good."

Sarah stared at him, an odd expression on her face. "You don't sound as if it's good."

He shrugged and picked up his plate. "My cousin was seen with a woman. I'm not sure how that warrants his being the topic of our Thanksgiving dinner conversation."

"It's obvious you haven't seen the photo."

Neither did he want to.

"Are you going Black Friday shopping tomorrow?" he asked, to change the subject away from Charles.

"You couldn't pay me to fight those crowds."

"You'll be home tomorrow?"

She nodded. "I plan to sit home all day, catch up on my favorite shows, and veg out."

"Sounds like a relaxing way to spend a day."

"Want to join me?" She gave him a hopeful look. "There's room for two on my sofa."

He'd promised to help Roger move furniture. His friend had said they could do that anytime over the weekend, but they'd agreed on the following day.

"How about I take you to dinner tomorrow evening?"

"I'd like that." She didn't hesitate to agree.

"And Saturday evening? Do you have plans?"

She shook her head. "Hoping to spend as much time as possible with you."

Her words spread warmth through him. Sarah didn't play games, just said what she was thinking. Most of the time he liked that quality.

He liked a lot about the woman he spent most every free moment with. Roger had commented on how much time he was spending with Sarah.

Enough time that he'd gotten to know the woman behind the glasses, the glasses she'd not worn around him all week. She still wore them at the hospital, but she wasn't hiding behind them with him. Not any more.

Which was quite telling.

"How about we stay in and I give you a cooking lesson?"

Her eyes widened with amused surprise. "You want to teach me to cook?"

"Somebody needs to," he teased, loving the light in her sea blue-green eyes.

"Okay, but I should warn you that I make a mean burnt toast and hummus."

"You know, lately I've been craving burnt toast."

Several nights later, Jude made plans for him and Sarah to visit Times Square. He'd noted how she'd gone on when they'd driven past it on the evening he'd taken her to *Phantom of the Opera*. Taking her there felt like the natural thing to do.

Watching her felt natural, too.

Excitement glittering in her eyes, she took a deep breath of the cold November air. "The lights, the people, the sounds, it's magical here. Like inside a snow globe."

He snapped his fingers with feigned remembrance.

"I forgot to arrange the snow," he teased, thinking everything with Sarah was exciting, new, magical. Like inside a snow globe. "Next time I'll remember."

"Ha." Her lips curved in a big smile that twisted his insides. "You know what I mean," she continued. "I know you do. I see it in your eyes when we're sitting on your sofa, staring out at the city. There's a life pulse to this city that is intoxicating."

"That might be the fumes."

"You aren't going to deter me from my appreciation of New York." She shook her hat-covered head. "No way."

"I wouldn't want to." He kissed the tip of her nose, grateful she'd quit hiding behind her ugly glasses.

Still smiling, she glanced around Duffy Square. "Where are we going?"

"To the top of that hotel." He pointed to one of the large skyscrapers facing Times Square.

"I bet the view is amazing."

"Have you been?"

She shook her head. "I've heard the restaurant at the top spins so you have a three-sixty view of the city."

"You heard correctly."

Her eyes shone with excitement. "That is so cool."

He chuckled. "You're easily impressed."

"You think? I've always considered myself picky."

"You're here with me," he reminded her, holding her gloved hand within his as they went inside the hotel and headed to the elevator bank that would take them to the restaurant.

"Exactly."

When he glanced her way, she was smiling like a kid at Christmas. Warmth spread all the way through him.

"You're good for my ego."

She cut her eyes upward. "As if your ego needs stroking."

"It has been a while."

To which she turned to him with wide, accusatory eyes. "Whose fault is that? Not mine, because I'm willing. You're the one who's moving at a tortoise pace."

He laughed and bent to kiss her forehead. "It's going to be all the sweeter when we do, Sarah."

"For the record, sweet isn't the adjective I want to use to describe sex. Make a note of it."

The feeling inside Jude went from warm to inferno. "What adjective do you prefer?"

"Hot? Carnal? Sweaty? Needy? Intense? Desperate?"

Jude groaned at the images her words incited. "You make me want to forget our reservation."

Her eyes burned. "Nothing says we can't."

"Except that I want to show you the city."

"City Schmitty," she mouthed, drawing his gaze to her lips. "Seen one skyline you've seen them all."

Jude smiled, reminding himself he would have this woman, those lips on his body, his lips on her body.

Sarah's tune changed as they ate their dinner in the revolving restaurant. She gushed over the view and talked a mile a minute as she often did in true New York style.

"I do love a good view," she praised. "And it's a good

thing I'm cooking again tomorrow evening because otherwise I'm not going to fit into my new clothes."

Jude sat back and listened, thinking she had a long way to go before she wouldn't fit into her clothes, but he appreciated the thought of her not wearing any.

Sex would change everything. If they'd had sex early on, Sarah wouldn't have known the real him, wouldn't have recognized that she was special. Neither would she have believed him if he'd tried to tell her.

There had been too many women. None of them mattered. All had been a means to an end that hadn't worked. Because none of them had changed the past or filled the hole in his chest. None of them had been Nina.

He took the bite of dessert Sarah offered and was struck with a truth. He didn't want Sarah to be Nina.

He wanted her to be Sarah.

Which stunned him a little. A lot.

He didn't need to go slow. Not anymore. Sarah knew him. The real Jude. The flawed Davenport firefighter. She liked him. Wanted him. Was smiling at him as if he was the center of her world.

Only her smile had twisted into a frown and she eyed him suspiciously. "Jude? Are you paying attention to me?"

Staring into her eyes with a clarity he hadn't felt in years, he said, "Absolutely."

Not convinced, she challenged, "What did I just say?"

"That you want to go home and make love to me and use lots of vivid adjectives to describe the experience when I've finished having you all the ways I've dreamed of."

Her jaw dropped. "I didn't say that."

He leaned across the table, stared into her lovely eyes, and arched his brow. "Didn't you?"

"I…" Her eyes darkened to a tumultuous sea color and, without letting her gaze break from his, she nodded. "You're right. That's exactly what I said."

"There's no going back, Sarah. You're sure this is what you want? That I'm who you want?"

He knew the answer. Deep in his gut he knew, but he wanted to hear her say the words.

"Positive." She stood from the table and motioned to their waiter. "Check, please."

Jude hailed a taxi and they rode in silence.

Sarah's brain told her she should feel awkward or nervous, but all she felt was excitement. So much so she couldn't look at Jude because she knew the moment she did she was going to gobble him up.

Literally, figuratively, emotionally, and every way.

So she kept quiet during the taxi ride, during the elevator ride to their floor, and when they stood outside their apartment doors.

"My place or yours?" he asked.

She wasn't sure it mattered, but she immediately answered, "Mine."

He nodded as if he'd known that's what she'd been going to say.

She unlocked her door. They stepped inside. Sarah turned to Jude.

Not to ask him if he wanted a drink.

Not to take his coat.

Not to make polite conversation.

She turned to show him she wanted him, to lead him to her bedroom, and perhaps to keep him there forever.

Jude was way ahead of her.

The second she faced him, he pulled her to him, kissed her lips, her face, pushed her scarf away so he could trail kisses along her throat.

"I want you, Sarah."

"Good." She wanted him to want her. She wanted him to need her. The way she needed him.

Matching him kiss for kiss, she fumbled to get his overcoat off, managed to get the material loose and off him to where it fell to the floor. Her coat quickly followed, as did her hat and gloves.

Grateful for the skin-to-skin contact, she touched him, cradled his face as she kissed him, savored the taste of him, realized how very hungry she was. Starved.

Starved for something she hadn't even known she needed until she'd kissed him.

She tugged at his shirt. "Show me those December abs."

Pulling back, unbuttoning his shirt, he chuckled. "You won't let me live that down, will you?"

"No plans to," she breathed in a husky admission as he finished with the last button. Impatient, she pushed the material back, off his shoulders and down his arms, letting her fingers trace over the bulging muscles in his arms.

She'd touched him before, his shoulders, his arms, but always with his clothes on. Seeing him shirtless, touching his bare skin, burned her alive.

"Are you real?" she asked, her voice catching. "You can't be."

"Real enough that I'm going to carry you to your bedroom and kiss you all over."

"Okay," she agreed, shivers covering her body at his words. "Hurry."

He laughed and scooped her up.

"Oh!" she squealed. "You didn't really have to carry me."

"Afraid I'll throw my back out and not be able to make good on my promise?"

"If you throw your back out then you just have to lie there. I'll do the work and you can just…lie there."

He groaned. A deep growl that came from low in his chest. "Sarah."

"Jude," she countered, wanting to say his name, to hear it on her lips. Jude. Her Jude. Hers.

Although Jude had never been inside her bedroom, he carried her straight there, laid her gently on her bed.

Staring up at him, Sarah waited on his next move.

"This is what you want? Once we do this, there's no going back," he reminded her yet again.

Was he kidding?

"I don't want to go back. I want you." To prove her point she reached for the shirt she wore and lifted the hem upward, glad when Jude helped pull the material free from her body, exposing the underwear her new BFF at the mall, Cher, had suggested.

She didn't boast any phenomenal curves, but beneath Jude's hot gaze Sarah felt sexy, beautiful, feminine.

"I'm almost afraid to touch you."

"We're going to have a major problem if you don't get over that," she warned, her eyes feasting on him.

"Noted." He undid her pants, slid the material over her hips, down her thighs. He sucked in a breath when he took in the barely there black lace that didn't begin to cover her bottom.

"Sarah," he groaned, tossing the material onto her bedroom floor. "No granny panties for you."

Heat rushed into her cheeks. Yep, she'd be sending

Cher tickets to that concert she'd mentioned wanting to attend for having insisted Sarah buy underwear to go with her rapidly expanding new wardrobe.

"I feel as if I've waited for this forever."

"You have." Or maybe it was her who'd been waiting for this forever.

When he undid his pants, pulled them off and, rather than crawl into the bed beside her, instead tugged her around to where her bottom was at the edge of the bed, he lowered to kiss her throat, her chest, her belly, lower, yeah, Sarah was feeling forever.

Forever and ever and ever.

Oh, my.

CHAPTER TWELVE

JUDE WASN'T SURE how sexually inexperienced Sarah was, but she'd told him she'd never been kissed the way he'd kissed her that first time. So at best she'd had a less than pleasurable sexual encounter, but he suspected she'd not even done that.

Which was why he paced himself.

Because what he really wanted was to be inside her. Deep inside her. Surrounded by her. Lost in her. Sarah.

Her whimpers of pleasure, her arches into his touch, her fingers curling into the quilt below her. Never had he experienced such pleasure at watching a woman, at giving pleasure.

He wanted to give Sarah everything. Every nuance of physical delight, emotional delight, everything.

When she looked back, thought of this night, he wanted only memories of perfection. He hadn't wanted her questioning anything, not him, not other women, nothing.

He wanted to be the entire focus of her world.

He was. He felt it in her touch, her kiss, the way she looked at him.

"Sarah?"

Her eyes opened. "Please."

Please. Such a hot word.

He trembled.

Not content to wait on him, Sarah reached for his waist, tugged on his boxers. "Now."

"Now?" Had that hoarse crackling sound been his voice?

She nodded.

Jude shucked his boxer briefs, covered Sarah while supporting his weight so he didn't squash her. He stared down into her lovely eyes and thought he was the luckiest man alive. Had to be. Because the way Sarah was looking at him made him so.

"Don't forget you're a safety guy," she reminded him.

A condom had been the last thing on Jude's mind.

How could he have forgotten something so crucial, something meant to protect himself and Sarah? Because she made him feel safe in ways that had nothing to do with her lack of sexual experience?

No matter the reason, he shouldn't have forgotten. It was his job to protect her.

Always.

Even from him. Shifting his weight to one side, he reached with the other to find his pants, to maneuver the condom out of his pocket, to tear it open while praying that when he looked back into Sarah's eyes reality hadn't set in, that she hadn't changed her mind about them. About him.

Because he was one hundred percent positive he didn't deserve to be with her.

That he didn't deserve the gift she was about to give him. Maybe that's why he'd had to wait so long, so he could give something to her even if that something was simply the new confidence she exuded in herself, in her femininity.

When he met her gaze, relief filled him.

Her desire hadn't waned. She. Wanted. Him.

"This is your first time, isn't it, Sarah?"

A brief moment of hesitation flickered on her face, then she nodded.

His heart slammed against his ribcage. "I don't want to hurt you."

Trust shining in her eyes, she smiled. "You won't."

"I will," he acknowledged, wishing there was a way he could take her pain instead. "But I'll make it up to you. I promise."

Still smiling, she touched his face in what he could only call a caress.

"I know, Jude. That's why you're here."

Making sure she was really as ready as he believed she was, he groaned at the wet heat his fingers encountered. "Sarah."

She strained upward, cradled his face, and kissed him, deep, intense, fully. He kissed her back, catching her cry when he pushed inside with more restraint than he'd have believed he had, almost bursting from the intensity of what was happening between the two of them.

Sex had never been like this.

This giving, this taking, this explosion from the inside out. Physical explosion. Mental explosion. Emotional explosion.

Afterward, as he cradled her in his arms, he was pretty sure there was nothing he wouldn't do for this woman, nothing he wouldn't give her.

She raised a sleepy head to smile. "That was worth waiting for."

Loving how she was looking at him with such happiness, he kissed her forehead. "Agreed. Get some rest because if you're able, I'm going to want you again. Soon."

Her eyes widened. "Really?"

"Is that your new favorite word?"

"Sex is my new favorite word," she corrected, then shook her head. "No, not sex. Orgasm. Orgasms is my new favorite word. Orgasms because that's what you did."

Jude swallowed, thinking she'd better be quiet because he was starting to stir in places that should be content for some time after what they'd done not so long before.

Tilting her head, she gave him a saucy little grin. "Do you think you can do that every time or was it a one-time deal because it was my first time?"

"Only one way to know for sure."

"That's what I figured," she mused, running her fingertip down his chest and into the groove along the center of his abdominal muscles, his ab muscles that had tightened into hard knots. Every muscle in him was hard. He was hard.

"You shouldn't do that," he warned. "You can't."

Her eyes widened in alarm. "I can't?"

"Not this quick."

She frowned. "Why not?"

"You'll be sore tomorrow," he reminded her.

"Is that all?" She shrugged her slim shoulders. "Then I guess you better make it worth it tonight."

Jude did.

"Charles and Grace got engaged!" Sarah gushed out the moment she burst into Jude's kitchen, her hair still wet from the bath he'd insisted she take while he made them breakfast.

He winced. He should have known Sarah would hear the news about Charles proposing to Grace on a sleigh ride in Central Park. Clearly, avoiding conversations about his cousin was going to be difficult over the next few days.

"I heard."

"Isn't it wonderful?" Sarah rushed on, her smile bright. "He sounded so happy when he called a few minutes ago."

Charles had called to tell her?

"That's nice."

"They love each other very much. It's so obvious when you see the two of them together."

"If you say so." Distracted, he lifted the pan lid to check their breakfast. Trapped steam rose and burned his fingers. Jude swore. "Can we not talk about Charles?"

So excited about the news, Sarah was oblivious to his mood and kept on talking. "He invited me to an impromptu engagement party Vanessa is throwing for them tonight."

Apparently, they did have to talk about his cousin.

Not looking at Sarah, Jude let out a long sigh. "How about those Knicks?"

"You must be happy for Charles, surely?"

"We're really not that close but, sure, I'm happy for him." Was he? Jude wasn't so sure.

"You're going to the party, too?"

Vanessa had called him just moments before. The news that Charles had asked Grace to marry him had shocked Jude. Had thrown him for a loop.

"No, I'm not going." When she looked ready to argue, he added, "Let it go, Sarah."

Unfortunately, she wasn't ready to let the matter drop.

"Why does it matter to you that I'm not going, anyway?"

Her gaze narrowed. "Maybe you weren't paying attention, but I was invited. I'd like to have a date."

"So you want to use me?" He was trying to lighten the conversation, to ease the annoyance he'd never heard in her voice before. To just spend the day with her and not think about Charles and Grace…and Nina.

"Absolutely." Sarah didn't crack a smile. "You found me out. That's all last night was. I was using you so I wouldn't have to go to Charles's engagement party alone."

"You're a terrible liar, Sarah."

"So are you," she countered, lifting her chin a notch.

He took a deep breath.

"I'm going whether you do or not," Sarah informed him, her disappointment thick. "Because I care about Charles and I want him to know how happy I am for them. Since no one but Penny knows about us, at least I'll be spared having to make excuses about why you aren't with me."

Did she really think no one knew about them except Penny? His father had called to ask about the woman Penny had flown around. His father hadn't asked him about the opposite sex in years. Fussed about how many women came in and out of Jude's life, yes, but never asked for details. Until Sarah. Which made Jude wonder what Penny had said. No doubt she'd sensed Sarah was special, that Jude wanted to make her happy, that he didn't want to disappoint her.

As he was doing by refusing to go to his cousin's engagement party.

"Is that it? Do you not want to go to Charles and Grace's party because you don't want your family to know about us?"

Old insecurities had appeared in her eyes and gutted Jude.

"They know."

More uncertainty flitted across her face. "Does that bother you?"

"No, and no, that they know about us is not why I'm not going to Vanessa's party."

Taking a deep breath, Sarah took his hand into hers and squeezed it tight. "Please, go, Jude. I can't imagine being with your family if they know about us and you aren't with me."

He opened his mouth to say no again, but his gaze met hers, saw the vulnerability in the depths, and when his mouth opened, the wrong words came out.

"I'll go."

"Really?" She practically leaped into his arms.

Jude wanted to take back those wrong words, but couldn't.

Not with how happy his mistake had made Sarah, but hell if he relished the prospect of seeing his cousin after all this time.

"You look absolutely stunning."

Sarah smiled at Jude's cousin Penny. "That's because you're comparing me to the pale, terrified woman who climbed into your helicopter."

Penny laughed. "You were stunning that night, too, but there's something different about you tonight."

Yeah, there was. Jude had introduced her to what all the fuss was about. The *ahhhh* of why people had sex, why sex sold things, why sex made the world go round and round and round.

He'd made her world go round and round.

She understood why Brandy had begged for more. Understood the constant flow of women in and out of Jude's apartment. When a man was that superb at giving pleasure, who cared if he was just using you?

Only not once had Jude made her feel that way.

Was she delusional?

Could a man like Jude fall for a woman like her?

He hadn't said he loved her, but when he looked at her…

Good grief, she was delusional.

Or something far worse. In love.

She lifted her gaze to Penny's and, unable to hide her surprise, her thoughts, Penny's eyes widened with realization, then a big grin cut across her beautiful face.

"Maybe we'll be celebrating another engagement soon."

Embarrassed that she'd revealed so much to Jude's cousin, Sarah shook her head in quick denial. "Jude isn't a settling-down kind of man."

Penny studied her. "But you'd like him to be?"

Sarah took a deep breath. "My guess is that every woman who has experienced your cousin's attention wants him to be the settling-down kind. He's a great man."

Penny nodded. "Until I saw him with you, I didn't think he'd ever be the settling-down kind either. He's had this restlessness about him. When he called to ask about showing you the city, that restlessness wasn't there. Something else was."

Don't let this go to your head, Sarah. Don't read too much into what Penny is saying. Just don't.

"What?" she whispered, knowing her heart was on her sleeve.

"Excitement. Hope." Penny shrugged. "Anticipation? You tell me. Whatever it is, it looks good on him."

Sarah glanced at where Jude talked with his father, an older version of Jude. "I've yet to find anything that doesn't look good on him."

Penny laughed. "You have it bad."

Sarah didn't bother to deny it. Why bother? She did have it bad.

"Lucky for you that he's just as smitten. Congrats."

Sarah knew it was way too early in her and Jude's relationship for anyone to be issuing congrats, but Penny's words fueled hope. Whatever was between them, she was different from any other woman he'd been with.

He'd shown her she was and she believed him.

He glanced toward her, and she smiled, letting everything in her heart shine because there was no point in trying to hide how she felt.

She was crazy about Jude.

Unfortunately, he didn't smile back. Or respond in any way other than to turn back to his father.

Okay, not what she was expecting, but maybe they were having an unpleasant conversation.

Only when she joined him a few minutes later, after he'd finished talking to his father and was finally alone, he was still scowling.

And abrupt in his responses.

Almost angry.

When another family member came over to talk to him, he dismissed them just as abruptly. Good grief, what was wrong with him?

Taking her arm, he gently guided her away from the crowd to where they stood off by themselves.

"Finally, I can breathe," he practically growled.

He hadn't had any problems with crowds on their other public outings, quite the opposite, so Sarah just stared, not sure what to say or do. She wanted to comfort him, but he didn't look welcoming of anything she might say or do.

"Remind me how you convinced me to come to this damn party again?"

Ouch.

Annoyed at his growl, hurt at his accusatory question, confused at his attitude, she lifted her chin and fake smiled. "How could you forget? I held a gun to your head this morning until you finally gave in and said you'd go for fear of your life."

His eyes flashed quicksilver. "Not funny."

"Yeah, well, neither is your attitude tonight."

"There is nothing wrong with my attitude. I told you from the beginning, I don't want to be here."

"So you're determined to make everyone have a bad time?"

"Are you having a bad time?" he snarled. "You seem to be buzzing from one person to the next and are all smiles."

Who was this stranger who'd taken hold of the sweet man she'd awakened next to that morning?

"Did I miss something?" she asked, totally confused. "You don't want me to smile or have a good time?"

He closed his eyes, raked his fingers through his hair, then took a deep breath. "I want you to have a good time." His tone wasn't thrilled, but at least he hadn't growled. "I was just ready to leave before we got here."

"I'd never have guessed."

"Normally, I appreciate that sharp wit of yours, but at the moment you'll have to excuse me." He glanced around the room, almost desperately. "I'm going to go find something to drink. You want something?"

Yeah, she wanted the man she'd made love to back and this belligerent stranger gone.

Not that he waited for her to answer.

She watched him walk away, watched as people came

over to talk to him. He shifted his weight, didn't make eye contact, and just looked awkward.

What was wrong with him?

CHAPTER THIRTEEN

COMING HERE HAD been a mistake.

Jude had thought going to Charles and Grace's engagement party would be okay, that he could deal with seeing his cousin.

He'd been wrong.

He'd rather be in the middle of a burning building than in the same room as Charles.

Time hadn't changed that.

Jude supposed it never would.

He finished talking to family member after family member who cornered him on his way to get his drink, and finally made it back to where Sarah patiently waited. He'd felt her watching him, and he'd bristled, not wanting her to see beneath the surface. Not that the surface was shiny and attractive.

Far from it. But what was beneath was bitter and hurt and didn't want to be in this room full of partygoers.

"Are you embarrassed to be here with me?"

He cut his gaze to her. Why had he said he'd come? He should have let her come and been sitting in his apartment, watching the sunset over the city. That would have been relaxing, enjoyable, pleasant, not this.

"You know that's not the case," he finally said, wishing she'd say she wanted to go home.

"Then why are you acting so weird?"

Because seeing Charles laughing, touching another woman—her hand, her back, her face—and looking at another woman with love felt all kinds of wrong. Felt like a betrayal to Nina.

How could he? Nina had loved Charles. Had died giving birth to his twins.

Had broken Jude's heart.

Charles had moved on, was in love with Grace, was going to raise Nina's children with Grace, was happy.

His cousin had found genuine joy in life again.

Joy in love again.

Which made Jude itch to escape because he knew how quickly that joy could be ripped away.

Being here felt wrong, felt like a betrayal to Nina's memory, like a betrayal to himself.

Maybe last night with Sarah had initiated that sense of betrayal, of guilt.

He'd been with other women, but they'd meant nothing.

Sarah meant something.

A whole lot of something.

That scared the hell out of him.

He wanted away from this party.

Everyone was celebrating love and happiness. Had Charles forgotten how quickly that could change?

How quickly how all hope could disappear?

Not that Nina had loved Jude. Not as more than a friend.

Neither did he fool himself that Sarah loved him.

She cared for him. He saw it in his eyes, but this was all new to her, and she was enamored with the sexual bliss they gave each other.

"Don't say you aren't acting weird, because you

have no clue what I just asked you," she interrupted his thoughts.

"You asked why I was acting weird," he countered, feeling a little off kilter inside.

"Yeah, three questions ago." She gave a little shake of her head. "This is your family, Jude. Your amazing, wonderful family who are glad you are here, who want to talk to you and spend time with you. Smile."

"If you like them so much, you can have them."

"I wish." Realizing what she'd said, Sarah turned a bright shade of red. "That could be taken in all kinds of wrong ways, so let me clarify that I just meant I wish I had a big loving family like yours. Not that I was implying I specifically wanted your family to be mine."

Well, as long as they were straight on that.

"They're not all they're cracked up to be," he assured her, taking a long drink from his glass.

"At least they're family and they love you."

Not wanting to talk about his family anymore and knowing he was digging a hole he didn't want to be in, Jude changed the direction of their conversation. "Do you not have family, Sarah? Is that what this is about?"

Her face a little pale, she shrugged. "My mother lives in Queens."

She'd mentioned her mother a few times, briefly, but no one else.

"What about the rest of your family?"

"There is no rest of my family," she told him, toying with the diamond earrings he'd given her on the night he'd taken her to the Broadway show. Why had he done that? He'd not bought jewelry for a woman ever.

"My mother ran off with her boyfriend when she was sixteen and lost all contact with her parents. If they are still alive, I've no clue. Apparently, she contacted them a few times early on, but they'd written her off as dead and refused to let her back into their lives. When she told them she had a baby, they wanted nothing to do with me, telling her she'd made her bed and to lie in it. Over the years, she worked about every kind of job there is, usually waitressing. Until she got involved with some loser again, that is, and then we'd end up in a homeless shelter or at one of her coworkers' homes until she could save up enough to get us back off the streets again."

He'd gotten the impression she'd come from humble beginnings, but he hadn't realized the scope of Sarah's childhood, of what she'd had to overcome to achieve those academic scholarships she'd mentioned.

"She lives in a group home for abused women. I used to offer to let her live with me, but she never would. She leaves the home from time to time, but always goes back. This last time, she took a job at the shelter. It suits her. She feels safe there with other women who hate men."

A bit stunned she'd revealed so much in the midst of a party, Jude stared. Yet again, this woman amazed him. He wanted to take her into his arms, protect her from the world, and tell her how proud he was, but she was as bristly now as he'd been minutes before.

"So, yeah, your big, loud, but loving family looks pretty good to me because it's something I've never had and grew up dreaming of." Every word dripped disapproval of his behavior.

"I'm sorry," he said, and meant.

"Don't be. Just appreciate what you have, because I don't believe you do."

"I like my family."

She looked him straight in the eyes and asked a question that told him she saw further beneath the surface than any other person ever had. "Just not Charles?"

The question, the answer, gutted him.

"I don't want to talk about Charles."

Because seeing Charles reminded Jude of how quickly everything could change, of how he had so much guilt over everything that had happened after he'd lost Nina to his cousin.

Sarah's lips pursed with disappointment. In him. He didn't like it.

"Like I've said before," she continued, not backing away from the subject despite his desire that she would, "Charles is an excellent man, an excellent boss and doctor. He's a fabulous father and just look at how he is with Grace." She cast a longing glance toward the couple. "I've met few better men in my life and none I admire more, especially at the moment."

Which was a direct dig at him. Jude bristled.

"With the way you talk about him," he barked, full of dislike at both her words and the way she was looking toward his cousin, "I'm surprised you didn't sleep with him instead of me."

It was a low blow. Jude knew it was a low blow. He'd like to retract the stupid words, but couldn't.

Staring at him in wide-eyed horror, Sarah's jaw dropped. "Did you really just say that?"

Yeah, he had. He shouldn't have. His words had been crass and hateful and stupid.

What was wrong with him?

He'd felt like the luckiest man on earth right up until Vanessa had called him. How could going to a party to celebrate Charles's engagement throw him so far off center?

Make his head cloudy and old hurt, old fears, abound?

Or was it how happy he'd been a few hours ago that was getting muddled up with the past that was messing with his head?

"While you think about what you just said, I'm going to give my congratulations to Charles and Grace." With that quiet scolding, Sarah gave him another disapproving look, then walked over to hug Grace and kiss Charles on the cheek.

Jealousy erupted within Jude the likes of which he'd never known. Irrational jealousy because he knew Sarah wasn't attracted to Charles.

He also knew that Charles was in love with Grace.

Yet jealousy blinded him.

Just as it had before he'd opened his mouth and spewed stupidity.

Blinded him.

To rational thought.

To reason.

To everything.

He found himself behaving with even more stupidity, because before he knew it he was at Sarah's side, wishing his cousin and Grace a mumbled congrats, then guiding Sarah away from the party.

"We're leaving."

She squared her shoulders and looked ready to insist on staying. She must have seen the finality in his demand because she narrowed her gaze and said, "Fine."

The taxi ride to their apartments was silent. Not a silence of gleeful anticipation as it had been the night before, but just stone-cold quiet that dug more and more distance between them.

Sarah was upset and well within her rights to be.

He was acting like a jerk, knew it, but couldn't seem to rein in whatever devil drove his lapse into insanity.

When they reached their apartment doors, she didn't look to him in question, just took out her key and let herself into her apartment. She didn't invite him in, but left the door wide open, so he followed.

She dropped her coat, bag, and scarf onto the sofa, then turned. "Okay, we're away from that 'damn party'. I think it's time you tell me what is going on between you and your cousin."

"What makes you think you have a right to demand anything of me?"

She flinched and Jude hated his words, hated that he'd hurt her. Again. Hated that he felt the way he did, that his insides were black.

Could betrayal and guilt eat away a man's reason?

"Fine. No arguments from me. I have no rights where you are concerned." She gestured to the door they'd just walked through. "Leave."

Pain ripped through him. He shut his eyes. "Don't."

"Don't? Are you kidding me? Don't?" She practically screamed. At least it felt that way. In reality, her voice wasn't much higher than normal. It was her tone, the hurt, the anger, the seething, the fear and uncertainty, the total disillusionment, all negatives that he'd caused.

Just as he had with Nina. The argument they'd had rushed through his mind. He'd been a jerk then, too, when Nina had tried to salvage their friendship.

He wasn't good at this relationship thing. Maybe that was why he did one-night stands.

No, he knew why he did one-night stands.

That had been abundantly clear when he'd seen Charles. He didn't want to get attached, to care again, ever.

Because he didn't want to get hurt, again.

He used Nina as a shield, a defense, a reminder to never let himself care.

He'd failed.

He cared about Sarah.

He didn't want an argument to be his last conversation with Sarah as it had been with Nina.

Which was why he was going to have to admit some things he'd never admitted to anyone, never said out loud.

"Don't make me go," he began. When she looked ready to toss him out anyway, he rushed on. "At least, not without letting me explain."

"You owe me no explanations," she bit out, her gaze shooting daggers. "We've already established that."

He'd done that, caused her anger, her lashing out, and he deserved her to toss him out rather than hear him.

"I shouldn't have said what I did, Sarah."

"Actually, you should have, because I'd gotten everything all tangled up in my head and thought you actually had feelings for me, that I was different from the female parade coming out of your bedroom. Ha," she scoffed, pacing across the room and shaking her head in dismay. "What a fool I was."

"You weren't a fool."

"I wasn't smart."

He took a deep breath and said what had to be said to break through her ire and disillusionment.

"I was in love with Charles's wife."

As he'd expected, Sarah's expression changed, went from hurt and angry to stunned.

"What?"

"I loved Nina." There. He'd said it. Admitted the truth out loud. For the first time ever.

To Sarah.

Probably not the best person to admit that particular truth to, but he'd never been tempted to tell anyone else. Besides, how else could he explain his unacceptable behavior at Charles and Grace's engagement party? To make Sarah understand the dark swirling emotions inside him?

She stared, wide-eyed and with a mixture of pity and abhorrence. "But that's…"

"I introduced Nina to Charles. I brought her to a party with me and was showing her off to my family, thinking our friendship was blossoming into something straight out of a fairy tale. Instead, I got to watch as I introduced my cousin, as she blushed, as she looked at him with an excitement in her eyes that had never shown there when she looked at me. I watched while the woman I was planning to spend the rest of my life with fell all over herself for my cousin, that 'most excellent man', as you call him."

Maybe he shouldn't have thrown Sarah's description of Charles at her, but the words spewed from his mouth.

"I got to watch while she married him, while they shared excitement over their announcement they were going to be parents. I got to grieve in silence when she died giving birth to his children and to fall apart later, in private, when I could let out the pain in my heart. So you'll understand that seeing my cousin fawn over another woman, betraying Nina's memory, then listening to you go on about him, well, tonight wasn't the best of nights."

"Why did you say you'd go?" Sarah whispered, dropping against the back of the sofa, as if her legs would no longer support her.

Good question. Why had he agreed to something so idiotic?

"Because you wanted me to," he said truthfully. Maybe he'd also wanted to see Charles and Grace with his own eyes, because he hadn't quite been able to believe Charles could love again after Nina. Jude's insides shook more than a little as he continued. "You gave me something precious and I wanted to give you something you wanted. Agreeing to go to that party was the only thing I knew that you wanted from me."

Jude had felt guilty that he'd taken Sarah's virginity, had felt obligated to give her something in return, had decided not to make her suffer through another party as the odd man, woman, out.

Great.

If Sarah had known how the night would unfold, she'd have begged him not to go.

Because now so much made sense.

Jude wasn't in love with her. She wasn't the one.

He was in love with a ghost.

Nina Davenport.

Sarah remembered the woman, had always understood why Charles had so completely loved her. She'd been beautiful, gracious, kind, intelligent, and had glowed with happiness. Sarah remembered how much joy Nina had shone with at her pregnancy, how she'd vocalized her happiness that she and Charles were going to be parents, how everyone at the hospital had mourned her unexpected death after the twins had been born. How Charles had grieved his loss.

Somewhere in the privacy of the playboy persona he exuded to the world, Jude had been grieving his loss, too.

Because he'd been in love with Nina.

Was still in love with her.

Sarah could hear it in his voice, in the pain that was still so very raw.

"I… I don't know what to say."

"I don't expect you to say anything." He raked his fingers through his hair, glancing around her living room without really looking. "I just felt you needed to know why tonight was the way it was." He closed his eyes. "Why I'm the way I am."

Her heart pounded in her chest at the gravity of their conversation, at all the implications of his admission, of all her silly hopes and dreams that had taken life over the past few days and how they'd come crashing back to cold, harsh reality. She'd known better. She had. Stupid, silly her. A lifetime of preaching from her mother and yet a few flirty words from a sexy neighbor and she'd gone all stupid. Had gone from being content with her successful career to thinking maybe she could have more.

She swallowed her wounded pride and shook her head. "You failed, then, because I don't understand your behavior any more now than I did then. Nina is gone. Charles has every right to love again. It's what she would have wanted him to do."

"I know that."

"But you blame him that he has?"

He hesitated just long enough that, no matter what words came out, Sarah knew the real answer.

"It's obvious you do. Because you can't move on, you condemn Charles because he has." She didn't need a degree to know that she'd hit the nail on the head. Jude was still in love with Nina and seeing Charles happy had undone him. "Maybe you need counseling."

"I don't need counseling."

"Having sex with half the females in Manhattan hasn't cured you."

His gaze narrowed. "I don't need counseling."

"You're grieving another man's wife. You need something."

"She wasn't his wife when I fell in love with her," he reminded her, sounding defensive. "She didn't even know him."

"She chose him."

"You say that as if you think I don't know that." Anger laced his words. "You think I don't? I lived it every single day. It doesn't matter now."

"Sure it does. You're still living it." She said the words softly, but they echoed around the room as if she'd screamed them from a speaker phone.

Jude opened his mouth to say more, but his cellphone rang.

It wasn't a normal ring but the specially programmed one that she'd never heard but which he'd warned her about. It meant there was an emergency that required him to get to the fire hall as soon as possible.

He pulled his phone out, glanced at it as if he considered ignoring the call, which surprised her, but then let out a resigned sigh as he touched the screen to answer.

Which was just as well.

There was no reason for him to ignore the call. He was in love with a ghost and Sarah couldn't compete with a dead woman. Competing with the beauty queens he usually dated had been intimidating enough. Competing with the memory of lovely Nina Davenport, well, that didn't even tempt.

Jude loved Nina.

Those three little words summarized everything. There was nothing else that needed to be said. Or done.

He hung up his phone. "I've got to go, but this conversation isn't over."

He was wrong. It was over.

They were over.

He was in love with another woman.

Maybe that wouldn't matter to some women, but it mattered to Sarah. She wasn't going to have sex with a man, have a relationship of any kind with a man, knowing that he loved another woman, that he'd given his heart to a woman who hadn't even wanted it, and that Sarah would always be second best, if she was even that.

Maybe when she'd started this she'd had no real expectations from him, but over the past few weeks, expectations had sprouted roots and blossomed. Expectations that, no matter how much she hoped and prayed, could never be met because the man she'd fallen for loved a woman who would never grow old, would never falter or mess up, because she was eternalized in his mind as the perfect woman. Even in real life, Nina had been as close to that as a living breathing woman came.

Sarah couldn't compete with that. She wouldn't.

Better to cut her losses now and move on before she became so entangled with Jude that she couldn't function without him, before every warning her mother had ever preached came to be.

He must have seen that truth in her eyes, because rather than leave he hesitated. "Sarah, I—"

"Please, don't." She stopped him. "There's no need. We both got what we wanted and there's nothing more that needs to be said. Not from you and not from me."

"I disagree. I—"

"You need to go," she reminded him. "Goodbye."

They both knew she meant for more than just the moment.

Still, he hesitated, then seemed to accept the reality of whether it was now or Christmas, as he'd previously suggested, they would be saying goodbye. Apparently he agreed now was as good a time as any, because he nodded.

"If that's how you feel. Bye, Sarah."

With that, he left. No goodbye kiss, no hug, no "It's been fun", nothing. Just bye.

Sarah stared at the door, waiting for the tears, waiting for the misery to rip at her chest and tear her to bits. It was coming. She could feel it.

Oh, she'd survive. She'd move on. She'd go back to her rather mundane existence, but on the inside she'd never be quite the same.

Thinking Manhattan would forever be changed as well, she walked over to her floor-to-ceiling view of the city, meaning to stare out, to draw comfort from what usually filled her with inner peace, but instead her reflection in the glass caught her eye.

The reflection that was very different from that of the drab woman who'd done her best to blend into the background a mere three weeks ago.

No, she would not go back to her mundane existence.

She would live, would embrace life, would embrace the city she loved, and maybe if she got lucky, someday she would find someone who could love her the way Jude loved a woman who'd died years ago.

If not, she would still embrace the woman reflected back at her. She wouldn't hide herself away.

Not because of her mother's warnings, not because of bad dating experiences, not ever again.

She couldn't imagine ever wanting anyone the way she wanted Jude, but they said time healed all wounds. It looked as if she would be testing that theory.

The first tear rolled down her cheek. She didn't fight it, knew more were to follow, and they would have, except her phone buzzed.

Was it…? No, it couldn't be. Neither did she really want it to be. Even if he wanted to continue their affair, she couldn't. The longer she let this go on, the more difficult recovering would be. She'd done the right thing.

She walked to her purse, pulled out her phone. The hospital. That only meant one thing.

With Charles and Grace's engagement party, a lot of the ER staff were at the party so staffing was tight. Her phone wouldn't be ringing unless she was needed.

Just as well, a busy night in the emergency room would keep her distracted from her broken heart.

CHAPTER FOURTEEN

JUDE AND ROGER made their way up a stairwell, one of the few still accessible in the burning apartment complex.

It wasn't known yet what had started the fire in the older high-rise, but the fire had quickly escalated and now encompassed several floors.

More than a hundred people had been evacuated, but there were many more still missing. How many wasn't even known at this point. Several had called in to 911 and were trapped on a particular level where part of the floor above had caved in.

A communication center worker had been on the phone with an elderly lady in one of the apartments for about ten minutes prior to losing the connection.

They'd cleared out known victims on lower floors, getting them to the stairwell, then had been informed of the elderly couple and at least one other who were trapped a few floors above them.

Command hadn't ordered them out yet. "Yet" being the key word because it was coming. Roger and Jude had taken off up the stairwell that so far was still passable. Jude prayed it stayed that way, that they could use it to get the rest of the tenants out.

At least two had died in the fire already. Jude didn't

want there to be a third added to that number and Lord forbid more than that.

But this building had him on high alert. Not that he wasn't with every fire, but tonight every instinct told him he shouldn't be there.

Probably his stupid heart whining that he'd walked away from Sarah.

That he'd left with Sarah thinking that he was still in love with Nina.

He wasn't.

He wasn't in love with Nina.

How freeing it was to think that. To know that.

He was no longer in love with a woman he could never have.

At least, he hoped he wasn't.

Because the walls Sarah had been throwing between them tonight sure weren't reassuring. Far, far from it.

How quickly she'd thrown their relationship away.

That bothered him.

But it was his own fault.

She believed he was in love with another woman. A woman she couldn't fight against or even think ill of.

But she believed wrong.

He had loved Nina. In some ways, he still loved her and always would. But he wasn't in love with her. When he'd stopped and the guilt over their argument, over the strain on his relationship with Charles, had taken over, he wasn't sure. Years ago. Perhaps even before she'd died, although he'd not realized it at the time because he'd been so hurt, so caught up in the idea of being in love with Nina that he'd not let himself see the truth.

Until Sarah had forced him to see the truth.

In such a short time she'd come into his life and turned his whole world upside down.

Made everything brighter, clearer, better.

"Man, watch what you are doing," Roger warned, when Jude reached for a doorway without checking it first with the thermal imaging camera. "Don't open that until we know what's behind it."

Yeah, he knew that.

He also knew he needed to get his brain in gear until they got out of this death trap. Being distracted wasn't doing Roger or him any favors.

He checked the door for heat, determined that the hallway was passable so they could get to the known trapped elderly couple and check for any additional trapped victims. Getting low, he opened the door and they made their way into the smoke-filled hallway.

Knowing which apartment the elderly couple had called in to the emergency communication center from, Jude and Roger made their way there as quickly as possible. Their door was unlocked, but the woman had wisely stuffed towels around the floor, which helped keep the smoke out of their apartment, but made open-ing the door more difficult.

Time was of the essence.

Jude used his shoulder, and shoved hard against the door. It gave and he went flying into the room. Quickly, they located the elderly couple hunched in a bathtub and cleared a path to them.

The man had fallen and injured his leg while try-ing to get them out. Unwilling to leave him, his wife had managed to drag him back into the apartment on a sheet, pulled him into the bathroom, and somehow gotten him into the tub. She'd pushed towels up around the doorway, trying to keep the smoke out, and they'd huddled together, thinking they were probably going to burn alive.

A hellish feeling for sure.

Thank God, they'd found them.

Roger called for back-up and to check the accessibility of the stairwell they'd come up. It was still open and help to get the Johnsons out of the building was on its way.

Unfortunately, Clara Johnson said there were more people trapped on their floor.

"Betty Kingston lives two doors down. I called her earlier, when I got Ed back to the bathroom," the woman fretted, looking as if she might drop from stress and exhaustion any moment. "She said part of her ceiling had collapsed in front of her door. I told her we were in the tub and that's where she was going, too. To her tub."

Two doors down.

"There's another couple who live in the corner apartment. Stanley and Estelle Miller," Mrs. Johnson continued. "Betty said they have to be trapped, too, because the part of her ceiling that caved in knocked part of the wall down with it and would have blocked them in, too, if they weren't already out." The woman gave Jude a horrified look. "What if they aren't out?"

Jude glanced at Roger.

"On it," his best friend said, calling down to Command to see if a Betty Kingston or the Miller couple had been located.

As they'd feared, neither had.

Jude grabbed Mr. Johnson, having the man hold on around his neck. Roger took hold of Mrs. Johnson.

"This is quite embarrassing, you know," Mr. Johnson mumbled.

"I bet you've experienced worse." Despite the severity of the situation, Jude grinned as they made their way back into the hallway. Smoke billowed thickly, so he got low, having Mr. Johnson hold onto his back as he hunkered down and moved them as quickly as possibly down the hallway and toward the emergency stairwell.

"Yeah, when that blasted woman of mine dragged me into the bathroom and refused to leave me, despite me begging her to go save herself."

"Helluva woman you got there."

"Don't think I don't know it."

The man coughed so fiercely Jude feared he was going to have to stop moving and beat on the man's back.

"Sixty-one years and I'm grateful for every day of her stubbornness driving me crazy."

"I understand."

"You got a stubborn woman, too?"

"Oh, yeah. Stubborn and smart. Sarah's a doctor. Works in the emergency room at Manhattan Mercy so you may meet her to get that leg checked before the night is up."

Before they got out of the hallway, the heat had intensified, as had the smoke.

Finally, they made their way to the stairwell and carried the couple down the flights until they met up with other crew.

Other crew who wanted to go the rest of the way up and get out the other missing people.

"We already know the layout of the apartments and where the one woman is hiding. Take the Johnsons down, get them to safety. We'll get the others."

At least the ones on that floor. Others from their crew and from several stations around that section of Manhattan were working other floors in the building, fighting the fire, trying to keep it contained and from spreading to the cracker box apartment buildings that were all around. This fire could easily get out of control and take out the entire block. Or worse.

"Thank you," Mr. Johnson said as he transferred to the other firefighter. "You want me to put in a good word for you if I run across your Sarah?"

"Yeah, if you run across Dr. Sarah Grayson, you do that. Tell her I'm sorry and that I'm crazy about her, while you're at it," Jude called, as he took back off up the stairwell, Roger close on his heels.

Jude and Roger made their way back to the floor, back down the smoke-filled hallway, and had to bust into Betty Kingston's apartment using their axes.

Fortunately, they rescued the terrified frail little woman from right where Clara Johnson had said they'd find her. Her tub. She'd inhaled a lot of smoke and was slightly asphyxiated, but otherwise appeared okay.

Except that she was too weak to make her way out of the apartment. Which wouldn't be a problem, except Ms. Kingston wasn't the only victim still on the floor.

"The Millers," the woman said, amidst a hacking coughing spell.

They needed to get her out, but get to the other couple, too. The other couple they weren't even for sure were there, but who might be trapped in the apartment next to Ms. Kingston's. The woman certainly was convinced they were in the apartment.

"Let's get her to the stairwell," Roger said. "We'll hand her over to back-up, then go back for the Millers."

As they made their way out into the floor hallway, they heard a crash from one of the apartments a few doors down from where they were. Not the apartment where the couple might be but close.

Just then the fire truck's horn blare could be heard above the fire. Once. Twice. Again.

Roger turned back, his gaze meeting Jude's. "Not this time, man. We've got to get out of here, and you know it. I've a bad feeling. This building is about to go."

Jude cursed.

"You're right," he said, knowing there was no time to waste. "Let's get out of here."

Roger's look of relief that Jude wasn't insisting they clear the other apartment was almost palpable.

Roger loaded up the woman and they made their way to the stairwell.

They were leaving a couple to die. A couple they were in fairly close proximity to.

Someone's family.

Someone's father, mother, sister, brother, cousin.

Cousin. Jude needed to apologize to his cousin.

To tell Charles he was sorry he'd shut him out of his life despite multiple efforts on Charles's part to heal whatever rift that had come between them.

Despite Nina's efforts to heal the rift.

Of course, Charles had never understood Jude's distancing himself. How could he have when he'd never known how Jude had felt about Nina?

Yeah, he needed to apologize to his cousin.

And to Sarah.

He needed to tell Sarah how he felt about her.

Sarah. Beautiful, sweet Sarah.

She might think their conversation was over, but he knew better, had known better when he'd left her apartment. If it took him the rest of his life, he'd make tonight up to her, would prove to her that he was a better man than the one he'd shown her at Charles and Grace's party.

He was a better man.

He was a man who did the right thing.

The right thing wasn't leaving a trapped elderly couple to burn alive.

Jude stopped, waited to make sure his partner made it to the stairwell, then saluted his friend, who had realized Jude wasn't immediately behind him and was shaking his head and mouthing all kinds of foul words.

Jude turned back to get the Millers.

A risky, foolish move. You didn't go off on your own in a burning building. You stayed with your partner for the safety of both of you.

His partner would do the right thing, too, would get Betty Kingston down those stairs and to safety. Roger would be all right. If all went as planned, Jude would have the Millers busted free and would be down those stairs with them before Roger had time to attempt coming back for him.

If Jude died in the process of making an exit for the Millers, then so be it.

There were worse things than laying your life down for others.

CHAPTER FIFTEEN

"Earlier I meant to tell you how fabulous you looked, but now you look as tired as I feel after being here all day. You okay?"

Sarah glanced at Shelley. Fabulous wasn't how she'd have described herself at any point that evening. Well, prior to Jude and her arriving at the engagement party Sarah had felt a bit like a belle on her way to a ball. As if she'd been the star of the evening, shining for Jude.

Ha. If so, that star had burned out and now there was a painful gaping black hole where hope had once shone.

"Even before I got here, it had been a long night," she admitted, squirting hand sanitizer on her hands and rubbing them together as she readied to go to the next patient. "But I'm fine."

"It's just getting started. Sorry you got called away from Charles and Grace's party. Especially with as glam as you looked when you got here."

"I was in scrubs when I got here," she reminded her.

"Yeah, scrubs and make-up and a fancy hairdo. You looked like a movie star doctor."

"That's funny." But neither Sarah nor Shelley were laughing. Or dallying to talk as they quickly moved from one patient to the next.

"Hot date?"

Her date had been hot. He'd also been a jerk. And admitted he was in love with another woman. No biggie.

"I went out with my neighbor, but it wasn't a big deal. We're not dating."

Not anymore.

But for the past few weeks she'd felt…alive. Wonderfully, femininely alive.

The night before she'd felt amazingly alive in Jude's arms. Then, poof, he'd transformed into someone totally inconsistent with who she'd believed him to be.

Because he'd gotten what he'd wanted and was ready to move on?

He was usually a one-night-stand man, but maybe he'd given her a few weeks because she'd been a virgin?

He probably had treated her more delicately because of her inexperience, but she believed his reasons for his bad behavior. He'd been in love with Nina and had shut off a part of himself when she'd died, had shut himself off from his family.

On autopilot, Sarah treated another patient, deeming the young man's severe abdominal pain to be a renal stone.

Sending over a prescription to manage his pain until he could be seen by Nephrology in clinic, Sarah typed in discharge orders and stepped out of the bay.

The emergency department was crazily busy. People, both patients and hospital personnel, were everywhere. In addition to the usual influx of patients, an apartment building filled mainly with low-income elderly had caught fire. Two people were confirmed dead. Dozens more had been rescued and brought in for smoke inhalation and minor burns. The hospital was still on standby as more were trapped inside the building.

Last she'd heard the fire was running rampant and out of control.

Was Jude there?

Of course he was.

That had to be the emergency call he'd gotten right before he'd left her apartment.

He was there. Probably inside that burning building, risking everything for strangers.

Because that's what he did.

Risked everything for strangers.

That's why he had the steady flow of different women.

Because he wouldn't let anyone get close.

Why he had invested more time with her than he generally gave, she wasn't sure. No doubt he regretted having done so, regretted having admitted the truth.

Not that he had to worry that she'd tell Charles. Jude's secret was safe with her. It wasn't her place to try to heal the rift between the two cousins, or to try to get Jude the counseling he so obviously needed that he couldn't let go of a dead woman's memory.

He'd put Sarah in her place tonight.

Her place wasn't to interfere in his life in any shape, form, or fashion.

He didn't let anyone interfere in his life, not friends or family or women. He kept them all at a distance and preferred it that way.

"You okay?"

Sarah blinked at her nurse. "Fine."

"You zoned out on me for a few seconds. You've been running since you got here. You need a short break or a drink or something?"

Sarah shook her head. "Sorry. Got lost in my thoughts, but I'm fine. Who's next?"

Every bay was full of smoke inhalation victims. Some with burns, some not. Every respiratory therapist in the hospital was administering oxygen and nebulizer treatments and whatever else was needed to keep airways open. Fortunately, so far only a few had had to be intubated, but from the calls they were getting from EMS, more victims were on their way.

Other hospital personnel were talking to family members and less critical patients who they'd stuck in the waiting area, offering drinks, blankets, and just a comforting pat on the hand in some cases.

All the acutely critical had been seen to and were being appropriately cared for. Now Sarah and the other providers would start chipping away at the overflow of minor injuries and other anomalies that had sent folks into the emergency room on a Saturday night.

Or so she'd thought.

At that moment, a gurney came rushing in, with another close on its heels. An elderly man and an elderly woman.

Paul was the paramedic with the elderly man who appeared to be in worse shape than the woman on the second gurney. Both wore oxygen masks, but the woman kept taking hers off to talk to the paramedic pushing her.

They had no empty bay to put either of the new patients, but hopefully the kidney stone patient would be out of his room soon. Plus, the transport crew was on their way to admit another patient up to the medical floor. Goodness knew the emergency room was giving them a workout with so many more than normal admissions thanks to the smoke inhalation victims needing respiratory observation at least overnight.

Sarah rushed over to meet Paul since the elderly man

appeared to be more critically injured. "There's not an empty bay. Let's pull him over this way so he's not in the direct line of traffic and you can give me report while I do my assessment."

"Ed Johnson and his wife, Clara…" Paul gestured over to the other gurney "…were trapped in their apartment bathroom. Like almost everyone brought in tonight, Ed is suffering from smoke inhalation, but his main injury is from a fall that occurred when he and his wife were trying to get out of the building."

"Tripped over my own two feet," the man said between coughs, his words muffled by his oxygen mask.

"His wife is a retired nurse and took a rolled-up bed sheet, put it under his arms, and dragged him back into their apartment. She blocked their doors with wet towels, and barricaded them in their bathroom where she called 911 and begged for help."

For a brief moment Sarah tried to imagine the pure terror the couple had to have felt. She shuddered.

"Thank God someone got to them."

Paul nodded, then a light dawned on his face. "Actually, it was my buddy, the one you met with the little girl a couple of weeks ago, who pulled them out."

"Jude?"

"That's him." Paul grinned. "Figured you'd remember him. He's that kind of guy."

Jude had rescued the couple, had saved their lives.

"Were they the last of the victims?" she asked, hopeful.

Paul's smile faded and he shook his head. "There were still others trapped. They'd called for everyone to evacuate the building as we loaded the ambulance with the Johnsons."

"Jude was out then?" she asked, praying that he'd heeded the warning.

Paul shook his head. "I don't think so. Like I told you before, that man is first one in and last one out." Paul finished giving report, then took off to get back to the fire scene, ready for the next load.

"Good man," her patient said through his oxygen mask after Paul had left.

"Paul? I only know him from coming into contact with him here, but, yes, he seems to be."

Mr. Johnson shook his head. "Didn't mean him."

It took Sarah a few seconds to realize Mr. Johnson meant Jude.

"I'm glad he got you out."

Mr. Johnson coughed so hard his oxygen sats dropped several points and Sarah began to wonder if she was going to have to suction, then intubate him.

When he finally cleared his throat, he grabbed Sarah's hand. "You're Dr. Sarah Grayson?"

She blinked in surprise. "I am."

"Said he was sorry."

"You must be…" She started to say "confused", but why else would Mr. Johnson say something of the sort unless Jude had indeed talked about her?

The question was why? Why would he say anything about her at all? Much less tell a virtual stranger that he was sorry?

"He said I might see you here." Mr. Johnson paused to cough and this time Sarah did suction him to clear the mucus from his throat.

When the man had caught his breath, he continued as if nothing had happened. "He told me if I saw you here to put in a good word and tell you he was sorry and that he was crazy about you."

Sarah's head spun. Jude had sent word to her? Why?

"He was going back for Betty Kingston. She was in her bathroom, too. Whole place was up in flames." The old man coughed again. "I hope he found Betty. And the Millers. And got out of that inferno."

Sarah's heart pounded. Jude was inside a burning building. He was in danger.

The thought gutted her. Made her want to call him and beg him to get out of the building if he wasn't already.

She closed her eyes, took a deep breath.

Examining Mr. Johnson, Sarah ended up admitting him to the medical floor and consulted orthopedic surgery. Bedside X-ray had shown he'd fractured his right hip when he'd fallen. Mrs. Johnson had suffered mild smoke inhalation and had been discharged. As Sarah expected, the woman stayed with her husband rather than leave.

Then again, her home had burned. She might not have anywhere else to go. Not that Sarah thought she'd leave even if she did.

Ambulances dropped off victims from a motor vehicle crash. Pedestrians came in with abdominal and chest pain. The ER stayed crazy. Sarah was swamped. But her heart wasn't fully on what she was doing.

Because no Betty Kingston or Millers had come into the emergency department and if they were who Jude had gone back for, surely they should be out by now? Should be in the emergency department, being given a good once-over even under the best of circumstances of being trapped inside a burning building.

Had Jude gotten them out?

Had Jude gotten out?

"Oh, God!" Shelley breathed, catching Sarah's attention. Her friend had just been at the unit desk and her face was pale. "That building that was on fire collapsed."

Collapsed.

Jude!

"Was everyone out?" she managed to squeak from her tight throat.

Shelley shook her head. "Per the call that just came in there were people still inside. Firefighters, too."

The room spun around, making Sarah think she might fall to her knees.

First one in. Last one out.

Wasn't that what Paul had said? Please, no.

Please, just, no.

"Sarah?"

Insides shaking, she stared at Shelley. "My neighbor works for the fire department."

"Your neighbor?"

Jude was so much more than her neighbor. He was... her heart.

Sarah's personal life never interfered with her work. Never.

But for the life of her she couldn't focus.

Couldn't think.

Could only feel.

Jude.

"Sarah?"

"I...um...sorry. I'm feeling a little light-headed. I'm going to grab that drink, Shelley. Be back in a few."

Sarah slid into the break room and leaned against the doorway. Breathing hurt.

Everything inside her hurt.

She couldn't think the worst. Jude might not have been in that building. Even if he was, he could be just fine. She had to pull herself together. She had patients to see, had to get through the night no matter what happened.

She needed to get back out there because she could hear nearing ambulance sirens wailing. Grabbing a cup, she filled it to the brim from the water dispenser, then downed it.

She needed something much stronger, but that would have to do.

She had this. Whatever the night brought. She had this.

Only when the doors opened and an elderly woman and a badly burned couple were rushed in, Sarah had to mentally brace herself.

The Millers and Betty Kingston.

No Jude.

Which probably meant that he was fine. He'd rescued them and was still there, fighting the fire.

Only Sarah's inside hurt and couldn't let go of the fear inside her.

Sarah and two other docs examined the new patients, taking over their care. Sarah had just gotten Mr. Miller ready to admit when there was another commotion as a group rushed in.

A group of firefighters carrying an unconscious Jude.

Sarah rushed over to the group, trying to get close enough to examine the man they carried.

"Bring him in here," she insisted, thanking God that the transport crew had just come and emptied the room minutes before.

Shelley was there, wiping down the bed and throwing a clean sheet over it even as the men set Jude down. Immediately, Sarah had oxygen on him, helped

Shelley undress him to get telemetry hooked up. She flinched at the deep purplish bruises across his ribs, across his shoulder, but said a silent little thank you at the strong beep that filled the room with its reassuring sound.

"He insisted the three ambulances at the scene take the others, rather than him, that he'd wait until another showed up," one of the men she'd met at the fire hall said.

"When he lost consciousness, we decided there wasn't time to wait for another ambulance to show," Roger said, his gaze focusing in on what Sarah was doing and helping her get Jude situated on the bed as she cleaned a spot to start an intraosseous line. "So we loaded him up and brought him in the fire truck."

"Got him here faster than another ambulance could have gotten to us," another of the crew Sarah had met at the fire hall party piped up. "Much less have gotten him here."

Even while she listened to his crew tell about how Jude had gone rogue to rescue the Millers and had them almost out when another section of the building had caved in, she, Shelley and another nurse worked on him. They started the intraosseous line and got only a grunt from Jude.

That grunt was priceless, though, because it meant he had felt pain, that he was in there.

"He managed to clear a path to get them out by holding up a beam for the Millers to crawl beneath. After the couple had cleared the building, they were that close, he tried to clear himself of the beam to get out, but triggered another cave-in that trapped him beneath rubble."

"Roger there had tried to go back in the moment he had the Kingston woman out, but Command restrained him. There was no restraining any of us when the Millers came out and we realized he was trapped twenty feet or so from an exit."

Thank God Roger and whoever else of Jude's crew had gone back in.

His blood pressure was low, his pulse slightly elevated. His oxygen was lower than it should be but not dangerously so. Yet.

Sarah gave another order to Shelley, preparing to establish an airway. She needed to get Jude stable, to be prepared for any scenario, so they could get scans to check for internal injuries in case of hemorrhage.

Please, don't let him be hemorrhaging.

Please, let him be okay.

Please, guide my hands and my mind as I do this.

Oh, God, how could she do this? How could she not? She didn't want anyone working on Jude other than herself. She needed to make sure everything possible was done, everything.

Sarah intubated Jude, not quite believing she was doing this to him. Her hands shook. She panicked just a little when the tube met more resistance than it should have. Mentally talking her way through what she was doing, she got the tube situated, sighing in relief when she checked placement and it was good.

Heartbeat low but steady. Airway established. Fluids going. Meds going.

Vitals stable for the moment.

She glanced around at the haggard, dirty crew who'd carried Jude into the emergency department. "I'm taking him for imaging to check for internal injuries and fractures. Other than insisting that he wait for the next ambulance, did he say anything particular before he went out? Mention somewhere he was hurting? That kind of thing?"

"We carried him out, but I don't think he'd broken anything. He'd had the air knocked out of him by the debris that fell on him."

"What kind of debris?"

"The big kind. Beams, ceiling tiles, dust, who knows what all that was? Visibility was next to nil and we were digging him out as quick as possible because the upper floors of the building were gone. We could hear explosions going off and although that ground floor wasn't on fire, the weight of everything above was pushing down hard and stuff was falling almost as fast as we could clear it.

"We cleared him of the building. Had him lying on the ground, but he was talking some. He kept saying your name."

She placed her hand over Jude's, squeezed the warmth she found there.

"He's going to be okay, isn't he?"

Sarah's gaze met Roger's. "He has to be."

Which said it all.

CHAPTER SIXTEEN

JUDE'S HEAD HURT. So did his body. But it was a strange hurt, almost as if he were experiencing the pain from somewhere far away from reality.

Breathing wasn't easy and his lungs felt full of dust and smoke.

The smoke put hazy thoughts into his head. Hazy thoughts of being in a burning building, weighed down in his gear. No, it wasn't his gear weighing him down. It was the building itself.

On top of him.

He couldn't move.

He tried to call out for help, but words wouldn't come. He tried to call for Sarah. He needed to tell her he was sorry, to tell her he wouldn't let their last conversation be an argument, as it had been with Nina. But no words sounded. Nothing. Just silent screams in his head.

Nina was there, too. Holding her hand out to him, telling him to come with her.

His voice wouldn't work or he'd have told her he didn't want to go. Not with her. His place was beside Sarah.

His heart belonged to Sarah.

He tried to tell Nina but smoke choked him, gagging him, making him feel as if he couldn't breathe.

But he must be because his chest was rising and falling. He could see it doing so, felt the pain with every expansion of his chest.

Even in his fog he realized he shouldn't be able to see himself, shouldn't be seeing the rise and fall of his chest. Yet he did.

He was lying in a hospital bed. His eyes were closed. He wasn't moving other than that chest rise and fall.

But he wasn't causing that excruciating rise and fall.

A machine breathed for him.

Somewhere in the fog he knew that should alarm him, but instead his attention went to the group huddled around him. His work family. Each and every one of them.

And Sarah.

Then they were all gone and a loud noise spun around him, sounding as if it was closing in on him.

Above that, Nina's voice came to him, calling him again.

"Sarah." He tried to answer, but couldn't. He went to reach for his throat to find out why he couldn't speak, but couldn't move his hands.

Nina's voice grew louder, beckoning him.

The radiology crew got the computerized tomography scans and X-rays and had Jude back in an emergency room bay in record time. Sarah stayed at his side except for the few minutes he was in the CT machine and then she waited next to the tech, ready to act if anything changed on Jude's vitals.

She'd consulted Pulmonology to assess his lungs. Neurology to assess his lack of consciousness. And wished she had a dozen more specialists to check him over in case she'd missed something. Logically, she'd gone over everything she knew to go over, was trying to look for any unknowns, and now it was a waiting game. If he stayed stable, she'd eventually have to transfer his care to the intensive care unit, but until she had to, she planned to keep him as close as possible.

The imaging tests showed no internal bleeding but lots of swelling and contusions. His chest images also showed that he'd fractured two ribs when the debris had fallen on him. Fortunately, they weren't displaced and hadn't punctured a lung or caused any significant soft-tissue damage.

"Thank you for what you're doing for him, Sarah."

She glanced over at where Roger stood, looking dirty, exhausted, ready to drop. Actually, all the fire crew did. No wonder. They'd gone from fighting fires and rescuing people to rushing one of their own to the emergency room.

"Roger, I'm going to take you guys to a private waiting area. It's actually where Jude waited the night we met when he'd brought in a little girl he rescued."

"I remember," Roger said. "But if it's all the same to you, we'd like to stay here with him."

"I understand. At least let me see if I can rustle up some chairs and some drinks, then."

"That would be great."

Sarah turned to go in search of vacant chairs and bottled drinks, but when she let go of Jude's hand, he grabbed her hand back.

"Oh," she gasped, shocked at the movement. Thrilled at the movement. "Did you see that?" she asked of no one in particular. "He moved."

"That he did, Doc. I think he wants you to stay right where you are. I tell you what," Roger said. "If you'll send us in the right direction we'll take you up on that drink and maybe a bathroom where we could wash up a little."

"Of course. Get the nurse who was in here earlier. Shelley. She'll take care of everything."

Roger nodded, then touched Jude's upper arm. "Wake up, my brother. I had a hot date tonight and I'm late, thanks to that fire and your nap."

Jude's hand jerked against hers and a noise came from somewhere deep in his chest as the crew each said something to Jude before leaving the room.

Sarah's eyes watered at the bond between them.

When she was alone with him, Sarah laced her fingers with Jude's. "Jude? Do you hear me? It's Sarah."

His hand jerked against hers again. For a moment she wondered if his movement was reflexive rather than intentional. However, when he squeezed her hand in a few rhythmic pulses her heart soared.

Intentional. Thank you, God, intentional.

"Jude," she said, fighting to keep her voice clear as tears almost choked her. "This is Sarah. You're in the emergency room. If you hear me, open your eyes."

Nothing.

She squeezed his hand a little tighter than normal. "Open your eyes for me, Jude."

He squeezed back again.

Sarah pulled her hand away so she could do a quick neuro check to see if he reacted to stimuli.

Pulling out a sharp point from her scrub pocket, she pressed it against his fingertip. Jude grimaced. Sarah smiled. She'd not gotten any response when she'd checked him prior to his imaging tests.

She ran through several other neuro tests, getting reactions to each one, then moved on to the one she'd been saving for last. Mainly because looking into his eyes earlier and seeing nothing but a blank stare had almost sent her into sobs.

She pushed his eyelids open, stared into the most beautiful blue eyes she'd ever gazed into and shone her light. As before, they responded appropriately to light, but he wasn't seeing her.

Or maybe he was because his stare wasn't blank. Not like before.

Jude saw her.

Some might think it was her imagination or wishful thinking but she knew better. Jude was seeing her.

She leaned closer, her face about six inches above his. "It's time for you to wake up, Jude Davenport. Do you hear me? Wake up."

Jude heard Sarah. Loud and clear. She was telling him to wake up.

Which didn't make sense because he was awake.

"Wake up, Jude," she insisted, louder.

His throat hurt. So did his head. And his body. He hurt all over.

"You know, tonight has been a really sucky one for me. First, you act like a total jerk at Charles and Grace's party. Then we argue and you break my heart. As if that isn't enough, you have the nerve to show up in my emergency room unconscious and I have to be nice to you. That's really not fair when I just want to not like you."

They'd argued.

Sarah had told him goodbye.

She wanted to not like him.

His heart hurt to go along with everything else.

He and Sarah had argued. He had to tell her he was sorry—tell her he hadn't meant to break her heart.

"And your crew are all worried and refusing to leave. You sure you aren't just playing possum to get attention?"

Jude tried to say her name, thought he might have, but she didn't respond if he had. Great. He'd try again, but couldn't because of his throat.

He reached up, pulled at the tubes.

"Stop that," Sarah ordered. "I worked hard to get that in place."

Sarah had done that to him?

His hand fell away.

And his eyes opened.

She was right there in front of him. Mere inches from his face. Sarah.

Sarah's breath caught. Jude was awake, was looking at her, tracking her with his eyes, seeing her.

He was seeing her!

"Hello, there," she whispered, not caring that tears streamed down her face.

He wanted to say something back, but couldn't, seemed irritated at the ventilator tubing. She glanced at his oxygen saturation. With the vent delivering oxygen, he was satting at ninety-nine percent.

She wanted to take the vent out.

If she did and he wasn't ready, she'd have to put it back in, would be risking injury, might not be able to re-establish an airway and would never forgive herself.

But truth was if it had been anyone else, she'd have pulled him off the vent already because she didn't think he needed it. Not anymore.

Maybe he never had, but she hadn't been willing to risk not maintaining an airway.

"I'm going to pull the vent, Jude. Don't you dare

make me regret doing so," she ordered, gloving up and pulling the tubing from him.

He groaned during the removal, but sighed once he was free of the tube.

His hand went to his throat and rubbed the area as if that would somehow help.

"Your throat is going to be scratchy and sore for a while from the tube," she warned, as she put oxygen on him.

"Sarah."

Her hoarse name on his lips weakened her knees. "You shouldn't be talking. Just be quiet and use your energy to get better."

He shook his head, put his hand to his throat, and hoarsely whispered, "I'm sorry."

"Hey, Sarah, I put those firefighters— He's awake!" Shelley stopped short just inside the emergency room bay.

"Yes." Straightening from where she'd leaned closer to him, Sarah forced herself into professional mode, doing another quick neuro examination, checking sensation and movement and reflexes.

Other than obvious intense pain with movement, all good.

"If you wanted to play with my feet—" his voice was raspy, but understandable "—you could have just told me you had a foot fetish."

Sarah rolled her eyes. "You wish."

He cleared his throat. "I do."

That had her pausing in her examination. "You wish I had a foot fetish?"

His gaze bored into hers. "That you had a me fetish."

Sarah's breath caught. Shelley, who was still in the

room, cleared her throat from the other side of the gurney where she checked lines.

"You've had a rough night, Jude," Sarah reminded him, trying to shake off all the emotions bombarding her. "You should focus on breathing deeply and not talking. Really. Just be quiet and breathe."

"Breathing hurts."

"Try not to and what I'll do to you will hurt a lot worse," she warned in the sternest tone she could muster.

"Mouth to mouth?"

"There you go wishing again. I'll shove that tube down your throat again and this time I won't be so gentle," she threatened. "So be quiet and conserve your energy for more essential things, like breathing deeply."

"I take it you two know each other?" Shelley asked as she jotted down numbers from his telemetry.

"He's my neighbor," Sarah explained.

At the same time Jude said, "We're dating."

Sarah's gaze cut to Jude. "In case you forgot, whatever was between us ended earlier tonight."

"What's between you and I hasn't ended. Never will." His oxygen monitor beeped, indicating his oxygen saturation had dropped below ninety percent.

Concern filled Sarah. She needed to focus on his health, not be having a personal conversation with him. He shouldn't be talking at all.

"Jude, please, stop," she pleaded, adjusting his oxygen tubing. "Just stop talking and breathe deeply or I really will put the vent back in."

"I could make a corny joke about you taking my breath away if it would help," he offered.

"You taking a deep breath would help. Several deep breaths." Sarah turned to Shelley. "Go tell his crew he's awake and they are welcome to come back in here so long as they can keep him quiet."

Shelley nodded and went to get his coworkers.

Jude sucked in a deep oxygen-rich breath, grimaced in pain, no doubt triggered by his fractured ribs and bruised chest. Then he took another, and another. His oxygen saturation instantly rose and Sarah sighed with relief.

"I tell you I'm sorry, that I don't want to say goodbye to you ever, and you tell me to breathe?"

She took a deep breath herself, then blew it out slowly. "You don't know what you're saying, Jude. You suffered multiple injuries, were unconscious for who knows how long. You're not yourself."

"Then who am I?"

"Injured. Tired. Confused."

"I need you in my life."

She needed him, too. So very much, but it wasn't enough. Would never be enough. Not knowing what she knew.

"I can't do this, Jude. Maybe you don't understand, but I won't be second best. Not even to a dead woman."

Proving just how quickly he was recovering now that he'd regained consciousness, Jude scooted up in the bed.

"Have you not heard anything I've said?" His voice was still scratchy but getting stronger. "You are not second best. You are best. You, Sarah. You and only you. There is no second best."

Fresh tears ran down her cheeks. "Please, don't."

"Don't tell you how much I need you? That had we not been interrupted earlier tonight I'd have told you at your apartment? That I've known from the very first night, here, that you were special? That I wanted you to know you were different from anyone I'd ever known? Which don't do you mean?"

"I… But Nina…"

"Nina was an amazing woman, but I'm not in love with Nina." At Sarah's open mouth, he held up his hand. "Hear me out. Maybe I was always more in love with the idea of Nina and I than I was with Nina to begin with. Or maybe I didn't want to acknowledge what a jerk I was to her after she chose Charles. I don't know. What I do know is that when I thought I was taking my last breaths, I didn't want Nina. I wanted you, Sarah. Just you. Always you."

Trying not to let his words poke too many holes in her shabby defenses against him, she arched her brow. "This isn't some traumatic brain injury talking nonsense that you're not going to remember tomorrow?"

"I loved you before I left your apartment, before I made love to you last night. I think I loved you even before I took you to see your first Broadway show."

Sarah's jaw dropped and she grabbed hold of the bed railing to steady herself. "You love me?"

"I've never felt the way I feel about you. Not for Nina. Not for anyone. Just you."

His words sounded too good to be true.

"How do you know what you're feeling is real?"

"Because I feel it with every beat of my heart. I feel you with every beat." He took her hand into his and placed it over his chest. "Feel it? Sa-*rah*. Sa-*rah*. Sa-*rah*," he said in unison with his heartbeat.

Eyes blurring at the enormity of what he was saying, at what he was doing, Sarah shook her head. "You're crazy."

"About you."

She fought back a major sniffle. "So I heard."

"Mr. Johnson?"

Despite the hot-poker pain that moving obviously caused to streak through his body, he lifted her hand to his lips and pressed a kiss there. "That's what I want, Sarah."

"You want Mr. Johnson?"

This time he shook his head. "I want what he and his wife have. I want that with you."

"I love you, Jude, but—"

"Thank God," he said, pulling her down to him despite whatever pain and trauma her landing against him caused.

"I'm going to hurt you," she insisted, trying to pull away, certain she was going to do major damage that she'd never forgive herself for.

"Yes, you are. Stop trying to get away and kiss me."

"But—"

"No buts, Sarah. Just you and me. Forever."

That had her staring wide-eyed at him. "Forever? I thought you just wanted me through Christmas."

"Haven't you figured out the truth yet, Sarah? I want you *for* Christmas," he corrected. "Not through Christmas."

"A doctor under the tree, eh?"

"A fireman in your stocking."

A fireman in her stocking. She closed her eyes, let herself dream a little, imagining what if what he was saying was true.

When she opened her eyes, looked into his, the truth shone so clearly that she was the one needing to be told to breathe.

"Forgive me, Sarah," he said. "Let me spend the rest of my life making tonight up to you."

The rest of his life. Jude and her forever. It's what she saw in his eyes, what she felt in her heart.

Being careful to try not to hurt him, she pressed a kiss to his cheek. "I'm the one who should ask you to forgive me. I was so scared of getting hurt that I almost threw everything away."

"I wouldn't have let you," he assured her, cradling her against him. "What we have is too special. I'll always fight for you."

"I'm dreaming."

"Then dream that my body doesn't feel as if a building fell on it so I can do all the things to you that I want to be doing to you."

"A building did fall on you." She placed her hands on his cheeks and stared into his eyes. "Please, don't forget you said all this, Jude. I need you not to forget."

"I love you, Sarah. Yesterday, today, and tomorrow. I'm yours."

"Yeah, and we all heard him say it and will hold his sorry butt to it, right, guys?"

Sarah turned to see his crew standing just inside the bay.

Jude grinned at his guys. "You won't ever have to. All she has to do is say she's mine and I'm the luckiest man alive."

"You are lucky to be alive," Roger corrected. "Two minutes more and you'd have been buried under the entire building. Not sure if you remember, but the whole thing came down."

"Thank you for getting me out."

"Wasn't just me." Roger gestured to the others in the room. "Guess we'll all be getting a chewing from Command."

"Won't be the first time," one of the other crew said.

"Won't be the last," Jude finished, then returned his gaze to Sarah. "Think you can put up with having these guys around constantly?"

Sarah looked into his amazing blue eyes and let herself drown in what she saw there, the need to love and be loved.

"I've told you I always wanted a big family."

Cheers went up from around the bed, but neither Sarah nor Jude looked at his coworkers or heard their teasing words.

They had eyes only for each other as Jude said, "Yeah, well, there's more than one way to give you that."

Sarah smiled, because she knew what he meant and looked forward to each and every moment of the rest of their lives.

Together.

Forever.

*   *   *   *   *

MILLS & BOON®

MEDICAL ROMANCE

THE ULTIMATE IN ROMANTIC MEDICAL DRAMA

A sneak peek at next month's titles...

In stores from 2nd November 2017:

- **The Spanish Duke's Holiday Proposal** – Robin Gianna *and* **The Rescue Doc's Christmas Miracle** – Amalie Berlin

- **Christmas with Her Daredevil Doc** *and* **Their Pregnancy Gift** – Kate Hardy

- **A Family Made at Christmas** – Scarlet Wilson *and* **Their Mistletoe Baby** – Karin Baine

---

Just can't wait?
Buy our books online before they hit the shops!
www.millsandboon.co.uk

Also available as eBooks.

MILLS & BOON®

EXCLUSIVE EXTRACT

Dr Hayley Clark and Sam Price's holiday romance was unforgettable – and unrepeatable! Then risk-taking doc Sam arrives at her hospital… Could their fling become something more?

Read on for a sneak preview of
CHRISTMAS WITH HER DAREDEVIL DOC
the first book in the MIRACLES AT MUSWELL HILL HOSPITAL *duet*

'Hayley, meet your replacement, Samuel Price. Sam, Hayley's just been promoted to senior registrar and you've taken over from her. You'll be working together.'

Of all the places…

Sam hadn't told Hayley that he was about to start a new job in London, and she hadn't told him where she worked. London was a massive city with quite a few hospitals. What were the chances that they'd end up working together? The way her pupils expanded momentarily told him that she was just as shocked and surprised as he was.

This was going to make things awkward. They'd had a fling in Iceland, agreeing that it would be nothing more than that, and they'd said goodbye. What now? Would she want to see if their fling could be something more, something deeper? Or had he just been her transition person, the one who'd helped her to move on after her partner's death, so she wouldn't want to pick up where they'd left off?

The problem was, he didn't know what he wanted, either. He'd really liked the woman he'd started to get to know in Iceland. But then again he'd liked Lynda, too—and his ex-fiancée had let him down so badly. Could he even trust his judgement any more? Would he be making a huge mistake if he started seeing Hayley?

She recovered first, holding her hand out. 'Welcome to Muswell Hill Hospital, Dr Price.'

Don't miss
MIRACLES AT MUSWELL HILL HOSPITAL:
CHRISTMAS WITH HER DAREDEVIL DOC
THEIR PREGNANCY GIFT
by Kate Hardy
Available November 2017
www.millsandboon.co.uk